EIGHT FOR
ETERNITY

By the Same Author

NOVELS

MISCELLANEOUS

EIGHT
FOR ETERNITY

BY

CECIL ROBERTS

HODDER AND STOUGHTON LIMITED
LONDON

FIRST PRINTED, DECEMBER, 1947

DP 2963

*Made and Printed in Great Britain for Hodder & Stoughton, Limited, London
by Wyman & Sons Limited, London, Reading and Fakenham*

To

BEATRICE CARTWRIGHT

CONTENTS

CHAPTER I

CHARLES AND MARY

I

He put Turpin in the stable, walked down the long yard, sad with all its unpainted doors and empty stalls. He glanced up at the clock, quite uselessly in the matter of learning the time, for its hands had stood at a quarter to ten for these last twelve years. They had stopped on the day his father had broken his neck at Cutter's Close, and been brought home dead, six foot two of him, handsome in his washed-out pink coat and glossy top boots. Nothing would shake the conviction, the country-side over, that the clock had stopped at the time of the death of his father. It was utter nonsense, but once an idea lodged in a Leicestershire head it could not be uprooted. Charles remembered how, a boy of fifteen, he climbed up to the clock to find out why it had stopped, watched by a disapproving groom who thought he was tampering with Fate. The reason was plain. A shingle had slipped from the dome and, lodging between the wheels, had stopped the clock.

"Yes, sir, perhaps so—but who made the shingle fall?" asked Havers, still unshaken by the evidence Charles held before him.

"But my father died at about eleven!"

"Ten or eleven—it wor near enough, I'd say. An' that clock ain't never stopped! It wor a goer like your father, sir," said the persistent Havers.

9

No one had started the clock again. It was left as a monument to Fate. The stables too had stood still since that day, for all the horses save two, one for Gervase and one for himself, had been sold under the crushing burden of the Death Duties. Twenty boxes were going to rot and ruin. Cobwebs festooned the windows of the saddlery room. At one end of the oblong cobbled yard the riding school had been converted into a garage. It still looked an intruder after fifteen years. It held only one car. It had never had more than two, except when visitors brought their cars. When Gervase was killed at Vimy Ridge they sold his Daimler. The old weather-beaten Rolls used by his mother, and driven by the tight-mouthed and rebellious Havers, was then the sole occupant. It was horribly uneconomic but no one would buy it at a price that would procure a dignified successor. Unlike the clock it never stopped. Havers hated its unbroken health. Cattle could get foot-and-mouth disease, but this thing would wear him out. His gloomy foreboding was fulfilled. Havers had died last January. Since a chauffeur of the new expensive status was impossible, the Rolls had been sold, and a Ford of gymnastic agility had taken its place, perilously driven by his nervous mother.

Charles had no need of a clock to tell him the time of day. He knew, on this April evening as the sun slanted through the elms, vivid in their spring foliage, that it was nearing seven. How often as a boy he had watched from the nursery windows the golden shafts that gilded the boles and underlit the branches as they struck the spaced sentinels of the drive. Turning from the gravel path into the forecourt he knew the gleam in which he would find the weather-vane burning on the Tudoresque tower. Now he looked at it with a deeper love, because of the change to come upon him so soon, for the eve of a young man's wedding draws a line across the account of his life. He never looked at the tower, the vane with its stencilled date, the great door set in the stone solidity of this east face, without lamenting the over-reaching ancestor who had added on the southern front. It was Georgian, designed by Adam, with all the spaciousness of the eighteenth century, when these Leicestershire fields supported the squirarchal mode of life. But what a nightmare it was now, when the exhaustion following the Great War had doubled the cost of living and halved the supply of servants !

Conscious, as he looked up at the gilded vane, of the immense change marching on them, he felt a little gust of fury sweep over him at the inanity of that stodgy Mrs. Cannon who had said to him, in a bronchitical spate of congratulation, " We all hoped, of course, you'd marry some rich American ! " What a cliché ! What made women like that advocate prostitution in the cause of feudal stagnation ? Mary had laughed when he told her. " Charles, you should have married some *poor* American—how indignant she would have been then ! I suppose she never imagines poor young Americans do fall in love with poor young Englishmen ! "

" We're not poor, anyhow," said Charles, looking down at her bright sweet face.

" We're the richest young people in all the world, darling, and we know it ! " she cried, radiantly.

Yes, how rich and fortunate he was ! Here he was, alive. At any moment in those past four war years, the thing might have happened. In Belgium in 1914, in France, in the Dardanelles, and in France again ; four years of unbelievable luck and, mud and blood apart, four enjoyable years of fierce health, good comradeship, excitement, variety and freedom from all worries outside the bodily cares. What sentimental nonsense, wrapped up in the fudge of hero-worship, people talked ! You did your job, you were killed or you were not killed, and it all came in the day's work. As for bravery and all that stuff the poets and politicians played up, bravery was the commonest quality of the race when the test came. England had survived, had come out of it, as she would again.

Again ? Charles remembered the horrified look on the parson's face when he had suggested such a thing. They had walked away together from the village war memorial, after the bugle-blowing and speechmaking had finished, and in a remark that he knew was a mistake the moment he had uttered it, he had asked, mischievously, where they would place the next memorial now the last space had been used up. Father Marshall's eyes had almost popped out of his head. " My dear Captain Conway ! You can't believe anything like this could happen again ? It isn't possible ! " And when he had suggested it was not only possible but probable, it was clear the old boy thought the war had damaged him mentally.

Charles had refrained from asking him to look around their own church. There lay the broken effigy of old Sir Richard Conway, who at eighty had ridden off with King Charles to Nottingham, to raise the Standard and start a Civil War on a windy August day in 1642. His son William had fallen at Naseby, later a Charles died at Malplaquet, a Richard in the Crimea, a Gervase at Lucknow, another Charles at Gibraltar, another Richard at Spion Kop in South Africa, and now poor Gervase at Vimy Ridge. " Their name liveth for evermore." It was a brave gesture to futility. The next generation would not care or know what it had all been about, caught up in their anxieties and duties. But you could not tell people that. They would crucify you to perpetuate their delusions. Just now it was a League of Nations that was the current craze. How much of its philosophy would those Germans imbibe? Anyhow, why worry? For his day the thing seemed settled and the next generation must look after itself. *Carpe diem.*

Suddenly he halted in the gravel courtyard as if something had hit him. He might become the next generation, or so much a part of it that he would be involved. A new sensation pervaded him at the thought, and a shadow like the wind over the wheat swept across his happiness. He might be a father, vulnerable. In the house there, his mother lived in the past in which Gervase walked even while he and his sister stood so lovingly close to her. In this old home whose walls had nursed four centuries of Conways, Richards had lamented Charleses, and Charleses Gervases, dead on various fields in various causes, all forgotten now, but all pressing and honourable once. Why should he hope to escape the burden of human destiny?

The face of the old house was grey in the shadow, darker for the bright evening sky over it, and the lights within. He stood for a time, motionless, contemplating its face like a lover whose happiness is touched with the fear of too great a possession. He watched, a slim figure in his brown riding kit, tall and hatless, the dark bridegroom of the morrow, intuitively conscious in this farewell hour of his youth and singleness that he was but a link in the procession of his ancestors. Conways behind and before seemed to be watchful in this changing tide of evening. Prescience of the unknown touched him in a brief moment of limitless consciousness. So brief a moment was it that when it had passed it seemed only the shadow of a shadow. He was too young and robust and triumphant for any mood of sustained apprehension.

He stepped forward, comforted by the loud crunching of the gravel beneath his feet, and the sharp ring of metal as he lifted the heavy latch of the great oak door.

II

His sister Beryl greeted him as he came out of the cloakroom. She and her husband had come from Bath for the wedding. Young voices rang in the old nursery, for she had brought Gervase and Ann, seven and five. Beryl was the executive of the family. It was she who had superintended the wedding arrangements. Three motor charabancs of villagers were being despatched to Brent Abbey for the service and festivities. There was a fête in the school for the children too young to go, with fireworks on the lawn. There would not be one person neglected, nor one allowed to encroach, so thorough would be Beryl's staff work.

It was Beryl who had worked out the time-table for the day, down to the time the car would leave the Abbey to take him and Mary to catch the train at Melton Mowbray en route for Venice. There were times when Beryl's precision and infallibility drove them to revolt, but they knew well what a skilful captain she was amid the shoals that beset them. It was Beryl who, ten years ago, fearing the storm, had let Winton for five years at a good rent, settled them in at Lodge Farm, and by various stratagems cut away the mortgage choking out their life in the old place. She had urged Charles to follow his bent for architecture when all tradition demanded he should farm, for which he had no aptitude. His career, even at twenty-seven, seemed assured with a junior partnership in a flourishing Leicester office. He

knew she had been a little dismayed by his choice of
Mary Firth, of a stock as tradition-burdened and im-
pecunious as their own, but once his determination had
been realised she became a loyal ally.

Strange that her efficiency was absent in the direction
of her own affairs. John, her husband, was kind, lazy
and careless. He was constantly being prodded by his
wife, but all her remonstrances floated over his head.
How he maintained any practice as a solicitor was always
a marvel to the family. He sat and smoked in an office
littered with deeds, in a disorder that never bothered
him and out of which he could retrieve the required
document, given time, with a certainty that seemed an
undue reward for such inefficiency. Things came to
pieces in his hands. Machinery appeared to achieve
almost human consciousness of his ignorance of all
mechanical principles. Nevertheless, he was easily the
best chess-player in the county, and on the croquet
lawn, if he could find victims for this dying exercise, his
skill was almost diabolical. He lived in a constant
tangle with the three pairs of pince-nez on three black
cords. His hair was too long and his trousers too short.
He was infallibly good-humoured and adored by all
children. He was twelve years older than Beryl, nothing
to look at, but was the father at fifty of two children
of incredible loveliness. The rewards of Nature, it
seemed to Charles, never followed any logical plan.
Who could have foretold that a gooseberry bush
would produce such roses, if he might mix his
metaphor?

"The children are calling for you. How's Mary?"
asked Beryl at the foot of the stairs.

"Like me, a bundle of nerves. There's a lot to be
said for a register office," commented Charles. "Is
John in the nursery?"

"No—he's missed the train and won't be here until after supper," replied Beryl, smiling tolerantly.

"I'll go up," said Charles, leaving her. He bounded up to the second floor and went down the wing corridor he had known from childhood. The evening sun fell, as always, on the mildewed engraving of Queen Victoria's Jubilee. He had once counted all the figures in it, two hundred and ninety-eight, on an occasion when he had been sent supperless to bed for telling the parlour-maid she was a fool. It had seemed an act of injustice from the grown-ups, for he had heard his father say the same thing a dozen times, though he was never candid enough to say it in front of the subject.

The children were not in the nursery. High young voices told him they were in the bath. Wet, gleaming faces turned to him. What a pair, chubby, fair-haired, like rain-dewy roses! Their Nanny was mopping up an overflow.

"Soap me! Soap me!" yelled Gervase.

"Me! Me!" shrilled Ann, bouncing up and down.

"Oh, Mr. Conway, you'll have to do it. You started something last night—they're quite out of hand," said Nanny.

"Ah—give me an apron!"

She gave him one. He tied it round his head like a turban instead of round his waist, to immense applause from the water-nymphs.

"Please, sir, not all the water on the floor," said Nanny, retreating to the cupboards, as pandemonium broke out, for Uncle Charles was on his hands and knees, approaching the lake, Indian fashion, to the screams and water-threshing of two steam-wreathed cherubs.

III

Charles woke in the early dawn. He was surprised at himself, for he was a sound sleeper and he had retired late. For a while he lay contemplating this momentous day of his life. His eyes travelled over the familiar objects. It had been his room through boyhood. He used to think of it as he kept watch in Flanders trenches through bitter starlit nights of winter and in misty birdless dawns amid the tortured woods. Clean linen, breakfast in bed, a book to fall asleep on, suits hanging in line in the wardrobe, mauve branches of wistaria framing the white window, they were the real treasures of life in those days when the sky belched fire and the earth shook. Somehow he had survived that organised hell. His eyes roamed over the chintz curtains. The light came through a gap.

Then above the twittering of birds came the cold, sharp sound of a bell. He knew then it could only be six o'clock. It came from the church belfry, calling people who never went. Father Marshall was High Church and severely criticised for it. He kept a candle burning constantly in the Lady Chapel, used a Latin breviary, wore sandals and a black gown, belted. "He's a Roman," said critics in the village. There had been uproar at vestry meetings. "I don't approve, but he's a good man," said Mrs. Conway, refusing to sign a petition to the Bishop against him. It was an offence because he called himself Father Marshall. He never wore a hat and kept his grizzled hair close cut. His hands were red with housework, for he had no maid. He looked famished and pinched with cold, for which there seemed no reason, for the living was a good one, though the Adam rectory had been designed for parsons with large broods. In the eighteenth century a Parson Ford

B

with a family of twelve had competed with a Squire Conway with a family of sixteen. Both had run level in the deaths of their children, eight each, all before six years of age.

Frugality marked the habits of Father Marshall. His rectory was often inhabited by humourless young divinity students from a Midland theological college. Like their host, they were sandalled and cassocked, devout, early risers, and participants in a high and elaborate church ritual. Rumour said that Father Marshall divided his income among these junior brethren. A daily charwoman was the only feminine intruder in the rectory. It was sparsely furnished, never heated except for a small log-fire in the rector's study in the depth of winter. He was a tremendous worker and every house in the scattered parish was regularly visited, even where the reception was frigid. The Conways had been genial with him throughout the twenty years of his rectorship. Charles's father complained he could find no red blood in the fellow and was irritated by the incessant bell-ringing. "It's 'Christians, awake, salute the foggy morn' with that fellow," he complained. He had responded to all appeals, nevertheless. Mrs. Conway attended some of the services, received communion, but firmly repulsed all invitations to make confession. " If I wanted to go ' over ' I'd do it wholesale and get all the etceteras," she once said, and then apologised, ashamed of her levity.

The bell tolled and gave a pleasant melancholy to the growing day. Then another sound came with the bird-song and the bell. Feet were crossing the gravel below his window. He knew whose feet they were. Sometimes, on occasions of trial or change, his mother went across to that cold, lonely service at daybreak. He knew it must be she, for this day of days was an occasion.

He got out of bed and crossed to the window in time to see his mother pass through the iron gate by the laurels along the churchyard wall. A mist lay over the Leicestershire fields. It was mostly grazing these days and the rolling country was verdant and lightly spaced with trees, the grand Fernie country. The cold air was sweet with the opening day. There was not a whisper in the leaves.

Suddenly he felt an impulse to join his mother. She would be as surprised as he was, but this was no ordinary morning and his last as the single son of the house. He slipped on some flannel trousers, socks and shoes. A shirt, with knitted pullover and tweed jacket, served his swift resolve. He went down through the still house out into the sharp dawn. The bell had ceased to toll. As he reached the open door of the church he heard the voice of the rector intoning the prayers.

Stealthily he moved up the aisle towards the pew where his mother was bent forwards on her knees. A grey light pervaded the large empty church. The yellow feeble flames of two candles on the altar gave emphasis to the space and chilliness. He thought he had slipped down beside his mother unobserved, but she gave him a quiet smile before resuming her devotions. The murmur of the rector's voice died down the aisle, yet it was clear enough for Charles to hear the Latin prayer. Thus once, long ago, it had sounded in this same church, for in the sixteenth century the historian Polydore Vergil had ministered here before returning to his native Italy, to die in Urbino.

Charles did not pray. He was alert as seldom before, the moments vivid in their rotation. He looked about him, taking note newly of what had long been familiar to him. Above him, on the left, was the memorial window, to a Richard Conway fallen in the South

African War, an uncle he had never known. Beneath the window, in its alcove, lay the marble effigy of old Sir Richard, feet and hands shattered by Cromwell's vandals who had no liking for the sturdy Royalist who at eighty had ridden in King Charles's Commission of Array. Near him his son William, who had ridden in that same army, kept him company, along with his spouse, and a frieze of three sons, two daughters, and four children in swaddling clothes denoting deaths at birth. 1644 was the date on Sir Richard's tomb. How far off, and yet how near these owners of Winton seemed. He wondered briefly what might be his own date, in turn. Now it was 1920. Certainly 1970 would see his record all told. Then, whimsically, he found himself wondering if some successive Charles would ever kneel here on his wedding morn, a son of his, adding to the human tally, like a recurring decimal in the sum of life.

   . . . . Grant us so to put away the leaven of malice and wickedness, that we may always serve Thee in pureness of living and truth. . . .

The prayer was in English now. Mrs. Conway rose, and Charles with her. The voice of the priest at the altar went on in its monotone of devotion. They moved noiselessly down the aisle, through the old porch with its parish notices and wire screen out into the morning. There was warmth in the air with a freshness and a sense of things stirring in hedges and boughs.

" Thank you, Charles, that was dear of you," said his mother as they went down the path.

He made no reply, but pressed her arm. They came to the hall door. There, for a few moments, they stood looking out across the long lawn to the fields and the misty copse. The birds clamoured joyously in branches overhead. A golden finger of light touched the old stable clock and a gargoyle on the square church tower above the lime trees.

" You will never love anything as you have loved this, will you ? " asked his mother.

" No—but it's not the end of loving it, or seeing it," he said.

" No—I feel somehow we shall always return," she responded.

A thought came as his eyes followed the line of copse whose far side looked upon Brent Abbey. Was Mary awake, too, caught like him in the exaltation of this day of days ? Only five more hours and they would stand on the threshold of their lives together.

Perhaps something of his emotion showed in his face. Mrs. Conway, about to say something, checked her words. She looked at his face, young, sensitive, eager. All the oncoming richness of life lit his dark eyes.

She left him and went in alone, mounting to her room. A little later she heard the water running in the bathroom and his voice singing joyously. Then followed a sudden scurrying and banging, and squeals of delight as feet rushed along the corridor. It was Uncle Charles being baited again. The house was up.

IV

At twelve-thirty the limousine came to the door. Charles, accompanied by Vincent Shore, his best man, was waiting for it. His mother, together with Beryl and John, had gone on ahead.

" A perfect morning. How do you feel ? " asked Vincent as the car moved off down the drive.

Charles looked at his friend and laughed.

" Not as nervous as you, old boy," he said, for he noticed how tensely Vincent was clutching his gloves and fidgeting with his pearl-grey waistcoat. They had spent twenty years of their lives together, preparatory and public school, then two good years at Oxford, interrupted by the war, then the army, in the same regiment. It was difficult to believe that their ways must now part. Vincent had been a perfect friend, feminine in intuition, graceful and delicate, yet possessed of a high courage, moral and physical, that had always made him feel inferior. Only this year he had achieved sudden acclaim with a biography of Voltaire. It was a strange subject for one who by nature was a mystic and whose spiritual quality had always made Charles feel a stranger to certain aspects of Vincent's character. He was now living in London and his small, almost monastic apartment in Sloane Street had always been Charles's *pied-à-terre* when in town.

Vincent smiled at the accusation of nervousness, but made no reply. He turned his face away to look out over the fields rolling by them, but not before Charles had detected a slight twitching of the nostrils. It betrayed the immense reticence with which Vincent crushed his emotional nature, infuriating sometimes in its secrecy. Mercilessly Charles now fixed his gaze on his friend, until his face turning again, their eyes met with a candour that could not be left unexpressed.

" It's hard to lose you, Charles."

The simplicity of the confession did not hide from his friend the controlled emotion beneath it.

" Nonsense—you're not losing me ; you're coming into the family ! Mary thinks the world of you," said Charles, with the heartiness with which he always attacked Vincent's apprehensions.

" Yes—I know that—but it can never be the same.

I realise things can't remain static—it's against Nature. I suppose the church'll be packed. Oh, those tickets for the Lyric to-night will be waiting for you at Claridge's. I could only get them for the fourth row ; I hope they're not too near."

Charles wanted to laugh and bang Vincent on the back. The mental manœuvre was so characteristic. He had bolted from the emotional abyss that had loomed up and taken refuge in that service of a friend, the procuring of a room for them at Claridge's Hotel, two seats for the comedy at the Lyric Theatre. Reliable in every detail, he had entrusted to Vincent their honeymoon programme, the theatre and the hotel for to-night in London, the tickets through to Venice on the morrow, the itinerary to Florence, Rome and Naples, through the Italian springtide, one whole month of absolute felicity. Vincent had done all this with characteristic care for detail, and a devotion to his interests that had never failed him. Now, in his heart, as he looked at his friend, knowing that a break in their lives had come, Charles felt troubled for him. He had never forgotten the long vigil Vincent had kept when, following the terrible winter of 1917 in the trenches, he had gone down with rheumatic fever. There was a moment when Vincent had threatened desertion rather than suffer separation. Day after day, through mud and rain, across the shell-smitten country, he came to the hospital where he lay in that first crisis. There was steel binding his human frailty, and Charles knew well the rare quality of this loyalty without alloy. He hoped the theatre seats were not too near ! Dear old Vincent ! What a desperate mask he put on to hide his sense of loss !

They were nearing the church now. A flag waved gaily from its tower. On the turret of Brent Abbey, deep in its elms, another flag waved. The vast Firth clan would be thronging the pews. They lived for weddings and christenings and there was never a lack of them, three sons, four sisters, a stream of nephews and nieces, providing occasions for lavish feastings. How those feastings, those wedding receptions of prodigal hospitality, were financed no one knew. An estate throttled with mortgages, deep financial embarrassments, these things failed to check the open heart of Colonel Firth and his fat, jolly wife, Lady Alice, fifth daughter of a bankrupt marquis. They had the best horses in the field, they kept open house. The crash seemed as certain as the thunderclap in the blackening storm, but somehow the crash was deferred. The prophets of doom were wearied with unfulfilled expectations, and began to make a joke of this unnatural survival. Two hopes seemed left. Mary and Frances might make good matches and retrieve the position. And now Mary, with paternal approbation, had turned down that very rich Henry Foulds, personable and madly in love with her, for Charles Conway, as impoverished as his bride. This bold fact, known over the countryside, and particularly in the villages and on the estates of Winton and Brent, hourly threatened with dissolution, had added to the gaiety of the wedding. This young couple had given dismal Fate a smack in the face, and they all applauded this recklessness.

As Vincent had anticipated, the church was packed to the doors. No Archbishop of Canterbury could have achieved such a congregation. The overflow by the lych-gate and the porch cheered the bridegroom and his companion as they stepped from their car. A murmur of delight went over the congregation as they went towards the altar. Everyone knew Charles Conway, a saucy lad with bold brown eyes and a merry laugh,

and very good to look at. In this dismembered age he
would keep the breed of the Conways running somehow,
they felt. He would hang on to that ruinous old home,
as they had seen him hang on, year after year, in the
annual point-to-point, winning or losing. And those
Firth girls had shed their beauty like may-bloom over
the countryside. It was good to know they were not
losing young Mary. Hers was the prettiest face of all
that peered in the shop windows of Market Harborough
and Melton Mowbray on market days. She was the
Leicestershire lass beyond compare.

There were some tense moments for Charles, waiting
there at the altar rail for his bride. The verger was
going up and down the aisle. Whispering and nervous
coughing broke the silence. Behind him sat his mother,
Beryl and John, and the Winton cavalcade. He noticed
how bright was the April noonday sun as it lit the stained
glass windows of the south wall : St. Augustine blessing
a sick child, St. Paul preaching in a luminous purple
robe.

A sound came from the outside. A sense of commotion pervaded the congregation. Charles half turned.
They were there. A pause, a patchwork of light and
shade in the western door, a glint of the silver crozier,
of the canon's scarlet hood, and then, as his heart jumped
a beat and a lump came into his throat, music burst
forth from the organ loft, tremulous and piping. The
congregation rose, and towards him, on the arm of her
father, he saw Mary, a radiance of white satin and point
lace, move down the aisle. Charles glanced from his
bride towards Vincent. He stood, erect and chaste as
a Sir Galahad. His mother, human, smiled at him.
But it was Mary whose warmth flowed through him as
she came to his side and stepped forth with him, lovely
and confident.

V

They were glad to get on the train at Melton Mowbray. They had a reserved compartment, and it was good to be alone after the exuberance of these last two hours. The whole county had been at the reception. For three-quarters of an hour they had stood in the Long Gallery, backed by the Van Dyck of Charles I raising the Royal Standard at Nottingham, in which both a Conway and a Firth had played their part. The long line of guests flowed past them, with congratulations, and sentences cut off by impatient successors. They had smiled, and said, " Thank you," and been kissed and photographed. At long last they had each escaped upstairs to the rooms where they put off their wedding garments. Then they made a public exit across the terrace to the waiting car. To their dismay there was another snowstorm of confetti. Now in the train they shook the tell-tale stuff from every crevice of their clothes.

" Oh ! " said Charles, leaning back as the train slipped out of the station. " Well, I must say your people did the whole show marvellously ! "

" *Our* people ! *We* did it ! Oh, Charles, I'd like it all over again. It was gorgeous ! " cried Mary, tucking away a curl.

He looked at her for a moment, a mere girl in her grey coat and skirt, with the thin rope of pearls his mother had given her around the lovely throat. He moved from the opposite seat and sat beside her, his arm enfolding her. They did not talk, the green level fields of the Midlands with the hedgerows in white blossom slid by them. The small villages nestling in trees, old grey church spires, the afternoon sun burnishing eastern windows, stone manor-houses, and Georgian brick mansions, trim little railway stations with flower-beds and bold name-plates, spaced telegraph poles that hurdled their wires, it was all England in peace and springtime again. Two years ago, in the mud and blood of Flanders, all this had seemed a fantastic dream. Charles remembered a dead German lying with his face in a roadside puddle outside Maubeuge. He was a blond youth, and had a posy of fresh flowers in his hands. The flies festered around his eyes and red young mouth. It was so incongruous a sight that he had never forgotten it. Some tribute of love from an enemy ensnared by Cupid? He would never know and always wonder.

Through the fair cloud of hair brushing his cheek he looked down on his bride. Mary's eyes were closed. His hand folded over hers and the possessive gold symbol he had placed there this noonday.

"Your mother was wonderful, Charles—I feel very mean to take you away," said Mary. "She says she will live in London. That means a little flat and a maid—Alice, I suppose. Isn't it strange, and a little cruel—she once had a day like this."

"She'll be happy—don't worry about mother. She wanted this for me, darling."

Mary did not answer for a while. She looked up into his dark eyes, and with a finger pushed back a black lock on his brow.

"I wouldn't have her courage—if anything happened to you, Charles darling," she said, her eyes smiling at him.

"Now, now, Miss Morbid. What can happen to me? Four years of every hazard and Fate's kept me for you —and you for me. Foolish little girl—*When we are old and grey and full of sleep*—what about that Keats you're always quoting?"

"Yeats, darling."

"Sorry. Oh, my sweet!" he cried, crushing her to him. "I don't know anything in any poet to tell you how I love you! The words haven't been made, my darling."

The landscape faded in the crimson and grey of dusk. Lamps shone starrily through the darkening world. Another hour and they would be in London, with just time to change, and a hurried meal and the theatre. The next day they would be less rushed. They were leaving Victoria Station in the afternoon for Dover-Calais and the Orient express. In Venice old Mrs. Trentham, Mary's grandmother, had lent them her apartment in the Palazzo Sangradin. They had neither of them been there, and Charles had been a little reluctant about accepting the offer. "It's all a bit too honeymoony—gondolas, moonlight and serenading—like a French novel," he had scoffed. But Mary's wish had prevailed. "It'll save money," she said, at which Charles laughed derisively, and made a deal. "Very well, then, we'll hire a car in Rome and do ourselves handsome on the saving!"

VI

If the reception clerk at Claridge's knew anything when Charles signed the register, and stared a moment at his unfamiliar signature, "Mr. and Mrs. Charles Conway, Winton Hall, Leics," he gave no sign, impervious to a thousand and one bridal nights. Nor did the porter or maid show one glimmer of romance in their demeanour, though somebody's frightful extravagance in flowers for their small sitting-room proclaimed the event to anyone entering it.

"Vincent's touch, this," said Charles when their last

piece of luggage had been brought in and the door closed. " I should have thought of it, but I didn't. No credit, darling ! "

They were in one another's arms for a moment.

" It isn't true, is it ? " he asked.

" No ! " she replied breathlessly.   " It's taken twenty-two years to reach this moment."

" Lucky child—it's taken me twenty-seven ! Darling, we have to change. Do I valet you ? " he asked, loosing her and looking at her bags.

Mary laughed and gazed at him with such a strange expression that he half anticipated her question.

" Charles—can I dress first ? You wouldn't help much ! "

She blushed as she spoke, and he took her again in his arms.

" Certainly, and I'll sleep on the doormat if you wish ; but I warn you, to-morrow it's a *wagon-lit* ! "

" Idiot-boy ! " cried Mary, patting his cheek.

" I'll go and have a drink—I'm a little dizzy with too much happiness. In twenty minutes the room's mine ? "

" I'll try," said Mary as the door closed on him.

VII

The next morning when their breakfast trays came in there was a bowl of rosebuds on one of them. Charles, coming out of the bathroom, surveyed them, smelt them and said, " That's not old Vincent ; that's the management. Lovely ! " he said, sniffing, and drawing up a chair beside his wife's bed. Mary leaned forward and sniffed in turn at his black head bent over the rose-bowl.

" Ah—a clean-man smell ! "

" After-shave lotion, darling. Like it ? "

" Yes. Oh, Charles, isn't it fun, you and I and the breakfast trays ! "

" And the roses, and the clean-man smell, and the loveliest little woman in the whole wide world. Gosh ! I'll be running to poetry soon ! That'll stun you from an old leather-saddle like me ! "

He took an egg and cracked it, opening the top. He buttered a piece of toast, he poured tea for her.

" Of course, Mrs. Conway, being an intelligent woman, you'll know this won't go on. I shall not notice what you're wearing, I shall read *The Times* and eat kippers and complain the coffee's cold," he said, popping a spoonful of egg in her mouth.

" I shall dislike your blue bristly chin, the black hair on your hands, your smelly pipe everywhere, and, above all, the bores you bring back to dinner."

" Ah, and the lovely ladies I might bring ? "

" I shall scratch their eyes out," cried Mary, choking with toast and laughter.

" Aren't we silly kids ? "

" Um—happy, silly kids ! "

The French clock on the mantelpiece struck ten.

" We're disgracefully late," said Mary.

" I'd call it gracefully," he corrected, catching her hand. " And the whole of Time's ours—except we must catch the boat train this afternoon."

" More tea ? "

" Please," he said, holding up his cup. " Do you know the last time a woman poured tea for me in my bedroom ? "

" Will you be quite truthful ? "

" Yes—it was a lady with a mole and one white whisker in it. My nanny, when I had measles."

" Charles, you are a great idiot ! "

" Wasn't it Vauvenargues who said that idiots are the inheritors of complete happiness ? "

" Did he—and when did you read Vauvenargues ? "

" Never—I heard his name and liked it, so I attribute everything I remember, or invent, to him. Vincent wrote a monograph on him."

" Poor Vincent ! "

" Why poor ? "

" I don't think he can ever be happy, he's too sensitive and reserved. I've dealt him a dreadful blow. He should hate me."

" Nonsense, my dear. Vincent would fight for you to the last ditch."

" Yes, because of you. Oh, yes, I know he's terribly loyal, but——"

" But ? " he asked as she hesitated.

" I can't quite explain. We must keep him with us, Charles, somehow."

" Darling, of course we will. Don't you worry about that," said Charles. " Vincent will always be in the family."

CHAPTER II

ROMAN SPRING

I

THE boat train from Victoria was crowded. Everyone appeared to be going to the Continent. Post-war travel was being restored. A disrupted Europe was pulling itself together. Those knitters of civilisation, the through expresses, began to run again from chill northern ports, through France, Switzerland, Austria, Italy, to the warm Mediterranean and the blue Adriatic.

It was Mary's first cross-Channel journey. She belonged to a generation whose usual " grand tour " had been destroyed by a long war. In August, 1914, she was going to France, chaperoned by Mlle Lefevre, whose ecstatic prophecies were about to be tested, for Mlle Lefevre, the French mistress of her school, had never left them in doubt that civilisation began at Calais and ended at Marseilles, with Paris the seat of all culture. How she would have disapproved of this honeymoon which ignored the great city ! But they were redeeming themselves by taking in Paris on the way home.

" I wonder if we're the only pair ? " asked Mary, when they were seated.

" Whether we are or not, we are *the* pair," asserted Charles. " Now those, for instance ? "

A young couple went by the window. The woman

was beautifully dressed, the young man seemed to have walked out of a tailor's shop. They followed a porter with a trolley of piled-up baggage.

"They look nice—they might be," said Mary.

"No, they're not," replied Charles definitely. "Look, they've got a dog. People don't go on honeymoons with dogs! They acquire those later—dogs and children."

She laughed at him; it was a typical Charles remark. Then she saw an expression of astonishment on his face.

"Good God!" he exclaimed, rising. "There's Vincent; he's looking for us! How on earth has he got here?"

Mary followed her husband out on to the platform. In a few seconds they had overtaken Vincent Shore.

"Charles! Mary—you don't mind, do you?" he asked, taking off his hat. "I felt I had to come and see you off."

"Why, it's wonderful of you, Vincent—how very kind of you," exclaimed Mary, wondering at this very moment why she had never before realised how very handsome he was with his shy, well-bred air.

"You old dog—when did you come up?" cried Charles, slapping him on the back.

"This morning—it was a sudden idea. You don't mind, really?"

"Mind! You silly ass, we're flattered to death," said Charles.

It was then they saw Grant, his man, waiting a little apart, with a bouquet. Vincent took the flowers and gave them to Mary. They were orchids.

"Vincent—how lovely, but how extravagant of you!" exclaimed Mary as she took them.

C

"Nothing's good enough for you, Mary—not even Charles," he added, with a difficult attempt at boldness.

"Of course, you've given us away!" complained Charles playfully. "The whole train's looking at us. Well, thanks for not hiring a band, old boy!"

"You look very happy," said Vincent to Mary. He was immediately conscious of the banality of his remark.

Mary said nothing. She just looked at him, her eyes telling him the whole story. They were closing the carriage doors now, the train was leaving.

"Well, here she goes. Good-bye, Vincent—a thousand thanks!" exclaimed Charles, wringing his friend's hand.

Mary stepped forward, and with a swiftness that surprised him, kissed Vincent on the cheek. "You are a darling!" she said.

He held her for a moment, a little embarrassed as their eyes met, and then, in a low, tense voice, as if afraid Charles might hear, "Good-bye, good luck. Mary, look after him, look after him, my dear!"

"I will!" she said fervently, and before he could turn and go she detected how near the tears were to his eyes. Briefly she halted, watching him walk away, hat in hand, his neat head proudly tilted in a manner characteristic of him, which Charles playfully called "The Guards' March."

"Mary!" called Charles by the coach door, anxious, for the train was moving.

She hurried to him; a porter closed the door on them. Vincent's orchids filled the table in the Pullman car. They seemed to have multiplied into a cascade.

"How sweet of him, Charles, to make that special journey!" she said, turning over the bouquet.

" He does nice things like that—I've always known my luck with Vincent."

Presently Mary looked at Charles, a thought in her mind. She could still hear that intense plea " Look after him, look after him, my dear ! " and see the anxiety in his grave face. " Charles," she asked, " hasn't Vincent some Scotch blood in him ? "

" Yes, his mother was Scotch—from Fife, I think. That gives him his Presbyterian gravity, I always imagine," said Charles, smiling over the paper he had opened.

" It explains something else, I think. I feel he's a little—fey ? "

" Fey ? If you mean by that he sees things, you're quite wrong. He's the most level-headed fellow I've ever known—and I know him inside out ! "

" I wonder if you——" With a sudden intuition of the male mind she changed the sentence before she uttered it. " I wonder if we should have these orchids put in water ? " she asked.

II

It was dark when the train drew into Venice over the long bridge across the lagoon. Mary, eagerly peering out, was disappointed. There seemed to be nothing but a low, black outline of buildings with a few lights. The railway station was drab and without any character. Bedlam broke out among the soft-slippered porters who fought for the luggage.

But out on the platform of terraced steps overlooking the dark stream, the lighted pavements and the glimmering façade of a church, the first note sounded in a growing orchestra of enchantment. There, rocking side by side, black and steely-prowed, were the famous gondolas. Helped down into one, she noticed the black leather cushions, the shining brass ornaments, the long, lean beauty of this craft, half swan, half punt.

Mary's grandmother had sent her gondolier, Mario, to meet them. He was a tall, saturnine fellow with Dantesque features, some fifty years of age. He wore a white and blue sailor's blouse with a red sash around his waist. His manner was grave, courteous and possessive. The swarm of mendicants, toothless old men with grappling hooks, redundant porters and uniformed hotel touts who effervesced about them as they came down the steps to the *fondamenta* were scattered by a stentorian blast of Italian from Mario. He firmly took the money out of Charles's hand, seeing his bewilderment, and paid the porters. They sullenly vanished. The gondola left the quay, gliding towards the low-arched bridge spanning the canal. Immediately the scene changed from their twentieth-century Europe to another world and era. Vivid life swarmed on the pavements on either hand. A hundred lights danced, a murmur of voices, the soft chug of a steamer, the lilt of a guitar, the lapping of water were mingled in this nocturnal theatre-piece. Speechless, Mary held Charles's hand. Yes, it was all that songs, de Musset's poetry and the cinema had striven to suggest.

" I suppose we shall get a good old Venetian whiff soon," said Charles brutally. " My God, look at that palace ! Why doesn't it crash into the water ? "

A towering façade of columns, balconies, Gothic stone windows, rose like a dark mountain against the sky, its front glimmering from the reflective water, a marble reality dissolving into a dream.

" Palazzo Vendramin. Riccardo Wagner, he died there," said the deep voice behind them.

" You speak English ? "

" *Si, Signore*—a leetle. I take you long way home to see all ? The canal maka long serpent curve. I cross it, or go long way home ? "

" As long as you can make it, please ! " cried Mary.

" *Si, Signora.*"

Mary gave her husband a playful dig.

" You see, he knows we're married."

" Why ? "

" He called me *signora*," whispered Mary, " not *signorina*."

" You needn't tell me that. I'll bet the whole Grand Canal knows we're honeymooning. It's their natural industry ! " scoffed Charles.

" You must be romantic, darling ! "

" If you really knew, I'm oozing it at every pore, but I'm damned if I'll let 'em see it. So I'm going to be brusque with 'em, my girl ! You don't think they'll burst into song and dance when we arrive, do you ? It's all rather *Madame Butterfly*, isn't it ? "

" We're in Italy, not Japan, Charles."

" We're in grand opera—just look at that ! "

" Palazzo Cà d'Oro," said the voice behind them.

" He understands everything we say. Be careful," whispered Mary.

" That will be a great handicap. Whoever designed these gondolas belonged to the Eavesdroppers' Union."

They were silent now for a long time. The pageant floated by them. The gondola slanted to the water, proceeding dog-fashion. Mario cursed a motor-launch that left a swamping wake. Its exhaust bombarded the marble walls of the canal. Then all was quiet again except for the murmuring life flowing along the café-illuminated pavements. The gondola rounded a point. Charles suddenly gripped Mary's hand.

"Look—it's there ! It's true—Shakespeare, Shylock and all the rest of it ! " cried Charles.

Before them a great arch, massively balustraded, spanned the dark water. They knew it at once, familiar as St. Paul's, and greeted it with a lift of the heart. There was no need of the voice behind them that gravely said, " The Rialto, *Signore* ! "

In about half an hour they turned off the widening canal, where a diamond crescent of light ran towards the dark horizon. They entered a side canal, silent, forbidding, where the unlit façades of houses rose cliff-like on either side.

" Rio San Vio, we come almost home," said Mario. " We have all for you ready, *Signore*."

" Thank you, Mario. Signora Trentham is away ? "

" *Si, si*. She go Tuesday to Cortina, to leave you alone. We know you want aloneness."

" Thank God for that, Mario," exclaimed Charles.

" It is solemn occasion, *Signore*," said the deep voice above them.

Mary and Charles looked at each other. The gondola noiselessly touched some steps and halted. Instantly a door opened, but it was so dark they could see nothing at first. Mario gave them his arm as they alighted. They mounted some steps, passed into a vast arched hall that resounded to their feet and followed a small smiling woman to a broad stone staircase up which ten men might have marched abreast. A great lantern hung from a dim ceiling, its faint light falling on dusky tapestries and two armoured knights flanking a double mahogany door. They passed on into the *salone nobile*, an immense room, with a high gilt-coffered ceiling. At the far end were six Gothic arches. The window of one of these was open, giving on to a romanesque balcony. A tall *cinquecento* fireplace, with carved armorial bearings dominated one side of the salon. A great tapestry, softly lit by two galleon lanterns, and a long table filled the other side. Persian rugs were spread over the wine-coloured marble floor.

They were not allowed to examine this exciting room. Their cicerone hurried, soft-slippered, before them. A short corridor brought them to a green enamelled door. They followed her in. It was their bedroom, mirrored, with painted panels, and flooded with light from an immense Venetian chandelier. The twin beds, with coverlets of crimson damask, had elaborate throne-heads from which fell the looped muslin mosquito nets. The woman hurried over to the window, unbarred it, and threw back the shutters, exclaiming, " *Bella vista* ! "

In the next few weeks they were to become familiar with that exclamation, but never with more justification than that evoked by the sight before them. They looked into a dark garden in which the sound of water rising and falling in the silver jet from a stone Cupid poised above a basin broke the cloistral quiet. Over the green darkness of the garden they beheld against the starry sky a tremendous dome, and twin towers scarcely credible to the sight. It seemed more a mountain than a monument of human creation, crowned with a winged angel, faint in the starry heaven.

" *Santa Maria della Salute*," said the woman in lyrical veneration, knowing she had brought them to a sublime revelation.

The gondolier appeared with their baggage, followed by a black-haired boy like a page stepping forth from a Veronese fresco.

" Thees is my wife, my son, *Signora*," said Mario briefly. " Dinner, it ees *pronto*, but as you are to please." He turned to his wife and son, smiling at the bridal pair. " *Venga!* " he commanded, and shooed them out of the room. The door closed. Charles and Mary surveyed the room, the bed-thrones, the great glass chandelier, the garden vista and the night sky filled with that towering dome of the church.

" The correct expression, I believe, is *Dio mio!* " said Charles. " *Il mio zio è arrivato!* "

" That's beyond me ! "

" It's the first Italian I learned in a play at Melton Mowbray. It means, " My God, my uncle has arrived ! "

" And my grandmother has departed ! " retorted Mary.

" Your family was always famous for tact. Oh, my darling ! " he said, pulling her to him and turning to the window. " Forty million poets can be wrong ! This is Venice ! "

To ecstasy they added industry. For a week they worked steadily through the sights, not as they had intended, with Baedeker loosely guiding them, but with Mario firmly ordering their progress. The architect grew daily in Charles and stirred him to almost frenzied excitement as the splendours of Sansovino and Palladio crowded their April days. The pageant of sunlit lagoon, palace and piazza passed swiftly as an enchanted land-scape seen from an express. They would have lingered, affectionately held by Mario and his obedient family, but Florence, Siena, Rome and Naples awaited them in the inexorable calendar of the orthodox honeymoon.

After Venice, Florence evoked her particular enchant-ment of peach-blossomed hillside, terraced vistas, domes, and towers along the Arno valley and in the Tuscan heights. Then came, too briefly, storied Siena. The Tuscan landscape detained them ere they hurried southwards, to achieve Rome in its Easter ecstasy of flower-filled piazzas, bright fountains and sonorous belfries. The gay crowds spilled over the Pincio and hummed in the bright Piazza di Spagna. Under high domes they heard the swelling Gregorian chant, the organ-burst of Pergolesi. They threaded the stream of black-garbed pilgrims, the corded and sandalled monks. They chartered canopied carriages to villa gardens and terraced restaurants. They watched from the Pincio and its sentinel pines the crimson evening fade over Rome, as though the winding sheet of day were dipped in the blood of its martyrs. They breakfasted in the hillside garden of the Hotel de Russie, they climbed to the rim of the great dome of St. Peter's, and dined *alfresco* as the evening tipped with its stars the cypress and ilex-haunted slopes of Frascati.

Meanwhile the portfolio of the architectural student grew to threatening dimensions, as Mary, pursuing her own passion for fine linens and porcelain, brought up the Conway cavalcade. They entrusted their spoils to the confident service of an agent, and, fearful of imminent ruin, made daily new self-denying ordinances, all futile under this southern sky whose bright splendour permitted no cautionary cloud. And as they explored this vivid world, new vistas of human relationship were revealed to them. Their joys were increased by the sharing, their fatigues lessened. It was soon as if there had never been any life apart and nothing could ever exist whose foundations were not united in their single consciousness. At night, when they lay in each other's arms, faintly visible in the moonlight threading the latticed shutters of their garden-haunted balcony, they had no lament for time past, no anxiety for time to come. The inevitable sorrows of the human pilgrimage would find them serene, they were sure. The coldest wind of Fate could only lock them more surely in a fast embrace. Their fortitude would never fail. People smiled, seeing them pass by or sitting at table together. They were provocatively happy, young, graceful, and full of energy and adventure. To others it might inevitably seem an illusion, but they knew this inbreathing of the spirit came from the deep reality of a perfect union.

"Can one be too happy—are we taking too much from life?" she asked Charles during the silence of content that bound them one evening as they lingered on their balcony, while a far campanile bell tolled midnight.

"Oh, the Greek moment," he said, smiling at her.

"Meaning? Charles, I never knew you were so erudite!"

"That sounds a horrible accusation! 'Count no man happy until he's dead,' they said. The Greeks always argued themselves into a state of uncomfortable intelligence."

"But is that intelligent—to believe in Fate?"

"I would not be sure, but intelligence is not all," he said, taking the pipe out of his mouth.

"You have lots of faith, Charles, haven't you?" she asked, leaning her head against the lattice as she watched a man's hand knock out the ash, in a familiar gesture now part of her being.

"Not as Father Marshall would regard it, but faith enough to make me grateful," he replied quietly, reaching for her hand. He rose, pulling her up with him. "Listen!"

Someone down in the darkness below began to play

a guitar. Then Italian voices expostulating and laughing came up to them. They listened. The player was skilful.

"Bed, darling," said Charles after a time.

They closed the shutters. The music rose faintly from the garden until sleep overtook them.

CHAPTER III

THE MONASTERY

I

FOR the southward journey from Rome Charles hired
a car and chauffeur. The hundred and fifty-five miles
between Rome and Naples offered a panorama of hill
towns perched above the olive-filled valleys, russet-tiled
farmhouses and meadows of young maize. But they
could not linger. Some eighty miles south lay another
bait for the architectural student. Near Cassino, high
on its mountain-top, stood the great medieval Benedictine monastery of Monte Cassino, a town in itself,
massive with courtyards and cloisters and domed church.
This was their destination for the day.

The road out of Rome brought them in the vivid
morning to Colonna. They took the eastern road, the
old Via Casilina that led through the foothills of the
Tiburtines, instead of the coastal route of the Appian
Way. The small hill towns shone in the morning sun.
The air was fresh at Valmontone. They came to
Frosinone, a little town laid out on a hill above the olive-
green Cosa valley. They stopped the car before an
albergo with a bright awning. It was too alluring to
pass, its balconies buried in mauve wistaria. They
wanted a reprieve from their demon driver, a sleek
young Roman whose ambition seemed to be the killing
of all livestock on the road. Charles dubbed him

" Orlando Furioso." He tore through the mountain villages, oblivious of life and scenery. At Frosinone he disappeared into the *albergo's* kitchen, hidden beyond a vine pergola, and by the cries of delight that came from that direction he had evidently found much entertainment.

Mary and Charles chose a table in the sun, not too near a lean young man who was sketching. He seemed to welcome company. His easy, slow speech marked him for an American. In three minutes he had from them all the biographical details he required. Charles became inquisitive in turn.

" Place you never heard of—Denton, Texas. Yessir, the home town boy's gone astray," said the artist, smiling. " An American's a rare sight for the folks up in these hills. Been here three years—arrived like you one morning, had a drink in the sun, and Ah've sat here ever since ! Don't paint much, enough to amuse myself, but Ah'm a creative artist. Like to see my works ? "

" Thank you, we would," replied Mary, amused, but fearing the worst.

" Giulietta ! " he shouted, looking upwards.

A girl, bare-legged and almost bare-breasted, came on to the balcony and looked down. She was a young Juno, in black muslin, not more than nineteen, sun-ripened as a peach, bright-eyed, with black curls framing a face of cameo-cut beauty.

The Texan talked in rapid Italian to her. She shook her head violently, but her eyes and mouth laughed, a vision of luscious youth. They argued, then she went in.

" She's bringing 'em," said the lean young man, rising. " They're being washed. She washes 'em like a cat ! "

At that moment the young madonna of the balcony emerged. Charles and Mary gave a gasp of delight.

In either arm the girl bore a naked infant. Dark eyes, black curls, red pouting lips and chubby limbs adorned the smiling girl-mother ; it was an altar panel from the brush of Fra Lippo Lippi, framed in sunlit wistaria blossom.

"That's Houston and Jefferson, aged one and two. Fine kids, eh ? Ah'd like to keep 'em like that, but kids shoot up here like beanstalks. Yessir ! Fine mother, too. Speak to my friends, Giulietta—she's a shy kid with company," he explained, turning to them, " but boy ! she's a temper and teeth, a little wild-cat, but Ah've got her so ! " He pressed his thumb down on the table. " Number three's coming up—want a girl this time, and Ah guess Ah'll be lucky. Say hello, kid ! " he shouted up the balcony.

" Good morning ! " said the girl. " Pleesa to excuse the *bimbi* no clothings."

" There—just cute, ain't she, folks ? Now Ah like to see their rosy toes, round bottoms and plump bellies— but oh, no, nothing in the nude for these natives."

He cooed at the babies who gave him the white of their eyes. " They'd sure have a public in Denton ! " exclaimed the delighted father. He blew the trio a kiss. The mother withdrew, smiling.

They paid the bill. The Texan followed them to the car and shut the door on them.

" Nice seeing you ! " he said. Lean, scarcely thirty, he had reddish hair and a puckish smile. He rode life easily, it was clear to see.

The sleek young chauffeur began to talk, half turning while he drove furiously.

" The Americano much amusing, *Signore ?* He maka *bimbi* alla up and downa the mountain. *Un giorno* he find mooch trouble with angry papa—so ! " He drew his finger across his throat and grinned delightedly.

" Keep your hands on the wheel—and slower ! " commanded Charles peremptorily.

" *Si, Signore.*"

" I suppose they are married. What lovely children," whispered Mary.

Charles laughed. " *L'après-midi d'un Americain*, perhaps. Did you notice the points on his ears ? Our scallywag at the wheel's probably right—*La Vie de Bohême, Murer* in the mountains ! The girl's luscious— what children ! "

He looked at Mary with candid eyes. She laughed a little, embarrassed by the unspoken thought.

A few miles further on they crossed a bridge over a slatey grey stream.

" River Liri—we are in the Liri valley," said the chauffeur. Later, nearing Aquino, he pointed ahead to a bleak chalky ridge cutting the skyline. " Monte Cassino, *il monasterio, Signore.*"

They looked. On the skyline a great wall of masonry covered the mountain-top like a guardian fortress. A quarter of an hour later they approached the town, entering along the Rapido River past a Roman amphitheatre. They drove up to the hotel where they planned to stay the night.

II

The *Albergo Monte Cassino* was clean, unpretentious and almost empty. It seemed as if their arrival had stirrred the place to sudden life. Cats scurried into hiding, the padrone and his wife, all smiles and chatter, bustled and bowed their way before them. A half-naked cook peered out of the kitchen and had the door slammed on him. They mounted a staircase of heavy stone, past an alcove with a jaunty bust of Garibaldi. An oleograph portrait of King Umberto, epauletted and medal-laden, glowered amid the palms on the landing. They were ushered into a dim bedroom, and the inevitable pantomime followed. There was a grating of hinges, a sudden burst of light and then the ecstatic *Bella Vista!*

They stepped on to a balcony above a rapid stream that washed the foundation of the hotel. Before them, across the narrow valley the mountain rose steeply, and there, dominating the high skyline, was the great monastery, towered, domed, many-windowed, stretched out in the noonday sun, a presence never to be forgotten or dismissed.

Charles and Mary came back into the room. It was spacious and comfortable, but they quailed before the bed. There was no question of its capacity, its Vittorio Emmanuele era. It was immense, brassy, the head-rail embossed with plaques of saints, a *letto matrimoniale* for ever alien to an age of twin beds and pyjamas. Charles suppressed a smile.

" *Il campo santo,*" he commented.

The padrone and his wife gave him a frightened look and then broke into effervescent mirth. They trilled like a pair of roller canaries in delight at the wit of the *Signor Inglese.*

" *Si,* you laya down and you not wanta get oop ! " exclaimed the little man, wiping his eyes. " *Buon riposo!* "

A dwarf brought in their baggage, a maid appeared with towels. Yes, lunch would be ready in a few minutes. They were alone at last. An exclamation from Charles made Mary look up from her portmanteau.

" See who's here—the G.O.M. ! "

Mary looked. On the wall over the writing bureau hung a large coloured portrait of W. E. Gladstone. The wide, tight mouth, the baleful eye, " chokey " collar and bow were unmistakable.

" What on earth is he doing here ? " asked Mary.

" Ah, then you don't know what Mr. Gladstone said in 1866 ? I have it here." Charles took out the loose-leaf notebook in which he kept his data, a repository that seemed inexhaustible on their tour. He opened it.

" This is what Mr. Gladstone really did say in 1866, or rather wrote, when the Italian Government began to suppress the monasteries. Monte Cassino seemed doomed with all the others. It was too much even for that resolute Anglo-Catholic. He wrote pleading for the Monastery. Here are his words : " The foundation and history of Monte Cassino have the interest for us which the Americans of the States feel in Alfred, in Edward III, in Henry V. They are part of the great current of Italian civilisation which has been diffused and distributed all over European lands." They used to listen to Gladstone. He was the Voice. So they left the monastery alone, and now it's a national monument. Darling, are you as hungry as I am ? "

Mary made no answer, but looked at him. Her hands went up to his shoulders. Her eyes rested on his face, so eager and boyish. " Where did you find that, Charles ? Where do you find all those odd little bits of knowledge that make me feel such an ignoramus ? I begin to know now why Vincent loves you so. You feed him all the time, like me—and you make each day so exciting."

He laughed and drew her to him. They stood together while Mr. Gladstone glowered at them out of his mahogany frame.

" They say his wife was devoted to him," observed Mary. " And now it's all over for them."

D

" But not for us."

" No—it can never be over for us, never, Charles," she said, almost fiercely. " Can it ? "

" Never," he said, smiling at her intensity. " Ready ? "

She nodded and slipped from his arms. They went down to lunch. At two the car was coming to take them up to the Monastery.

III

Orlando Furioso was waiting for them. They were soon out of the town and began the long zig-zag ascent of the mountain before them. Slowly as they turned on the hairpin bends the town and the Liri valley spread out below them, with the blue vein of the Rapido winding southwards to its confluence with the Garigliano and the Mediterranean sea.

The mountainside was clothed in firs and mountain pines. The scene grew in magnificence as range after range came into view. The site of the monastery had been well chosen for safety and power. It commanded the valley, the town and the Rome-Naples highway from its height of seventeen hundred feet.

They had expected to see a large monastery, but as they drew near to the vast rectangular pile it seemed like a walled city. What a cavalcade of history it had witnessed through the centuries ! Down in the little town where Roman Casinum had given place to medieval San Germano, emperors, kings and popes had resided, plotted, made war and peace. Here in 529 came young St. Benedict to destroy idolatry in the pagan temple on the hill and found the abbey that became the seat of Western monasticism. Five times destroyed and rebuilt, its fame spread across Europe.

" One wonders how it has survived human rage and folly," said Charles as he outlined its history to his wife. " Lombards and Saracens sacked it, but it was always rebuilt."

They were not the only visitors. Half a dozen cars stood in the parking-place. They entered under a massive arch into the central cloister and came to a passage with a guardroom. A monk approached them, coming out of the office labelled *Padre forestieraio*.

" English ? " he asked, and when they replied he summoned a monk in a black robe and sandals. " You would like to see everything ? " he asked in excellent English. He was about twenty-five, of strong physique, with a young athlete's head and clear eyes. His close crop gave him the appearance of a boxer.

" Everything, if it's not too fatiguing—the mosaics, most of all the library and the chief architectural features," said Charles. " This lady is my wife."

The young monk gave her a grave bow.

" Your English is very good ! " said Mary.

" I am English—I'm a lay brother. I teach in the seminary."

" There is a school ? " asked Charles.

" Yes, we have over two hundred boarders. This way, please."

They passed through the Cloister of the Strangers, with its twin-columned cistern and baroque statues of Saint Benedict and his sister, Saint Scholastica. A grand flight of steps brought them level with an upper terrace and the Portico. Through this in growing wonder they were led to the Cloister of the Founders. It was strange in the general stillness of that mountain air to hear the raucous cawing of jackdaws who were privileged to inhabit this court, following a tradition of Saint Benedict's homily to them. They came to the door of the

cathedral, bronze inlaid with silver, made in Constanti-
nople in 1067. They entered the church, proceeding
to the altar over the tomb of the saint, overawed by the
lavish ornamentation, the mosaics, the paintings, the
marbles, the carved choir, the rococo side chapels and
seventeenth-century organ. Centuries of loving and
intricate workmanship had gone to the creation of this
basilica cathedral. The young monk thoughtfully paused
and never intruded with the patter so customary in church
guides. They visited the Sacristy and the crypt. Emerg-
ing into the vivid day again, they traversed arcaded
corridors, passing processions of dark-eyed boys and
masters proceeding from the seminary. They came at
last to the great library.

"It would take years to explore our treasures," said
the lay brother, with the first touch of pride in his speech.
"We have 80,000 volumes, 12,000 manuscripts, and over
40,000 ancient records kept here—centuries of classical
and ancient lore on which the brethren have worked.
See," he continued, coming to a stand, "this is the auto-
graph of Pergolesi's *Stabat Mater*. This was a great school
of the medieval copyists. But for the Abbot Desiderius,
who became Pope in 1086, many classical treasures would
have been lost to the world—Varro, Tacitus, Apuleius
and others. We have Origen's commentary on the
Epistle to the Romans, dating from the sixth century
and the *Vision* of the monk Alberic, dating from the
twelfth. Except for this there might have been no
Dante, for it is believed his poem was suggested by
Alberic's *Vision*. Dante himself alluded to Saint Benedict,
our Founder, and to this monastery, in the twenty-
second Canto of his *Paradiso*. We have here also
some eight hundred documents of emperors, kings,
and princes, and many papal bulls relating to the
Abbey."

"They're all in a much better state than when Boccaccio came here, I'm sure," observed Charles, looking down the vista of bookshelves.

"Boccaccio? Was he ever here?" queried the young monk.

"Ah, you've not read your John Addington Symonds? Can I give you the passage?" asked Charles, pulling a slim volume out of his pocket.

"That would be very instructive," said the young monk, showing two rows of perfect teeth as he smiled. "Our reading is restricted, and I'm no scholar."

He motioned for them to sit on the wooden bench in the deep recessed window that commanded the valley, the town and the distant mountains.

"What do you teach?" asked Mary, growing ever more curious concerning this strange young man in a monk's habit.

"Gymnastics," he said, smiling faintly, and aware of the effect of this reply. "But I study also. I am a lay brother."

"If I may say so, you look more like the boxing ring than the monk's cell," said Charles, laughing.

"Not a bad guess!" responded the young monk, laughing also. "I was considered pretty good at Sandhurst."

"Sandhurst?"

"I was once in the army."

"Good God! I beg your pardon," said Charles hurriedly. Their eyes met. There was a moment of embarrassed silence.

"Boccaccio?" asked the young monk. "You were saying——"

"Oh, yes—it's here somewhere. Yes, here we are. It's about Boccaccio's quest for the lost manuscripts of

Cicero. He made a visit here, some time in the fourteenth century."

Charles began to read : " ' When he was in Apulia, attracted by the celebrity of the convent, he paid a visit to Monte Cassino, whereof Dante speaks. Desirous of seeing the collection of books, which he understood to be a very choice one, he modestly asked a monk—for he was always most courteous in manners—to open the library as a favour for him. The monk answered stiffly, pointing to a steep staircase, " Go up, it is open." Boccaccio went up gladly ; but he found that the place which held so great a treasure was without door or key. He entered and saw grass sprouting on the windows, and all the books and benches thick with dust. In his astonishment he began to open and turn the leaves of first one tome and then another, and found many and divers volumes of ancient and foreign works. Some of them had lost several sheets ; others were snipped and pared all round the text, and mutilated in various ways. At length, lamenting that the toil and study of so many illustrious men should have passed into the hands of most abandoned wretches, he departed with tears and sighs. Coming to the cloister, he asked a monk whom he met why those valuable books had been so disgracefully mangled. He answered that the monks, seeking to gain a few *soldi*, were in the habit of cutting up sheets and making psalters which they sold to boys. The margins, too, they manufactured into charms, and sold to women. " So then, O man of study, go to and rack your brains ; make books that you may come to this ! " ' That's what Boccaccio saw on his visit here," commented Charles.

" I assure you we're much reformed—look ! " said the young monk, smiling. " But thank you, I have so much to learn."

They tramped along corridors, they climbed steps, they traversed cloisters, room unfolding after room in this great maze of monastery-cathedral-college. Skilfully, in a crescendo of wonders, their guide saved the *pièce de résistance* until the end. They came to a balcony on the east side of the second courtyard. It was the far-famed Terrace of Paradise. It was well named, for the panorama of plain and mountain spread out before them held them entranced. It was like a window in heaven. Southwards and westwards ran the broad village-dotted valley of the Liri river, with wave on wave of receding hills merging into the blue horizon, where they glimpsed the sea in the Gulf of Gaeta.

Eastwards, beneath them, lay the town of Cassino in its enclosed valley, guarded by the rocky summits of the Matese mountains, the Rapido river running through it like a blue ribbon, a terrain so lovely and peaceful, so rich with soft colour, that it seemed like a painting of the Primitive School. Northwards, almost brutal in contrast, rose the wild peaks of the Abruzzi mountains, with the great Monte Cairo dominating the foreground. The falling sun, under a crimson baldachino of clouds, took the day westwards, while, fold on fold, the oncoming night laid its sable cloak over the eastern hills.

They parted with their athletic guide. The mystery of him had monopolised their thoughts. By what strange events, so early, had he retreated from the bright free world for which he seemed so well equipped? They would never know the story of his renunciation. He had the air and manner of a courtier, and when Charles pressed upon him the little gift of the book from which he had read, it was received with a princely grace.

" I am Charles Conway from Leicestershire—we are on our honeymoon," explained Charles. " May I know your name ? Perhaps one day when you return to England we may meet ? "

" I'm Brother Sebastian. Thank you, but it is improbable I shall ever return to England—though a Benedictine must regard it as his particular parish," he said, smiling. Then, aware that they were puzzled by his allusion, he added, " The history of our Order is the history of the English Church. A Benedictine monk, Saint Augustine, established the first English Benedictine monastery at Canterbury, soon after his arrival in 597. The nine old cathedrals were served by our Order."

" It is a very large one ? " asked Mary encouragingly, for she found herself moved by the quiet ardour of this young man.

" In the fourteenth century there were thirty-seven monasteries serving the Church. We have numbered twenty-four popes, two hundred cardinals, seven thousand archbishops, fifteen thousand bishops, twenty emperors, ten empresses, forty-seven kings and fifty queens. And millions of the faith have served in the humblest stations."

" We must thank you for your kindness," said Charles as they came back to the entrance court.

" It's been a great pleasure. My heart is in England, and my love for it remains, quell it though I would," said Brother Sebastian wistfully, and then, as if to correct his human weakness, added, " I have found happiness here. May the blessing of Our Lady rest upon you through many years."

He looked at them kindly, and they saw briefly a shadow of sorrow in his clear grey eyes. Then he turned and hurried away.

Deeply moved, they watched his retreating figure, the square, proud head, the firm young shoulders and the athlete's form that not even the loose monk's habit could hide. There was a springiness in his bare sandalled feet, incongruous in one who had renounced the creative flesh and the vivid world.

"Well, that would give any novelist a theme," said Charles. "What a place it is! My dear, could you bear it? I want to go round again; there are some notes I must make, and our monk obsessed me—or are you too tired?"

"Darling, do; but I'm going to sit in the cloister. You want to be free. I'm perfectly happy," answered Mary.

"Sure?"

"Quite sure—a man's work, you know——"

He laughed, and went off happily.

The bell was tolling for vespers and the closing of the monastery when Charles returned, fatigued but happy.

"The old notebook's bursting," he said, elated, whirring its leaves. "I could spend a week here. Architecturally it's got everything. They tell me ten thousand people come here every year."

"We'll come back one day—and find out what's happened to Brother Sebastian. Do you think that's his real name?" asked Mary.

"It might be—but I suspect not. They take new names when they make their vows, I believe. Sebastian's an obvious choice for a fellow like that. Wasn't the original one, the saint fellow who seemed to enjoy having all those arrows shot at him, a vigorous young Roman officer? All those painting fellows with an eye for a torso always chose him. I think our Sebastian would strip very well and revel in martyrdom!"

"Oh, Charles, don't make fun of him, poor boy!"

"Sorry—I wouldn't for worlds. I like him immensely. Now where's Orlando Furioso?" asked

Charles as they passed out of the great door to the car park. " Ah, there he is ! Darling, I'm hungry again ! I hope there's a good dinner—with a bottle of *Lacrimæ Christi*."

IV

The light of the early morning, coming through the closed shutters in long pencils of silver light, awakened him. For a few moments Charles contemplated the unfamiliar room with its painted ceiling crowded with rosy cherubs tumbling amid cornucopias of flowers and wreathed statues. Later he became conscious of the great bed in which he slept, and the warmth of a form beside him. Turning, he saw the beloved face, the loose fair hair dimming the smooth brow and billowing about the slender throat. He moved an arm towards her, his hand slipping over the silk of her pyjama jacket until he had encircled her breast and gently insinuated himself into the yielding curve of her slender body. She stirred, turned drowsily towards him, a hand moving to the firm shoulder against her. They lay thus, relaxed, soft-breathing while the light grew and odd sounds of the day's awakening came into the dim room. How long they lay thus they did not know or wish to know, but when at last Mary's eyes opened, to scan the head cushioned against her shoulder, he was awake, and the greeting kiss touched her cheek as she spoke.

" Is it late ? " she whispered.

" I don't think so—and don't care. I like this double bed," he said, nestling against her. " Why are we going to Naples ? "

" Oh, darling, we must keep our programme ! "

" There's no ' must ' for us, sweet. The whole world's

ours. Nothing matters with a bed like this—it's double bliss ! "

He gave a deep sigh and snuggled deep, his face half hidden in the curve of her arm, while with a free hand he playfully traced the line of her throat.

" Weren't you terribly tired last night—I don't remember falling asleep," asked Mary.

" I'm still terribly tired—let's spend the day in bed ! "

" What would Orlando Furioso think ? "

" He can't think—he's just a mechanism in a state of constant acceleration."

" Perhaps they've double beds in Naples," suggested Mary, " so we'll get it out of our system."

" No, we're going to the Palace Hotel, which will be *de luxe*. It caters for the plutocracy, and the plutocracy insists on twin beds."

They lay in blissful silence. Then Italian voices sounded outside from below their balcony. Later someone dropped a tin that rattled in a resounding diminuendo.

" I love our Italian friends, but they have no eardrums. Remember those hellish motor-boats on the Grand Canal—and now some sorcerer's apprentice is tin-canning the morning ! " complained Charles.

He sat up, hanging over her while she laughed at him. He moved out of bed, went across the room and threw open wide the shutters.

" *Bella vista !* " he cried as the silver morning flooded the room. " The old monastery's there—you know, it quite bullies the landscape. You can never get away from it, it's so dominant and immense. What a pile ! It looks bigger than ever this morning." He crossed to the bed, put one knee on it, and looked at his wife.

" Oh, Mary, you——" The sentence went unfinished as his mouth pressed against hers. She ran her fingers

through his hair, laughed at him, and said, banteringly,
" Get thee to a monastery."

" Poor Brother Sebastian ! " he said, leaning over her.
" If only he knew ! "

" Perhaps he did, and that's what he ran away
from ! "

" Crazy and monstrous child," said Charles, tweaking
her nose.

" We must get up, darling."

" I'll inspect and report on the morning, my lady,"
he said, rising from the bed and walking towards the
balcony.

He stood in the sunlight there, while she lay looking
up at the rosy riot on the ceiling. Then she heard his
voice reciting, the rich, full voice she knew and treasured :

> Morning's at seven ;
> The hill-side's dew-pearled ;
> The lark's on the wing ;
> The snail's on the thorn :
> God's in his heaven——
> All's right with the world !

" All's right with the world." If only it could always
be so, she pondered. If others could be happy, as they
were happy, if this could go on undiminished by custom.
That was asking too much. Love could not breathe
for ever on such heights. It must go on pilgrimage and
be strong to walk through storms. Not every woman
was so blessed, had such a companion for the unknown
journey.

She let her reverie run, then spoke to Charles, who
made no answer. She spoke again and then sat up.
She could not see him on the balcony.

" Charles ! " she cried to him beyond the shutter.

He made no answer. " Charles ! " she called, louder,

and then, moving from the bed, " Charles ! " she cried again with a note of fear. " Charles, aren't you———"

She reached the empty balcony, saw the great monastery on the hill above her, and then, in the corner beyond the folded shutter, a man's form strangely collapsed.

" Charles ! " she screamed. " Charles, darling ! "

She bent over him and lifted his head. It lolled terribly between her hands, with unseeing eyes. She stood up, trembling, and then, in the blackness of panic ran, crying, out of the room, along the corridor, to the staircase, where a startled maid encountered her.

There was a half-hour of nameless anguish. Two women, vainly seeking to comfort her in a language she could not understand, detained her in a strange room. But even before the distracted landlord came in, raising his hands and crying, " *È morto ! Povero Signore ! È morto !* " she knew the dreadful truth.

V

It was a wet summer. From the window of a third-floor flat in Cadogan Gardens, Charles Conway's mother stood looking out upon the shining pavement and dank trees below her. A steady drizzle fell from the leaden July sky. It was not the rain Mrs. Conway was watching, but the almost empty street, hoping every moment to see a taxi draw up at the door below. Half an hour ago Mary had telephoned her to say she was coming in to tea. She was quite surprised to learn Mary was in town. Since that dreadful tragedy of her honeymoon she had gone back to Brent Abbey, her old home, and had refused to go anywhere. The Hall stood empty, its future undetermined. Later, they must face the problem. Mrs. Conway had been to visit her daughter-in-law twice. She had met her on her return to London with Vincent Shore, who had gone out to Italy at once. After a night at the apartment they had travelled down to Leicestershire together for the funeral. Only a month ago she had gone there again, and was happier on seeing the resignation with which Mary was facing life. The telephone call this afternoon had been quite unexpected and she wondered what had brought her so suddenly to town.

At twenty minutes to five Mrs. Conway's vigil was rewarded by the sight of Mary stepping out of the taxi that had halted below. A few seconds later the apartment bell rang, and Alice, her maid, ushered in young Mrs. Conway, slight and neat in her black coat and skirt. She kissed her mother-in-law and gave her the bouquet of flowers she was carrying. Alice brought in the tea. It was not until the maid had completed the service and left the room that Mary looked at her mother-in-law and began to talk.

" You wonder what I'm doing here ? " she asked, smiling.

" Darling, it's not my business," said Mrs. Conway, not willing to have her eager curiosity challenged. She poured the tea and passed the cup. " But I am surprised—with such short notice."

" I only decided to come yesterday. I rang and got an appointment for two o'clock to-day."

" An appointment ? "

" Yes, in Harley Street, with Dr. Appleton."

" Oh, Mary—you're not ill, there's nothing wrong, darling ! " cried Mrs. Conway, apprehensively.

Mary put a hand on her arm and smiled.

" Nothing wrong, mother," she said quietly, looking at her. " Nothing, darling. But I know now—God answers prayer."

Mrs. Conway stared at her daughter-in-law, bewildered by this calm assertion. Then the light in the girl's face as their eyes met made the revelation clear. There was a moment of deep silence as they looked at each other in wordless happiness.

" Oh, Mary, my darling," cried Mrs. Conway, putting out trembling hands towards the young face shining before her. " What happiness for you, for all of us ! " she exclaimed, her sight dimming as she leaned forward to kiss her daughter-in-law.

CHAPTER IV

BROTHER SEBASTIAN

I

EVERYBODY knew and liked the Carters. It was one of those families that seemed to have everything. They lived in a large, beautiful house, set in spacious grounds half-way up a hill that looked over the Sussex Weald. The size of the family was just right—two boys, one girl. There was no lack of money, though they spent it freely. Mr. and Mrs. Carter were the best-dressed couple around Grinstead, and they were almost famous because of the beauty and turn-out of the " Carter kids," as they were known. From birth they commanded attention. When they took an airing in their prams they excited comment, and a proud Nanny was stopped in the course of shopping and asked how old they were, and whose children they were. Fair as angels, blue-eyed, with masses of curling hair and chubby limbs, they were a threat to any baby contest. " They're poster kids ! They look like baby-food advertisements. I'll bet they grow up into horrors ! They always do ! " prophesied Colonel Candy, the town's cynic. Time proved the Colonel wrong.

Their angelic beauty faded, but Jack, Gerald and Janet remained through childhood and youth a remarkable trio. " They're so full of fun and good-tempered, not a bit spoilt," people said of them. The Carter

parents were the most popular pair in the neighbourhood. Mrs. Carter was quiet, soft-voiced, small-limbed.
She looked like a woman always on the verge of invalid-
ism, so frail that any current epidemic seemed a threat
to her existence. Everyone wondered how such a
woman could produce such offspring, for Jack, at nineteen, was over six feet and well-proportioned, Gerald,
at eighteen, was tougher and heavier, Janet, at seventeen,
had the fresh beauty of an opening rose.

Mr. Carter's vital contribution was perplexing. Physic-
ally, he simply did not belong to the family. He was
short, swarthy and taciturn. He lived in an atmosphere
of infectious high spirits, good looks and improvised
gaiety. He was always left outside the family activities
and was quite bewildered by the ever-changing interests
of his inexhaustible children. He was successful in
making money and spent it lavishly. Perhaps ten years
in the Detroit automobile business had given him the
American standards of expenditure. At a time when
one car in the family was considered adequate there
were five in the garage, communally owned and used
with the exception of the Rolls-Royce, the family omni-
bus and driven only by Davis, the family mechanic.
Mrs. Carter had a plain Ford, Jack had a Bugatti that
thumped over the countryside, Gerald drove a sports
Alvis, while Janet was content with the Morris-Cowley
discarded by her mother. Mr. Carter was Daimler-
minded. There never seemed an hour of the day when
the low bleat of an exhaust did not sound in the drive
or in the long Tudoresque garage beyond the tennis-
court.

The diversity in the choice of cars was paralleled in
many aspects of the Carter menage. Mr. Carter, a
Dundee Scot, a son of the manse, and descended from
a line of Presbyterian ministers, had chosen for his bride

E

lovely young Kitty Delaney, met on a boat coming from Buenos Aires. Everything and everybody was against the marriage. Her parents were strict Catholics, large landowners in the Argentine, and intensely ambitious for their only daughter. In this their wish seemed about to be fulfilled, for at twenty-one Kitty was engaged to the second son of a marquis, of one of the oldest Catholic families in England. John Carter, with no money, no looks, and no youth, for he was thirty-five and a Presbyterian to boot, performed the miracle. He supplanted the aristocratic fiancé, defied the parents and took his bride, reared in luxury, to a grim Lancashire town, where he was a works manager on a small salary. The compromise with the Church was unusual. The boys were to be raised in the Catholic faith, the girls as Presbyterians. Contrary to all prophecies, the marriage was a great success. John Carter prospered and adored his young wife. She, equally in love, presented to him the renowned Carter kids.

Never did one man with apparently so little achieve so much. He had hidden resources of character not visible to the casual eye. A tremendous worker, he was almost reckless in the little things and fanatically tenacious in pursuit of the main object. At fifty-five he was a comparatively wealthy man. He knew his limitations. He had a masterly grasp of a blue-print, but was utterly bewildered by the spontaneous unconventionality of his family. He never opposed it and bought peace and affection by a complete surrender to their unpredictable wishes. When Mrs. Carter took a sudden dislike to the old Oxfordshire manor house on whose restoration he had spent a fortune, and suddenly expressed a wish for a flat in Knightsbridge, he sold up and moved without a murmur.

Three years later the family sighed for a country life

again, so to Sussex they moved. Any morning at breakfast-time he was prepared to hear a family decision to move again, which he would not oppose. In gratitude for all that life had given him—a woman he loved and a family that filled his days with gaiety and bewilderment—he was willing to surrender everything except his passion for speculative business. In this they showed the utmost loyalty and fortitude. Twice he had reduced them all to comparative poverty by unlucky adventures. Their beautiful homes had vanished with servants, cars and horses. Dismal flats had housed them during temporary eclipses, but all this had never impaired their faith in " the old Dad."

He was more cautious now. A man nearing sixty had not the same power of recovery ; moreover, his ambition was less over-reaching. " I charge thee, Cromwell, fling away ambition, by that sin fell the angels," Shakespeare had made Wolsey say, but John Carter knew that the threat had a medical term. Coronary thrombosis was what the doctors warned ambitious men of, in the sixties. In ten more years his three lovely children would be established, their course in life chosen, married, and happy, he hoped. He wanted to live through those next ten years ; it would all be worth beholding. In 1924 he would be sixty-six, time to retire and sit watching Jack, Gerald and Janet.

He put the two boys through Beaumont, and sent Janet to a French convent school. Contrary to expectation, it was Gerald who evolved as the family athlete. He achieved the school eight, rowing at Henley in his last year. He had a compact body, muscular yet graceful, with a neat square head that was Roman in appearance, so that he looked like the young Cæsar Augustus. When he decided to be a soldier, and after a brief stay at the crammer's, went on to Sandhurst, no one was surprised.

It was Jack who astonished them all—Jack, six feet two, a young giant with the head of the Archangel Gabriel, an impetuous talker with a first-class brain that promised for him the highest scholastic distinction. He came back from Cambridge in his second year expecting to rock the family with his proposal. Since a child he had shown astonishing virtuosity with pencils, crayons and brushes. Now all he desired to do was to paint. Art was his career, he announced to the family at breakfast one morning.

"Dad, I don't want to go back to Cambridge. I want a couple of years in a Paris *atelier*," he said.

"But, darling, shouldn't you finish at Cambridge, take your degree and then——" began Mrs. Carter.

"Mummy darling, what's the use! I'm going to be an artist, not a schoolmaster. Do you agree, Dad?"

They looked at Dad. Gerald and Janet knew this bombshell was coming. The trio had held long and passionate discussions on the subject. They thought Jack crazy, but they failed to shake him. In a month's time he would be in receipt of a small legacy from an aunt. He said he could live on this—he was not asking anything from the family.

Mr. Carter did not seem startled. He buttered a piece of toast, munched slowly and then gazed gently at his son. He had hoped that Jack would go into the business, suppressing misgivings as to his fitness for it, but, a wise man, he knew the folly of compelling sons to follow their father's footsteps.

"If you feel you must paint and if you have considered how remote is the possibility of success, in any financial sense, then I can't stop you, my boy. I would have liked you to finish at Cambridge, but I can't compel you, and I won't try. You'll manage on that legacy of yours?" he asked.

" Of course, I wouldn't dream of asking you to support me," responded Jack at once.

" I think your vow of poverty will have a salutary effect," observed Mr. Carter, not without a touch of grimness.

In the study, when they were together, Mrs. Carter did a little pleading. Couldn't Jack's allowance be continued for a year or two ?

" Not a penny, my dear, not a penny. Let him finance his own folly," said Mr. Carter. " He has a thousand pounds from his aunt's legacy—that may last him four years, and he should know then whether he can earn his living or not."

" And if he can't ? "

" We might be able to talk sense together then—the young have to get things out of their blood, my dear," said Mr. Carter, smiling.

" You've no faith in his career as an artist ? "

" He has a thousand to one chance. I'm not more pessimistic than that, and of course he might be the one ! " said Mr. Carter with a chuckle.

So it was settled. The jubilant Jack set off for Paris and for a time the family circle was enlivened by a series of sparkling letters narrating the adventures of a young man in the gay capital. " If he can paint as well as he can write he may get somewhere," said Mr. Carter one morning when his wife had finished reading the latest chronicle.

It was arranged for Gerald and Janet to go over with the car, join Jack in Paris, and then, together, motor down to the Riviera and spend August there. Already in Cannes, staying with his aunt, there was Richard Falmouth, Gerald's great friend at Sandhurst. That holiday, so ecstatically planned, never took place. In mid-July Gerald was " warned " not to leave the country, owing to the tense situation in Europe. On August 4th England was at war with Germany. A week later Jack came back from Paris. By Christmas, 1914, Mrs. Carter was the mother of two lieutenants in the army and Janet was driving a car for a colonel at the War Office. Mr. Carter had obtained a big contract for war materials. " I shall make a million, but they won't let me keep it," he said laconically. He was working twelve hours a day and enjoying it. His growing factories began to eat up the countryside.

For more than five years the Carter kids had been the life of every party in the district. They were a prominent trio at every dance. " Who won the tennis tournament ? " someone would ask, and the answer came, as ever, " Oh, those Carter kids ! " They were splendid amateur actors, they could run, swim, sing, paint, and rattle the dice over the backgammon board against all oncomers. They were incessantly in love, but their passion was more general than particular. Janet's swains revolved dizzily and hopefully around her. The fancy of Jack was fickle as an April day, and as full of sunshine and tears for the temporary recipient.

It was Gerald, " the boxing kid," as he was now known, having fought his way into the Army amateur championship class, who loved with a fixed passion little Estelle Warren, the local doctor's daughter. They were the best dancers ever seen within twenty miles of home. It was always Estelle, wrapped up in a brown camel-hair overcoat, sitting by his corner of the ring, who attended Gerald's fights. In all the excitement of these contests, to which Richard Falmouth always went in the rôle of a faithful second, Estelle sat very quiet. She was dark and vivid, with fine features and high colouring, so that men turned to have a second sight of one so striking in appearance. She was not popular with her own sex, partly because she ignored other women, partly because she always had a court of enamoured youths about her. Her tongue could be sharp, but her smile suffused the cold, classic beauty of her face with a radiance that was unforgettable. She had the alertness and delicacy of a gazelle. She responded to Gerald's quiet possessive ardour with a firm independence.

In the third year of the war, when he returned from the trenches and begged her during a hectic leave to become his wife, she still put him off. " I love you very much, Gerald, but I don't feel this is the time to settle anything—it's all too difficult."

" But why ? " he protested. " Everybody's marrying—our time might be so short, Estelle. One must snatch happiness these days ! "

" Oh, I don't mean that, Jerry—I know you'll come through. When it's all over we'll be able to make plans."

" When ! But, Estelle, don't you realise we're getting older. Time's rushing by ? "

She laughed at him then, a silvery peal of laughter that was uniquely her own.

" Darling, we're twenty-two, with lots of time to love one another in."

So he prepared to return to the muddy horror of the trenches. The day before he left news came that Jack had been wiped out with his battery. Janet was far away in the Mediterranean with her Red Cross unit. There was a terrible leave-taking from his distracted mother. His father was on some mission to America. Again, in a last ten minutes, just before the leave-train left Victoria, he made a final appeal to Estelle. " Jerry, I must think it over—I can't say now, darling. Give me time," she replied.

"The next leave I'm coming back to marry you," he said, passionately. He held her in the strong embrace she knew so well, looked at her a little desperately, smiled, and whispered hoarsely, "Oh, God, how I love you!" and then was gone through the gate into the khaki medley of returning soldiers.

A month later, in the trenches, he received a letter that stunned him. It was from his father, enclosing a letter written in French, with a Paris address. They had just received it and it would explain. Could he get a few days' leave and go to Paris and report? They felt something must be done, certainly for the child if not for the mother. Gerald read through the enclosure slowly. It was a well-written letter, and had dignity despite its astonishing contents. It was from Madame Louise Perron, as the name written across the heading carefully announced. Since October, 1913, and until Jack had been killed in July, 1917, she had been his mistress. She had last seen him in Amiens in that month as he went through to his regiment. She did not write to embarrass them, but she felt she could not remain silent upon a loss affecting them both, particularly as Jack had left behind him a young son, a most beautiful baby and very like *pauvre cher* Jack. If they wished she would send a photograph of *le petit Jacques*. She hoped they would forgive her this letter, but she was greatly troubled in her mind by the thought that perhaps they had no knowledge that Jack had a two-year-old son.

Three weeks later Gerald succeeded in obtaining a few days' leave in Paris. He went to the address in the Rue Wilhem. After much questioning, the spider-like conçierge admitted him into the hall. Madame Perron lived on the top floor. *M'sieur* would have to walk. Electricity was rationed and the *ascenseur* only ran between six and ten in the evenings. It was a quarter to six.

Gerald climbed the concrete stair of this modern apartment house that stood in a wedge between the Rue and the Quai d'Auteuil, overlooking the Seine. On the sixth floor he touched a bell and heard it ring in the apartment. After a few moments feet slithered across the floor, and when the door opened a few inches an old woman's face peered at him. He asked for Madame Perron. He was looked at suspiciously for a few minutes as he haltingly explained he was a friend. "*Je suis le frère de M'sieur Jack Carter,*" he added, wondering if it would have any effect on the dragon at the door.

The response was immediate. Her wrinkled face lit up with pleasure. "*M'sieur Jacques? Mais oui! Entrez, entrez, m'sieur!*"

She flung wide open the door, ushered him through the tiny hall into a long room with three windows. It was pleasantly furnished. The apartment comprised a kitchenette, a sitting-room and an alcove bedroom, across which a curtain was half-drawn. The floor was covered with a red Turkey rug. On the walls hung copies of Millet, Daubigny, and Renoir. There was a small balcony beyond the window, with a view across the Seine towards the Eiffel Tower, whose lights were beginning to shine in the dark of the October evening.

The old woman asked him to be seated. Madame was out, but she would be back in a few minutes. She retreated into the kitchen, having switched on the sitting-room light. Could this be the place where his brother had lived with this French girl? He was not wholly surprised by the disclosure of the letter. There had been an evening, during leave in 1916, their last together at home, when he had felt that Jack was trying to tell him something and could not bring himself to the point. At first he had thought it was a money matter, for Jack seemed to have no interest in any girl at home. " There are things I want to tell you, old boy," said Jack as they went out in the car to a party at Estelle's home. But nothing more had been said the next morning, for they had both slept late, people came in to lunch, and at four o'clock Jack left for the front. Why had it never occurred to him that Jack, in his life in Paris, had had a liaison ? It was all in the tradition of the Latin Quartier.

Gerald found himself wondering what this girl was like. Thus far nothing had conformed to his expectation. The place was not dowdy, it had none of the attributes of the fictional *fille de joie*, being neither garish nor disorderly. Everything was neat, and, he observed, rather masculine in design. It might have been a bachelor's apartment.

He got up and peered into the bedroom. A woman's toilet things filled the mirrored dressing-table. There was a double bed and in one corner a child's cot, with baby linen hung on a rack.

A sound in the hall made him start back. Someone had come in and was talking to the *bonne*. He turned and saw a young woman advancing, a child with a blue knitted bonnet at her side. She gave the child to the *bonne*, held out her hand and addressed him.

" Captain Carter—ah, I see you are Jack's brother ! " she cried excitedly, her eyes shining as she gazed at him.

He could find no adequate words for a few moments. She was so completely unlike the kind of young woman he had expected. Slender, fair, with an exquisite complexion, this was not the prototype of the loose woman or the female harpy, for which he had prepared himself. There had been a moment when the speculation of blackmail had entered his mind. He stood now, confused and tongueless, as he looked at her. No young woman could have had an air of better breeding, of more conventional respectability. She was dressed in excellent taste, combining modesty with expense. Her tailor-made coat and skirt, her shoes, gloves, the string of pearls on the throat, her manner and voice were all characteristic of the fashionable well-bred young women one encountered in the lounge of Claridge's, the Savoy and the Ritz. She asked him to be seated, taking off her jacket and removing her hat.

" I'm so sorry not to be here. I got your telegram this morning. I always take Jacques out for an airing as soon as I get back from the shop. Ah, you must see him—your nephew ! "

She clapped her hands, and called to the *bonne*, who came forward with the child. Taking him in her arms, she showed him to Gerald, proudly.

" Is he not lovely ? He has Jack's eyes, and hair ! Ah, *mon petit trésor !* " she cried, kissing the child.

" He is very young ? " observed Gerald, forcing some expression through his dry lips.

" Two—and such a big, heavy boy—feel ! " she cried, holding out the child.

He took it, apprehensively, feeling utterly foolish for some reason. The whole scene had no relation to life as he had conceived it. He nursed the child a few moments, while it regarded him silently, with solemn blue eyes. Then he passed it back to the waiting *bonne*. With a sign the mother dismissed her.

" Let me give you a drink—but help yourself—everything is there just as Jack liked it, I have changed nothing," she said, opening a door in the sideboard.

" Can I make you one ? " he asked.

" Please—a Martini."

There was a silence while he made the drinks, then, as he sat down again, she looked at him and spoke.

" You cannot know how much I have wanted to see you, Captain Carter—I——"

" Gerald—please."

" Thank you—and I'm Louise.   Oh, I can see you are the Gerald he talked about so much !   I know you all so well, Mr. and Mrs. Carter, Janet, yourself, Estelle—— "

" Estelle ? "

" Isn't she your fiancée ? "

" I still have hope."

" He talked so much of the family at Grinstead—I know all the history of the Carter kids ! "

She laughed gaily.   Her eyes had a singular light in them when she laughed.   She must be about twenty-six or seven.   Her voice had a thrilling quality to the ear.   The hands were beautiful too.

" You must want to ask me so many questions—am I a bit like what you expected ? "

" No, not in any way.   You speak very good English."

" My grandmother was English, she brought me up when I was sent here from Martinique by my parents. Now, you can ask me anything you want to know. How I met Jack, how long we lived together, how I became what I think you call ' a loose woman,' how——"

" Oh, please.   I have not said that ! "

" But of course you must all have thought it !   Why shouldn't you ?   It must have been very shocking for your parents.   Now, the questions please.   I will be very truthful.   You see I had to write.   I could not keep Jack's boy all to myself.   It is all we have of darling Jack, you understand that ? "

" Perfectly."

" So I wrote. Oh, it cost me nights and nights of thinking. I wrote letter after letter, and tore them up. It was not easy. I knew it would mean pain—give pain?" She smiled apologetically for her English. " And I was afraid, too."

" Afraid ? " asked Gerald.

She gazed into his face, her serious eyes holding his as her thin fingers played with the cocktail glass.

"He cannot, he must not be taken from me ! He is everything I have," she said, intensely. " You understand ? "

" Absolutely."

" *Enfin*, now all your questions."

" It's half past six—could we dine together ? This is my one night in Paris. I leave at 2 a.m."

" For the Front ? "

He nodded. She looked at him, wordless for a moment.

" I know so well these few hours—and the train that pulls one's heart with it. If you please, I will bathe Jacques and put him to bed. We always do that, Marie and I. Then we can go out. You do not mind ? "

" If I can watch the performance," he replied, smiling. " I suppose Jack helped you."

" When he got leave—but it was such a short time. He had to go home, to see your parents. Sometimes I wished he would tell them. I did not mind, but he always hoped somehow we could be married."

" You wished to be married ? Then why——"

" Gerald, you can't understand—I was married. I had a husband living. That was the trouble."

" You have a husband ? " stammered Gerald.

" I had—the irony of it ! He was killed a month after

Jack. It was never a success—he was so grim, so much older, a Captain. My parents forced me into it. You know our *mariage de convenance*. He would not have an annulment. He hated us."

The *bonne* appeared out of the bathroom with a large tin bath filled with hot water which she placed on a mat on the table. Then she brought towels and soap and powder, and stood smiling before her mistress.

"We must bathe Jacques—then we can go. Excuse me," said Louise, disappearing into the bedroom. A few minutes later, clad in a waterproof apron, she carried in the naked Jacques. A little embarrassed by this nursery ritual, Gerald sat by and watched. It was most complacently endured by this chubby infant who began to prattle. A thought of his brother officers, sitting in filth at that moment, passed through his mind. The grim joke of man's civilisation, that bathed, perfumed and powdered infants destined, twenty years on to live lice-ridden in mud and be blown to bloody shreds by shrapnel ! The seven ages of man that came to such a violent end in the third age, from one of those fuse-caps his kind father was making a fortune out of !

"Feel him, feel the weight," said Louise, holding out the boy after he had been dried and powdered.

He took Jacques in his hands, nervously, feeling the satin softness of the child's skin. Serious blue eyes looked serenely into his. The boy laughed and talked in French with his few words.

"He's a great lad—what shall we do with him ? " observed Gerald as he passed back the precious burden.

Louise did not answer for a time, as she began to dress Jacques with Marie's assistance. Later, raising her head as she pulled on the infant's bed jacket, she said——

"That's why I felt I must write. He is Jack's son. Are your people terribly strict? Why couldn't Jack mention our affair? Are they terribly shocked?"

"I don't know whether they're shocked or pleased. You see, I haven't seen them. Father sent on your letter asking me to look you up. I should say they're both surprised, and pleased, in a way."

"In a way—yes, I hope that is it. Something of Jack remains. I would never have written had I not thought I might be robbing them of something. But Jacques is mine. I don't want any help, any conditions," she said, intensely.

"I can understand that," he agreed.

He watched her deft fingers complete the task of robing the boy. He had an impression of independence and great competence. He knew so little about her but already he began to know how Jack must have found her efficiency useful, excluding any passion. Jack had never been a manager, he was spontaneous, generous and disorderly in his mode of existence.

The boy left to the care of Marie, Louise appeared dressed for going out. Again he noticed her quiet elegance. Her beauty had a warmth that was perturbing. More and more he wondered what her story might be, how she and Jack had come together. He would hear the whole account soon, he felt.

They found a taxi and drove to a restaurant he liked near the Rond Point des Champs-Élysées. He ordered an expensive menu, despite her protests. It was not until the coffee came that she smiled at him with her candid eyes and said, "How old are you?"

"Twenty-two."

"You're very young for a captain."

"Thank you—or should I feel reproved?" he answered. She laughed and toyed with a coffee spoon.

" It's strange, but if that bullet had found my husband earlier you would now be my brother-in-law and an uncle."

" Aren't I ? Jacques is my brother's son, after all."

" So you accept that without questioning—some people would be very suspicious. Thank you. I was prepared for you to want definite evidence, though I don't know how I could produce it."

" Oh come—anyone can see you're not, you're not ——" he paused in search of a word.

" A little prostitute who picked Jack up in a night-club," she said candidly. " But there's no reason why you all shouldn't have thought so. I was married, and I lived with a man who was not my husband. It started with simple physical passion, though something else came." She paused, and rubbed the spoon over the cloth, watching it. " You see—we found we really loved each other and that made it complicated," she said, looking up with a look in her eyes that he found perturbing. " I hadn't bothered about Etienne—my husband —before that. I will be very truthful with you—you can think the worst of me. There had been others before Jack."

" Others ? " he repeated blankly.

" Two. Short affairs, never satisfactory. A lonely girl in Paris need not be lonely, and they helped to blot out the nightmare of Etienne. I'm not unattractive. It is difficult to live alone when things have gone wrong and you want sympathy and you are hungry for something, and there are always men seeking you."

" Are you trying to shock me—to make the worst case for yourself ? "

" No," she replied, shaking her head. " I want to

be very honest with you. It isn't easy—you are so young."

"Oh, come—Jack was only a year older!"

"But there's been no woman in your life?"

"If you mean in that sense, no. But I'm not a fool. I've seen a good bit. I can understand."

She put a hand over his on the table and pressed it.

"Gerald, I find you very sympathetic—I could wish you were not so nice and—and——"

"Innocent? I'm not censuring you or Jack. I'd have done the same most likely, in this city—it's made so easy for one," he added.

"Oh, no!" protested Louise. "You must not think that! I've cut myself adrift from most of my friends and relations. They condemn me; how could they do otherwise? Most French women stay with their husbands, even when they know their husbands don't stay with them. Now let's go back to the beginning."

It had begun quite conventionally. She worked in a Paris beauty specialist's establishment. One evening in 1913, to a party given by a girl she worked with, her brother, an art student, brought with him a young Englishman, working in the same *atelier*. He was very tall, very young, with charming manners. She danced with him, and after midnight he asked to see her home. They began to meet regularly after that. He came to her little apartment in the Rue du Bac where he played the piano and they made coffee and discussed books and pictures and plays. He brimmed over with zest for everything. "I soon knew the life history of the Carter kids, you and Janet and your adorable mother," said Louise, smiling.

The visits to her apartment had grown so frequent that a time came when their friends had no doubt about their relationship. As it happened, they were quite

F

wrong. Then one night very late, in June, 1914, there was a heavy thunderstorm and such a downpour that Jack could not go back to his own apartment in Montmartre. He stayed with her. From that time on they were never separated. They were breathlessly happy in each other's company. After a time Jack found a bigger place for them in the Rue Wilhem. It was airier and they loved the view, and with their combined money they could just afford it.

" We were in heaven—but with one big cloud. I didn't seek for Jack to marry me, for I knew Etienne would oppose an annulment. I was willing to go on as we were, but Jack fretted about it, poor boy. There was always the troubled ghost of the family standing behind him. I suppose that was why I was never mentioned in his letters home—I never was mentioned, was I ? "

" No. He never told us anything," replied Gerald.

" But he wanted to tell you, I know that. I'm sure in the end he would have told you all, he hated the duplicity he had to practise on you. That was all that ever troubled us. We were completely happy—completely ! " she emphasised.

" And your people ? "

" My parents are dead, but I have a darling old grandmother at Senlis. We kept nothing from her. She adored Jack. She came to visit us, we couldn't go to Senlis. Everybody knows everything about everybody, it's too small. When Jacques came she sent me Marie —her old servant."

" And how does she explain Jacques ? "

" Her granddaughter's a war widow, with a child. Some believe it, some don't, she doesn't mind what they think. Jack was her idol."

" What are we going to do about Jacques ? "

" We ? " she asked, quickly.

" Well, he's part of the family. I'm sure my people will want to do something. I would, if they didn't."

The moment he had spoken he knew it was a mistake. She threw him a quick, frightened look and her voice changed instantly.

" They can have nothing to do with him—they can know of him, see him if they wish. I do not want anything. I can bring him up. My grandmother has a little money—it will go to him, I know. No, there is nothing I want you to do, please tell them that," she said, decisively.

" But what will he be called—you'll have to consider that," asked Gerald, a little perturbed by the strength of her will.

" He'll be Jacques Carter. Why not—he has nothing to be ashamed of. And I shall be proud of him."

" I feel that is a little unfair to the boy—it will make difficulties," said Gerald, slowly.

His companion smiled at him, mockingly he thought.

" You are very English, aren't you ? I see you think I am very shocking," she said, teasingly, her beautiful eyes touched with derision. " Perhaps I did wrong to let you know anything, perhaps Jack was right."

" Oh, come," responded Gerald, with impatience in his voice. " Of course we understand, my people will be very nice about it. They'll——"

" Nice ? Nice ? " Her voice had an unpleasant note, strident and combative.

" I don't mean—" began Gerald.

" I think we will not talk of it any more. Jacques is my boy. I shall always be glad for your family to see him, but he is mine ! "

Gerald made no comment. He glanced covertly

at his watch. It was nearly eleven o'clock. She must have seen his action.

"I'm tiring you—please don't be angry with me," she said.

"How could I be—it is all for you to decide."

She smiled at him, and her charm touched him again, like the sun coming out of a cloud.

"Let us go and dance somewhere—you like dancing? It is so soon you go back—you poor boy!"

"I should like nothing better—and don't be sorry for me, there are millions of us in the same boat," he said. "In a few hours this will all seem unreal—one cherishes these memories."

He paid the bill, and a taxi was called. She gave the driver an address.

"Jack and I always went there on our last nights when his leave was up. May I come to the station with you?" she asked.

"Oh, please don't if you——"

"I want to," she said, quietly. "It will hurt me to go there again, as so often with Jack, but I want to."

He made no answer. He found her baffling at moments. She was direct and hard, mentally, yet there was a warmth in her, a courage that touched him.

The night club was dark, crowded and noisy. There were many allied soldiers in uniform, too many of them, somewhat drunk. A negro jazz band blared on a dais under a blue light. There was no air, the side tables were crowded, everyone appeared to be drinking champagne. When the floor show came on he had no more doubt that he was in one of the hot spots of Paris night life. Could Jack have liked this place? Perhaps it had changed with the war. Louise seemed to know a great many people there, but she refused to dance with anyone else. She was a superb dancer. Her rhythm flowed

into his, they moved as one body.   She scarcely talked,
her eyes half closed.

" You dance well," she said.

" Thank you ! "

" Do you make love as well ? " she asked, archly,
her eyes mocking him again.

" Oh, that—well, I don't know, I—" he paused for
words. She clung a little more closely and laughed at
him.

" You are so unlike Jack—but nice," she said, almost
with a sigh. " You don't know much about women,
do you ? "

" I'm not a baby," he retorted.

She put up a hand and pinched his ear.

" *Tiens !*—I've made you angry ! " she laughed.

" Not at all—you're only twenty-six yourself ! "

" But I've lived, Gerald. I've had lovers, I've——"
She saw him flinch at the word.

" Now don't be silly and so very British—and don't
jump to conclusions ! "

" Then why tell me ? "

" I like shocking you ! Gerald, you are a great
boy."

" I'm not a boy, and not as green as you think."

" Green ? "

" Inexperienced."

She looked at him quizzically and seemed about to
ask him something but checked herself. The music
grew more hectic. The floor was suffocatingly crowded.
She danced so superbly it was a pleasure to move with
her, to hold her, to feel the impulse of their perfect
rhythm. He found himself wondering if the pearls on
her throat could be real. It was highly improbable,
for after all she was only a shop girl. She had a beautiful
throat, her voice, too, had at times an alluring quality.

It was not difficult to understand how anyone as susceptible as Jack would find her attractive.

They sat out the next dance. They did not talk but watched the floor. War, the mother of disorder and the mistress of opportunity, had gathered a mixed brood here to-night. The imminence of death goaded the hectic animality of these swaying dancers. Swift intimacy, swift finality gave desperation to the fleeing moments.

At a quarter to one Gerald took Louise on to the floor for a last dance. He had ordered champagne but she drank very little of it. Now, as they began to dance, she pressed herself to him, silent, her face averted.

" You are tired ? " he asked.

" Oh no. I'm enjoying every moment of it. Gerald— about Jacques. If your people want to see him they can come to Paris some time. I won't go to England. I should be on the defensive, and it would be awkward. I won't be apologised for. Explain that to them, if you can."

" It won't be easy, but I'll try. Can they help ? "

" In what way ? "

" Well, financially, at least," he said.

" No, I'll manage quite well. Tell them, Gerald, I should like to see them, and for them to see Jacques, but I must be quite free."

" Very well—I'll try to explain," he agreed.

" You'll come to see me again ? "

" Oh, certainly."

" I like you very much."

" Thanks, I like you."

She smiled up at him, her hair against his cheek.

" You are such a polite boy," she said, softly.

" Boy ! " he expostulated.

Five minutes later they left the club and drove through the black city to the station. They did not talk but sat in silence in the dark taxi, holding each other's hand, like children. As they drew up to the station, thronged with soldiers and their relations, the tension between them grew unbearable.

" Gerald, it's so strange to be here again, to—" Her voice choked.

" Don't ! " he said kindly, close to her in the darkness.

She moved against him and they were in each other's arms. Their mouths met in a long kiss. The night roared about them. Then the taxi stopped with a rattle.

" We're here," he said, as calmly as he could unloosing her with hands that trembled. He paid off the taxi. She went with him to collect his kit. Then they stood before the gate, with five minutes to spare. All the hardness had gone out of her now. He felt sorry for her. Had she been desperately building up a façade of independence ? The last moment came.

" Good-bye, Louise—I shall write to my people. They're very nice—and understanding."

" I'm sure they are. Gerald, shall I see you again ? "
" Of course—unless—" He gave a short laugh.
" That won't happen—it can't ! Good luck, good-bye ! "
He held her hand, thin and warm.
" Good-bye," he said.

She watched him through the gate, and waved in answer to his farewell salute.

II

The day before they were sent into the line Richard Falmouth arrived back from leave. Slender, reserved, he was a good soldier, though inclined to severity with his men. He never spared himself and perhaps because he had a fear of losing discipline he never achieved the easy, warm relationship that made Gerald such a natural leader. A growing bitterness with the war, based perhaps on the lack of promotion which he felt to be his due, increased a natural reticence. For the past six months Gerald had been troubled by a feeling that Richard was brooding and withdrawing more and more into himself, try as he would to keep their friendship as close as of old.

The moment Richard walked into his billet on his return from leave Gerald knew something was wrong.

" How are they all at home ? " he asked.

" Oh, quite all right. I saw your people. Janet's home," replied Richard.

" That's good. How's she looking ? "

" Splendid—I only just saw her."

There was a pause. Once it seemed as if there was something between Richard and his sister.

" Jerry ! " Gerald looked hard at his friend, hearing the odd forced note in his voice.

" Jerry, I must talk to you," he said, and added, glancing around, " Not in here, someone might come in. Let's go outside."

" Very well," replied Gerald, rising and lighting his pipe. What could the trouble be, he wondered.

They went outside and walked some distance from the shelled farmhouse that was their billet. They came to a wall by the blasted orchard, a macabre wintry scene of branchless splintered trunks. A plane angrily hummed overhead. The dull roar of the guns came on the wind.

" Well, what is it, Dick, what's troubling you ? " asked Gerald quietly, instinctively taking shelter by the wall. His friend looked white, his lips compressed. He did not respond at once but searched the sky, not purposely but in nervous agitation.

" I don't know how I'm going to tell you this," he said,

hoarsely, wetting his lips. " She wanted to write first, but I said I would tell you."

" Who ? " asked Gerald sharply.

" Estelle. Estelle and I are engaged to be married. I know it's a blow, Jerry. God, don't I know it ! "

Gerald stared at him. He heard a plane whine down the sky. Some poor devil had got it, but he did not look up, he watched Falmouth's hand fidgetting with his belt. Then he looked at him.

" Go on—tell me the whole story," he said, in a low voice.

" There's not much to tell. Jerry, I hate to hurt you like this."

" Go on, man ! "

" For a year we've been in misery about it. For a long time Estelle wouldn't admit it——"

" Admit what ? "

" That we were in love with each other—we even kept it from each other as long as we could, knowing what it meant to you. But we're terribly in love, Jerry, and I know I couldn't come back here again and keep you in the dark. So I insisted this time that we should tell you."

" We ? "

" Estelle is writing—but she agreed I should tell you."

" Do her people and mine know ? "

" No—not yet. We felt you should be told first."

" Thanks."

" Jerry, I'm terribly sorry. That's what's been the matter all these months. I didn't know how to talk to you."

" I understand."

" Do you ? " asked Falmouth, anxiously.

" Quite. Well, there we are," said Gerald, moving away from the wall.

" Jerry, you must say something—say what you like," cried Falmouth, following him.

" What should I say—these things happen, don't they ? I've read of it in books, seen it in films.   Well, here it is. Do you expect me to bawl ? " he asked, fiercely.   " Give me a little time and perhaps I'll behave like a gentleman and congratulate you both."

Falmouth looked at his friend despairingly.

" Jerry, I'm just miserable about the whole thing. You believe that, old man, don't you ? " he asked.

Gerald stood still and looked at his friend.

" You're in love with her ? "

" Terribly, Jerry."

" And she's in love with you ? "

" Yes—absolutely. She's fond of you, Jerry. She's——"

" Oh, cut it out !   When are you marrying Estelle ? "

" The next leave."

" You won't expect me to be best man, I hope," said Gerald savagely.

Falmouth quailed.   He hesitated for some reply, but before any words formed on his lips Gerald had spoken.

" That wouldn't be wise. Estelle might change her mind again, at the altar. Women can do those things, you know. I've something to tell you. Old Jack got himself a son on a French flame—but at any rate she went through with it. Some women are faithful in their fashion."

" Jerry ! For God's sake, don't talk like that, old man. It's not like you ! " cried Falmouth, walking with him as his friend hurried on.

" How the hell do you know what I'm like—or any of us are like ? Oh, don't let's discuss it any more ! "

They reached the farmhouse in miserable silence.

*   *   *   *   *

Could that all be only three years ago? thought Brother Sebastian. It seemed in one way to belong to another world, something that had happened to him in an existence so apart that he wondered if ever he had been Gerald Carter. He stood looking down on Cassino, this fair May morning of 1920, from a window in the great monastery which now sheltered him from a world he had found too nauseating to live in. He had not yet achieved tranquillity—that he might never achieve. His sin was too heinous to hope that, in whatever mortal span was alloted to him, there could be happiness or peace. He did not seek these : he only sought to scourge his spirit, to attain afar off, in God's mercy, some hope of atonement. Still too anguished by the thing obsessing and torturing him, he eagerly awaited the fuller renunciation when he ceased to be a novice and gained the greater seclusion through the vows of Stability, Conversion and Obedience under the rule of Saint Benedict. This noble place had been his refuge now for seven months. He hoped that in its tranquil life his own might be merged until, all identity lost in the vows of poverty, chastity and obedience, the consciousness of sin oppressing him would be alleviated.

He had been sent down to the town this afternoon on the Abbey's business and there he had learned of the sudden death of the young man whom, together with his lovely bride, he had conducted over the monastery only yesterday. He could hear now that eager voice reading the passage on Boccaccio's visit to Monte Cassino. Death had touched him and the business of life was no more his domain.

He had found comfort in an impulse that had made him ask if he might offer a prayer beside the body of his countryman lying in the shuttered hotel bedroom. His prayers for one not of his Church, his words of solace to that poor young woman who had knelt with him, had brought him, briefly, a respite from his own obsession. For an obsession it was, that might be mitigated only by long contrition and a continuous plea to God for grace in his sinful state.

The valley below him lay in the blue shadow of evening. The sun had sunk below the mountains whose peaks were sharply silhouetted against the waning golden light. Evening after evening this splendour heralded the oncoming night. If anywhere in the world he could find peace of mind it would be here in the high silence of these mountains, within the walls of this noble monastery. He had come here from Rome, seeking this retreat. Eight years ago, motoring with his people up this valley from Naples, *en route* to Rome, he had first seen the monastery dramatically crowning the mountain and had wondered then what kind of a place it was, for what reason men withdrew themselves from the world and all its vivid delights. He had found the answer now for himself.

Thou shalt not kill. He had killed, purposefully, vilely. When he had sent out that wiring-party on the night of October 20th, 1917, he knew all the risks. No one could condemn his act. Either of the two lieutenants must lead the party. One had to be chosen. There was no accusation, no suspicion in Richard Falmouth's eyes when he spoke to him just before they went out into No Man's Land. The night, with no moon, was perfect for the essential task of repairing the wire defences. He had led out parties himself. He had given Richard their most experienced sergeant and six picked men. He had every chance.

He would never forget how, fighting the voice that whispered within him, he had waited and waited, how, at that sudden clatter of machine-gun fire, following the glare of the Verey lights above the place where the wiring-party was working, he had cried to himself, " It can't happen ! " There was a terrible half-hour while they awaited the returning party. Then came the reporting of name after name, the long wait, and two more names. Eight had gone out, six were back. Six ? Yes, sir, six. Lieutenant Falmouth and Woodward were not back. They would not be back. The machine-gun fire had riddled them both. They lay over there, in the darkness, huddled against the third post where the light and the fire had trapped them. In the morning it would be possible to see them. In the morning . . .

The third night Gerald had gone out himself, unable to bear the torture any longer, the accusation of that inert brown form huddled against the post. Earlier that afternoon, through his glasses, he had seen the rats begin their loathsome business. By daylight they could be shot at, but by night. . . . The sergeant went with him. " We all liked him, sir, and we know what it means to you, sir," he said as they covered over the rain-soaked body, having gone through the pockets to add to that small, pathetic collection in the dark dug-out.

Richard died gallantly. His men loved him. He was deliberately sent to his death by me. I selected him for the wiring-party, knowing all the risks, knowing what would happen. He had stolen Estelle from me. She had always belonged to me.

That letter was never written except in his heart, where every accusing word was engraved in fire. Somehow he wrote a letter to Dick's mother and father, and another to Estelle—triumphant lying, if ever there was such a thing.

The war ended at last. They tried to put together again the broken pieces of life. His parents made a journey to Paris, to see Louise Perron and the boy, but the mission was a failure. She was suspicious and slightly hostile. She had sent the child to her grand-mother, at Senlis, and had to be persuaded to produce him. She refused every kind of offer made by the Carters, fiercely independent. She wanted nothing of them—the boy was hers. They wondered why she had ever revealed the existence of young Jacques. So they had returned, hurt and disappointed. There was nothing, it seemed, they could do about Jack's boy, a splendid little fellow, most plainly a Carter, with his vivid eyes and fresh colouring.

Estelle came again into Gerald's life. She knew she had hurt him, but he carefully avoided any reference to Richard Falmouth. When he had been dead for more than a year it seemed as if he were fading out of their lives, but she knew that the Gerald who had returned was not the same Gerald. He had brooding phases, and days of deep, unnamed depression. Yet Gerald turned to her.

There came an April day, down in the beech wood, where the stream rippled past the daffodils the Carter kids had planted, when Gerald had suddenly laid his head in her lap and cried like a little boy. She ran her fingers through his hair, soothingly, and kissed him and sought to know the nature of his deep trouble, but he could not be comforted. It was when they rose, in the dusk of the evening, with lights shining in the house above them, that he asked her the thing she had waited for. He wanted to marry her. He could never love anyone else. They would go and live in London, where he had joined a stockbroking firm. With their joint private incomes and what he would earn they could be quite comfortable. So she accepted him and they set a day in June. She loved him and wondered now whether Richard, after all, could have made her happy.

It had been a wayward intoxication. Something within her had been hypnotised by poor Richard's flame-like passion. It all seemed so unreal now, in these less dramatic days of normal values.

The two families were delighted. What had seemed inevitable for so long now was to be fulfilled. The Falmouth episode had distressed both families, but now there was to be a happy ending.

A week before the wedding, as the presents began to arrive, the Carters and the Warrens had another shock. Gerald had thrown up his position, gone to Paris and thence had written to Estelle, saying he could not go through with the wedding. He loved her, but he knew he could never hope for any happiness from their marriage. She must try to forget him, without bitterness if she could.

Those terrible months of indecision had seared his soul. He had desperately tried to fight back to the normal life. There had been moments when he had clung to Estelle, like a lifebuoy in his sea of misery, but he knew how vain was his hope. Again and again he came to a point of confession. He must tell Estelle he had sent Dick to his death. But his will failed him when the dread moment came. He suffered in a hundred ways. Places and people crucified him with poignant memories. The Falmouths lived in the district and they were so kind to him that he felt at moments that he must scream out the real truth of their son's death.

So he had fled, cowardice companioning guilt. He had a little money from the same source that had enabled Jack to go to Paris. He decided to seek the anodyne of travel. In his sudden flight he avoided all explanations, all harrowing scenes. He would be condemned for his treatment of Estelle, but so many of his former friends had withdrawn themselves from him. He had learned, too, that those glad reunions dreamed of in the war proved bitter illusions in peace. Men developed other contacts and loyalties, sympathies veered, old associations lost their glamour in the anxieties of the new day. Time inexorably worked its alchemy of change. It was mental as well as physical, and the little chill wind of loneliness blew over the landscape of a cherished dream.

Taking his car and a minimum of baggage, he crossed the Channel. Exiles always went south, and for the moment his ultimate destination seemed to be Italy. It was June in Paris, cool and leafy. The city was resuming the natural gaiety of her life quicker than any other capital. So he lingered, choosing a small hotel on the left bank.

Again and again the thought of Louise Perron and her child came to him, but he resisted an impulse to look her up, recalling the chilly reception his parents had received. Then one evening, sitting outside at Fouquet's, on the Champs-Élysées, he saw her. It was the *aperitif* hour and the tables were crowded. She was not alone. A tall, elegant young man was squiring her. After some searching he procured a table, and they sat down, a little distant. They were obscured by other customers, but at odd moments Gerald could glimpse her. Almost two years had elapsed. With a start it came to him that Jacques must be about four years old now. It would be interesting to see the boy, how he had developed, what characteristics of his father had begun to assert themselves.

Those two years had been more than kind to Louise Perron—they had increased her beauty. She was exquisitely dressed, with that air of neat expense achieved by Frenchwomen. He could see only her profile, a part of the brow obscured by the brim of a white straw hat. Her blond hair was drawn tightly back above the ear, from whose lobe hung a large pearl. She wore scarlet kid gloves, which she had not removed, and she held a long ivory cigarette-holder in her left hand. She was in great enjoyment with her companion. They talked animatedly. He was well-groomed, a long-faced man of about thirty-five, French probably, certainly not English.

Gerald resisted a strong impulse to go over to her. They sat on and on, until the tables on the pavement emptied and he had an undisturbed view of them. He had removed his own hat and possibly, at some moment, she might look his way and recognise him, for he had not changed so greatly, though out of uniform now. As he waited and watched, he recalled again the vivacity with which she talked. He could hear her voice, pleasant to the ear. There were only half a dozen customers on the pavement now. The dusk was deepening into night. Lights rimmed the long boulevard, twinkling between the trees. At last they rose, but they passed him unseen, crossing the pavement to the smart green Isotta-Fraschini racing car parked by the curb. The man opened the low door and helped her into it. Gerald could see her full-faced now, but the light was poor. It was not too poor to withhold from him a sense of her beauty and unique daintiness. With a deep throb of the exhaust, they were gone into the night.

He sat on, disturbed by this brief encounter. His thoughts were confused, his motives contradictory. He wanted to speak to her and not to speak, to be seen and not to be seen. That incident in the taxi on the night he left for the front came vividly back. It was so clear, yet so absolutely part of a life that had no relationship with the present. Then the terrible thing had not happened. He was young, in love, unfettered by remorse and free of any guilt. The danger of life then gave it an intoxication. Above the mud and blood of that existence he had known the exaltation of comradeship, the wild throw of the dice with Fate, the vague hope of a rewarding new world when the present madness had passed. Scarcely two years ago, and now here he sat, terribly lonely, a wanderer to no known end. He paid the bill, rose, and sadly walked away.

III

Daily the impulse to call on Louise Perron grew more strong. She might not be at the same address. It was possible she desired no further contact with the Carter family. Her reception of his parents had been less than cordial. She might think he was after the boy, an emissary of the family. One evening, motoring back from Versailles, he found himself on the Quai d'Auteuil. He had an impulse to find out whether she still lived in that apartment overlooking the Seine. He turned off the Quai and stopped before the door he remembered. " Yes," said the concierge, " Madame Perron still occupied Apartment 5." She showed him the way to the tiny *ascenseur*. He touched the button and it wheezily ascended. Glancing at his watch, he saw it was almost seven. With luck she might be at home.

He rang the bell and waited with a quickened beating of the heart. A wild idea flashed through his mind. A growing consciousness of the loneliness of life had begun to perturb him. Louise Perron had no part in his past life and yet he felt a tie in her association with Jack and in her son Jacques. If he married her he would give a name to the boy, a name that was rightly his, and for himself he would gain an attractive companion. The idea came as he heard the bell ring within the apartment, and its extravagance made him smile. In his present state of mind he was not safe to plan his future. He wondered how such a wild idea would strike Louise.

There was no answer. He rang again, and waited. He had rung a third time and was about to turn away when he saw through the frosted panels of the door that a light had been switched on in the little hall, and some-one was there. Presently the door was opened. A man stood there, clad in a dressing-gown and wearing slippers. His chest was bare, and his thick, dark hair was dis-ordered. He seemed slightly annoyed by the visitor, whom he examined before he spoke. He was a robust man of about thirty-five.

" Yes—what do you want ? " he asked abruptly, in French.

" I'm sorry to disturb you. Is this Madame Perron's apartment ? "

" Yes—but she is not in, *m'sieur*."

" Oh—I just called on the chance I might find her here."

" No, she is not here, *m'sieur*."

There was a long pause. The man in the dressing-gown held the door half-open and without further speech looked hard at the stranger before him.

" I am sorry to have disturbed you," said Gerald again, lamely.

" I was in the bath—so I could not come at once. Can I give Madame a message ? "

His annoyance had vanished. He was pleasant in appearance, tall and well-featured. His black hair was roughly pushed back from the brow where it made a peak.

"Thank you, no—or you might say I called. Mr. Gerald Carter," said Gerald.

"Mr. Gerald Carter—of England?" asked the man with the first glimmer of a smile.

"Yes—I knew Madame Perron during the war."

"Ah, yes," responded the man in the dressing-gown.

There was another awkward pause.

"Well, thank you. Good night," said Gerald, turning toward the lift and ringing for it.

"Good night, *m'sieur.*"

He waited politely at the open door until the wheezy lift arrived, and Gerald had entered. Then, as he closed the gate, the apartment door was shut and the light was switched off.

In a state of confusion Gerald reached the vestibule. He was out in the street and something there gave him the answer to the question filling his mind. By the curb, in the half-light of the summer evening, stood a sports Isotta-Fraschini car. It was the one into which Louise Perron had stepped two evenings back outside Fouquet's. The man who had driven her away was the fellow in the dressing-gown.

Who was he? Obviously he had been taking a bath, and was very much at home there, even when the owner was out. Suddenly Gerald stopped in his walk. It might be that he was not having a bath. It was a curious hour to be taking one, unless he was changing for dinner. But why should a man be changing for dinner in Louise Perron's apartment? Perhaps Madame was not out, perhaps . . .

"Well, I'm damned!" he exclaimed with emphasis. He hailed a passing taxi and gave the man the address of his hotel. In the taxi, rehearsing the extraordinary scene, he realized he had left no address with the fellow at the door. She could not reach him if she wished. It was very improbable that she would desire to.

Back in his room at the hotel he found it very hot. He threw open the window. His hands were moist and his brow was damp. He was actually shaking with nerves. Why, because of this demi-monde? For he had no doubt of it now. It explained the fairly expensive apartment, so much beyond any girl who worked in a shop, and her clothes which even a man's inexpert eye told him were very fashionable and expensive. Why had he been such a fool as not to recognise the situation at once? He began to understand now the strange conduct regarding the child.

Let him be fair. The facts concerning Jacques were possibly in her favour. Some kind impulse, perhaps a genuine love of Jack, had prompted her to inform them of this living legacy of the past. He must absolve her from any plan to profit by the situation. Her independence had been unchallengeable. The boy was proudly hers and she would not let him go. It was easier now to understand why she had cut herself off from any consequences of her communication. She had no desire to divulge her mode of living.

The revelation filled Gerald's thoughts for the next three days. His curiosity grew with the accumulation of questions to which he sought answers. He finally succumbed and wrote to her, suggesting she should dine with him one evening before he left. The response was surprisingly prompt. She called him the next morning, and they managed to meet the following evening. He suggested the place where they had dined almost two years ago, the restaurant he liked near the Rond Point des Champs-Élysées.

She was prompt when the time came and, as she stepped

from the taxi that brought her, he was again aware of her *chic*. She was a figure of grace and great distinction. All eyes watched her as they progressed to their table by the wall. She had a little blue hat trimmed with lilacs, and long suede gloves of a colour to match. Her bodice was cut to set off her exquisite throat and bosom. Her eyes had probably set the note of her dress, for they were violet. Her hair was a mass of soft fair curls that gave an impression of the head of some classic Greek youth of almost feminine beauty. The mouth was wide and when she laughed her lips curled back—a fortunate characteristic, for they revealed two rows of perfect teeth. Gerald wondered why he had not been aware before of her very real beauty, or had two years given her something she had not then possessed? Her poise was perfect and the general effect quietly aristocratic.

They dined and discussed a dozen topics. Young Jacques was at Senlis, with her grandmother.

"I thought your people charming, Gerald," she said. "Your mother is very sweet and gentle. But I couldn't bear the thought of losing control of Jacques. They wanted to help, but if I accepted I would have to accept advice and defer to their wishes. Perhaps I should never have written, and they would never have known anything—I obeyed an impulse."

"It was the right impulse, I'm sure. Perhaps one day you'll let me do something for the boy. Anyhow, here we are—I've your impulse to thank for that!" he said gaily. It was the first time any gaiety had shown in his manner.

She looked at him curiously. He had seemed a mere boy when last they met. Now he was a man, quite different in some indefinable way. His voice had lost its eager note, his face had a strained look.

" You've altered. You've become very serious. Are you angry with me ? " she asked.

" Angry ? Why should you say that ? "

" Perhaps not angry—but different. You are wondering about the man in the apartment when you called ? "

" Your life has nothing to do with me—I was surprised, shall I say ? I should not have called. I've no desire to pry into your affairs," he answered slowly, his eyes on the table.

" Then why have you asked me to dine with you ? You can't help but wonder. Well, I'm going to tell you, and after that we can say good-bye. He was one of my lovers."

" One ? "

" One of several," she answered unhesitatingly.

" Are you trying to shock me ? If so, you've failed. I never imagined Jack was the only one," said Gerald with brutal candour. " But why discuss it ? "

" I must discuss it. In one thing you're wrong. Jack was not the first, but he was the only one. I loved him as I shall never love any man again."

" Oh, nonsense—you never know ! " protested Gerald. " And your husband—did he ever exist ? Look, my dear, I don't want to be curious. Let us have a pleasant little dinner together. I felt lonely, and I like you— you are very attractive and beautiful."

She made no reply for a few moments and toyed with her wine glass.

" Gerald, what's happened ? You're not the same boy. There's something in your eyes—they were beautiful, kind eyes—that's the first thing I knew and liked about you. You're unhappy. Anyone can see that. Why are you in Paris ? Don't tell me anything unless you want to."

He pushed the coffee-cup and his napkin away. Glancing at his wrist-watch, he said abruptly, " Let's go and dance somewhere. We're getting morbid."

" You asked me a question. I'm going to answer it. My husband did exist. That part's quite true. He was thirty-two when I was married, at seventeen. For two years I had a wretched life. Then I consoled myself with lovers—two, before I found Jack. My husband went his own way also. When I wanted to be free to marry Jack he revenged himself for his injured pride. Perhaps he was justified. I am a passionate woman. I like men. A young woman with any beauty does not have to be alone in Paris. The man who opened the door to you the other evening was one of my friends."

" Friends ? " queried Gerald.

" Lovers, if you wish. He had been staying there three days. He comes up from his estate near Le Mons."

" So you pick rich ones ? "

" I deserve that, I suppose. No, not always rich—those I happen to like."

" They are—remunerative ? " asked Gerald, searching for the least pleasant word. " Tell me, do you really do any work—or is that beauty parlour a bluff ? "

" I do work there. It isn't a bluff, but of course I could not live and dress on what I earn there."

" You dress exquisitely—in perfect taste."

" Thank you. You must admit I am very frank with you."

" Most honest. But why should you dine with me to-night ? I am not remunerative. I can't give you clothes or diamonds."

" Why did you ask me—surely you could not have had any doubts about me after your call ? " asked Louise, drawing on her gloves. " Gerald, the first time

I saw you, I liked you because you were Jack's brother
then I began to like you for yourself—now I like you
because you are so *simpatico* in a rather brutal way. I
would talk to no other man I know like this, nor allow
him to talk as you do."

He watched her as she spoke, thinking, " How wrong
all those moralists and dramatists are ! Here is an
unabashed man-chaser, but she has the face of an angel,
with an aura of purity and great refinement. Her voice
is not hard, nor her manner assertive. She is very
feminine, and beautifully delicate, like a flower undashed
by violence. When she bathed the infant Jacques she was
the Madonna, Bouguereau's Madonna, warm-blooded,
lush, unlike those anæmic madonnas crowding the altars
of cinquecento churches. One could not simply say,
' Here is Vice.' That did not meet the problem of
beauty's true foundation, which one was assured was in
the soul. Louise's eyes were so full of soul, just as her
face was full of grace, and her voice of innocence's
gentleness."

" I am very ambitious, Gerald," she continued, as he
watched her sensitive face, her lovely, candid eyes.
" When Jack was killed I made a vow to take everything
out of life I could—since I'd lost everything."

" You loved him so much ? " asked Gerald, unable
to doubt the sincerity of her avowal.

" Yes, so much—curious, isn't it ? But there's one
man in the world somewhere every woman would go to
the stake for. And now about yourself ? " she asked,
placing her gloved hand on his own.

" There's nothing to tell. Like many men, the war's
made me restless and dissatisfied."

" Very well, if you won't tell me, let's go and dance."

" You don't believe me ? "

" No. You've been terribly hurt somchow, and at

your age since it isn't a bad marriage, or misfortune in business, it must be a woman. I'm sorry for you."

He made no reply. They rose and went out, hailing a taxi that took them to the night club.

IV

From that moment it was as if the hand of Fate had been upon him. As he stood by the window of the monastery, at the hour when the light left the valley, another scene came back to him in memory, dismiss it though he would. He remembered how the light faded over Paris, how the Eiffel Tower, its base lost in the twinkling dusk, soared up to the bright rose-flushed heaven where it hung a few cold sentinel lights. For two whole weeks he had seen that Tower from Louise Perron's apartment; lamp-festooned in the dark sky until past midnight; ethereal and grey in the morning mist when he got up and drew back the blinds, for Louise rose early to go to her shop. Then came the telegram that shattered their tranquillity, the news that little Jacques had been drowned in the lily pool into which he had fallen, in the garden at Senlis.

There were four days of nightmare, with an almost hysterical Louise clinging to him. It had never been the same again for either of them. After a fortnight he announced his departure, and met with no resistance. The parting was unemotional, though they were gentle to each other. He left Paris by car early one morning. A week later he had got as far as Florence, where he went to collect his mail. At Cook's office a re-directed telegram awaited him. His beloved mother had died suddenly of a stroke. The telegram was a week old.

He did not go to bed that night. He walked the dark streets of Florence until he saw the dawn come up and the light touch the towers and domes and spread over the valley of the Arno. He remembered sitting far back in an unknown church, crying to himself while the old priest celebrated early mass for half a dozen poor worshippers. That morning he bought a ticket for London, sent a telegram announcing his return, and then cancelled it by another. He could not go home. The judgment of God was upon him.

For two days he stayed in his hotel bedroom in such anguish of spirit that the hotel-keeper's wife, who spoke a little English, came up to his room to inquire if he needed a doctor. Was this a nervous breakdown, he asked himself, looking in the mirror. Yet he felt quite clear-headed, and analysed every step in his progressive derangement.

One night he went to the opera, desperately seeking diversion. It was *Aïda*, splendidly sung. When they came to the entombment scene, he wished it were a reality, with himself eternally shut out from the light of day. Within a week he found himself in Rome. It was in Rome, after ten days of lonely misery, of such depths of despair that he did not think it possible for the mind to sustain its reason, that he began to apprehend his course. A priest, after confession, a gentle white-haired confessor, had spoken to him kindly. A week or so of tranquillity might bring him to a consciousness of God's unfailing grace. Would he like to go into retreat for a time? He could arrange for him to be received at the monastery of Monte Cassino, some sixty miles away. The brethren were very sympathetic. The quiet, the keen air, the timelessness of that great monastery would soothe him. "It will give you strength to face the future, my son," said the kind old priest.

So he had first come to the monastery. When he left it after two weeks his decision was made. He returned to Rome. For three months he lived obscurely, preparing for the fulfilment of his great decision. He studied, he prayed, he slowly withdrew himself from the affairs of the day. At length his desire was granted. He was admitted as a novice of the Order of Saint Benedict in the monastery of Monte Cassino. He was appointed to the boys' seminary.

The calm of that place and his task as a physical instructor began to heal him. On the morning that he left the Eternal City, so early that the soft dawn was breaking over its storied domes, towers and palaces, it seemed as if at last the light was breaking through the darkness of his tormented spirit. " I do not know what has made you take this step," wrote his father. " It seems to me as if you have run away from life for some reason. I am disappointed, but I do not reproach you, though it is sad that I should lose both my sons. There must be some very compelling force that has brought you to this decision, so young, and, as I felt, so well-equipped for life. We can none of us know another's heart, and before that mystery I must bow my head. My blessing goes with you."

Gerald read and re-read the letter. It was in a manner a revelation of the nature of his own father, the worldly industrial gambler, who made fortunes and lost them. Since his belongings could be few, Gerald destroyed almost everything he possessed. But this letter he saved and cherished, his only tie with the warm familiar life that had enveloped the Carter kids in those happy days before Armageddon destroyed their way of life.

A last letter from Estelle he burned, tears dimming his sight before the flames that consumed it. How little they knew, that happy pair he had conducted yesterday

over the monastery, the disturbing tumult they had
awakened in his heart at the sight of their happiness!
His prayer in that dim room at the hotel had been deeply
heartfelt. He had besought peace for the soul of his
countryman and comfort and grace for the sorrowing
young bride. *In te, Domine, speravi.*

CHAPTER V

RUDI AND FRANKIE

I

It was eleven o'clock in the morning, dark, rainy and cold on this November day. The inhabitants of the houses in a small street near Cadogan Square were full of indignation. In the little newsagent's shop on the corner of the street Mrs. Adams, who 'obliged' the people round about with a little cleaning, expressed herself forcibly across the counter to Mrs. Westell. "I call it a shime and a scandal, 'im a-playing like that, when we ought to 'ave a 'oly 'ush ! He's as drunk as an owl again, that's what it is ! " she exclaimed.

Mrs. Adams put the matches into the apron she was holding, already weighted with groceries bought for the cook at No. 7, Maple Street. In the absolute silence of the morning the music of a piano streamed down the street. A milk cart and two delivery vans had come to a stop, the roar of the buses down Sloane Street had faded out. Over the Square, over the west end of London, over the metropolis, over the whole of the United Kingdom there was a deep silence as if the human race had suddenly died in its habitations. Two minutes of absolute silence at eleven o'clock on this morning of the eleventh of November, reminded the world that the war to end all war had been terminated fourteen years ago.

" He can play—I'll say that for 'im. But so could I if I'd been at it all them years," commented Mrs. Adams.

" Sh ! " warned Mrs. Westell, watching the clock over the desk where postal business was transacted.

There was a glissade of notes, falling like leaves in the listening street. Outside, people halted in their missions were looking up at the flat-fronted house across the way. The French window on the Victorian iron balcony was open. Inside, someone was playing the piano brilliantly, quite oblivious or neglectful of the memorial silence that gripped all London. Then, the two minutes concluded, the dull murmur of life filled the air again, people began talking, buses started up with a churning of gears, taxis whizzed by and the rattle of milk bottles being collected in an area made the morning normal again.

" I should say he's drunk again, that's the explanation," asserted Mrs. Adams. " But that don't excuse him— why didn't his housekeeper stop 'im ? He's allus very polite to me—he's a gentleman all right, but he's a terror for the bottle. Drunk at eleven—and on this morning of mornings ! It's a shime, someone should say something to 'im."

There was a crash of bars, a crescendo and then silence. Mrs. Adams paused at the door on her way out, her thin face cocked on one side as she listened intently.

" It wouldn't surprise me if he'd fallen off the stool. I've seen that 'appen. Well, I must get on ! " she called, and hurried out of the shop.

Mrs. Adams was only partly right. Mr. Rudolph Allington was drunk, but he had not fallen off the piano stool. He had got up to fetch another whiskey and soda. He poured it noisily, gulped it, scratched himself in his dressing-gown, and went back to the piano, slithering his slippers over the parquet floor. Plato, the Siamese cat, scurried out of his path. Mr. Allington seated himself at the piano, meditated for a few moments, rubbed his eyes with the back of his hand, swayed a little, and began playing again.

It was obvious he played with the command of a master. There was authority in every phrase, and perfect artistry. He could have been a great pianist, but he had chosen to be, according to some, a great composer. Twenty years ago his *Symphony in A Minor* had swept through the capitals of Europe. He had conducted it himself in Berlin, Vienna, Budapest, Rome, Paris and London. Then his appearances began to be more rare. Inability to arrive at the concert hall punctually, and at the podium soberly, had affected the number of engagements. He conducted brilliantly, in whatever state he reached the platform, but the uncertainty of his arrival outweighed the advantage of his presence. The world waited for the new concerto on which it had been announced he was working. After ten years its hopes subsided into indifference. Half the world believed Rudolph Allington dead. The other half seldom saw him sober.

A few friends still believed in him, hoped for him. He tried them sorely. He spilt food down his clothes, he never answered letters, he was always anything from ten minutes to two hours late, he smelt of drink, he dropped things, broke them, fell over them. But drunk or sober, he had exquisite manners and an alluring smile. It was impossible to resist him. Animals, babies, policemen, postmen and such odd creatures as he consorted with loved him. A nocturnal creature, his day began when others were thinking of bed, so that he rose late. His breakfast was rarely brought into his room before eleven when old Lulu the housekeeper answered the bell and came in with the tray. Breakfast never varied. It consisted of hot coffee and rusks, which he soaked in the coffee and sucked. His teeth had always been troublesome. He had four sets which he kept in a musical box in the bathroom. He would change them two or three times a day as the whim took him, and Lulu knew when this was taking place, for the musical box, a present from Switzerland, played a tune when the lid was raised.

Out of doors the whole neighbourhood knew him. He blinked at everybody and wore a flat black felt hat, almost a sombrero, which he had bought years ago at San Sebastian and refused to give up, despite its age. Then he always carried a malacca cane with a silver top and he had a habit of weaving his hands in the air when he sought to describe anything. He moved about the country in taxis, and it was well known that when the desire came to him to go to Brighton and take the sea air he would hire a taxi. He always succeeded in persuading the astonished driver to send his wife a telegram saying he was spending the night and bringing his fare back on the morrow. Such absences from home in no way surprised old Lulu. She was French, having been with Mr. Allington ten years as housekeeper. She had originally been maid to Mrs. Allington and on her sudden death had continued with the Master, as she always called him. She ran the house with the help of Mrs. Adams, who came in to clean.

It was difficult to believe that Rudolph Allington had ever been married. There was nothing domestic about him. Actually the marriage had been a very happy one and a spring seemed to snap when his adored Alice died. His eccentricities grew from that day, and with no restraining hand upon him, drink and sloth ate up his time. There were days when he never got out of his pyjamas and dressing-gown. On the large desk in his study the sheets of the new symphony lay for years, it being a fiction piously accepted by Lulu that the Master was going to finish it soon. For ten years she carefully dusted the untidy and the bottle-stained paper.

On the study wall hung Laszlo's portrait of Mrs. Allington, third daughter of Lord Bedlow. Laszlo's sparkling brush had caught her in all the beauty of her youth, long-fingered, long-necked, with brilliant eyes and a lovely brow under the clustering blonde curls. Their marriage had created a sensation and everyone prophesied early disaster. No one could understand why this well-born beautiful girl of twenty-one had chosen the untidy haphazard composer fifteen years her senior. He loved her passionately for ten years, reformed his habits, dressed as neatly as he could and squired her wherever she chose to go. Then one day, while visiting her parents at Aix-les-Bains, she died. Rudolph was playing at a concert at Brussels the night she died. They did not dare to tell him until he had come off the platform. He hurried to Aix, escorted the body home, and after the funeral shut up the house for two years and took Eulalie Lafitte, his wife's maid, with him to Berlin, where he lived in an apartment off the Kurfürstendamm. It was said he was working on a new concerto, the ever-unfinished concerto that now littered the desk in No. 10.

He grew shabbier and shabbier, drank more and more, worked less and less. Gradually his name vanished from the concert programmes. Few people ever entered the slip of a house with the twin French windows and iron balcony on the first-floor drawing-room. But occasionally, when one of the windows was open, a passer-by would hear a piano being played. Invariably he halted, for there was a commanding quality in the performance of the unseen pianist.

II

On the eleventh of November, 1932, the day on which Rudolph Allington's playing had shocked Mrs. Adams, standing in the corner shop kept by Mrs. Westell, at about seven in the evening there was a crash on the two steps leading up to No. 10, Maple Street. There was the sound of breaking glass, and a querulous voice making protest in the still, dark street. At that moment a boy passing by saw a man sprawling over the steps. He went to him and recognised the figure at once. It was Rudolph Allington, stunned and leaning up against the railing while a dark wet patch spread over the steps. Obviously the liquid darkening the steps was whiskey. Mr. Allington's pocket and half of his trousers were saturated with the strongly smelling spirit. The boy stooped over the prostrate figure.

"Are you hurt, Mr. Allington?" he cried in his thin boy's voice.

"What the hell do you think I am!" exclaimed the figure, with a baleful glare. "Ring the bell and don't stand gaping!"

The boy straightened himself and rang the bell. Presently old Lulu appeared. She seemed in no way surprised at what she saw.

"You help me with him!" she said curtly to the boy.

Together they heaved the grumbling figure to its feet. Mr. Allington was tall and angular. His black sombrero was crushed down over his eyes. The boy retrieved the malacca stick from the area into which it had fallen.

"Mind the glass in my pocket. I've broken the damn bottle—what a waste, what a waste!" complained Mr. Allington as they got him to the door.

"You should be grateful you haven't broken your

bones," said the housekeeper as they lifted him over the steps and moved him to a chair in the narrow hall. Mr. Allington took off his hat and rubbed his hand down his wet trouser leg.

"Now if I'd drunk the stuff there'd be reason and sense in it, but to break a perfectly good unopened bottle of whiskey is beyond all reason," he growled, looking from the housekeeper to the boy.

"You might have killed yourself—you smell horrible !" said the housekeeper.

"Lulu, don't be a fool ! I only slipped—and horribly, not horrible," he remarked testily.

"Let's get you upstairs—you're badly shaken, and wet through."

Mr. Allington growled.

"I'm more mad than hurt. I can get up the stairs myself. Who are you, boy, haven't I seen you before ? Lulu, give him a shilling and warn him not to drink too much."

"Oh, no, Mr. Allington, it's quite all right," responded the boy, politely. "I'm glad you're not badly hurt."

"So you know me, eh ? Your face is familiar."

"I'm Frankie Westell, sir. We keep the shop on the corner. I've often seen you come in," said the boy.

"That explains it. Your mother's a nice woman. You've been well brought up. Lulu, give him half a crown."

"Oh, please, Mr. Allington !" protested the boy.

"Be quiet ! You know you'd like it. You can help me up the stairs," said Mr. Allington, rising with difficulty.

The housekeeper smiled. Together they assisted him to the stairs. They got him up to the second floor and into a back bedroom. The housekeeper took off his coat and waistcoat and brought a fresh pair of trousers.

" You'd better get into those, sir, you smell terrible," said the housekeeper.

" Terribly—not terrible, Lulu. Your grammar is appalling," exclaimed Mr. Allington, raising his finger like a schoolmaster.

" You help him—I've got the dinner spoiling downstairs," said the housekeeper.

" Off you go ! " he cried. " Dinner, for God's sake, don't spoil my dinner ! " He turned to Frankie. " Undo my shoes, like a good boy."

The housekeeper left the room. The boy undid his boots. After something of a struggle Mr. Allington changed his underwear and his trousers. It was nice silk underwear, Frankie noticed. When Mr. Allington had dressed he surveyed himself in the mirror. Then he turned to the boy watching him.

" How old are you, Frankie ? " he asked.

" Nearly fifteen, sir."

" At school ? "

" No, sir—I work at Harrod's, in the packing department."

" Have you a father ? "

" Yes, sir, he drives one of Harrod's vans."

" You are a polite boy, Frankie. Politeness is a great quality, never forget. I went to Winchester to acquire it. With you it is innate—though your parents have had something to do with it."

He looked at the gawky boy standing before him. He was tall with a pleasant face and carefully brushed black hair. Apple-cheeked and dark-eyed, he gave promise of a handsome youth.

" Have you any sisters ? " asked Mr. Allington, spraying himself with eau-de-cologne.

" No, sir, I'm the only one."

" That's a pity—a great pity, an only child is doomed

to be odd or odious," commented Mr. Allington. "Now let's go down to dinner. Give me your arm, I'm shaky still."

They went downstairs. At the entrance to the dining-room, where the table was set for one, Frankie said he must be going.

"Nonsense—it's not your bedtime," said Mr. Allington, and leaning over the stairs descending to the basement called, "Lulu, set another place, we have a guest!"

Lulu appeared and set another place. To the boy's relief she did not seem annoyed. She smiled at him and said, "It's very nice for the Master to have company."

"You see, you're approved of," said Mr. Allington, seating himself with the boy on his right hand.

Lulu brought in the soup, and placed it before them. Frankie was bewildered. He had never before seen so many spoons, knives and forks. He chose the spoon behind the plate, diffidently.

"No, boy, that's for pudding. The large spoon at the side," said Mr. Allington.

The boy's face crimsoned with embarrassment. When the fish came he waited and watched his host. So it was the broad-bladed knife, like a small scimitar, one used. He managed to commit no further error until the coffee came. The two silver pots puzzled him. He filled his cup to the brim with milk.

"No, my boy—you've left no room for the coffee."

"Oh," exclaimed Frankie, crimson again.

"Let me pour it back," said the maid, kindly. "There, now help yourself to the coffee and add some milk."

"You've done very well, Frankie—I shall always tell you what to do—it's the privilege of age. Now let's go up to the study. Give me your arm. Don't think I'm drunk, I'm merely shaken." He turned to the table.

"We'll take this bottle with us," he added, lifting up a full bottle of whisky, "it won't interest you but it will me."

The study was actually the drawing-room of No. 10. It ran from the front of the house, with its two long French windows and balcony overlooking the street, to the back, where a stained-glass window hid the dismal small yards and desperate gardens of the kitchen side of the rows of houses backing each other. In the drawing-room, between the French windows and the fireplace, stood a full-sized Steinway concert grand. It was the one Frankie Westall had heard so often when he stood outside in the street below listening in the darkness to Mr. Allington's playing.

A fire burned in the grate. Bright rugs covered the floor. Deep easy-chairs and a great divan by the wall increased the note of comfort. The marble fireplace was beautiful. The boy could not help commenting on it. The paintings on the walls also pleased him.

"Is that Venice?" he asked, looking at one of them.

"Yes—Canaletto, the Orologio and the Piazzetta. Does that mean anything to you?"

"No, sir, but it's very beautiful."

"Oh, you've the sense to know that! Canaletto was the name of the artist, at least he liked to call himself that—*settecento*, the best period."

"*Settecento?*" echoed the boy.

"Eighteenth-century, from *sette*, seven, and *cento*, hundred."

"But that's seven hundred, not eighteen," said Frankie. Mr. Allington chuckled.

"That catches everybody. The Italians drop the first nine hundred years, and they start counting with the first year of the thousand. So anything from seventeen hundred to eighteen hundred they call *settecento*, and we call it the eighteenth-century. And people expect nations to understand each other. Can you pull a cork ? ''

Frankie looked at him, startled by the sudden question.

" There's a corkscrew in that drawer. Get it and open this bottle for me.''

Mr. Allington sank with all his weight into the red leather chair by the fire. He turned out a light by his head. A cat jumped up on his lap.

" Plato, we've got a visitor. Your best manners, please,'' he said to the Siamese cat. There was a pop as Frankie pulled the cork. " Good boy, that sounds a clean job. Now pour me two inches into a glass, and then water up to the middle. Doesn't it smell good ? ''

" No, sir. I don't like whisky.''

" Keep to that opinion, better for you and better for me ! ''

Frankie brought him the tumbler. Mr. Allington took a gulp and sighed.

" Sit down,'' he said. " It is polite to remain at least an hour after you've eaten a man's dinner, but I'll let you off with a half.''

" Oh, I'm enjoying every minute, sir. The beautiful room, the wonderful dinner—and you, sir.''

" Thank you for the addition. You are diplomatic as well as polite. To many I am a trial. Do you play dominoes ? ''

" Yes, sir, but if you wouldn't mind, I'd rather you played the piano.''

" Yes, you are a diplomat,'' exclaimed Mr. Allington, regarding the boy steadily for a few moments. The shape of the head was good, the eyes wide apart, the brow broad. The accent was bad, but there was promise in the young colt, properly trained. These boys never got any real training, they were too soon out of the paddock pulling vans and carrying parcels for a few shillings a week. Even so, the parents had done a good job with him, he was clean, well-mannered, well set up. Mr. Allington knew the little shop on the corner, he bought his stamps and writing-paper there and chatted with the smiling little chubby-faced woman who ran it. He remembered now he had seen a man there in the evenings, a little, bald-headed fellow with black eyebrows, who assisted like Frankie. Fortunate pair to have produced such a boy, while he . . .

"So you want me to play—what makes you think I can play?" demanded Mr. Allington, breaking his reverie.

"Oh, I've heard you, sir. I often stand under the window at night and listen. I heard you last night, playing Chopin."

"Good God! How did you know it was Chopin? You'll tell me you've heard of Liszt next."

"The *Third Rhapsodie*—you played that also last night."

Mr. Allington pulled himself up in his chair, took a drink and looked hard at his young guest.

"So you've learned to play—you're a pianist?" observed his host.

"Oh, no, sir, not really. I've never learned proper. We only got a pianner last year."

"Properly, Frankie, please—properly. And never pianner—there's no such instrument. Pi-ah-no, from the Italian, meaning soft or light. The instrument's a piano-forte, a light treble, a loud base, from *forte*, strong. Now say ' piano '."

"Piano," repeated Frankie gravely. "Thank you."

Mr. Allington liked the boy better and better. He got up, emptied the tumbler, gave it to the boy and said, "The mixture as before." Then he went over to

the Steinway and sat down in front of it. Frankie
brought the tumbler and stood by him. He noticed for
the first time, with surprise, how stubby the pianist's
fingers were. He had always imagined they must be
long and slender.

Mr. Allington began to play. He snorted a little with
the labour of it. There was amazing dexterity in those
stubby fingers. When he had finished he looked at the
boy standing by him.

" Do you like that ? " he asked.

" No, sir, not very much," answered Frankie
slowly.

" Ignorant, but at least honest ! I thought you
wouldn't. It's beyond you. It's Prokofiev—a Russian
modern. Anyone can like Chopin—though I'm not
disparaging him. Well, here's your *Polonaise*. Sit
down."

Mr. Allington played the *Polonaise*. He played two
Etudes, then something by a man called Bach, and
something by one called Debussy, a filmy, waterfally
kind of piece that Frankie thought he liked, but couldn't
be sure. It was rather like a foggy morning in October.
He told Mr. Allington so and the man at the piano
chuckled, played a few arpeggios, and stopped. He
picked up the empty tumbler.

" *Encore, s'il vous plaît*—do you know French ? " he
asked.

" No, sir, but I know it means you want another,"
laughed Frankie.

" You are beholding a very dreadful example. Don't
chatter to your mother about encores."

" My mother admires you, sir. The other day, when
you came in for some notepaper——"

" My boy, I never went in for some notepaper ! "
interrupted Mr. Allington. " Only ignoramuses talk of

notepaper. Notepaper is paper you make notes on. The paper you write on is writing-paper. I went in for writing-paper, Frankie. To resume, my boy. The other day, when I went to your shop for writing-paper, your mother—— ? "

" She said you were a very great gentleman."

" She must have said something else, being a discerning woman. She must have added to that pleasing eulogium the word ' but '—nevertheless, Frankie, I appreciate the appreciation. Have you watered this down a little ? " added Mr. Allington after drinking. He pulled the boy's ear and smiled at him.

" If you don't mind, sir, I think I should be going. My mother will wonder——" began Frankie.

" Of course, my boy, of course. Please thank her for this pleasant visit." Mr. Allington looked down at his young guest's boots. " Your boots are excellently polished. Do you do them yourself ? "

" Yes, sir."

" My Lulu, who began life as a French maid and has developed into a wonderful *bonne-à-tout-faire*—or housekeeper, as we dismally say—has every virtue, but her pride stops short with my silver. She doesn't like polishing and the condition of my silver depresses me. Now you seem to be a good polisher, Frankie, so I'm willing to make a bargain with you. If you will contrive to keep my table silver bright, I will give you a piano lesson once a week. It will be manual labour for both of us, so don't feel insulted."

The boy's radiant face left him in no doubt of the answer.

" You couldn't have too many spoons, sir ! " he added joyously.

" Ah, wait until you've counted them. Now, you may come when you like. Lulu will lead you to your task. And would Tuesdays, at seven, say, with a little supper afterwards, suit you ? "

" Oh, Mr. Allington—that would be marvellous ! "

" Very well, and since we have now arrived at what I hope will be the affectionate relationship of teacher and pupil, I feel something less formal, though not less respectful, would be helpful. My name Rudolph I have always detested, though the reason of it was pleasant, and I have reduced it to Rudi, which is less Hapsburgian. So Rudi let it be. Can you show yourself out ? "

" Oh, yes, sir. Good night, and thank you ever so much, sir," called Frankie at the door.

" No—no. Thank you very—not ever so. Thank you very much."

" Thank you very much—Rudi," said the boy shyly.

" You know," exclaimed Mr. Allington, as he stood by the door, " it does sound rather like a music-hall turn—Rudi and Frankie ! "

With a chuckle he closed the door on his guest.

III

Faithful to their agreement through the next six months, Mr. Allington gave Frankie a piano lesson, and Frankie polished Rudi's silver. Frankie did something else for his teacher—he gave him a new interest in life. Lulu was quick to notice the change. On Tuesdays it was seldom that Mr. Allington was in a regrettable condition. There had been two bad lapses—one when the teacher couldn't get out of his chair, and one when, at the keyboard, he was incapable of instructing his pupil. Even so, the record was remarkable. Frankie's visits were no longer restricted to Tuesday evenings. He was now an accepted member of the family. He had the run of the library, he never ceased asking Mr. Allington questions, he met many of his friends and became more confident in manner. Little by little he assumed a degree of control over his elderly friend, who delighted in extending his quick mind. They began to go to concerts and theatres, and when the summer months came they made excursions to the country. There was one perfect day, a Saturday in July, when they went to lunch at " Frenchways," in Surrey. It was a high-water mark in Frankie's life, though the ordeal was exhausting. They were met at Guildford by a car and motored out to a Tudor house on a hillside looking over the beautiful Sussex landscape. " Frenchways " was the property of Sir George and Lady Frant, who were Rudi's oldest friends.

Lady Frant was a terrifying woman to meet. She had large black eyes and wore a black lace mantilla on her head. Her bony hands were twisted with arthritis, and she hobbled about with the aid of a heavy rubber-tipped stick. She was never out of pain, but an indomitable will drove her on. In her early years she had had some fame as a pianist. She and Rudi had studied under the same master, Leschetizky, in Vienna. Born the daughter of a bishop, she had shaken ecclesiastical circles by marrying, first, a jockey, who broke his neck in a steeplechase, then an American brewer of great wealth from Milwaukee, by whom she had two children before getting a divorce, and then, in middle age, George Frant, a judge in India, whom she had met on an Hellenic cruise and married after only one month's acquaintanceship.

This last marriage had been a great success, but Geraldine Frant's earlier episodes had produced some unusual ties. The jockey had been a comic little man from Newmarket, whose horsey relations, employed in training establishments, were always welcome at "Frenchways." Her favourite was a tall, wall-eyed nephew, who ran a grain business at Peterborough, and was also a renowned horse-coper. He played the flute with astonishing facility and had a prodigious memory for Restoration poetry, much of which was quite unrepeatable except on carefully chosen occasions. Then America walked into the house in the form of a nephew, a Rhodes scholar at Oxford, whose home was near Laramie, Wyoming. Lanny from Laramie, his aunt called him. He had a passion for backgammon and played her for high stakes, with varying fortune. Also in the American contingent were two grandchildren, Spencer and Marcelle. The youth was at school in Lausanne, the sister at a finishing school in France. Between them, Frankie learned, they would one day inherit twenty million dollars. Their mother had married three times, their father twice. The mother lived in a château near Pau, and was now married to a French marquis twenty years her senior. Their father, Lady Frant's son, had married, secondly, an Egyptian, by whom he had four more children and was financing an archæological mission near Kut-el-Amara. Frankie's head reeled as these relationships were revealed to him.

Sir George and Lady Frant were down at the swimming pool when they arrived. There was a great bathing party going on, with a slim brown youth, Spencer's schoolfellow from Lausanne, the son of an Italian prince, providing an astonishing exhibition of diving. Frankie was invited to take off his clothes and join the party, whereupon he achieved immediate renown with a jack-knife dive, to Rudi's utter astonishment.

" Who is the boy, Rudi ? " demanded Lady Frant, looking critically at the performer on the diving-board, who was now doing a couple-dive with the Italian youth. " His accent——"

" Geraldine, keep your claws in. I don't want the boy frightened. He's my pupil."

" But where does he come from ? " persisted Lady Frant.

" A most respectable home, you old snob ! " retorted Rudi, with a comic snort.

" Rudi, that is the last thing you could ever call me, with my menagerie ! " She poked her stick at him. " We much prefer him to that terrible young woman you brought here the last time."

" Lucy Thomas—but, my dear, she's brilliant—she writes all the musical criticism for the *Daily Post*. Her book on Brahms——"

" George and I disliked her at sight, Rudi. There's only one woman I dislike more than one who knows nothing, and that's one who knows everything. She spent her whole time improving us."

" Very well-dressed," observed Sir George, a man of few words.

Up on the terrace a bell rang. " Tea ! " said Lady Frant, struggling to her feet. " I don't suppose they'll want to leave the pool. Rudi, give me your arm. What have you been doing this last few months ? We see nothing of you now."

" Composing a little."

" The old yarn ! Is this a musical prodigy you've discovered ? "

" No, he's not a prodigy. If you must know, his people keep the newsagent's shop on the corner of my street. I slipped one evening on the steps outside my house and Frankie helped me up."

" You were drunk, I suppose."

" Geraldine, dear ! " exclaimed Sir George.

" Rudi has nothing to hide from us. We love him, drunk or sober," said Lady Frant.

" Thank you for those kind words. I assure you that on this occasion I was not drunk, only unsteady. I asked the boy in—he is now my faithful attendant. A very sharp lad."

" He looks it—he's lots of charm," said Lady Frant, panting up the steps to the terrace.

" Too much, I fear. He's seduced Lulu and Plato. They are his slaves."

" What sort of a pupil is he ? Are you seriously teaching him ? "

" Yes—a good ear, fair executive ability. Time is his great defect. It's not the musician I'm interested in, it's the mind. It's a thirsty one. I like to watch it opening."

" Rudi, it was a great tragedy you had no children," said Lady Frant, seating herself before the oak tea-table on the flagged terrace. " They might have reformed you—there always was a strong element of the school-master in you. I remember what a tyrant you were when we played duets."

Rudi Allington made no reply. Lady Frant looked at him sharply. He was gazing down at the swimming pool, where the young people were splashing about. She saw then that her remarks had opened the old wound and she was immediately contrite.

" I'm sorry," she said, giving the back of his hand a pat.

He smiled at her, and she, aware of the ghost of Alice she had raised, felt guilty. Was this great ideal of one love such a desirable thing after all ? It was putting all your eggs in one basket, and Fate had a trick of knocking the basket out of your hands. She had put eggs into three baskets, and though some of them had proved somewhat addled, she had found it a rewarding policy, as witness that horde of shouting youngsters down by the pool.

IV

Since Wednesday afternoon was the time when the shop was shut the Westells could breathe a little on Wednesday evenings. It was then they asked Mr. Allington to take supper with them. Once a month he sat down at the square table in front of the kitchen-range in the little parlour behind the shop. Mr. Westell put on a stiff collar and tie and flattened his black side tufts with a little brilliantine. He also spent some time over the kitchen sink with a nail-brush and some ammonia under Mrs. Westell's strict instructions. Mr. Allington had the seat of honour, the high-backed Windsor chair with the wooden arms. On the upright piano by the wall, for which the last instalments were now being paid, stood his photograph in a bright tin frame. Since he had been giving Frankie music lessons the instalments had been increased. Hitherto, Miss Spinks had been paid two and sixpence an hour for a piano lesson, much of which was wasted, since Frankie was so bad at practising. Mr. Allington had changed all that. The pupil practised faithfully.

Mr. Westell was critical and said Frankie should help his mother a little oftener in the shop, but then Mr. Westell was often critical of his son. He could never quite understand him, and the boy's contrariness infuriated him. " He'll contradict you just for the sake of it—and where does he get all those words from ? Told

I

me last night I was inimical to music. What does he mean by that? Was he being saucy?" grumbled Mr. Westell.

"You should be proud of him. Don't you like to see a boy improving himself?" asked Mrs. Westell, impatiently.

"He's getting a bit beyond himself, playing that grand pianner, and the four-course dinners, and reserved seats at the theatre, and all that!"

"Very well, we'll tell him he can't go any more to Mr. Allington's. We'll keep him in our own world and break his heart, Mr. Westell," said Mrs. Westell sharply.

"You do carry on," retorted her husband, puffing at his pipe. "I've nothing against Mr. Allington. He's a gent. But I don't want Frankie's head to swell."

"Well, I do. You're just a jealous old man. You should be proud to see the boy stepping out in the world and holding his own. He's ambitious. Young people nowadays aren't content to go along in the same old rut. Look at us, scratching all the time and never a week ahead with our living expenses."

"You'll be saying you made a mistake in marrying me next," said Mr. Westell dismally.

Mrs. Westell closed the oven door after basting the shoulder of mutton that sizzled appetisingly. Then she put down the oven-cloth and went to the back of her husband's chair. She leaned over and kissed the top of his bald head.

"You silly old man," she said. "I hope when Frankie marries the girl 'll be as pleased with her bargain as I've been!" she said, smiling at him.

Mr. Westell caught at her and pulled her on to his knee.

"Dad, don't be silly. I've got the dinner on my hands. Mr. Allington will be here in a quarter of an hour," she cried, but she was content for him to hold her for a few minutes and peck at her cheek.

"You're a good-looking lass still," he said, surveying her. "Pity we haven't had a girl to keep the pattern going!"

At this moment Frankie came in and observed them with a smile. Mrs. Westell stood up and straightened her apron and pushed away a wisp of hair.

"Frankie, fetch me some coal," she said, as much from embarrassment as necessity.

Frankie went out into the yard and into the coalhouse, where he filled the scuttle. He did this a little resentfully always. He was the family heaver and hauler, for his dad had a "heart" and must not lift anything. Every Monday, being wash-day, he had to haul in from the outhouse the dolly-tub, the scrubbing-board, two large wash-tins and a portable mangle. It was always a desperate scramble so that he should not be late at the warehouse. The condition of his father's heart had always been a shadow over the family. There were periods when Mr. Westell had to lie still in bed, uneasily, for there was always the menace of losing his job. Mrs. Westell, a confirmed optimist, found consolation in her husband's affliction. "Who knows, they might have taken him off for the war, and then I'd have had no husband," she said, never forgetful of her favourite brother's death in the fighting around Soissons.

Unlike his family, Mr. Westell had no patience with his heart. He was prepared to lift anything, to run up and down stairs, and do all the strictly forbidden things. In his youth he had been a gay dancer and had fallen in love with his wife at one of the shilling "hops" to which he had gone every Saturday night. She was the lightest-footed girl on the floor, as well as the best-looking. But those days were over. Dancing was strictly forbidden, as also hurrying for buses, and carrying in coals. "If you're careful, you'll live to be an old man," said the doctor. "I'd rather 'go' young and have some fun," replied Westell rebelliously. His wife and Frankie watched him at every turn, determined to keep him alive.

Frankie realised he would never be reprieved from the coal-scuttle and wash-tub heaving, and he smothered his dislike. His one anxiety was that Rudi should never see him in the act, and his parents had been implored never to divulge the fact. They responded, aware that the boy had curious facets of pride. Two years ago there had been that curious passion for gloves to be worn on Sundays, when he went to church and Sunday school. "Why on earth is he clamouring for gloves?" exclaimed Mr. Westell irritably. "He'll be asking for a tail coat next!"

"Oh, let the boy have 'em. It's growing pains," said Mrs. Westell, who at Christmas had responded to a prayer for a pair of patent shoes. She had had to fight her husband over that desire. "Box calf's always been good enough for me. I wore boots with nails in 'em at his age," he said.

Up in Frankie's bedroom Mrs. Westell had found a little book, obviously bought in a second-hand shop, entitled *Manners for Men*. She examined her son's secret reading, and found a clue to recent curious behaviour, such as always waiting until she was seated, and pulling the chair out for her when she rose.

"What the dickens——" exclaimed Mr. Westell, observing this performance on the third occasion.

"Ssh——" went Mrs. Westell, and added, when her son was out of the room, "You silly old goose, what do you want to make fun of the boy for!"

"But all this jumping up and down, and pulling in and out the chair, and rushing to open the door, for you, not for me!"

"We've got a young gentleman in the family."

"I thought we'd got an errand boy, and not so willing at that, for all I hear," said Mr. Westell. "I must say he's a rum 'un. Wants me to make him a trouser-press now!"

"Well, make it for the boy; it's no crime to have a crease in your trousers—and you know you like making things for him."

She did not reveal the clue to Frankie's strange behaviour. In *Manners for Men* it said that gentlemen always waited for ladies to be seated at table, assisted them to be seated, and withdrew the chair on their rising. *The hallmarks of a gentleman are good gloves and shoes. Even if the clothing is shabby it should be unostentatious and well-pressed.* So that explained it. She fought hard to get Frankie his gloves and patent-leather shoes. They were most reverently treated.

Alas, there was a scene one Sunday evening as they went to church. Frankie resolutely walked behind.

"What are you dawdling for, are you ashamed of us?" exclaimed Mr. Westell, turning round.

"Yes," replied Frankie, brutally. "Oh, Dad, your hat's awful!"

"What's the matter with my hat?" cried Mr. Westell angrily, removing his bowler and looking at it.

"It's too small, and you wear it too far on the back of your head."

"Well, of all the cheek!" burst forth Mr Westell.

"Frankie, how dare you be so impertinent to your father!" cried Mrs. Westell.

"But, Mum, it really——"

"Not another word! You should be ashamed of

yourself. You come and walk with us properly," said Mrs. Westell firmly.

But that night when Frankie had gone to bed, under a cloud, and his father had burst forth about the bowler incident, Mrs. Westell shook him.

" Frankie was quite right, though I wouldn't admit it. I've never liked you in that bowler. It's too small and it makes you look like a comedian," protested Mrs. Westell.

" So you're another of 'em. I'll wear it till it's green, my good woman ! " retorted Mr. Westell.

He never wore it again. A few days later she traded it with a man in the street who had a barrow-load of potted geraniums. Mrs. Westell wanted some flowers for her four empty window-boxes. Her husband, returning home one evening, remarked upon the festive windows and learned what his bowler had procured. A few days later she went with him to purchase a Homberg hat. " Now, don't you make any comment on it," she warned Frankie.

This phase had just been concluded when Mr. Allington came into their lives. They had known him as a customer for a number of years. He had certain distinctive marks as a customer. He bought his stamps in sheets of one hundred at a time—one hundred penny, one hundred halfpenny. He could not resist pencils, and as Mrs. Westell was always stocking new cards of pencils brought by the travellers, Mr. Allington's collection was increasing. He bought them with metal caps, he bought them with rubber erasers, he bought them hard, soft and medium, black, blue and red. " I can't think what he does with them all," observed Mr. Westell one evening when he had just sold him a new collection. " He must have a load of 'em."

About a year later Frankie was able to report on the

mystery. "They stand in jars, Dad, in dozens, all over the house, on the top of memo. pads. Then if a bar of music comes into his head he can always jot it down. He's got them in the bathroom, even."

Mr. Allington arrived just after Frankie had washed his hands and brushed his hair. There was no doubt that their visitor enjoyed his supper. He brought his own bottle of whiskey with him, and Plato also came across the road and sat peacefully on the snippet rug in front of the fire. After supper, when Mr. Allington had reached his fourth glass of whiskey and radiated happiness, he talked about his travels, his adventures as a musical student in Berlin, Prague and Paris. He talked a lot about Paris on this particular evening. He had conducted there on several occasions. He was going again in May, to conduct one of his compositions.

"When do you get your holidays?" asked Mr. Allington, turning to Frankie.

"Either in July or October," replied Frankie. "I could get them changed," he added quickly.

Mr. Allington turned his tumbler slowly.

"If you have the kind of parents with courage enough to let a young son go to Paris, I might arrange something," he said with a twinkle.

"Oh, Mr. Allington, of course we'd let him go with you," exclaimed Mrs. Westell. "Wouldn't we, Dad?" she asked, turning to her husband.

"If he can get his holiday shifted, yes. You know, Mr. Allington, it's very good of you, but Frankie mustn't neglect his job. We're working folks, and I don't want Frankie to imagine——"

Mrs. Westell cut him short.

"It'll be a wonderful education for him! If only someone had taken me to Paris!" cried Mrs. Westell.

" I'll take you there, Mum, one day," said Frankie.

" You notice they don't want me—wouldn't trust me, I suppose," commented Mr. Westell slyly.

So it was arranged. As Mr. Allington was leaving he turned to Frankie.

" You'd better get hold of Plato and bring him across. I don't want him out all night."

Frankie seized Plato and walked across to No. 10.

" Well, our little plot came off very well," said Rudi as he opened the door, and Frankie put down the cat.

" Rudi, you're a wizard ! I can't believe it now, that I'm going. I think I must be the luckiest boy that was ever born."

" I hope you'll always feel like that. I started off with that feeling," said Mr. Allington. He gazed a little sadly at the eager young face before him. " Well, good night, my boy."

" Good night, Rudi. And thanks ever so much ! "

A severe look warned him of the offence.

" Sorry, thanks very much ! " he cried, laughing, as he closed the hall door after him.

Mr. Allington stood still for a few moments after he had hung up his black felt hat. He had dreaded the idea of going to Paris alone. As he got older he grew very lonely and disliked journeys. But was it kind or wise to be giving Frankie glimpses of a world that in comparison must make his own seem humdrum ? Some of his friends had scolded him. He defended his action. He knew his own pleasure in watching a bright young mind expand accounted for much of what he was doing. The warm enthusiasm of this boy gave him a new interest in life. But there was another reason, he told himself. This was a very singular boy, sensitive, on whom nothing was lost. It was early yet to know just how gifted was this protégé of his, or in what direction his gift would demonstrate itself. He would wait, encouragingly. It was like putting a plant in a pot, watering it, and waiting for the bloom.

" You're making a great mistake. It never pays," warned a friend, who disapproved of Frankie.

" Pays ! Who wants to be paid ? " remonstrated Mr. Allington. " I'm getting far more than I give— I'm in the family, bless 'em ! "

V

But Fate stepped in. Two days before the excursion to Paris was due there was a ring very late in the evening at the door of No. 10. Mr. Allington was dozing before the fire in the study. Plato was asleep in his lap, Lulu had gone to bed. Grumbling at this unexpected caller, Mr. Allington made his way unsteadily downstairs. It must be a telegraph boy and he had a singular dislike of telegrams because they always brought him bad news or desired him to do something in a hurry. Without turning on the light in the hall he opened the door to find Frankie standing there.

" Good Lord, why aren't you in bed ? " exclaimed Mr. Allington, irritably.

The boy did not answer but stepped past him into the hall, and then rushed up the stairs, leaving his bewildered host down in the hall. With much labour he followed after him, to find Frankie all his length on the lounge sobbing his heart out.

" Now whatever is it ? " said Mr. Allington, sitting down by him and putting a hand on his head.

The boy lifted a tear-stained face.

"Rudi—Rudi! My Dad's dead! My Dad's dead!" he cried.

"Oh dear," exclaimed Mr. Allington, holding Frankie to him. He said no more but just patted the sobbing boy gently. Presently, when Frankie had recovered a little from his grief, he heard the direful story. Mr. Westell had gone to Hampstead to spend the evening with a married sister. When he departed for home, a little before ten o'clock, he caught a bus. It was surmised he must have hurried, for, mounting to the upper deck, he suddenly collapsed. The alarmed conductor saw that his passenger was dead. He stopped the bus, a police ambulance was summoned and the body was taken to a mortuary. There the contents of the dead man's pocket were examined and in a wallet was found a health club membership card with Herbert Westell's name and address. About ten o'clock a policeman had called at the shop and broken the news to Mrs. Westell. She and Frankie had gone off at once in a taxi to identify the body. Mr. Westell would be brought home on the morrow.

Little by little the boy sobbed out his story. Then he grew calmer and said he must go back to his mother. His aunt was with her and he declined Rudi's offer to go home with him.

"I'm sorry to have made such a scene," he said, standing up and wiping his eyes. "And I'm sorry to come so late, but I had to tell you, Rudi."

"Of course! Of course! Tell your mother I will come across and see her in the morning. And I know you'll be brave and be a comfort to her."

He watched Frankie go, sorrowfully. Neither of them had made an allusion to the Paris trip, but it was now impossible for the boy to go. A problem presented itself. In homes like these the death of the breadwinner was a

serious economic question. It was unlikely the shop
would support them adequately. Meditating upon this,
Mr. Allington went slowly upstairs and back into the
study. It was nearly midnight. He poured himself
another drink and sat staring disconsolately into the dying
fire. Plato came and rubbed himself against his master's
leg and then leapt into his lap, peering with his squinting
green eyes into the face above him.

Mr. Allington returned the inquisition. "We've got
a problem, Plato," he said gravely, rubbing the cat's
head. "Something's got to be done for our young
friend." He reached unsteadily for the whiskey decanter.
Long ago he had learned to drown his sorrows and
disappointments. The world had never been much to
his liking and he had a painful patience with his fellow
men. They were a mixture of the heroic and the mean,
the logical and illogical. What a mess they were making
of the world to-day! Having scarcely ended one war
they were squabbling over the peace and getting themselves set for another. In the past their bloodthirstiness
had sprung from greed and bigotry. Now they dressed
their bureaucratic tyranny in high-sounding sociological
terms such as world-parliaments, democratic liberty,
international brotherhood. It was no longer kings
grabbing kingdoms, it was nations grabbing markets.
For bows and arrows and papal bulls they had substituted
tanks and trade treaties and economic blocs, but it was
the same avaricious spirit trafficking with human folly.
The ruthless will of the powerful few was now substituted
by the futile conferences and resolutions of a hoard of
gallivanting delegates. No, it didn't make sense, and
to Rudi Allington's way of thinking it would never make
sense, not until this planet was as cold as the moon.
Amid all this nonsense he tried to follow his own philosophy, to be honourable, tolerant and kind. That was

all one could do. That one should feel so was perhaps the witness of the living God.

"One must be kind, Plato," he said, his voice husky, as he raised his shaking hand to drink again. Then he fell asleep, snoring loudly, while the clock ticked and the fire died.

CHAPTER VI

NOW THE BLOSSOM

I

In five years a boy sweeps into the full flood of youth, and the pattern begins to shape itself inexorably. It was difficult to recall the shy gawky boy in the confident young man who so often was the life and light of Rudi Allington's table. There were those who resented the manner in which at times he eclipsed his host. Rudi seemed to get fainter and fainter as Frankie grew more and more assertive. He ran Number 10. Rudi, never a domestic soul, was happy to have someone who was willing to assume the burden of a house and see that everything functioned to perfection. Old Lulu, more devoted than ever to Master Frankie, was given the assistance of a cook. The shy little boy who had come in to clean the silver now wrote out the menus for the dinner-parties that Mr. Allington gave with such success.

The house was brighter in both spirit and decoration. Frankie had developed a flair for furniture, hangings and pictures. The upstairs study was no longer an untidy lounge. The Steinway still kept the place of honour but new divans and chairs had replaced the heavy old-fashioned leather furnishings. It was characteristic that Rudi now drank his whiskey out of a cut-glass tumbler and a decanter instead of the cheap tumbler and bottle as of old. In a back cupboard Frankie had discovered one day a great wealth of beautiful old glass. In long unopened drawers he had found layers of Irish linen. A casual remark of Rudi's about a box at the bank had resulted in the reappearance of a wealth of Georgian silver locked away after Mrs. Allington's death. A Raeburn and two Romneys wasting their glory in back bedrooms had been hung in the study. The music books that had been scattered in such disorder over the tables and chairs now stood tidily and in sequence in convenient bookracks.

Frankie was not so successful with Rudi's personal appearance. After long insistence the greasy old black sombrero had been replaced by a more respectable hat, of the same shape. A watchful eye was kept on Rudi's waistcoats which hitherto had carried evidence of many repasts. He was urged to buy himself new overcoats and shoes. He smiled at the exaggerated compliments by which Lulu and Frankie sought to encourage him ; all his clothes soon took on again the old shapeless outline. The house itself was renovated outside as well as in. There was a new bright blue enamel-painted door with an artistic No. 10 and a brass Adam knocker. There were window boxes gay in spring and summer with marguerites and pelargoniums.

That Mr. Allington was happy, the whole street knew. Cars drew up to the door and young people ran up the steps and went inside the house. Often late at night music poured out through the French windows and young voices were heard laughing and talking. The music that came out of the windows was often very different from that heard by a rather wistful little boy who had once stood listening in the street below. It was now gay and syncopated and its origin was clearly transatlantic. Rudi amiably tolerated the noise these youngsters made on the piano. The people who could drink such things as cocktails could like this noise they termed jazz. They called it music just as they called shuffling up and down the floor hugging each other dancing. But at sixty one could not be expected to appreciate the tastes of twenty. One could only be tolerant.

So Rudi smiled and was glad to see these boys and girls enjoying themselves. They were Frankie's friends, nicely mannered and good to look at, and their zest for life warmed up the old house and filled it with laughter. Some of his old friends thought it all dreadful. That commonplace young man had Rudi completely under his thumb. How else could he have been persuaded to buy a sports car and be rushed across the countryside at sixty miles an hour? He had even figured in the police court and been fined for exceeding the speed limit. Sir George Frant raised his hands in despair. " It's all that young upstart who's ruining him ! " he exclaimed.

" Stuff and nonsense ! I like Frankie. He's given Rudi a new life and brightened him up. The boy has good manners—it's not spoilt him in any way," said Lady Frant.

" Well, I think he's a swelled head. What else can you expect ? "

" I expect quite a lot, he has a head on his shoulders. Anyhow, he's gay, and he's nice to look at ! " said Lady Frant.

" How like a woman ! " growled Sir George. " He hasn't stopped Rudi drinking or made him work."

" No one could do that, but Rudi does drink less, and he is clean and produceable again—we owe that to Frankie. Everybody here likes the boy and I admire him for the way he stands by his mother. His great danger is his looks. I'm not surprised Marcelle made a dead set for him when she came here this summer."

Sir George put down his paper and twisted in his chair.

"There are certain frank things can be said about that young woman though she is your granddaughter. Three husbands at twenty-five! Ruined with money, spoilt to death, and no morals. It's no compliment to any young man to be marked down by that nymphomaniac!" protested Sir George.

"While I dot every *i* and cross every *t* about Marcelle, I still say Frankie is an attractive boy," answered Lady Frant. "He's much too sensible to let Marcelle turn his head—though I don't expect they'll ever see one another again now she's in Honolulu."

Frankie had an equal liking for old Lady Frant. She was often brutally frank but he never doubted her friendliness. Visits to "Frenchways" in these past five years had always been enjoyable despite Sir George's critical eye and aloofness. Marcelle Legrande on one of these visits had paid him some attention but in his eyes she was a creature of another world. Elegant young men with expensive cars and a considerable background gyrated around her. She rushed through Europe as she rushed across the United States, her exhausted French maid dragged with her, guardian of a quarter of a million dollars' worth of jewellery, and ten great trunks. Yet Marcelle never looked anything but the freshest of maidens, dewy-lipped, starry-eyed, and all innocence. Too much of everything and Time would destroy her, but for the moment Paris, Palm Beach, Mexico City, Honolulu, Arizona, Rome, Vienna, Deauville, and very briefly London, were her happy hunting grounds. Somewhere on her route she had met and discarded an Italian husband, a Swedish husband, and had acquired a French husband. She was unique as a transitory bride of great wealth in that not one of her grooms had

a title. " She's funny that way," complained a Rouman-
ian prince to an Hungarian count, after a futile and
expensive siege. " I suppose it's a craving for originality."
It seemed very unfair. It was cheating the purpose of
Christopher Columbus who had discovered the New
World that it might come to the rescue of the Old.

At twenty Frankie had not experienced passion.
Variety and independence marked his course. He
brought a series of young women to No. 10, where Rudi
most hospitably entertained them. He liked young
society and was happy to watch the quest of young love.
" When you get married, Frankie, I shall present you
with a grand piano," he said. " I don't think I shall
ever get married—well, not for a very long time,"
responded Frankie, solemnly. Rudi laughed derisively.
" We all said that ! " he commented. Already he had
noticed one girl, Cynthia Sloan, who was establishing a
monopoly.

When Frankie's father died and the boy's future
became a pressing problem Rudi had bestirred himself.
Mrs. Westell, brave and independent, said she could
manage with the shop. It seemed clear to Rudi she
could not, and on this excuse he made himself responsible
for young Frankie. He took him away from the packing
department and sent him back to school for three years.
When the boy was eighteen his career had to be decided.
Rudi secured him a position in a City export business
with excellent prospects. This step was much discussed
for Frankie had advanced so greatly as a pianist that a
musical career was under consideration. Frankie himself
decided the point.

" You've spent quite enough on me, Rudi—it's time I
earned my living. I want to help mother as soon as I
can." So a very earnest and ambitious young man went
down on the Metropolitan Line to the City every day.

K

It was an excellent opening. " Rudi, why are you so good to me? There's nothing I can do for you, it's all so one-sided ! " he exclaimed after they had come away from the momentous interview that had gained him the opening, and were dining at Rudi's club.

" You have a very pleasurable gift, all too rare these days," said Rudi, as they lunched at his club.

" What's that ? "

" You always say ' Thank you ' so nicely."

" But no boy ever had a friend like you ! "

" No lonely old man ever found such a delectable shrub on his doorstep. I potted you, I've watered you these five years, and now I'm just beginning to get the bloom."

" It was a lucky day for me when you slipped on that step, Rudi ! "

" Ah—and now after these mutual compliments, my boy, let's sample this *Château Latour*, in reverent silence, it's one of the Club's best." He raised his glass. " Here's a health to a future City magnate."

The boy raised his glass but he made no answer. Rudi, looking at him, saw there was a mist in his eyes though he was smiling.

II

1938—that was the year of their holiday in Belgium, and a note of tragedy. Rudolph Allington went to Brussels in October to conduct his new symphony, finished at last under Frankie's unceasing insistence. They spent two days of glorious sightseeing. Rudi grew increasingly nervous as the evening of the concert drew near. In the afternoon, after a successful morning rehearsal, Rudi said he would go to his room and lie down. It was arranged that they should dine lightly at half-past six. The concert began at eight o'clock. The hall was sold out.

Frankie went to the cinema. At half-past six he went to Rudi's room and tapped on the door. There was no answer. He opened it and entered. The room was in darkness. He switched on the light. It was empty. After waiting for about twenty minutes Frankie went down into the hotel vestibule, and then into the dining-room. Rudi was not at their table. He inquired at the desk. No, they did not know whether *m'sieur* was in or out, his key was not in the rack. At seven o'clock Frankie began to get alarmed. What could have happened? He sat down in the lounge and waited, keeping an eye on the door. It was now a quarter-past seven. Rudi had to dress, to dine and reach the concert hall by eight o'clock.

At seven-thirty he went to the desk again. The clerk was sympathetic. *M'sieur* Allington had certainly not come in. But he would page the reception rooms. Five more terrible minutes passed and then a stout elderly man in a tail coat came up to him.

" *M'sieur*, you attend *M'sieur* Allington? " he asked.

" Yes—we can't find him ! "

" Oh, if you please—will you follow me. We have found *M'sieur* Allington."

" What? Has there been an accident? " cried Frankie.

" *Mais non, m'sieur*—but *M'sieur* is indisposed."

" Indisposed ? "

" He is in a corner of the bar, where we find him at last."

" In the bar? You mean he——"

Frankie did not finish the sentence. His heart sank within him. The manager looked at the youth before him sympathetically, and shrugged his shoulders.

" It is regrettable, *m'sieur*," he said, quietly, leading the way.

The bar was a part of the hotel Frankie had not seen before. He blamed himself for not having thought of it, but even had he done so it was unlikely he would have seen Rudi. There was a series of little alcoves, hideously draped with tasselled curtains and dimly lit. In one of these sat Rudi. At one glance his condition was obvious. He smiled at Frankie with glazed eyes, and muttered something.

" But why did you let him have so much ? Good God, he's conducting an orchestra at eight o'clock ! " exclaimed Frankie.

" *M'sieur*, it is deeficult—how we know ? *M'sieur* sits here quietly and orders," said the manager.

" We must get him up to his room—and call a doctor at once."

" A doctor—but *M'sieur* ! "

" Good God, man, don't stand there shrugging your shoulders. Get a doctor, and help me out with him ! " cried Frankie.

The manager summoned a waiter, gave an order and hurried away. They approached Rudi.

" Oh, Frankie ! " he murmured, as they lifted him to his feet. Frankie made no reply. Anger, disgust, misery welled up in him. Slowly they made a horrible passage to the door and out into the corridor, their burden hanging heavily between them. They reached the lift. Mercifully it was empty, as also the corridor on the fifth floor where their rooms were. They laid the inert figure on the bed. Rudi tried to say something quite inarticulate. Frankie tipped the waiter, who departed.

It was already a quarter-to-eight when the doctor appeared, accompanied by the manager. He was a precise little man with a red beard and large horn-rimmed glasses. No, not for an hour at least would *m'sieur* be in any condition to move.

" *Hélas, m'sieur*, he is very—" He did not finish the sentence but looked sympathetically at the despairing youth before him. He saw the young Englishman was almost in tears.

" He is conducting an orchestra. He should be on the platform now ! " cried Frankie, distracted. " What can we do ? What can we do ? "

" I suggest, *m'sieur*, you telephone to the hall. Your father has had an accident—what else is possible ? " said the doctor. " My very great sympathy is with you, *m'sieur*. It is most sad. *C'est disastreux !* "

" You mean it is impossible to get him fit for the concert ? " asked Frankie, despairingly.

" Quite impossible, *m'sieur*, I assure you."

" Will you please do something for me ? My French is poor. It will be difficult for me to explain to the concert director. Will you speak to M'sieur Lemaire and say there has been an accident which prevents Mr. Allington appearing ? I am his assistant and I will take the responsibility for this."

" Ah, *pardon !* I thought you were his son ! *Mais, certainement, m'sieur*. I will speak to the director," replied the doctor.

While he telephoned, Frankie stood by the bed, his mind in tumult. The stark tragedy of a ruined life could no longer be dismissed. All he had heard and wished not to believe was now irrefutably proved. How could one explain it all ? A great gift had been given to Rudi ; for some inexplicable reason a brilliant mind snapped at the moment of tension. He felt paralysed by the cruelty of Fate.

III

1939—that was the year of their holiday in France, and Frankie's engagement. It would be their last holiday together. In June Frankie had broken the news. He was engaged to Cynthia Sloan. They were to be married at Christmas. Rudi was delighted. Cynthia was a fair-haired girl, twenty-one years of age, the daughter of the senior partner, an old friend, in the firm of solicitors employed by Rudi. The boy had brought her to the house for the past year. She was intelligent and pretty. Her quiet demeanour was somewhat overshadowed by Frankie's exuberance. Well-educated, after finishing at a French convent school she was now acting as secretary to a member of Parliament. Her quietness and reticence masked a firmness of character, as Frankie discovered. Her mind was exact. She was a corrective to his easy and often indefinite generalisations. He was often content with something like, she required the clear definition. Sometimes they clashed and he was invariably defeated. Frankie never resented this, instead he gave her an increased admiration. "You can't get away with it with Cynthia," he would say proudly. It was a tribute from one of whom all said he could get away with murder.

Mrs. Westell liked her prospective daughter-in-law, but she was uneasy in her mind, and one day, in conversation with Mr. Allington, her suppressed fears came to the surface. "She's very nice to me, she's a sweet girl—but I wonder if she isn't too much of a lady for Frankie?"

"What do you mean, Mrs. Westell?"

"Well, perhaps it's silly of me. I always have a feeling she's watching Frankie and a bit nervous for him. He won't like that when he finds out."

"Oh, no—I don't think you need feel like that about it," said Rudi. "And remember they're both very young." But the remark stuck in his mind, and later he began to see the shrewdness of it. Cynthia did watch Frankie. She tried to tone him down, but he was too much in love and too elated to be aware of it.

Early in August Rudi and Frankie set off in the car for the south of France. They were going for a holiday despite the Jeremiahs. "My dear, there's always going to be a war. If we let that fellow Hitler get on our nerves we'll forever sit at home with the jitters," responded Rudi to Lady Frant's warning. "Last year it was the Czech crisis, this year it's the Polish, next year it'll be the French, or the Dutch or the Russian."

They stayed two days in Paris and then motored south to Cannes. They stopped at wayside inns, ate wonderful food, drank delicious wines, and firmly declined to believe the rumours that fell upon their track like the threatening drops of a darkening storm. Frankie was in the seventh heaven of ecstatic youth. He drove like a demon. He wore a gay French pullover and beret. He looked very boyish. They were equally delighted when an innkeeper at Auxerre alluded to Frankie as M'sieur's grandson.

"I don't feel a bit insulted, for he thinks you're seventeen and I'm over sixty—which I am!" laughed Rudi.

"You're really only half that," said Frankie, with an affectionate smile. "You're the youngest thing alive!"

They raced down the long straight roads, they sang, the poplars waved, blithe rabbits popped into their burrows. Outside Avignon they stopped at an alluring little inn. It had a sad, sacred memory for Rudi. He had stayed there with Alice on his honeymoon. He showed Frankie their balcony bedroom. Mine host produced a *Château Yquem*. They lifted the golden wine and clinked glasses. " Here's to *la belle France et la vie heureuse !* " cried Frankie.

A motor bus noisily came to a stop. A little group came out of the inn. Two clumsy young men solemnly kissed two elderly men, and a half-a-dozen weeping women. They climbed up into the bus. It rattled off. There was much waving, and the women went in, with handkerchiefs to their faces.

" France is mobilising, *m'sieur*," exclaimed the waitress, tearfully.

They paid their bill, thoughtfully. When they got into the car they looked at each other.

" I suppose we'd better go on ? " asked Frankie. " We're almost there."

" Yes—we might as well," replied Rudi.

But the sun had gone out of the sky.

IV

For almost a week they tried to ignore the rumours and the nervous tension surrounding them but there came a morning when it seemed certain that the storm was going to break. They motored north through a France mobilising for war. The boat on which they crossed the Channel was thronged with the English hurrying back home. Some were certain it was Armageddon, some would not believe, after 1914–1918, the world could become a slaughter-house again. Through that last week of August men and women went about their work gravely. The holiday crowds were strangely quiet as the storm gathered. A politician went on the air to assure them the position was grave but not hopeless, and war was not inevitable, indeed it was unthinkable. " Blatherskite ! " said Rudi, switching off the radio.

He went down to stay with the Frants for a few days. It was there on Friday morning, September 1st, he heard that Germany had crashed into Poland. All England drew a sharp breath. Then came news that Russia had joined in the massacre. Soon now England and France would be in the lists. Mussolini spluttered in Rome. It was Armageddon. " Kind of makes all the village war memorials look silly, sir," said Frant's old gardener. Two of his sons' names were on the local memorial cross.

On Saturday Frankie called on the telephone. The Frants asked him down for the week-end. He arrived in the afternoon, less exuberant but not in any way dismayed. He was going to join up at once, but was not quite sure what he was going to join, if he had any choice.

On Sunday morning, the frightful tension ended. They heard, over the radio, England declare war on Germany. So it was here. There was almost a sigh of relief. Troop movements had been going on day and night all over England. Children were being sent out of the towns to their country billets.

They dined quietly on Sunday evening. Relations and neighbours came in. Rudi played a little. Frankie telephoned Cynthia, back from Scotland. They listened to the radio. Lady Frant looked around on the faces at her table. When, if ever, would they be gathered here again ? Frankie had brought down the car and he and Rudi would leave early on Monday morning.

About eleven o'clock, after Rudi had finished playing, he went out on to the terrace, leaving a heated argument that had sprung up over Chamberlain's policy at Munich. There was a bright moon over the tree tops, with a slight ground mist down in the fields. He walked along the terrace towards the garden-house, taking the night air, when he heard footsteps behind him. He turned. It was Frankie who came up and slipped his arm through his. They walked on without speaking, past the garden house, to the lychgate that led into the long rose garden. The night was beautiful, still and moonlit. They began to talk. This might be the end of everything. No one could foretell.

" I don't at all mind, now it's come. The uncertainty's been so unbearable. I shall rather like soldiering—it'll be a change," said Frankie. " All I hope is I won't be smashed up, I'd rather be knocked right out."

Then he was aware Rudi was saying nothing and intuitively he knew the cause of his silence. He pressed his friend's arm.

" Rudi, don't worry—we'll be all right. We've had some wonderful times together. Nothing can take away the things we've had, the lovely days—and all you've done for me. Rudi, I'll always thank God for you. Don't worry about me, please."

" I'll always worry about you, Frankie," said Rudi quietly, " I'll always be happier worrying about you. Well, here it is, and we're just the victims of a thing we'll call destiny. My life's almost over—at least there can't be any part of it worth living now. If you come through you'll inherit a new world. You'll get adjusted to it, for when you're young all change, disastrous or otherwise, means opportunity. But I've been through one war, and the pattern won't alter. The decent people will go under, the bravest and least selfish be ruined or killed. The scum will come to the top. They'll make money and somehow have a good time and get themselves advanced. And it'll wreck many of the younger genera- tion. When all the excitement's over, the dangers, the bravery, the glamorous uniforms, the decorations, the rush to marry in the face of a gamble with death, the young men will come home, demoralised many of them by a life of adventure, free love, easy money and brief authority. They won't want to sit on office stools and work regular hours. They'll be disgruntled and unusable and disillusioned. Some of them will expect the State to keep them for the rest of their lives. They'll be bitter. That's how it always goes. The last war left us exhausted, this war, even if we win it, will leave us ruined. I'd have to live to be ninety before anything like normal life will return to the world again. Perhaps it never will. It will be too hungry, too grim and disordered for anyone to care much about such luxuries as art, literature or music—the sense of values will be so changed. Yes, it's the end of my world, Frankie. Perhaps such as I aren't really necessary. But I mustn't be gloomy, and I'll end this long wail by saying I've been very fortunate. I've loved a beautiful woman, I've had leisure to pursue my own wayward course. And I've had you for a few years—too few, Frankie, but very dear to me, and I thank God, old reprobate that I am, for all the sweetness and brightness you've brought me. The bombs can't destroy memories, whatever else they shatter. There, I've got that off my chest!"

Frankie laughed and hugged Rudi's arm.

" I love you when you go off like that ! I shall miss your explosions, Rudi." His voice quivered, and he suddenly added, " What a lovely night ! " to change the subject.

They walked on in silence. They came to the end of the rose garden. There were a few roses still on the bushes. Frankie picked one and pulled its petals apart. There was not a sound in the night. The trees looked tremendous in the moonlight. It shone on the long roof of the old house. Here was the very heart of England,

strangely at peace.   It was as if the curtain had risen and
the stage awaited the actors in the drama.

"I suppose we should go in," observed Rudi, and
quoted softly,

> *I wept as I remembered how often you and I*
> *Had tired the sun with talking and sent him down the sky.*

"What's that?"

"A translation from a Greek poet—he wrote it over
two thousand years ago, recalling happy days."

"Rudi, I've something to tell you," said Frankie,
halting in the path.   "I've had a talk with Cynthia.
We are going to be married at once. Anything can
happen now and you have to seize your happiness while
you can. Mr. Sloan's been most helpful. He says we
can have the little flat in Bury Street that he keeps as his
pied-à-terre.   We'll move in the few things we've collected.
I don't suppose I'll be sent overseas for some time, not
until I'm trained. I hope you think we're right; after
all we would have been married at Christmas but for
this."

"You're quite right, Frankie, and God bless you both,"
said Rudi quietly.   "When is it?"

"Tuesday morning.   You'll come won't you, Rudi?"

"Of course I will."

"You've always been behind me, bless you!" said
Frankie, slipping his arm in Rudi's.   They walked slowly
back to the house, talking very little. The world they
knew was dying. It would never be the same again.

CHAPTER VII

THE STORM

I

THE ordeal began. It was a strange war at first, with long lulls of a half-peace between recurrent activity until the catastrophe of Dunkirk, when England was starkly faced with extinction or survival. Rudi refused to leave London. There was nothing to keep him there save an honourable obstinacy. As long as the door bell rang in Mrs. Westell's little shop he felt he too must keep some part of the old life going. So he refused the kind offer of the Frants and other friends to retire to the country. Lulu also wished to stay. A lifelong dislike of the country could not be changed by war. When at last the bombings came a belligerent spirit pervaded No. 10. They dug in until the last word with Hitler.

Slowly but inexorably the conditions of life deteriorated. Rudi played the piano in a room with blacked-out windows. He fumbled his way through the black streets to play at canteens and prostituted his musical soul with the loosest behaviour on the keyboard, to the great delight of his uniformed audiences. Through the blazing fires and uproar when London was transformed into an inferno he sat huddled up under the staircase with Lulu and Plato or went out into the night and performed his air-warden's duty. One dawn he looked across towards Mrs. Westell's and saw a ruin. The shop would never open again but its owner, sheltering at a neighbour's for company, had providentially escaped death. Mrs. Westell departed, to stay for the duration with a sister near Worcester.

Frankie was in India when this happened. His course had been erratic but progressively exciting. Commissioned eventually, a word in the right quarter had sent him off to India on a staff job. The uniform had transformed him into something of a dandy, he shone from head to foot. He wore his cap at a rakish angle, he had a handsome tan. His long slim body set off the excellent tailoring, the belt and strap of the Sam Browne accentuated the narrowness of the waist, the breadth of the shoulders.

But India, conceived by many as a great stroke of luck, irked him. He was not a toy soldier, he wanted action and danger. He fought his way home, and appeared briefly and resplendently at No. 10, where he asked to stay, greatly to Rudi's surprise. The Bury Street flat had been razed to the ground. Cynthia was living with her sister-in-law in Curzon Street. She was in uniform, secretary to a general at the War Office, efficient and more reticent than ever. Whenever Rudi met her he had an impression that she avoided talking about Frankie. Twice he opened the subject and received no encouragement. She was always loyal when she spoke of him but he could not escape an impression that something was troubling her. When Frankie came home and the young pair made no attempt to live together for his brief leave, Rudi's misgiving became founded on a certainty of disaster. He invited them both to come and stay with him.

"Thanks, Rudi, but Cynthia's on call all the time, and it won't be many days before I'm off, I'm sure."

"But that's all the more reason why you should be together. Frankie, what's gone wrong?"

" Wrong ? Why, nothing. What makes you think that ? "

He looked straight into Rudi's eyes, smiling at him, but there was something disingenuous in the tone. He changed the subject at once.

Two days later his orders came, for Africa. There was a swift visit to his mother, two hectic days in London and he was gone. Cynthia was not with him on the last day.

Gravely disquieted, Rudi called her on the telephone. He arranged to take her out to dinner the next evening. She met him at the Berkeley, very attractive in her uniform. Half-way through dinner he approached the subject obsessing him.

" He's not told you ? " she asked.

" No—told me what ? I knew there was something wrong ! "

" Frankie's asked me for a divorce. Of course, I'm releasing him," said Cynthia.

He saw by the trembling of her mouth how much emotion she kept controlled under her calm manner.

" A divorce ! Good God, but why ? He's never breathed a word of it to me ! "

Cynthia looked at him quietly.

" Rudi, you've known Frankie since he was a boy. Did he ever breathe a word to you about his inner self ? Frankie's the cat that walks alone."

" But Cynthia, I can't make it out ! Is there someone else ? He's never mentioned anyone to me. I was certain something had gone wrong, I was worried all the time he was home, but he denied there was anything. I couldn't understand why you weren't together. He said you'd just arranged it that way for convenience. Good Lord ! Why couldn't he tell me, why ? Who is it ? "

" I suspect a woman called Marcelle Legrande whom he met at Delhi. I'd heard rumours from my cousin there, but I just didn't believe them ! "

" Good Lord, that trollop ! " exclaimed Rudi.

" You know her ? "

" I know of her, and very little to her good. She's Lady Frant's granddaughter. Why, that woman's had three husbands already ! She's one of those rich gadabouts who're a menace to domestic happiness. What a fool, what a fool he is ! "

" No, Frankie was never a fool, Rudi. He told me quite frankly that he felt our marriage would never work."

" And what did you say ? "

" Perhaps, Rudi, he's right. Sometimes I feel I've never known Frankie. Something goes on inside him that you can never touch. There's an inner unhappiness, a baffling secrecy of soul, if I can explain it that way. I was aware there had been a change these last six months. His letters became fewer and fewer. I wrote every week for a long time. He swears he did also and says they must have got lost en route. I've tried to think that but letters from India don't get lost, at least very few. I heard from my cousin who was in Delhi quite regularly."

" I too complained about his letters," said Rudi, " but you know, my dear, Frankie was never a good letter-writer. I've had only two from him in five months. I got a little news from you. When his mother went to Worcester my news of him almost dried up. But I didn't think that meant anything serious. Cynthia, are you sure it isn't a phase—these are disturbing times. Marcelle Legrande may be only a temporary infatuation. I wonder if you should give him up so easily ? "

" Easily ? " she caught at his word, and he saw, with surprise, how deep a wound he had touched.

" I'm sorry," he said, placing his hand over hers, at the table where they dined.

" It wasn't easy, Rudi. I love Frankie, I shall always love him. But I couldn't hold him, and it wouldn't have been possible. Frankie was never really in love with me. He was in love with the background I represented. He's terribly afraid of all he's escaped from, and very ambitious. Sometimes he seemed quite desperate, he—oh, it's so difficult to put into words ! "

She saw he did not understand. It was difficult to explain and not be unfair to Frankie.

" You see, I brought him all he wanted for a time," she went on. " He walked right into the heart of my family, as he always does, in his irresistible manner. They were a bit prejudiced at first, particularly my brothers, but they soon ceased to be silly that way. I did little things for him, criticised him a bit, and he took it very well. But now he's found a bigger world. He's learned how to move around. I know this from little things he's told me. Some of those women at Delhi flattered him. Frankie's very vain in a childlike sort of way. My cousin Alan came back from India last month, he was on the vice-regal staff. He'd run across Frankie there. He said he was cutting quite a figure."

" You mean he's got a swollen head ? " asked Rudi.

" No, the reverse. He's got a very cool head. Frankie's intensely ambitious. My world no longer satisfies him. So we've said good-bye to each other."

" Oh, my dear—I wonder if you're right ? It doesn't sound like Frankie somehow—I don't understand it— I——" said Rudi, hesitatingly. " He seemed so much in love with you."

" Rudi, as you've said, this war does things to people—

L

there's no blame attached to anybody. These things just happen."

There were tears in her eyes and he saw she was struggling to preserve her quiet demeanour. She began to talk of her younger brother, Richard, who had gone to the Staff College.

II

Almost two years passed. Captain Frank Westell had a charmed life. He was getting all the fighting he craved. He had fought in Libya, in Greece, and in Crete, making an incredible escape to Alexandria. He was at Tobruk, mentioned in despatches, wounded, and then in hospital in Cairo. Meanwhile Montgomery had made history ; the Allies had landed in North Africa. England, battered, tired, hungry, felt a great lifting of the spirit. Had the tide turned at last ?

News from Frankie was scarce. An occasional letter reached Rudi. Ever since his last leave there had been a deepening mystery concerning him. The divorce had gone through but no word had ever been received concerning the affair with Marcelle Legrande. He had not married her, and sometimes Rudi wondered if their speculations had been correct concerning them. The break with Cynthia was complete and final. No word had passed between them. Mrs. Westell, after the first shock of the divorce, had said no more. Only once had Rudi referred to it, and then his reference had been completely ignored by Frankie. But he never failed to write regularly to the boy. Young men in these days were under stress and strain. They needed patience and understanding more than ever. Rudi suppressed all his fears and questionings. Frankie would come out all right in the end.

One morning, as Rudolph Allington sat at breakfast the telephone rang. He was tired, hot-eyed. He had been up all night at his air-warden's post, had come home at dawn and cat-napped in a chair, where Lulu had found him. She chided him, but he refused to go to bed, so she brought him breakfast on a tray into the study.

He picked up the receiver. It was Partridge, a friend who worked at the Rainbow Canteen in Piccadilly Circus, asking him when he could come in to play again, in a series of concerts they were arranging for the American boys. Just before Partridge rang off he said something that stunned and bewildered Rudi.

"Major Westell looked in wonderful form last night. Bring him in if you've time."

"Frankie?" asked Rudi.

"Yes. I saw him dancing at the Dorchester last night."

"You couldn't have done—Frankie's in Cairo!"

"Oh—well, that's funny. I'd swear it was he. Well, so long, Rudi."

He put down the receiver. *Major* Westell. No, there was a mistake, there must be a mistake. He sat down in front of the breakfast tray, but he was too perturbed to eat. Whatever made Partridge imagine he had seen Frankie dancing at the Dorchester Hotel? Frankie was still convalescing in Cairo.

He left his tea untouched. He went to the sideboard and poured himself a strong whiskey, gulped it, and slumped in the big chair. He tried to read the newspaper. When Lulu came in she scolded him for not eating his breakfast. "You've got a chill," she said, looking at him. "Go to bed and let me bring you a hot water bottle."

He refused to go to bed. She was arguing with him when the door bell rang.

" I don't want to see anybody," he said, petulantly. He looked at the clock. It was a quarter-to-ten. Lulu went out and down the stairs. A minute later there was the sound of excited voices. Rudi jumped up, hearing the voice in the hall below. A few seconds later there were bounding footsteps, and then in came Frankie, smiling. " Rudi ! " he cried.

He was good to look at, tall, bronzed, broader than ever in the shoulders, immaculate in his uniform, his black hair plastered down on his neat head. A crown on the shoulders confirmed Partridge's report. The boy was a major now.

The next instant they were holding each other, and then appraisingly surveyed each other in an excited silence.

Rudi's appearance gave Frankie a shock. He tried hard to hide it. He had aged terribly. He was shabbily dressed and dirty, with an old spotted tie and an ill-fitting shirt, frayed at the collar. His trousers were shapeless bags, his shoes were unpolished. The condition of his waistcoat was disgusting. He looked grubby, and smelt of whiskey. Why had Lulu let him get like this ? The room, too, was in terrible disorder. There seemed a week's ashes in the grate. Papers and books were everywhere, and dirty tumblers stood on the table. The room was depressing in the grey morning. Frankie tried to hide his dismay. All London was down-at-heel, people were tired and shabby, but he had expected nothing like this.

He sat down and explained his sudden appearance. He had been flown home for a few days' furlough. He was quite well again and had asked to rejoin his regiment, fighting now in Italy. He had arrived yesterday evening.

"I just didn't believe it when I was told you were seen dancing at the Dorchester, last night," said Rudi.

"Oh, yes, I went downstairs for some supper and ran into some people."

"Where are you staying?"

"I've got a room at the Dorchester."

"But there's always a room for you here, Frankie."

"Oh yes, thanks—but I don't want to trouble you."

"Trouble me! You know you can't trouble me."

"Well, I'll be going to see Mother in a day or two, so I might as well stay put, Rudi, thank you."

There was a moment's embarrassed silence.

"You're a major, Frankie. Since when?"

"Just before I was wounded."

"Why didn't you tell us?"

Frankie laughed. It was the old infectious laughter lighting his eyes and puckering his face.

"Oh, you've other things to bother you," he said, lightly. "They were giving out promotions, so I got one."

"You've had a bad time, though you didn't say so?"

"A bit bloody half my company wiped out in Crete. But I'm well now. Don't ever worry over me, Rudi. Gosh, it's good to see you—are you all right?"

"Of course, Frankie. We'll dine to-night—some sort of dinner's still going at the club."

"Thanks, Rudi, I can't. I'm dining."

"With whom?"

"With some friends."

"Oh," said Rudi, quietly.

"But I can lunch with you."

"Good! To-morrow night I'll gather some friends for dinner."

"I can't to-morrow night. I've got a dinner. You see, I have to get around quickly—it'll only be a few days."

A cold eddy went through Rudi. Time had produced a different Frankie. How different he could not define.

They talked for awhile. Rudi carefully refrained from mentioning Cynthia, but that moment would have to come. He hoped Frankie would mention the matter first. Later they took the old walk, through St. James's Park. As they mounted the club steps, Frankie smiled at Rudi.

"Like the old times," he said. "Oh, Rudi, if you don't mind, don't call me Frankie—it sounds a bit——"

"Shall I call you Major Westell?" asked Rudi, a little flame in his eyes but a tremor in his voice.

"Rudi, don't be silly, of course not! But can't you understand, I——"

"Westell! Where the devil have you come from?" cried the hearty voice of a young officer at the top of the steps.

The two young men wrung each other's hands and slapped each other's shoulders. In a few minutes' chatter they ran all round the Mediterranean. Rudi stood aside waiting. The young man went off.

"Who's that?" asked Rudi, as they entered the hall.

"A friend," said Frankie.

"He didn't look like an enemy," commented Rudi. "Let's go into the bar."

III

It was Frank from now on, but Rudi remained Rudi. After two days Frank returned from Worcester. He had a slightly strained air in Rudi's presence. He had an engagement for every hour but on his last night of leave he dined with Rudi at No. 10. The evening ended in an appalling scene. Looking back, distressed by the event, he was not clear just how it had rushed to such a frightful climax. Rudi had been drinking when he arrived and was very jumpy. He was aggrieved and caustic in some of his remarks. He deplored the destruction of Italy and its treasures. He thought the whole Italian campaign a colossal blunder. "The losses are simply criminal. What perversity, what utter ignorance of Italian geography! Haven't our people ever been in the Apennine or the Abruzzi mountains? If they had they'd know there wasn't a worse terrain to fight over in the whole Mediterranean basin. Now they're stuck at Cassino and along the Garigliano. Thousands of young lives thrown away! I know that country, I could have told 'em!" cried Rudi, filling up his glass.

"You may know something about music and whiskey, but you don't know anything about military strategy," said Frank, curtly, "so I can't discuss it with you."

Rudi looked at him as if he had been struck in the face.

"There's quite a lot of things you can't discuss with me, I notice," he retorted.

"Such as?" asked Frank, nettled.

And then the floodgates opened. All they had each penned up within them poured forth in a terrible, destructive spate. The name Cynthia came into the maelstrom of words.

" It's none of your business. I suppose you've all been encouraging her to bleat ! " raged Frank.

" What a monstrous thing to say ! Cynthia isn't the kind of young woman to bleat. Since you hadn't the decency to be straightforward with us and——"

" Decency—that from you ! Look at you, half-drunk and half washed as usual. You wonder I don't stay here ! When I'm out of the trenches I don't want to stay in pig-styes ! "

They stood up facing each other, quivering.

" You young bounder, you swollen-headed bounder ! " cried Rudi, shaking with anger.

" If you must know all about my affairs, I broke with Cynthia because I was not going to be patronised by anybody, understand that, the whole pack of you ! I was sick to death of the precious Sloans and the airs they gave themselves. What are they after all—a lot of middle-class snobs ! "

" Which includes me, I suppose ? "

" Yes, if you want to fit the cap," retorted Frank.

" But that wasn't the real reason."

" What do you mean ? "

" I mean that you wanted to be free to marry Marcelle Legrande. Why hadn't you the courage to tell Cynthia the truth when you came on leave the last time ? "

" Courage ! My God, who are you to talk about courage to me ! " cried Frank, bitterly. " If I did want to marry Marcelle Legrande what the devil had it to do with you, I'd like to know ! "

" Nothing, if you feel that way. But it's a sorry spectacle to see a man throwing away a good wife for a trollop with a bag of money."

" You filthy old swine, how dare you ! "

Rudi looked at him, holding on to the mantel, his face white and quivering.

"Yes, Frankie, filthy old swine if you like, but never filthy enough to trade my wife for dollars," he said with quiet scorn. "And it didn't come off after all!"

For a moment it seemed as if the younger man would strike him, but he checked himself. Without another word he turned and went to the door. It banged behind him with a loud reverberation.

CHAPTER VIII

MONTE CASSINO

I

IT was the road to Rome, one of them. It was also the road to death. Men had been going along it and not coming back for months, but it was always full of life also. It started, peacefully and beautifully, in Naples, where one could sleep in a bed, dine in a restaurant, and from a pergola terrace look over the blue bay to fabled Capri, or watch the wreath of smoke over Vesuvius, or the long blue-grey line of the bay running out towards Sorrento. At Mignano where the railway ended, signs of the grim business began. Cassino was miles away, through the mountain valleys. Highway Six took you there, but no further. The great monastery that had become a fortress blocked the way. The mountain that lifted it to the sky, that dominated the route to Rome along the Liri Valley, was the gateway of Death.

So far the most desperate assaults had failed to force it. Fifteen German divisions were in the line Garigliano-Cassino. The Germans must hold it at any cost. They were holding it. The German 10th Army had infiltrated into all the Allied positions. The mountain, the valley, the ruined town, became a vast cemetery smelling of death.

Major Westell and his men lay under the shadow of a farmhouse up a ravine that had become a charnel house.

They awaited their next advance. Below them, they could see the traffic speeding along the highway, like ants scurrying on their tasks. Trucks carrying soldiers, trucks carrying ammunition, food, petrol, American trucks and British trucks, jeeps, ambulances, all plastered with mud, were driven by grim, grey men through a quagmire made by ceaseless traffic, shellfire and torrential rains. Man's rage had descended upon this quiet Italian road winding through the mountains and the olive groves. Bivouacking along its route, in camps, shattered homesteads and wrecked villages, were the men of all nations, pressing forward to the impregnable fortress-abbey of Monte Cassino seized by the Germans. They were from the New World and the Old, they were Americans from the North and South, from Harlem to Texas, black and bronzed ; from India, Sikhs and Gurkhas, tall and bearded or squat and dark-eyed. The British Empire had flung in its quota, lads from Canada, New Zealand and Maoris lads, lads from Scotland, Wales and Ireland, and lads from the Midlands, lads from the Kentish fields and true Cockneys born to the sound of Bow Bells. The French too, with their Goums, were there, fighting for their occupied homeland, and dashing Poles fighting for a homeland lost.

Over all this seeming confusion of wrecked transport, dead men and animals, mud and blood, diminutive against the dark mountains, spilling over the grey valley, spread the 78th Division, signed with the yellow battle-axe. To the left lay the Rapido River at the foot of the Liri Valley. From a crest above the ravine, near Cervaro, Major Frank Westell, D.S.O., could sweep his glasses across the long battlefield. A line of grey rubble, endless it seemed, filled one part of the sodden valley. Once upon a time it had been Cassino, the ancient Casinum of the Romans, the San Germano of the Middle Ages.

Now it was a heap of broken houses, but alive with the threat of death, for men were grappling and fighting there day and night, fiercely contesting a pile of stones or the walls of a broken house. It was still a no-man's-land, serrated and grotesque, pitted with craters in which tanks were engulfed and men and mules were drowned. Across this war-riven landscape blew the stench of unburied bodies, the unforgettable sickly sweetness of decayed flesh polluting the air.

For three months they had thrown along that valley, against that mountain wall, the flower of their armies from the Old World and the New. Young veterans who had survived the desert heats, from Africa and Tunisia, Greece and Crete, Sicily and Calabria, from the shelled beaches and the cruel Apennines deep in snow, now fought along the high bleak valleys, on the freezing slopes and rain-logged plateaux. And ever they were mocked by the Abbey that watched them, by the towering five-thousand-foot Monte Cairo that defended the hell-gate of the Liri valley and its icy torrent. All through the grim winter of battle, month upon month, fought over yard by yard, shelled, bombed, the German line seemed impregnable.

1943 passed into 1944 through a procession of bitter bloody days. Was it a stalemate? Men of the American 34th and 36th Divisions, lads from Texas, Iowa and Minnesota, were thrown back across the Rapido with fearful losses. In vain had been their incredible courage. The French were forced off Monte St. Croce. The New Zealanders were blocked. For forty-six days of unparalleled valour the Gurkhas hung on to the peak of Hangman's Hill, without relief, isolated, within a stone's throw of the desperate German infantry. They drank a bomb crater dry and got K rations by American parachutes. Down in Cassino town the fighting grew more bitter. It raged from hand to hand, house to house, murderous, unavailing. From that high, inviolate Abbey eyes were watching all approaches. The great monastery became the deadliest menace, the king-pin of the German front. It was a watch-tower of the enemy. In desperation it was doomed. On February 15th, while the fighting raged in the blocked streets of Cassino, the Flying Fortresses, Mitchells, Marauders, Kittyhawks, two hundred strong in unchallenged flights through the cold blue sky, bombed the great monastery in waves. There were quick yellow bursts, eruptions of rocks and smoke. The southern and western slopes flickered with the bomb flashes. The great dome of the Abbey church crumbled, the massive walls writhed and toppled, the hilltop was engulfed in swirling black smoke five hundred feet high. When it cleared the great monastery showed her gaping wounds, but still she crouched, ruinous, massive, defiant, a deadly lair, still held by the Germans.

Two days later a terrific artillery barrage was turned on the smoking hillside. Americans, New Zealanders, Gurkhas went in to the north of the town. In the darkness of the night, before moonrise, the Gurkhas fought their way up the slopes, almost to the monastery. There were terrible struggles around the German concrete pill-boxes. Grenades and flame-throwers burned out the defenders. For two days the battle raged. When, on the 19th, it died down, Hill 596, commanding a ravine, was prised from the enemy. Meanwhile the New Zealanders had fought along the railbed into Cassino, as far as the station, but they failed to hold it. Up Monastery Hill men dug in and burrowed. The bloody siege went on, until, with heavy losses, the battle was called off. When a month later Cassino town was subjected to a terrific bombing it became a flooded ruin, a death-trap, a drowning pit of hell.

A month after the obliteration bombing of Cassino, Major Frank Westell, coming on from the railhead of Mignano, rejoined his regiment. Re-formed and only a fragment of its old strength, he was shocked to find how heavy had been the toll, how few were the old faces. By a great stroke of luck Parker, his old batman, was there. The word went round, ' Lucky Westell ' was back. " Ooh, sir, it does me 'eart good to see you ! " exclaimed Parker, grinning from ear to ear. Everywhere the grimy hard-bitten boys smiled. The Major was back. It was a bright moment in their grim lives. Depression and the ghost of defeat lay over the battalion. There had been terrible, costly blunders. The whole show had bogged down.

They rested by Cervaro. That night the jeeps would carry them further up the valley of death. Over them screamed the shells from the guns behind. Ahead of them, beyond the traffic on the highway, the charred vehicles, the burnt-out tanks, the rusty debris of the old battle-field, lay the no-man's land of hidden death, the domain of the patient infantry.

Darkness came. It was time for the relieving company to move up. The jeeps traversed the mud-logged terrain, over temporary bridges, through olive groves, to the last point of road communication. They were dumped. The painful ascent on foot began in the blackness of the night. Faint under the starlight they could feel more than see that behemoth lying on the hilltop ahead, waiting for them, watching them, the sprawling ruined monastery crowning the mountain of death. At dawn, exhausted, they reached the battalion head-quarters. They were relieving the Poles, who in turn had relieved the Gurkhas. The company commanders reported, the British take-over was completed. When the dawn came Major Westell and his company had inherited the slit-trenches, the holes and crannies that were to be their homes for a harassed month.

Parker took possession of a ruinous outhouse, remnant of a goat-herd's hut. There was a box turned into a work table with a telephone on it. Other boxes made seats. The mud floor was soaked, the north wall was simply the earthen hillside. There was no glass in the window, the roof was turfed. Murky, dank, it was overrun by insects of original and sickening varieties.

" Well, 'ere we are again, sir. Welcome home ! " said the ever-cheerful Parker when he had fixed the camp bed. Four officers shared the adjacent room. The men found holes and shelters and burrowed themselves in with a mole-like agility. Every few minutes the air was split by the obscene whine of a shell. Through the open window, in the dawn's light, there was a view of the Monastery, beautiful in ruin and menacingly near.

The command headquarters was a tortuous quarter of a mile away, past Tin Can Alley, Dead Mule Gulch and Delirium Tremens, names for death-walks left by the Americans. Their unburied bodies were strewn all over the hillside. One far-off day they might be brought in but now they must lie in the rain, shrivelled in their muddy rainsoaked uniforms, companioned by dead mules and live rats, insects and festering flies.

Lower down the hill was something that might have passed for a cemetery. It was an odd sight. The ground was patched with helmets and boots, a helmet at the head of each grave and a pair of toy boots at the foot. They were the helmets and boots of the little Gurkhas, fierce killers of Germans, brought from far Nepal to die on this cruel alien soil. But they had company, oddly mixed, for around them lay Canadians, Poles, English, Irish, Scots, Americans and New Zealanders. One day, such of them as were identifiable would be collected and

sorted, but for the present they were one with the earth
and the air, through storm and sunshine and the shell-
ravaged days and nights.

Food, water, ammunition came to the company on
mules every night. The route was marked by their
slaughtered carcases where a burst of shell-fire had caught
them, but even unseen their presence was felt ; the stink-
power of a disembowelled mule was high.

Major Westell's C.O. was a jumpy little martinet but
a first-class soldier who seemed to flourish on discomfort.
He was a great tea drinker. The spiteful said he sat
on an unopened crate of Bourbon whiskey inherited
from the American C.O. The Adjutant was from
Westell's old regiment. They had a joyful reunion.
They had parted in the sands of Libya, they now met in
the snows of Monte Cassino.

II

They settled into their neolithic life, giving out and
receiving death. Above them was the target, the ruined
monastery, but nearer, scarcely five hundred yards
distant, the enemy also lived mole-like on and under the
ground. They all knew one another's habits in that
tree-blasted terrain. It was largely a nocturnal life.
To show oneself was to get a ' packet.' The calls of
nature, however desperate, must be postponed until
darkness. Too many men had gone west on the latrine
route. Even so, they were a happy company, bound by
desperation, and unremarked courage. The normal
world ceased six miles back up the valley. Here was a
world self-contained, dug-in on a shell-smitten mountain-
side, with one simple aim, to kill and to survive. Intimacy was total, every meanness, every virtue was stark.

No counterfeit could pass the pitiless scrutiny of men bound by a brotherhood of courage. They had their hates, their loves, their oddities, their dreams. They joked at their postures lest they might appear heroic, so that it seemed at times as if they would barter all their virtues for a week's leave, a 'binge,' for five minutes' intimacy with a nameless woman. The mere animal, wrapped in dirt, worried with insects, smells, the cold, the rain, the monotony, seemed all that survived until, in one electrified moment, the image of God glowed briefly in a spontaneous sacrifice of self.

Those men had the measure of 'Lucky Westell.' To many he was a newcomer, but to some he was a legend, and the news spread. A major at twenty-six, and now a D.S.O., a veteran, it was not these things that gave him his status in the unsentimental judgement of the ranks. Others had careers more meteoric, battle honours more glowing, but it was known of Westell he never spared himself, and his men had his ceaseless vigilance and thought. The sense of him pervaded the company which moved as one man behind him, impelled by a quality of leadership founded in affection and discipline. Some boy-officer, despairing, shut out, suddenly felt himself touched by something that brought a glow into his young eyes. A scrounger, a shirker, a ruthless sergeant, the nourisher of a grievance knew the appraisal of the young major's glance. Others, with little griefs, or freezing into self-pity and despair, felt the warmth of his interest. It was lucky to be with him and under him, a good soldier with a clear brain and a warm heart. Pride, knowledge, and an audacity always rewarded, made him the unchallenged leader. They were lucky with Lucky Westell; he never missed a move or left them out of a good thing.

He was cool and grim these days. It seemed to the

M

devoted Parker that the major had lost a little of his gaiety but he attributed it to this winter-bitten terrain. The sun of Africa loosened you, the cold winds of these mountains congealed you. And the old smile, the warming word were there at times. He was jumpy about mail these days, noticed Parker. When the mules came up he always wanted to know if there were letters. His quick fingers broke the string and turned over the envelopes. Was it some girl who should be writing, wondered Parker whose quick eyes missed nothing. His own mail was often exciting. There was one day when he could not contain his excitement. He pulled a letter out of the blouse of his battle dress.

" Look at this, sir. I've got a photo of 'im. He's two, and I ain't never secd 'im. Nah, would you believe it, sir ? "

He unfolded a sheet of paper and brought out a photo print. A shock-headed young woman was dangling a baby in a backyard.

" He looks a fine fellow," said Westell. " What's his name ? "

" Same as mine, sir, Bill," replied the proud father. " And he's a true Londoner, 'e is, born in the blitz an' he's sitting it out with his Ma. Nancy wouldn't quit— that's my wife, sir, though my folks wanted to get her out of London when 'e was coming. A kind of pride, you might say. The Parkers are Londoners, and when the 'ome was blowed up last October not a brick standing, they moved over to me mother's. She's looking after them, my old mother. She keeps a nice little shop in Balham. She's a wonderful old gal an' they want for nothing."

" You're a lucky lad, Parker, with a wife and a son at your age."

" P'r'aps some day you'll 'ave luck, sir."

" I hope I shall," replied Westell, handing back the treasured photograph. And he thought, as his batman carefully put away the photo, how surprised Parker would be if he told him he too had a mother who had kept a shop in a little London street and was a wonderful woman. His men would never know how very close he was to them in many ways. His secret amused him somewhat.

The letter he awaited and hoped for never came. There was no reason why his hope should be fulfilled, for his pride would not let him break the silence. Four weeks, four long weeks had passed. Waiting in Naples, he had sat down and written to Rudi, but the letter was unsatisfactory. He had written it to justify himself, he found, on reading it over, and he tore it up. He wrote another, trying to balance things, but it was no better than the first attempt. It was not sent. There was so much to explain, so much that baffled any explanation, lost in multitudinous cross-currents of thought and feeling. The years had done something to them both, but more than the years, the change born of their separation, and his inheritance of a new world of authority and independence, there was the fierce determination that he would not be pulled back into that humdrum sphere from which the chances of war and the upheaval of society had rescued him. The boy in the corner shop, who once yearned for gloves and patent leather shoes, who was disturbed by his father's bowler hat and the way he wore it, was dead now. He could walk confidently into a drawing-room, up the steps of a West End Club, into expensive restaurants, hail taxis, and sign cheques on a banking account, a man of the world, an authoritative man in a world of position and power.

But it wasn't even that or the shock of seeing Rudi with candid eyes, a Rudi shabby, neglected and brought down by indulgence to a squandered career, an aged failure however much disguised by his transcendent charm and loveableness, that unnerved him. He had been challenged, unfairly he felt, in his weakest spot. In that terrible scene between them he had been driven by a nervous fear to stop Rudi's intrusion into his personal life. Even had he wished to confide in him, he was given no opportunity to tell him of the frightful emotional trial through which he had passed. He had breathed no word of that meeting with Marcelle Lagrande, in Delhi of all places. He could tell Rudi nothing of those days passed in her vivid presence, the sheer intoxication of her quick mind, her command of a world in which her flame-like beauty, her wealth, her zest for life, all built up a personality that swept him into her service.

When, with no effort at disguise, she had shown him preference over all others crowding about her, he had retreated, alarmed, but it had been in vain. Marcelle was accustomed to the fulfilment of every wish. Fate had killed the third husband she had tired of in a twelve-month. He had been spared dismissal. He had fallen gallantly and could now be proudly if fitfully lamented. Marcelle's lovely, innocent eyes looked with surprised interest at the amazing transformation of Frankie Westell. In this tall, dashing young officer, grown handsome, moving with such aplomb, it was not easy to find any reminder of that gawky, crude boy trailed down to the Frants by that singular bibulous old composer.

She wanted him. Her plan was simple, clear, and admitted no obstacles. He was going home. He must get his release from his wife. There could be nothing then to trouble them. They parted, in an ecstasy touched with desperation and defiance of the unpredictable course of these tumultuous times. Somewhere, somehow she would come to him, marry him. In her world no frontiers impeded her. Wealth and beauty were master-keys when skilfully used.

Thus it was, when he lay wounded in Cairo she came to him again, via New York, uniformed, practical but glamorous, on a Red Cross mission. He realised then she would have contrived a mission to the North Pole if her desire had required that destination.

Young, rich, beautiful, uninhibited, it was not surprising that with so many dashing men around in a vivid, war-excited Cairo, she acquired a court. Soon his wheeled chair had to penetrate a cohort of dapper colonels, brigadiers and even generals. There was a moment when his pride protested. His divorce had gone through. It was time for a definite announcement so that those bigwigs should know where they stood. Marcelle opened wide innocent eyes on him. " But, darling, I can help you so much more if I don't seem interested," she said. She seemed hurt when he showed indifference to this kind of interest. In another month, just as he was beginning to walk and get about again, she gave him his dismissal. " It's frightfully important I should be in New York. They're flying me back to-morrow. I wonder where we'll meet again, Frankie ? Life is so uncertain, darling."

" With anyone like you, yes," he said, looking straight into her lovely eyes. They met his unwaveringly.

" Don't be peevish, Frankie. It has been exciting and worthwhile, but we have worn it out a little, haven't we ? *C'est la guerre.*"

So Humpty Dumpty had a great fall. It would have been hard to explain all that to Rudi even had he been less the avenging angel of a broken-hearted girl, which Cynthia certainly was not. ' Swollen-headed bounder.' They were bitter words even if only half meant. With what frightful candour they had stabbed each other that terrible night ! Leaving the house he had trembled all the way home in the taxi. He sat long in utter despair in the loneliness of his room. But in the morning he was indignant, stiff with injured pride. At ten o'clock that night a message awaited him. He was being flown off to Naples at 6 a.m.

For half an hour he placed the room. Twice he picked up the telephone, and replaced it. At eleven he walked down the blackness of Park Lane questing a taxi. Succeeding at last, he directed it to the end of Maple Street. He dismissed it, and walked along, rehearsing his words, his fingers icy. He came to No. 10. Through the balcony windows male voices, singing, accompanied by the piano, poured out into the night air. He looked up but the blacked-out windows revealed no sign of the roysterers within. Then it was that he saw by the curb in the darkness two American transport vehicles. Rudi was entertaining American soldiers.

He stood in the street listening. He could not go in now and see Rudi. He had braced himself to this ordeal, never imagining this frustration. He waited there, dismayed, looking up at the balcony, listening to those hearty raucous voices. What ages ago it seemed since he had stood there, a small boy listening, enchanted, to the music of Chopin and Liszt streaming out of those windows. He turned and sadly walked down the dark street. He would have to write.

All that was four weeks ago. He had not written, baffled in his attempts. Somehow, here in this insect-ridden, shell-spattered hovel he must write that letter. He must break their silence.

III

The pattern did not alter, but something was happening, the day of their relief was drawing nearer. The thought of Naples, of soft clean beds, of good food, women, shops, music even, began to fill their dreams ; in two weeks now, in ten days, in six days . . . Someone coming up from Naples had reported spring in the valley, the sun began to be warm, an almond tree in blossom over a broken wall had been seen. In these cold bomb-blasted valleys and mountains it sounded like another world.

Major Westell was out near the observation post. The hillside was grey-silver in the moonlight. Above them the ruined Monastery was incredibly moving in its stricken beauty. Somewhere in its rubble German soldiers were having a sing-song, the strains of *Die Lorelei* were bellowed forth to the accompaniment of an accordion. That music would stop soon, thought Westell grimly. There were many sounds in this weirdly beautiful night. Death was abroad. The intervals of silence were broken by menacing noises. Down by the Castello di Cassino, a hot spot, shells were falling at regular intervals. The Germans had drawn a line on it. There was a sound of riven silk followed by a terrific burst and a blinding flash, missiles from the heavy batteries. Bren-guns barked, German machine-guns roared. Then all fell quiet. You could almost touch that quiet. Then singing came again, from the Germans.

Out by the post they had a machine-gun. Westell passed the word. There was a sudden rattle in the night air. *Lili Marlene* abruptly stopped. As expected, mortar-fire came back a few minutes later. The hillside was alive with strife, then went quiet again.

In the hut bad news greeted Westell. Their telephone lines had gone after a shelling. That meant a repairing party must go out. The men worked in pairs. They had buried sixteen on that work these last two weeks. Westell gave the order.

The mules came in with food and letters. There was one for him. He knew his mother's handwriting at a glance. He put it in his pocket. He was due to make a round with the C.O. They were being mortared heavily from the Monastery these days. The C.O. wanted a platoon with machine-guns moved farther out. It was suicide and he would tell him so. Their casualties were too high.

He came back from their tour of inspection pleased, for he had won his point with his rattled C.O. He had never thrown men away—he never would, whatever the pressure. His men knew that, so that they never shirked a call. Back in the hut the telephone rang. "Line repaired, all in, sir." "Good," said Westell with relief, and put down the receiver.

He hung the electric lamp by his side, took out his mother's letter and opened it. Her handwriting was as neat as her person.

The first line was a shock. He read on, his face rigid. He did not hear the scream of a shell, the distant thump of artillery, a sudden flurry of mortar-bombs from their own lines that silhouetted the skeleton of the Monastery in a brief glare. Parker came in with a cup of tea and, seeing him engrossed, set it down without comment and went out.

I have very sad news for you. Four days ago a bomb made a direct hit on Nos. 10 and 12, Maple Street. It was after midnight. It took the rescue squads five hours to dig down into the rubble. There was only one wall and half the chimney-stack left standing. They did not know how many were trapped. Mrs. Adams went round early the next morning. Old Mrs. Connick and her nurse were in No. 12. The old lady was killed outright ; the nurse was found in a bad state, but will live, they think. About ten o'clock that morning they came across the bodies of poor Mr. Allington and the housekeeper. They were hardly recognisable. They could not have suffered. I came up yesterday for the funeral. His friends, Sir George and Lady Frant, were there, and spoke to me. She said she was eighty the day Mr. Allington was killed. It was very plucky of her to make the journey in the bitter cold. Frankie, dear, what can I say? You have lost the greatest friend a boy ever had. What a blessing you saw him so recently. He lived for that day. I don't think you can ever really know how proud he was of you. He wrote me such a wonderful letter the day your D.S.O. was in the papers. You can be sure he . . ."

He read on, and when he had finished he read the letter through again. Somehow it wasn't true, it couldn't be true. He sat holding the letter in his hand. A centipede fell on it and wriggled across the sheet. Outside the silence was suddenly shattered by a terrific blast that brought down dirt from the roof. The Boche batteries, searching for the supply route, had dropped a short one.

Young Lieutenant Fremont came in, said something, got no answer, looked at his face, and went out. He stopped the sergeant about to enter. "Keep out for a bit," he said, "something's hit the Major."

"Hit? My God—badly, sir?" asked the alarmed sergeant.

"Not that way—bad news, I think," said Fremont.

"Very good, sir. Signal exchange reports line cut."

"Damn—again !" exclaimed Fremont, walking back with the sergeant.

Westell overheard the report, understood it, but he did not move. All the shells in the world meant nothing now. He was back in the past years : the lamp on the study table and the score sheets ; the happiness on Rudi's face in the Galeries Lafayette as he bought him a Basque beret, and shirts and espadrilles, for their holiday at Cannes ; the way he snorted at the piano in the heavy passages, the way, as he taught him at the keyboard, he marked the music with one of his hundred pencils ; the clink-clink of the decanter on his tumbler ; " ' very,' not ' ever so ' much, Frankie " ; the ecstasy on his face as he sat back in the Queen's Hall entranced by a movement of a symphony ; Plato on his knee, old Lulu coming in with the coffee as they sat by the fire ; and then, like a nightmare, the dreadful scene, " You swollen-headed bounder ! " " You filthy old swine ! ", the door banging behind him, the dark street, his anger, his misery.

He stood up, folded the letter and put it in his pocket, looked at Parker's cup of tea, ignored it, reached for his helmet and went out. It was dark, cold and starry. All the noises had died down. He made his way along the dug-out, towards the O.P., round to the point by Cookhouse Lane, past the last sentry and the redoubt with the Vickers machine-gun. He was utterly alone here. Above him the gaunt masonry of the monastery stood out in the moonlight, beautiful in its ruin. Below him, down the woodland, splintered, grotesque like a scene from Doré's *Hell*, he looked on the valley, towards the dim heaped waste that had been Cassino.

He had not written—he had postponed the ordeal. Now he could never write, say what was in his heart. What had gone wrong with life ? Cynthia lost, Rudi lost, by his own pride and folly. Into the gulf of Time he had thrown something precious that could never be retrieved. He stood there, isolated under the cold stars. In that moment of his grief he felt alone as he had never before been alone in life.

IV

Five more days, four days, three days. They would soon be moving out now, and, as if sensing the expectation spreading through the battalion, the Germans began to be increasingly nasty. They harrowed the lines, the approaches, the steep zigzag paths. Their fire mowed down the Indians who brought up supplies by mule ; it played havoc among the wounded on their stretchers, carried, bumping and slithering, down the treacherous slopes. Two medicos were knocked out. The relieving Polish advance parties were reported from the valley. The mortaring grew fiercer and fiercer. There was nothing to be done amid the shrapnel and flying rock but to keep in cover, take it, and hope. One more day now and they would be out of it. The Poles would take over again this patch of Hell for another month of torment.

On the last evening but one, in the dusk, news came over the line that the machine-gunners out beyond Dead Man's Gulch had caught " a packet." Three had been killed and one badly wounded. The communication trench was demolished. The sergeant was bringing the man in. It was death's alley watched by tne German O.P. Breathless, from their cover they followed the sergeant's course. A man hung limply over his back He sought every bit of cover, scurrying from rock to rock on that treacherous hillside.

" It's Harris and Parker," said Fremont, following their daring progress through his glasses.

" Parker ! What was he doing there ? " asked Westell.

" Went over with some tea, and for a chin-wag, sir," said a corporal.

Westell watched through his glasses. Harris was doing well. He was stocky and cool. He was carrying Parker.

When another burst came he lay flat. They waited. There was no movement of the unseen Harris. They waited while another round of fire churned up the ground. The air grew quiet again, but Harris did not reappear. He must be lying low with young Parker. A minute, two minutes, five went by.

"Christ! They've got it," said Fremont.

"Get the bearers up. Have them wait here. I'm going over," said Westell.

"But you can't, you——" began Fremont, but the Major was out of cover, crawling before he could finish his protest. Two dozen pairs of eyes watched.

Westell took his time. Every twenty seconds there was a round of fire. Their own machine-guns opened up. Soon he was over the ground and reached them. Harris's head was pulped. It might have been a cracked eggshell. A shell-burst had caught him. He lay across Parker, drenching him. Parker's leg was gone. Westell came to his side. The boy was conscious still.

"I'm done, sir, don't bother about me," he said very quietly, his grey eyes on his officer.

Westell made no reply. The light was failing rapidly. He pulled away poor Harris and got his arm under Parker. The boy was very light. He lifted him easily, ran with him and at the next burst of fire, dropped with him. He saw that Parker had fainted. He waited, then started off again. They watched him breathlessly. Lucky Westell. He was making it. He flattened again at another round of shelling, was obscured in the cloud of rubble and dust that leapt from the churned-up ground, and reappeared again unhurt. There were only two hundred yards to go now. He was Lucky Westell all right.

The stretcher party came up the trench ready. The Major started off again, Parker in his arms. With clockwork regularity the shells came over, the dust cloud rose. It settled slowly. When the air had cleared they could not find Major Westell and his burden. Was he keeping cover behind some rocks, waiting his chance? There was a lull, but nothing moved on that ravaged slope. The minutes went by. Darkness fell, broken intermittently by shell-flash. Then complete quiet settled over the scene. The Germans had finished their hate. Two parties went out into the no-man's land under cover of darkness. It was Fremont who found them. Major Westell lay dead with young Parker in his arms.

Next morning, before dawn, when the company moved out, leaving the Poles to take over, they passed two more simple wooden crosses in the ground which for a month had received their comrades. Fate kindly spared them the malice visited upon the graves of Major Westell and his batman, within two hours of their leave-taking. A shell exploded, churning up the ground, exhuming four of the bodies, mixing them in a heap of rubble. A Polish captain, standing near, suddenly found that his right arm had gone. He stared, bewildered. A second shellburst caught him, and he disappeared under the churned-up soil, rocks and disinterred bodies. Above it all, the old monastery was lit for the whole length of its façade of ruin by a golden shaft of spring sunshine. Somewhere, in a spell of silence, a lark sang in the clear blue sky.

CHAPTER IX

POLONAISE

I

HE stood on the steps of the terrace and looked through
the drooping fronds of the palm trees out across the
lake. On a little promontory someone had built here
in Palm Beach a reminiscence of Venice, a villa with
gothic stone windows and balconies, russet sun blinds,
a terrace, and striped *pali* against which a gondola might
well have been tethered to complete the illusion. The
January night was warm and breathless, a full moon
silvered the smooth face of Lake Worth. If the foreground was Venetian, with a sub-tropical frame, the
immediate background was wholly American. Five hundred members and guests of the Everglades Club dined
in the open air under the illuminated trees, while in a
great shell fronting the dance floor a Cuban orchestra
shimmered and crooned through the amorous rumbas
and two-steps. From time to time the floor was jammed
with the dancers. It being the end of January, when the
colleges had called back the younger generation, the
floor was a picture of the gay fifties, sixties, and even the
seventies.

Stanislas Morowski estimated that ten million dollars'
worth of diamonds, rubies, emeralds and amethysts were
oscillating on the throats, arms and fingers of the stout,
less stout and slim matrons piloted by their thick-set,

sun-baked beaux. Here and there a young woman
of exquisite beauty shone in singular splendour, watched
by others for whom fatiguing sessions in the beauty
parlours and hairdressing salons of Worth Avenue failed
to defeat the ravages of time.

They dined at innumerable flower-laden tables, while
overhead in the green tracery of leaves, orange, crimson
and blue electric bulbs twinkled in gay festoons. The
food was lavish in variety and quantity, a banquet of
Lucullus demonstrating the possession, on one side of
the submarine-infested Atlantic, of everything that was
missing on the other. The champagne of France flowed
golden in the glasses, the vintage of a year long before
the German boots thudded down the Champs-Élysées,
and regiments of rutted necks sat spaced along its café
pavements.

The January night seemed walled in with flowers,
scents, music, jewels, palm trees. The alcoves, domes
and balconies gave a stucco illusion of arabesque Spain.
Here luxuriant nature had been made more luxuriant.
Coloured limes flushed the curving trunks of the palm
trees with a wash of sunset-crimson, or pale-blue moonlight. Skilfully massed, banks of scarlet hibiscus, vermilion poinsettias, azaleas, orange blossoms, gladioli and
tuberoses distilled a hundred scents while the music
drifted, the lake frogs croaked and the cicadas trilled.
The eucalyptus seemed silvered in a passing breath of
air, the tom-tom beat through this premeditated jungle
of sub-tropical luxuriance. The richest playground in
the world touched its peak of planned extravagance.
Here was heaven achieved by the interior decorator,
the scenic architect, the florist, the chef, the modiste,
the manicurist, the jeweller, and, to weld it all in senti-
ment, the crooner and, to move it all in rhythm, the
musicians.

Round and round went a billion of dollars, contiguous, paunch-full, happy, unhappy, peevish, calculating, kind and callous. They read of bombings, of occupations, of concentration camps and hangings as the Nazis rolled across Europe and turned it into a charnel house. Here the warm wind blew from the azure Gulf Stream, the fireflies flitted in the moonlit patios, over the floodlit swimming-pools. In the courts of fairyland castles fountains coolly splashed, and the dice rattled at the backgammon boards and the cards fell on the bridge tables. In halls of French, Spanish, Tudor and Arabian design, in salons gazing over the blue Atlantic on one side and the sunset-crimsoned lake on the other, the happy winter tourists feasted and played.

Sometimes a chilling wind of apprehension blew over this halcyon scene. Was it possible that one small oasis of luxury could flourish in a world of so much violence and surging hate? The radio and the newspaper intruded with their horrifying reports in this earthly paradise. Some were deeply troubled, some were not; the bombings, the drownings, the cowering of millions in cellars under the terrors of the night, the migration of hungry populations, the slave battalions, the starved prisoners, the hanged hostages, seemed incredible here, where the roast turkeys on the weighted tables had their brown breasts decorated with roses sculptured from coloured turnips, and the juicy steaks were carried on flaming swords.

Outside in the drives and courtyards waited the long line of automobiles, the Rolls-Royces, the Cadillacs, the Packards, sleek, shining, valeted and chauffeured by men who knew the entrance to Longchamps and Ascot, the Rue de la Paix, Bond Street, the Graben, the casinos at Deauville, Cannes and Monte Carlo, as well as they knew Woodward, Detroit; Michigan Avenue,

Chicago ; Canal Street, New Orleans ; Sunset Boulevard, Los Angeles ; or Fifth Avenue, New York. For this was a new race of international couriers, the King's Messengers of a plutocracy whose empire was bounded only by the inexhaustible letter of credit.

Stanislas Morowski, standing on the terrace by the lake, hearing the seething roll of the rumba and looking upon the stars, cold and distant through palm branches that seemed cut out of black cardboard, so still and silhouetted were they in the moonlight, had at that moment an acute consciousness of the variety and romance of his life. To him the incredible had happened all in the space of twenty-five years. From a hovel on a Polish plain he had arrived here, with homes in Paris, Cleveland, and Palm Beach, the husband of a woman worth millions, who lavished upon him everything her adoring heart imagined would give him pleasure. He knew he was laughed at, scorned by some, treated with scarcely veiled contempt by a few, but popular with many. They all knew he was an adventurer, but cared little since his hospitality was unbounded.

At the mooring down the lake lay the *Osiris*, their yacht which had transported much of the *Almanach de Gotha* on free cruises around the Mediterrranean and through the Antilles and the Bahamas. It had been Mrs. Weissberger's pride, and had passed in successive marriages to Cyrus J. Cattling and Norman D. Flott, before it became the property of Stanislas Morowski. Unlike the bride, the yacht had kept its name through these successive ownerships.

How wrong the world could be in its estimates. He knew that the men who came so eagerly to their table, drank their champagne and smoked their cigars regarded him as an adventurer. He would admit to the rating of a gigolo, if that be the métier of a penniless, handsome

N

young man who married a very rich, fat old woman. He was twenty-two and Mary Flott was sixty, five years a widow, when she took him off the dance floor of an hotel in Nice one winter. He had never wanted for anything after that, living the life of a young millionaire, except that he had no millions.

A young couple came out on to the terrace as he stood staring over the still lake. He saw with pleasure that it was Julia Jansen. She seemed to him without any doubt the most beautiful young woman in Palm Beach, and he always found her interesting and charming to talk to. At twenty-two she had poise without hardness. She was intelligent, she swam, played tennis and golf with considerable efficiency. Her parents were solid, sensible people, rich but unspoilt, whose home on North Ocean Boulevard was one of the most hospitable places in this hospitable resort. The large dinner parties her people gave were carefully selected, ; they could even make a large cocktail party seem a personal compliment instead of a public cancellation of obligations.

Stanislas was grateful to them for their recognition of himself. It had been an achievement, even as the husband of Mary Flott, to pass their threshold, nor was it due, he liked to believe, to his ability as a violinist and Mrs. Jansen's passion for music. She had, of course, heard the gossip that he had been a street musician and played the violin outside cafés on the Riviera. If Mrs. Jansen believed it she chose to ignore it. Sometimes Julia had accompanied him on the piano. She was an accomplished musician. It seemed to him that on these occasions he touched such happiness as he could never surpass, for he was deeply in love with her. By a tremendous exercise of will power he had allowed neither Julia nor anyone else to know it. He had his code, and loyalty to his wife was part of it.

He watched Julia now as she came across the terrace
with her escort, fair and sylphlike, with the beautiful
colouring that proclaimed her Scandinavian stock.
The young couple sat down at a little distance and
chatted.

Stanislas Morowski reflected how utterly astonished
she would be if he announced to her his immediate
intention, and in support of it took her back, in a candid
revelation of his history, to the cause of his present momentous decision. Would she understand? He felt she
would. At midnight he would be gone from this scene.
It might never see him again, smiling, handsome, popular.
There would be no more lunching at the Bath and
Tennis Club, playing golf at the Seminole, dancing
here at the Everglades, shaking cocktails under the awning of the *Osiris,* turning his long-bodied Cadillac boldly
into the gravel drive of these ornate villas at the cocktail
hour. Up in the cupboard of his ocean-fronting room
at the Villa Moana a small bag was packed in readiness.
In the morning he was leaving for the races at Hileah
Park, but he would not see those races. He would be
in a plane flying north to Canada.

It was kindness that made him secretive, a desire to
spare the woman to whom he owed so much, and towards
whom, let the world say what it would, he felt a warm
devotion. Since passion had never been within the
means of his giving, since the bargain between them
had lacked dignity on her part and exposed her to
derision, he had been punctilious in behaviour, both
public and private. " You know, he really fusses over
the old girl as if he was fond of her," he had overheard
one man say to another in a locker-room. He found no
offence in the remark. It reassured him. An adventurer, a bounder, a gigolo, he had his code. In his
many sins ingratitude should not be found. His wife

had loved him and encompassed him with unfailing
devotion ; against that let all her faults and foolishness
be weighed.

He moved a little away from the laughing couple.
Julia's laughter was a music that touched an ache in his
heart. It opened a vista of the utterly impossible. Life,
after all, had not been kind to him, fairy tale that it
was. Standing alone there, while the revelry of this
artificial paradise filled the air with music, voices and
movement, he marvelled a little at the deep half-
analysed force compelling him to such a complete sacrifice of everything that most human beings would regard
as the acme of felicity. To have come so far, so swiftly,
and now to throw it all away for a rendezvous possibly
with death ! He was demented, obviously, and yet there
stirred within him a force he had never thought existed
and would never have credited.

The land of his birth had given him little. Two
rooms, of rammed mud in a straggling village on a
windswept plain of Poland had been his inheritance.
He could recall his father, a lumbering clod, a cowherd,
with watery-blue eyes and red hands, who seldom spoke.
His mother was the flame, a Jewess, out of Cracow,
black-eyed, tireless, a contriver and given to rebellion
against life until incessant childbearing and unbroken
poverty had worn her down. He was the eighth child,
the fifth boy, and two more followed him. At ten he
was driving geese up from the stream, at twelve milking
cows in the low stinking byre. A young priest came to
the village. He was almost as poor as themselves, but
he could read the newspaper and a few magazines that
found their way to his bare dwelling. Most wonderful
of all, he loved to play his violin in the early evening
while Stanislas stood entranced by the gate.

One evening he was called in and permitted to draw

the shining, pearl-handled bow over the strings. The voices of cherubim choired in that whitewashed room. The young priest had found a growing excitement amid baptisms and burials, confessions and masses, in teaching his protégé. Perhaps St. Cecilia more than Holy Mary possessed Father Hofmeyer's soul. He was removed to Lwow, but the seed had been sown. One month later a small boy lay asleep on the doorstep of his lodging in a mean street. He sent him home. Twice Stanislas came back. Finally, he was found a job, firing the boiler and delivering the parcels for a local laundry.

The Morowski family scarcely missed young Stanislas. The sleeping quarters and the communal beds were overcrowded. One more out of the nest was a blessing. His mother kissed him, wept a little, cut down a pair of an elder brother's trousers, and saw him depart in the local bus, with two shirts and some old shoes, carried in a bag made from a piece of carpet. He was thirteen. He never saw her or the village of Zarew again. For six months he worked in Lwow, and served faithfully as an acolyte to the young priest who gave him lessons on the violin.

One night, when Father Hofmeyer had gone away for two days to attend an ecclesiastical conference, he went to the priest's room, borrowed the violin, and played outside one of the cafés. In two hours he collected seven zlotys, went to the station and took the train for Warsaw. Two months later the astonished priest received back his violin in perfect condition with a note asking forgiveness. It had not been a theft, but a means to independence. Stanislas informed the priest he had earned enough to buy himself a violin.

Four years later Father Hofmeyer, sitting at a table drinking coffee in the Stadt-park in Vienna, was astonished to see a youth in the café orchestra waving a violin

bow at him. Short-sighted, he wondered at this demonstration. When the orchestra had finished playing the
youth came up to his table and addressed him. He was
bewildered until the stranger asked him if he recalled
little Stanislas Morowski who " borrowed " his violin.
They spent a happy evening together, sitting in a gallery
seat at the State Opera House, hearing *Die Fledermaus*.
After the opera they went to a *bierkellar*. At two a.m.,
feeling quite happy, they parted. Stanislas had grown
into an intelligent handsome youth. No one could
recognise in him the cowherd's pale little boy with the
dark eyes and black curls. Stanislas found his companion little changed, except that he had developed
quite a stomach, and he took snuff.

That was the last time he saw Father Hofmeyer. Seven
years ago now. He wondered what had been his fate
in butchered Poland. He recalled him now with some
affection and gratitude. The poor young Father had
the soul of a musician.

The atmosphere in Vienna became uncomfortable.
The anti-Jewish drive had come over the Austrian
frontier and the Viennese hooligans began to molest
the Jews in public. One night he was sitting in a café
near the Schwartzenberg Platz when half a dozen louts
with swastikas on their arms came in and ordered all
the Jews to stand up. For a moment or two Stanislas
did not rise with the Jews in the café. Somehow, despite
his mother, he had never thought of himself as a Jew.
He had been baptized a Catholic and at odd times went
to Mass. But when he saw the trembling Jews in the
café stand up, some stirring of racial affinity, of chivalry,
caused him to stand up also, although there was nothing
save his dark liquid eyes and black hair that might
arouse any suspicion of his Jewish blood. They were
all ordered to get out of the café and never to come

into it again. It was reserved strictly for Aryans, shouted
a bull-throated youth. The Jews meekly went out.
They seemed grateful not to be molested. This incident
and the failure of the authorities to stop the repeated
assaults on the Jews warned Stanislas that Austria would
soon fall under the heel of Hitler.

The young Austrian Nazis grew more and more
arrogant. He wondered where to go next. He spoke
only Polish and German and this restricted his movement
somewhat. Then fortune, as it seemed, came his way.
One afternoon as he was playing in the orchestra at the
Stadtpark restaurant, he noticed that he was being
watched by a young woman at one of the tables. She
sat alone smoking and there was something singular
about her appearance and dress. Their eyes met from
time to time and presently she smiled at him. He
responded shyly, for she was a lady obviously, self-
possessed and about thirty years of age. She came to the
café on three consecutive afternoons. On the third
occasion, as they were putting away their instruments,
his friend the drummer nudged him and laughed. " She's
after you—why don't you go over and speak to her ? I
thought it was me she was on to at first, but it's you."

Stanislas laughed shyly. Except for a few outings in
the Prata and a little clumsy kissing under the trees
when they went out in a party he had no knowledge of
women. He was eighteen and self-conscious despite
his mature appearance. Now, urged on by his experienced
friend, more as a challenge than as a desire, he went over
to the table where the strange lady was sitting. He bowed
and smiled. She invited him to sit with her. He could
not understand her German. It transpired she was
French. They had an amusing but difficult conversation
over their coffee. Presently she rose and they walked
through the tables to the edge of the park.

It was six o'clock on a July evening. He noticed his companion had beautiful rings and what looked like a genuine pearl necklace. She was fashionably and expensively dressed. At least her attire suggested expense, for he had no knowledge of these things. Her cigarette case was gold, studded with emeralds. She had a lighter also of gold. Her bag held other expensive attributes. She told him her name was Laurette. It sounded very foreign and pretty when she pronounced it, her beautiful hazel eyes smiling at him. The teeth behind the curve of her lovely mouth were small and pearly. It was the first time in his life anyone so well-dressed and beautiful had ever taken notice of him. The strange accent added to his enchantment. When he told her his name was Stanislas she said " Polish? " and when he nodded she added, " You all play like demons ! " He was not sure what this meant, for her German was quite funny. They laughed at their difficulty in understanding each other. When she looked at him so coolly but with admiration he felt terribly self-conscious.

She took his arm as they walked. Presently she turned towards the road and halted in front of an automobile with a foreign design. A chauffeur sitting at the wheel, seeing her, jumped out and raised his cap. Then he opened the door of the drop-head coupé. Recovering from his astonishment, Stanislas followed her into the car. She said something to the chauffeur, who resumed his seat in front, and they drove off.

For half an hour they drove round the park. It was obvious the chauffeur was strange to the place and Stanislas had to direct him on the circuit. A cool hand took his own, the thin jewelled fingers interlocked in his. How was this going to end, he wondered a little nervously, but he put a bold face on it, not wishing to betray his inexperience.

They turned later into the Ringstrasse, and so at last came to the Imperial Hotel. He had never been in it before, though he had often looked in, past the commissionaire, through the entrance to such luxury. Bracing himself, he walked in beside his new friend. She went straight to the lift and it rose with them to the fourth floor. Her door opened into a beautiful sitting-room, gay with chintz covers and garden-like with flowers. Motioning him to sit down, she went into an adjoining bedroom. He sat in a fauteuil, awkwardly, his heart beating. Presently she came into the room, having taken off her hat, smiled at him and picked up the telephone. She spoke in French, rapidly and decisively. Putting down the receiver, she tried to explain something to him and there was a laughing confused pantomime that ended in her kissing him lightly on the mouth. He was too unnerved to respond, a little intoxicated with the smoothness of her skin and its scent. Taking his arm, she piloted him into the bedroom and across to a mirrored door. She opened it and he saw an elaborate bathroom, pink-marbled and glittering with mirrors and bright taps. It was like a scene in an American film. She laughed and closed the door on him.

He looked at the shelf over the bowl. He had never seen so many bottles, so elegant and strangely labelled, in his life. Even the toilet lid had a fluffy white cover and the whole pedestal had a canework enclosure. He took off his coat and washed. Curiosity impelled him to take the stopper off one of the bottles, gold and green, with the number 4711 in gold. It smelt delightful. He rubbed a little on his hands and his face. Somehow it gave him confidence.

II

When he had been a week in Paris Stanislas wrote to Father Hofmeyer who had given him his address in Lwow. He begged him to make a journey to Zarew and find out if his parents were alive and, if he could find his mother, to send him news of her. He enclosed two hundred francs which she was to spend on herself. He did not know quite why he did this for in the five years since he had left home he had neither communicated nor felt any curiosity about the Morowski family. Perhaps there was a little pride in this overture, a wish to demonstrate that he had prospered and could afford to be generous. Three weeks later he received a letter from the kind Father. He had been to Zarew and seen the family, still crowded in their hovel. His mother, who could neither read nor write, sent him her love and hoped he would not forget her for so long again. His father was dead. Three of his brothers and two of his sisters were married. Father Hofmeyer had given his mother one hundred francs. He would give her the other in three months. So much money at once would have been squandered.

At the end of September a sudden distaste of Laurette Daumier seized Stanislas. She had set him up in a small hotel on the left bank. He discovered she was a divorcée and made her living as the buyer for a big American store. She went to New York once a year and spoke of taking him there on her next trip. But he did not believe her. He had discovered she was a cool, continuous but clumsy liar, and he was quick to realise she was a woman insatiable in her animal appetite. She made no pretence of love or romance. What had at first seemed to him a somewhat delirious adventure she had reduced to a thing of unvarnished sensuality. A nausea

grew in him and soon he hated her and became refractory.
There was a scene and she told him to get out. But the
next morning she sent the chauffeur round with a
message for him to meet her for lunch. He promised to
go. Instead he went out and found a cheap room,
packed two bags with the clothes she had bought him,
loudly gave a wrong address to the taxi driver in order
to fool the watching concierge, and thus dismissed
Madame Daumier. Besides his two bags he carried his
violin. He had six hundred francs in his pocket and he
was beginning to talk French.

A week passed and to his surprise he found no one
wished to employ a violinist. He tried all the café
orchestras down the Champs-Élysées and then the smaller
ones in the hotels and side streets. In two weeks he
began to feel desperate. When he was down to his last
hundred francs he tried playing his violin on the café
sidewalks. Both proprietors and police were hostile,
the patrons were stingy. He was lucky to make ten
francs with a night's fiddling. His shoes were wearing
out and his linen was dirty. He was always hungry.
He thought of the excellent restaurants in which he had
eaten with Laurette Daumier, of her cosy apartment
in Neuilly. He tried to get work as a waiter and was
just as unsuccessful.

He had his last seven francs in his pocket and stood
playing his violin outside a theatre when a tall fat man
stopped and listened. After a time he came up and
spoke to Stanislas, asked him where he lived, what he
did, and whether he would be prepared to travel with
him. He invited Stanislas to a *bistro* round the corner,
ordered something for him to eat, and began to explain.
He was a seedy-looking individual, a dentist by profession.
He specialised in painless extractions. He had no
surgery. He travelled through the country, sometimes

with fairs, more often on his own, going to the smaller town. He set himself up in the open air, made a speech on dental hygiene and offered a free examination of anybody's mouth. To attract the crowd he had had a young man who played the ukelele, but he had died suddenly of pneumonia. " I don't promise we'll get rich or fat, but we shan't starve and you'll escape the winter, for I'm making my way south to Nice."

Stanislas liked the engaging, seedy dentist. It would be an adventure and he would see the fabled French Riviera. He seemed likely to starve here in Paris, and he would soon be cold. They made a bargain. The next day they would take a train to Auxerre. " Sometimes we go by train, sometimes by bus, sometimes we walk." Professor Audubon's equipment, it seemed, consisted of a bag holding his wardrobe and dental instruments, a demonstration sheet, and a collapsible chair. He wore a crimson gown proclaiming his professorial rank. It also served to hide the bloodstains. " We have to travel light," said Professor Audubon.

In five weeks by devious ways and means they reached Nice. Once they were detained in the local gaol as vagrants but the Professor talked his way out, as he talked his way out of every difficulty. On this occasion he extracted a molar and collected fifty francs from the gendarme who had locked them up. " Moreover, we got a free night's lodging, and that excellent dinner from the gendarme's wife, who was enchanted with your playing, *cher enfant*, though I suspect in other circumstances her interest in you would not have been musical. Youth is a wonderful gift, *mon cher !* "

Professor Audubon had a touch of genius. He was a huge man with a big belly and a little pill-like head on the top of his great frame. He was surprisingly agile, and his gift was his astonishing power of persuasion. He almost talked teeth out of the mouths of his hypnotised audience. When Stanislas had attracted and charmed the audience with his violin the Professor took over. His lecture on the terrible evils of dental decay, and the miraculous recoveries, from arthritis and cancer, made by following the laws of dental hygiene, seldom failed to bring a patient to the portable chair. It was at this critical moment that Stanislas embarked on Paganini's *Witches' Dance* to cover the extraction.

The Professor revealed his genius in many ways. He could charm a free bed out of a sour-faced farmer, he could cook skilfully in any kitchen into which he infiltrated, he could persuade obliging motorists to go out of their way, or get the innkeeper's wife to wash his shirt and socks while he read a book he had borrowed from the village curé. With children he was a giant Pied Piper. He shamelessly used them to decoy some mother, aunt or grown-up sister to the portable chair. " I suppose no man ever left more gaps behind him than I," he would say with a twinkle. He could swap Latin with the curé and was learned in all sacerdotal ways.

There were times when Stanislas suspected Professor Audubon was an unfrocked priest. He never was certain whether the Professor had graduated from Grenoble University, or Lausanne, for he often referred to his youth in Switzerland and his days at Lausanne University. But at other times he talked of his studies at Grenoble. He once alluded to his dear little wife, and when Stanislas wished to know more about her the Professor's eyes watered. " Ah, that is a story, *mon enfant*," he exclaimed with a heavy sigh, but the story was never told in full except that she was very small, very sweet and fell from a trapeze. She was an *équilibriste*. " It was pride killed her, *mon enfant*, she scorned a net. All the Jouvels were like that. Her father, a lion-tamer, was killed by

one of his lions because he scorned entering the cage with
a revolver. You can understand why I dislike travelling
with a circus, though business is always better at fairs."

It was late October when they reached Nice, but it was
not their plan to stay there. Business in big towns was
bad, there was too much professional jealousy. Since
they had money in hand, they spent a pleasant week
making excursions, eating in little restaurants. They had
an apartment with a kitchenette at the back of a dilap-
idated villa belonging to a fat Indo-China princess who
had a jewel in her nose, and always carried a marmoset
on her shoulders. It was a rooming house, and sailors
used to arrive with their partners and dance to an auto-
matic music-box until the early hours of the morning.
Doors were always opening and closing in the corridors.

" I suspect the Princess is a broken-down *madame* from
a naval port. We will keep out of the house, *mon enfant*,"
said Professor Audubon. But twice he succeeded in
abducting two sailor clients from Madame, and extracted
their teeth at forty francs a time. " She was hostile,
I felt, so I had to show her what I could do ! " exclaimed
the Professor, rattling the extracted teeth in a matchbox
on the mantelpiece. The Princess, in a yellow kimono,
stockingless, slithered in her Turkish slippers down the
passage and beat angrily on their door. A stormy
verbal duel ensued. When it had ended and she had
gone, Stanislas asked what it was all about. " She does
not like the smell of our cooking," said the Professor,
" and has ordered us to leave. We shall leave when it
suits us. I'll have another of those sailors to-night and
teach her a lesson. Her Highness is not at all a pleasant
woman, *mon enfant*."

The Professor loved to go to market with his long
straw bag, where he haggled over his purchases with
tremendous vigour. He cooked the most succulent

meals. But one day towards the end of the week he would not leave the room, saying he was tired. He seemed very anxious and jumpy all that day. Stanislas went out in the evening alone. When he came back the Professor was missing. It was nearly midnight. They shared a large bed in the corner of the room. Stanislas waited up until two o'clock and then retired wondering what had happened to his companion. He had not returned at breakfast. About ten o'clock an urchin arrived with an envelope. Stanislas opened it and found a pencilled message inside. "*Cher enfant*, they have got me. Please bring my razor, shaving soap, a clean shirt, and two hundred francs that you will find in the lining of my portmanteau, on the right side. Come at once. The boy will bring you. Emile Audubon."

Obeying the instructions, Stanislas asked the boy where the Professor was. He was locked up at the central Prefecture.

There, in a dismal room, he found the Professor. "It is nothing. It will all be straightened out, *mon enfant*," he said, genially. He had been arrested for bigamy. "They are very vindictive," he commented with a sigh. After half an hour their interview had to be terminated. Stanislas promised to return on the morrow. On the way out he spoke to the inspector who was writing at a high desk. The official looked at him suspiciously, pulled at his long waxed whiskers and said, a little satirically, "*M'sieur*, you do not know *Monsieur le Professeur*?" He opened a file, and produced a sheet with a portrait of Emile Audubon. It was headed *Wanted for Bigamy*. There was an exact description of his friend.

"Yes, *m'sieur*. He is a remarkable man. He marries young girls as easily as he extracts teeth. This is his fifth offence. I do not think you will see the Professor again for a long time. It is a pity, he is a charming man, and this time he has had only six months' run. And we got him just in time. The girl at the tobacco kiosk on the Avenue Victoire had promised to marry him. Her father was suspicious, *et voila !* "

He put back the file, looked at the astonished young man in front of him, and then resumed his writing.

Stanislas never saw the Professor again. When he called the next morning the prisoner had been sent to Lyons. A pencilled note awaited him. "This is Goodbye, *cher enfant*. Dispose of my effects for what they are worth and keep the money left after settling the bill. It is sad to part so abruptly. You are a *bon enfant* and we had happy times. *Au revoir*, Emile Audubon."

Stanislas Morowski, standing now on the terrace of the Everglades Club, recalled the Professor with affection. He was a memorable link in the chain of events that had caused him, in the singular pattern of his life, to be here in Palm Beach to-night, the husband of a woman he was about to desert. There had been times when he wished he could find Audubon again and share a little of his own fortune with him. He had stayed on in Nice a whole year after the Professor's arrest. He had maintained himself in various odd ways. The first winter he had played in a café orchestra. In the summer, wanting sun and fresh air, he had obtained, owing to his superb physique, a job as a physical culture teacher at a beach club. It led to some miscellaneous adventures which he came to accept with nonchalance.

The second winter proved a bad season. He was twice out of work. He tried playing his violin at odd cafés but barely made enough to pay for his room and a frugal meal. Fortunately with his summer earnings he had purchased a good wardrobe. Clothes sat well on his

athletic figure. He was tall, handsome, with good
colouring and strong black curly hair. He had well
shaped hands, and soft dark eyes behind his long lashes.
Nothing of the Jewish strain had come out in him. His
nose was straight, his mouth firm and sensuous. He had
immediate success with women, he discovered, but was a
little scornful of their overtures. At twenty sex was a
fitful obsession, not a master passion.

Around Christmas he was becoming somewhat desperate. He stayed in his room reading Balzac and playing
the violin. Across the landing in his lodging was a young
German, handsome, blonde and always well-dressed.
He was a refugee from Germany, an anti-Nazi who had
found himself stranded in Nice after having been brought
there by a Dutchman to whom he had been chauffeur-
companion. He called himself Baron Franz von Klammer.
He wore a crested gold ring. Once a week he had his
blonde hair waved. He liked to gossip and listen to
Stanislas play the violin. Sometimes he talked of the
wonderful home he had had in Dresden, the high society
he had moved in. He wept easily. He regretted he was
not dark and strong like Stanislas. " You always suggest
passion," he said, enviously.

It was Franz von Klammer who came to the rescue
when Stanislas was about to be turned out of his room
for arrears of rent. Franz had a plan. He played his
gramophone and taught Stanislas to dance. Then he
took him to a large hotel on the Promenade des Anglais
where every afternoon at five there was a *thé dansant*.
He was introduced to the manager, inspected, and agreed
to hand over two hundred francs a week floor money.

He appeared at the *thé dansant* every afternoon, immaculate, and restrained. A floor captain superintended
and kept a sharp look-out for ' sharks.' These were
handsome intruders whose professional status was difficult

to define. They came in as self-paying guests. A few of them lived in good hotels. "They can afford to cruise and are quite unscrupulous. They only go for the big game. They are the real gigolos and they get us a bad name," said von Klammer.

It was hard work, Stanislas found. It was middle-aged and old ladies who hired him. Most of them danced badly and had to be pulled around. Some of them treated him like a hired automaton, some of them were coquettish. He preferred the former. A few of these elderly women were agreeable, and became regular clients. One old lady, departing after a month, presented him with a gold cigarette-lighter and thanked him for his services. She never attempted to squeeze his hand. There were some terrible old vampires who were indignant when their frank overtures were repulsed. It was inconceivable that a youth so handsome, earning his living in this manner, should not know what was expected of him, at a price.

Klammer coolly waited for the best bid. He liked a ' regular ' attachment. Stanislas only occasionally met a lady by later appointment. "You're much too particular," said von Klammer, when they compared notes one night. "I'm playing a wonderful old fish—I remind her of a young man she loved long, long ago, ouff ! "

For five months he made a fair living as a taxi-dancer. He was handsome, talked agreeably if encouraged, and had suave manners. He also went to night clubs as a free lance. He was scrupulously honest. He saw what happened to many of those who were not. They over-played their hands sooner or later.

One evening in February von Klammer came in excitedly and showed him a cable. He had a passage on a boat to New York. His old ' regular ' missed him dreadfully and had sent for him.   It was a great opportunity.   He sailed on the *Conte Biancamano* calling at Monte Carlo.   Stanislas saw him off.   He had a first-class cabin with bath.   Three years later Stanislas saw him again, playing polo, at Del Ray, Florida, monocled, austere.   The Baroness was young and pretty.   He had married the rich, divorced niece of his ' regular.'   His throat had thickened and his hair had thinned, but he was still a very handsome young man.

All through February and March, 1937, Stanislas had had a faithful client.   She was about sixty, a widow, rich.   She danced well, she talked to him, tipped him generously and treated him like a gentleman.   He dined with her several times, escorted her to the Casino at Monte Carlo, and made excursions with her in her impressive Lancia.   She often playfully said she enjoyed mothering him.   One day she looked at him and said, " Now quit romancing and tell me truthfully where you come from and what's your background."   He told her without any reservation.   " One good story deserves another," she said, and told him her life history.

She had been a manicurist who, at twenty-eight, married Mr. Weissberger, a Grand Rapids furniture manufacturer of sixty.   She was his third wife.   " He died of cancer four years later, and I cried bitterly, I was really fond of him.   Then I married Cyrus Cattling, a brewer in Milwaukee.   He was big money.   I had two sons and a daughter by him.   He was heavy, and always chasing young girls.   After twelve years I divorced him. He was quite generous, but poor Cyrus was a weak fool. He married a young thing who led him a dance and finished him.   When I met Harry Flott we were both fifty.   We liked the same things, and it was a great success except that he had a vinegary married daughter who hated me, afraid I'd skin him.   Harry died four

years ago and left me six millions for which I had to
fight a lawsuit with his daughter, not content with five.
I won it. So here I am, with four darling grandchildren, lots of friends, but very lonely and still full of
life."

Mrs. Flott departed at the end of March for Paris.
To his surprise she wrote to him regularly. That summer
he went on the beach again. He was twenty-one, a fine
figure of a man. He passed through a few desultory
affairs, but felt he was getting nowhere. He hired
himself out on the dance-floor next winter. Then, in
November Mrs. Flott returned to Cannes and came over
to see him. It was quite a happy reunion. " My,
you've grown—you're quite an eyeful. How have you
escaped ? " she exclaimed, laughing. They dined and
danced all that evening. As she was leaving, she said,
" Come to Cannes as my guest. It's quite on the level.
My daughter Nancy and her husband and the children
are with me."

He went to Cannes. He merged into the family
circle immediately and was adored by young Nicky and
Madelaine. The son-in-law looked at him shrewdly
and one day said, " The old girl enjoys your company—
and it gives us a break." At the end of a month Stanislas
said he must be going. The children cried at losing
Uncle Stan. He hated leaving them himself.

Just before Christmas Mrs. Flott came to Nice. The
family had gone on to St. Moritz for the winter sports.
" I'm sure they've had enough of me, and I've never
learned to ski." They danced, dined and went for drives.
Their relationship was easy and pleasant. In the middle
of January she informed him she had bought a villa
in Palm Beach, Florida.

" I'd love to see it," he said.

" Then do, come over with me."

" But how—wouldn't it—er—won't it——" he stammered.

" 'Cause quite a lot of gossip—yes, it will. But there's a way out of that. We can marry. I won't say I'm in love with you—it would sound silly. And I don't expect you to say you're in love with me, because I know you're not. I'm making the offer—I'm lonely, I like to have a man in the house, and frankly I prefer a young one. You're fun and you're good to look at, Stanny."

He looked at her with his dark, smiling eyes.

" How long should I last ? " he asked.

" If I said ' a lifetime ' it might frighten you—so let's say ' till Reno does us part '—and I wouldn't see you stranded," she replied.

" You must know you're buying me ? I'm sorry, let's put it the other way round. You know I'm selling myself—for the price ? "

They looked at each other in silence.

" Stanny, there's candour about you, added to your looks, that makes you irresistible ! "

" Thanks, and, Mary dear, I like you a lot."

" Then it's Yes ? "

" Yes," he said, and put his arms around her and kissed her solemnly.

She stroked his young dark head with her white jewelled hand. When she released him there were tears in her eyes.

" I know I'm an old fool. Be kind to me, Stanny," she said, in a choked voice.

That was over three years ago. The world laughed when it heard of their marriage in Paris. It stared when they dined at the Plaza and the Colony in New York. Mary Flott, always so level-headed, had made a fool of herself. " Well, she's bought one young enough," said the men. " How long do you give it ? "

For three whole years she had treated him with unfailing kindness. Sometimes he was alarmed by his power to make her unhappy. He watched himself strictly. He masked his occasions of boredom, his moments of impatience with her affection. He tried always to show pleasure in the presents she lavished on him. There were times when he failed, or came near to protest, or made an overture of independence, but these lapses were in private. No one outside had ever seen him inconsiderate or neglectful in public.

Slowly, they began to treat him with friendliness instead of toleration. He was a perfect host, affable, deft and intelligent. He was always good to look at, immaculately groomed and naturally well-mannered. Women who became romantic with him received no encouragement but were never humiliated. He went everywhere, enjoyed everything. Women loved his broken accent and deep voice. When he played his violin they found him irresistibly romantic.

It troubled him that he was going to hurt Mary. He knew the resistance she would make to his proposal and so he decided he must leave without warning, it was kinder so.

At the end of the terrace Julia Jansen and her partner had been joined by other guests. Behind him the dancers were jammed on the floor. Over them the bright stars shone in the clear night. Not a palm tree stirred, not a ripple broke the silver surface of the lake. Stanislas went towards the small tables under the fairy lanterns. He had left his wife there talking to some friends. The war threw its shadow over this gathering despite their gaiety, the food, the music, the dresses and jewels. England was being heavily bombed, France lay prostrate, Poland had been massacred. Everywhere the Nazis were invincible. The invasion of England seemed certain this spring. Would he get to England in time to join the Polish forces that had taken refuge there? Why, when he had everything here, security, luxury, position, was he throwing them away? He scarcely knew, and he would have denied it was patriotism. Poland had given him nothing but a hovel and poverty. Yet he was certain he could not rest here, in this gilded cage. Deep within him something stirred. For over a year now he had tried to hide his unrest. Every time he heard of some young American who had slipped over the Canadian border to join the Royal Air Force he had felt the irresistible urge. It could be denied no longer.

He could not find his wife. As he turned, searching, he was face to face with Julia Jansen, near the dance floor. She smiled at him.

" Going ? " he asked.

" No—not yet."

" Will you dance ? "

She moved into his arms. They did not talk, being serious dancers. She knew he was one of the best dancers on the floor, as he should be if what they said of him was true. Whether it was or not she did not mind. He was handsome and charming, and always interesting to talk to.

" Are you playing polo this year ? " she asked, after a time.

" Yes—I was at Del Ray yesterday. I saw your brother there. Isn't he going back to Princeton this term ? " he asked. He liked young Jansen.

" No—he's leaving us in a few days, he's been begging Dad to let him to go Canada and join the British Air Force. Mother's terribly upset. Dad's agreed, he'd go anyhow, he says."

" So that's another of them. Bravo ! " commented

Stanislas. "Julia, will you keep a secret if I tell you something no one in Palm Beach knows?"

She gazed into his eyes. He seemed so serious.

"I promise—what is it, Stanislas?"

"Let's go into the patio. I want to talk to you," he said abruptly.

She followed him into the leafy quiet of the arabesque patio with its shining marble floor, its arches and palms and white cupola ghostly in the moonlight. They sat on a stone bench, the dance music distant. They talked for a few minutes. Presently she asked him what his secret was.

"This is the last time you will see me, Julia," he said, quietly.

"How very dramatic—why?" she asked with a laugh.

"I too am going to Canada."

"You!"

"I'm on my way to England to join the Polish Army."

"I had forgotten you were a Pole—when do you go?"

"To-morrow—in the morning. Mary doesn't know—she won't know until I have gone. I don't wish to upset her."

"I am the only one who knows?"

"Yes."

She made no comment for a few moments. Then her hand moved over his as it rested on the bench. In the dimness of this leafy alcove she could see his eyes watching her face.

"It's good of you to tell me, Stanislas. I admire you. I shall pray for you," she said, softly, smiling at him.

"I've another secret. I am going to say something I have no right to say. You may think it disloyal of me, and feel angry. It is possible I shall never see you again, and I might always regret I had never told you my secret."

He paused. They heard the cars passing outside in the drive, the beat of the orchestra within, a babble of voices. He felt Julia's hand pressing his. Their eyes met and held each other's.

" You know that I love you ? " he asked, almost in a whisper.

She made no answer, but her face told him. They sat wordless. Presently she withdrew her hand.

" Shall we dance—once more ? " she asked quietly.

They rose. He led her to the floor. They moved into the throng. It had thinned a little, the hour was late. It was the last dance. When the music stopped, she clung to him for a moment or two and spoke so softly that it was almost a prayer. " I will wait for you, Stanislas, I will wait for ever ! "

There were tears in her eyes and she trembled as he released her. The chattering crowd left the floor. The band put away its instruments. In a group saying good night to one another Stanislas saw his wife, a diamond necklace glittering on her scrawny throat. He turned to the girl at his side as they crossed the court.

" Darling, I feel it has been very wrong of me to say what I have. Forgive me. I may not return. You may come to love someone, you are so very young and lovely. You must forget me if that happens. Good-bye, Julia darling."

Before she could find words to break through the tumult within her, he was gone.

III

From Canada he made his way to England. He was sent to a grim, windswept barracks in Fifeshire, where the Polish contingent was being trained. His fellow countrymen were strange to him. They had arrived after many perils, by devious routes, through Rumania, across to Syria, round the Mediterranean, but here they were, undaunted, turning the heads of all the Scottish lassies with their courtly airs, their hand-kissing, and debonair ways. Many a broken heart and many a bairn marked their passing to unknown graves in war-ravaged deserts, mountains and plains. Their hearts and hopes were always in Poland. His were in America. This was a life on another planet. The master current of Chance would now carry him to his unknown destiny.

He was commissioned. The day came when grey Scotland, the short leaves in Edinburgh, the blacked-out countryside of England were changed for a more foreign soil, a vivid sun and blue seas. So, at last, battle-worn, he came to see snow again in the Apennine mountains of Italy. Later spring came to their dug-outs on the ghastly slopes of Monte Cassino. Poland laid her bones on that treacherous terrain along with allies from America, India, Britain, New Zealand and France.

On a morning in April, when Captain Stanislas Morowski went up from Mignano, after furlough at Naples, to enter that rabbit warren of death above Cassino, he received some mail from the United States. Among it was a letter from Julia Jansen. It was the first letter he had ever received from her and when he turned to the name at the end of the letter to see who was the writer, he wondered why she had written across a silence of three years. The name brought back to him their last meeting that gala night at the Everglades Club in Palm Beach. How vivid it all was, though of another world of cleanliness, beauty and ease. There, the scent of tuberoses and night-blooming cyclamen, here, the stench of decaying flesh and the whining of shells.

A newspaper-cutting fell from the letter and he knew before he read it what news it bore. There were photographs of a girl and a youth. The text announced the marriage of Julia Jansen with Lieutenant Charles S. Condor, U.S.N. The bridegroom had left immediately for the Pacific. Mrs. Condor was making her home in Philadelphia.

He read the letter. She had met Charles at a graduation ball at Annapolis. It had all been very sudden. It had to be these days. They were married within a month. " Do you remember what you said, Stanislas, that last time—' You may come to love someone . . . you must forget me if that happens ' ? I did not believe then it could happen. Since it has, I feel you should know at once. I wonder where and when this letter will reach you. I got your address from Mrs. Flott, but it seems so far away, and these mysterious numbers and names tell me nothing. Wherever you are I hope you are happy and safe. Let us hope one day soon we can all meet. God bless you, Stanislas dear."

He looked at the date. The letter was seven weeks old. He read the cutting again. The lad was pleasant-looking and puppy-attractive in his uniform. So good-bye, Julia.

There were four other letters, two from Scotland, two from U.S.A. One of these was from his home in Palm Beach, but it was not in Mary's handwriting. He wondered who else should be writing to him from there. In a few moments he knew, and gripped the sheet, stunned. It was from Mary's son-in-law, father of young Nicky and Madelaine, now at Groton and Dobbs Ferry. " You will have received my cable. Mary will be buried in Cleveland. We leave to-night. It has all been a terrible rush. I had to fly down here with Nancy. It was a good end. She was writing to you, and they found her slumped at her desk . . ."

He had received no cable. Only a few days ago he had read her last letter, one of an unfailing sequence. In all the past three years she had never failed to write him her weekly budget of news. She was a good letter-writer.

So he was free, and a comparatively rich man. The thought gave him no pleasure. All her kindnesses were in his mind. An old fool and her gigolo, had been the verdict of the world. But his sense of guilt arose from a circumstance the world would never comprehend. His loyalty in a bargain had almost failed. It troubled his conscience now. Was it irony or justice that had brought him news of Julia's marriage by the same mail? He placed the letters in his wallet—letters concerning the two women who had played the most important rôles in his life.

Three days later, when his company took over from the English on Monte Cassino, the shelling caught him as he looked at the new graves behind the slit trenches. The fragment of shell that tore through the lung, just after he had lost his arm, obliterated his wallet. When they found him and went through his pockets there was no clue to the episodes of a singular history. Among his kit was the violin he loved to play. Its delicate case had survived three campaigns.

CHAPTER X

THE QUEST

I

CHARLES CONWAY lay in bed late. When you were a young harassed lieutenant in the army, lying in bed late was a luxury not to be missed if at all possible. It was possible this Sunday morning. A soldier taking his embarkation leave was very much like a man condemned to be hanged. He could be humoured in these last few hours before the jump into the unknown.

He finished the breakfast on his tray, aware that in the matter of butter, marmalade and sugar he had been favoured by those struggling with an increasing shortage of foodstuffs in this second year of the war. He opened the Sunday newspaper, which also showed signs of the progressive shrinkage in all the amenities of life, and glanced through the news. It was wholly dismal, but stoic in its presentation of the gloomy facts. Nothing seemed to check the success of those frightful Nazis, nothing except this English Channel, which they had not yet succeeded in crossing. The attempt might come at any hour. It was singular, in the face of it, despite the frightful night raids, the bombings, the fires, across the scarred face of Britain, how unchanged was this corner of Leicestershire. As he looked out of the windows of his room, across the green fields and the black leafless woodlands, misty but touched with weak sunlight on this February morning, it seemed exactly as it had always been through his boyhood and youth.

This room in which he now lay had been his father's bedroom. He, too, had looked out on the same scene through the windows, had heard the wind soughing through the elm trees, the bells ringing in the old church tower. It was here his father had spent his last night at Winton, on the eve of his wedding. Fate had destined that he should never see it again, that he should die far away in a little mountain town in Italy.

A posthumous child, Charles had never seen his father, but how vivid he was ! It seemed there had been no day in his life since he could remember that there had not been some reminiscence of him, though his father's years had been few in this house where Conway had followed Conway through the centuries. And here he was, lying in bed on this final morning in England. He was the last of the Conways, and, unlike his father when he had last slept in this room, it was not his bridal morning. If something should happen to him in these coming months the line came to an end at last.

He contemplated the fact a little sorrowfully. Everything was coming to an end these days. It was probable they would not be able to go on living in this old house. A hundred years ago it had sustained twenty servants, according to the house books. There had been six grooms and thirty horses in the stables. There was not a horse or a groom to-day. Downstairs, in the long passage leading to the servants' hall, there was still a coat rack numbered from one to forty. Not a coat hung on that rack to-day. Not a foot trod the stone floor of the vast kitchen with its great out-dated ranges. A modern kitchen, a little affair for the ministrations of a swift succession of cooks, had been installed in a former flower-room. At the moment there was not a cook in the house. A sad-looking woman from the village came in and " obliged." The evening meal was early and sparse, as she had to go home early. There were only two servants in the house, old and faithful Hannah, now very slow, and old and faithful Sarah, his mother's maid. It seemed to him that his darling mother worked harder in the house than any former servant.

" When this war's over I don't see how we can run the place—with all the prices so high, and our income so reduced," said his mother the previous evening. The strain must be very great to have wrung that confession from her. For this was Charles Conway's old house and his ghost still walked in every room.

How well he knew the legend of his father! His mother had kept his memory so vividly alive that there had never been a time when his own life had not been influenced by the man who had died so young and tragically on the balcony of that hotel at Cassino. He had one master-passion. One day, if he survived this war, he would go to Cassino and stand on that very balcony. He knew exactly where it was, the name of it, the floor, the number of the room. He knew how you threw open the shutters to the flooding light and there, crowning the great hill before you, was the immense ancient monastery. He wondered if in it there still lived that mysterious monk, the Englishman who had once been an army officer and a boxer, and who, for some unknown reason, had shut himself up for life within the wall of that great Abbey.

" A love affair? " said his mother, one day when he closely questioned her on the oft-repeated story. " Well, darling, I really don't know. He was young and hand-some, so perhaps it might have been, for we couldn't conceive that any sense of sin had sent him there. Your father and I talked about him on that last night of ours.

We were a little sad that we weren't going to see Brother Sebastian again. He didn't seem unhappy. When I did see him again, on that dreadful day, he was very gentle and comforting. I still remember how very boyish and English he looked as he prayed beside your father's body in that hotel bedroom."

" I shall go and look for him one day when this is all over," said Charles. " Perhaps, when I remind him who I am, he will tell me something about himself. Brother Sebastian. It's a bit odd, mother, isn't it ? I wonder what his real name was. I wonder if he has ever wanted to get out. I wonder if he remembers you and father."

" There's one thing you haven't wondered—whether he's alive still," said Mary Conway. " It's over twenty years ago, although to me it's only yesterday."

" He must be alive ! " declared Charles. He was always reluctant to believe that anyone who had known his father could not be living.

" If you do ever meet him, and he seems to have forgotten about us, you can try reminding him of a book your father gave him."

" The Symonds book, with the passage about Boccaccio going to the monastery library and finding it in such an awful condition ! " said Charles at once, every detail vivid in the saga of his father's life. " You know, Brother Sebastian's almost like a member of the family ! "

" I don't think you should remind poor Brother Sebastian you called your red setter after him, he might not feel flattered ! " laughed Mary Conway.

Italy was in the war now—poor, foolish Italy, drunk with bombast and speeches hurled at them from the balcony of the Palazzo Venezia by that mountebank Mussolini. Brother Sebastian might have become a

Fascist, he might now be fat, with dirty feet sticking out of his sandals.

It was a horrid thought : he lived so much in that world in which his handsome father and his beautiful young mother moved through the vivid days of their youth. He remembered how, when a boy of fourteen, he had been given his father's attaché case, he had asked his grandmother, then living, if his father was a good business man.

" He was good at everything, Charles. He wrote neatly, he had an eye for detail. He rode beautifully. He knew how to get on with everybody. And I'm not just a foolish old mother talking. Talk to your Uncle Vincent," said the old lady.

In her room she always sat under the portrait of Charles Conway in his hunting pink, by Munnings, done for his coming-of-age celebrations. He remembered how one morning he had seen two men carrying it along the corridor to his grandmother's room. He asked why it was being moved and was told she was dying and wanted to close her eyes looking upon the portrait of her son.

That painting was hung now in the study, over his father's desk, where hung most of the hunting pictures —the Ferneley, Stubbs, and Sartorius equine studies. One of the Ferneleys had always fascinated him. It was of young Squire Tidmas of Sutton Bonnington, Loughborough. He was an eighteenth-century buck, superbly mounted in front of his country house. He wore a bright pink coat, white buckskin breeches and glossy top boots. He had reddish locks waving under a rakish tall hat that was as glossy as the flanks of his mount. The Quorn in its palmiest days could not have had a more racy figure. He was his father's mother's great-grandfather. And there, opposite, a hundred years later, was Charles Conway, his great-great-grandson, equally

P

handsome under Munning's brilliant brush. How often he had stood in front of his father's portrait, a mere boy, hoping those lips would speak to him, trying so hard to bring to life the man who was a legend to him. A Conway of Winton stood before a Conway of Winton. Surely to him, the latest carrier of the torch, a word would be said ? In the strained silence Charles almost heard his father speak.

The male view of his father came chiefly from Vincent Shore. " Talk to your Uncle Vincent," his grandmother had said to him years ago. He could never remember a time when he had not talked to " Uncle Vin," his father's old friend. Many found him austere, " a regular old bachelor," with his precise manner, his courtly but stiff bearing, his beautifully furnished rooms in London. He was a constant visitor to Winton, both as a trustee of the estate and as a guardian. It was Uncle Vin who had given him his first riding lesson, taken him to his first meet and watched him at his ordeal of being " blooded." It had required a strong will not to cry when the huntsman, having cut off the fox's tail at his first " kill," had come over to him and smeared his cheeks with raw bloody " brush." Little Diana Burke, sitting on her pony beside him, had also been initiated. The cool demeanour of that young lady had shamed him into a stoic acceptance of the rite.

" Traditional barbarism," said Uncle Vin, referring to the ceremony some years later. He was not really a hunting man, though born in this horsey shire, son and grandson of M.F.H.s. It was Uncle Vin who had taken him down to his preparatory school at Worthing, it was Uncle Vin who never failed to turn up, accompanying his mother, at Eton's Fourth of June. It was Uncle Vin who had seen to it that he went to King's, Cambridge, and who had organised every detail of his coming-of-age celebrations here at Winton only last year. They were very much curtailed celebrations, with so many of the tenants' sons and daughters in the Services. But he had brought down some dozen of his fellow officers and the old house had been full again, and there was a small dance in the decorated hall. But there were no bonfires on the terrace, as was traditional. The Nazi bombers were lighting the bonfires across the Midlands.

Charles recalled how that evening, as they sat on the stairs during one of the dances, he heard a voice below him, belonging to old Major Bricker, say, " I can't think why he never married Mary Conway. He's been a father to Charles all these years. He should have made a complete job of it." Charles pretended to be listening to the girl sitting on the stairs at his side, but his ears strained. He knew it was Uncle Vin they must be talking about. Dr. Grant, a red-faced old Scot who had seen most of the local babies into the world, and their grandparents out of it, in the last twenty years, was sitting next to the Major, and wholly unconscious that the son of the house was behind them as they talked, said, in his gruff voice, " Perhaps he asked her and was turned down. You know, since that awful business out in Italy she's never looked at a man. A pity. My God, she was a beautiful girl. She's a beauty still, but then——" He threw up his hand. " I was at the wedding over at Brent Abbey. You never saw such a pair, and I've been at weddings, preparatory to my first job for newly-weds, for over forty years ! "

Charles remembered how that overheard conversation had hit him like a thunderclap. Why had it never occurred to him that Uncle Vin might have wished to marry his mother ? In a sense he belonged to this place and their lives here. All these years he had filled the rôle of a father to him. He had arrived last night from

London—a beastly journey these days of black-outs—in order to be with him on this last visit to Winton before he went overseas, a characteristic gesture.

Charles looked at his watch on the bedside table. A quarter to six. Eight more hours in the beloved old place and then he would start that journey into the unknown. He eased himself down into the warm softness of his bed, a softness he was not likely to know again for a long, long time. He was leaving England at last. He had awaited this day impatiently, tired of the long training, the constant postponement of the ordeal of battle for which they had been so rigorously prepared. Well, it had come at last. Their destination was unknown, but there was a conviction in the regiment they were going to the Mediterranean theatre, which probably meant Africa.

The daily help who had brought in his breakfast tray had turned on the meagre electric stove. The glow from it fell on the brass shoulder pips of his tunic hanging over a chair. A mere lieutenant yet, with not a single ribbon on the breast. With luck, time would alter all that. He wondered if he was a born soldier, how he would behave under fire. He had not heard the help's verdict when she returned to the kitchen. " Just a baby, that's what he is, with his nice curly hair. Looked like a little boy in his pyjamas. Fairly made me 'eart ache to think of 'im being shipped off to fight them Nazis."

Charles glanced at the newspaper, put it down, looked all round the familiar room, wondering just what his father had thought about on that last morning twenty-three years ago. Suddenly the quiet of the morning was broken by a peal of church bells. It was for the eleven o'clock service in the old church on the edge of the park. Turning, he could see its tower now through the bare elm trees.

There came to him a sudden desire. He leapt out of bed, hurriedly shaved, bathed and got into his uniform. The bells stopped just as he tied his shoe-strings. He slipped on his Sam Browne, ran a comb through his strong brown curls, surveyed himself critically in the mirror, and left the room. In the hall he picked up his hat, and hurried out across the gravel drive towards their private entrance into the yew-spaced old church-yard. He knew his mother would already be in the church and a sudden desire had come to him, not from any religious instinct, for he had long been a shirker in church attendance, to be present with his mother on this last Sunday together.

The congregation was sparse, the large church was cold. He could just remember frail Father Marshall, the ascetic-looking old priest who was criticised for being "a Roman." The grizzle-haired old man had died twelve years ago. His successor was a rubicund, red-cheeked parson, young, who rode about the parish on a rattling old motor-cycle. The Roman, it would seem, had been succeeded by a heathen, for young Mr. Portall, living with his short-haired wife in the vast vicarage, had bred greyhounds for racing until the war had closed his kennels. But he was a breezy preacher and kept his sermons short and cheerful.

The service had just begun and they were singing the opening hymn when Charles stepped quietly down the aisle and came to the family pew in which his mother was standing. She greeted him with a smile as he opened the little leather-covered hymnal in front of him.

When it came to the sermon, more robust than notable, his mind wandered. He thought of all the times he had been in this church since he was a child. He had been baptized at the old Norman font by the door, he had been confirmed at those altar rails by a visiting bishop.

He wondered how far scattered now were those village choir boys whose faces he had looked on, Sunday by Sunday, familiar with their names and families.

A thin shaft of sunlight came into the grey church. Beneath a stained-glass window lay the marble figure of Sir Richard Conway, the old Royalist, who, at eighty, had been with King Charles I at the raising of the Standard in 1642, the opening of the Civil War. In the next alcove lay his son William, also of that army. He knelt, in armour, prayerfully with his spouse, while below ran a sculptured frieze of sons and daughters, and children dead in childbirth.

Charles's wandering eye halted at the memorial window to Richard Conway, a great-uncle fallen in the South African War in 1900. They were all here, Conways who had served their country across the centuries —William, fallen at Naseby Field, Charles at Gibraltar, Richard in the Crimea, Gervase at Lucknow, and another Gervase, his uncle, at Vimy Ridge. And there, in the adjoining window, was the newest of these memorials, a stained-glass window, with a smaller panel depicting St. Benedict preaching, and behind him his foundation, the great abbey on the hill. The inscription below ran, " Sacred to the memory of Charles Somerset Conway, of Winton Hall, Leicestershire. Born Winton, March 3rd, 1893. Died, Cassino, Italy, May 2nd, 1920. *Requiescat in pace.*"

Charles read it, and at that moment, as he sat there beside his mother, his unknown father seemed very close to him. Death divided them, but so constant had been his mother's memories of him, so vivid remained the reports of all who knew and loved him, from Uncle Vin down to his groom and batman in the last war, that Charles would not have found a stranger had his father this very moment materialised and stood there in this pew with them. Twenty-three years ago he had sat here, beside his mother at the early service, on his last morning at Winton. Now his unseen son sat here, also on his last morning. Charles wondered whether the day would come when his own son would be here. The race went on, and, like recurring decimals, son followed father through the eventful centuries.

There came to him at that moment a sense of unfulfilment. Fate plucking him so roughly from his native scene had given him no time to assure the succession. Did it really matter, these unregenerate days, when old traditions were derided, when ancient loyalties and inherited responsibilities were on the scrap-heap, and a new generation of men, in a vociferous claim to equality, trampled roughshod over the pattern of centuries? Would anything worth having survive this present holocaust? As in musical chairs, the nations raced round and round frantically, none knowing where it would rest when the war drums ceased to beat. Could it matter much if an old line vanished, and an old house, impoverished and neglected, sank into decay?

His slightly melancholy thoughts were interrupted by the congregation rising to sing the closing hymn. Later, by the porch, many came up to greet him and his mother. They knew he was departing, and they wished him Godspeed and a safe return.

They walked back across the gravel courtyard. The sky had cleared briefly showing a patch of blue. The old place stood out sharply in the wintry morning, beautiful in every line of its grey stone. Briefly they paused and looked at it, the heavy oak door in the solid east face, the crenellated tower with the gilded weather vane, the long stone terrace on the south side, leading to the boxwood parterres and clipped yews. And behind it all, like an iron frieze, stood the leafless elms in the park, with their cawing rooks.

" It's a dear old place, isn't it ? " he said quietly, somewhat ashamed of his emotion.   " I wonder when I shall see it again ? "

His mother's silence gave him a twinge.   It was a stupid thing to say.   She remembered one who had loved it as he loved it, like himself the heir to it, who had not come back.

" Charles, darling, it was thoughtful of you to come to church this morning.   It will be a nice memory," said Mrs. Conway, smiling at him as she slipped her arm through her son's.   " As we sat in church your father was very near.   Your grandmother told me how, on our wedding morning, he went to the early service with her."

Charles made no answer for a few moments—he knew so well what she was thinking.   It would be futile for him to assure her he would come back.   To change the thought he squeezed her arm and gave a short laugh.

" Mum, I'm going to ask you a question I've never dared to, and always wanted to—about Uncle Vin."

" Yes ? "

" Would you have married him had he asked you ? He's so much a part of the family, he's been like a father to me.   He never fails us in any way, and he worshipped Dad.   You must be very lonely sometimes, darling."

" You've asked the question, Charles.   I will answer you.   Vincent did ask me to marry him.   He asked me one year after your father's death.   It was so like him. It was exactly one year and one day after.   I'm sure he had been marking the calendar to be certain he did his duty ! "

" Duty ? "

" Yes.   He felt, out of loyalty to Charles, it was his

duty to look after me and you. I knew that and, apart from the fact I was not in love with him, and could never love any man after your father, I knew he was not in love with me. When I challenged him the old darling confessed it at once. He blushed and was as embarrassed as if he had been caught cheating at cards. He felt we should be protected, that Charles would wish him to do this. Well, he's done it all without marrying me, and is much happier. Vincent is one of Nature's bachelors as well as gentlemen. You have only to visit his rooms to know that a woman's hairpin on the rug would fill the place with vibrations. He writes wonderful monographs—you've read his *Marie Antoinette*, *Princess Pauline Borghese*, and *Madame de Lamballe*—he understands women in book covers perfectly, but never women in skirts. God makes a few unselfish, lonely souls like Vincent to sweeten the ruck of humanity. Have I answered you, darling?"

"Overwhelmingly, Mum darling," cried Charles, laughing. "Only I wish it were all in print!"

"But why?"

"Well, I'd send copies to old Major Bricker and Dr. Grant. But for them I'd never have asked you the question. I overheard them discussing it when they were sitting out on the stairs below me at our dance!"

"They're a pair of old gossips—rather darling old gossips," said Mary Conway, smiling at the boy at her side.

They came to the door, paused, looked out across the lawns to the falling fields and the black copses.

"We've had a lot of fun, Mum, haven't we? Thank you, darling, for so many happy years," said Charles, touching her cheek with his lips.

Her eyes rested on the slim youth smiling at her.

"I thought life had ended for me that morning at

Cassino—but I know it never ends, Charles. *La vita comincia domani*," she said.

" Meaning ? "

" Life begins to-morrow," she replied, turning to enter the house.

II

The unpredictable chances and changes of war had worked what seemed a miracle. For a time when Charles Conway found himself carried from Africa to Sicily, from Sicily into Calabria, then through the southern Apennines towards the frozen German line, he could hardly believe Fate might fulfil a dream from a peace-time world. They were fighting along Highway Six towards Cassino. In a fever of excitement he had looked upon the town from a distance. Through his glasses it had come into his vision like a revelation from heaven, though in reality the approach to it was proving a veritable hell. Week after week, up that Liri valley went the troops of all the Allies. The road out of Naples was choked with transport. At Mignano, where the railway had been pulled up to make a track for the guns, the tanks and lorries surging forwards, evidence of the grim tragedy ahead, began to be visible. The ghastly wastage of war marked every mile with charred vehicles, deserted bivouacs, dumps of collapsible boats and Bailey bridges, and, in pathetic succession, the little cemeteries of the hastily buried.

Up and down that highway went the urgent trucks, Red Cross trucks with wounded, trucks with ammunition, trucks with petrol, trucks with food, trucks and tanks with infantry ; Americans from Minnesota, Texas and Harlem ; Britishers from England, Scotland, Wales and Ireland ; from her far-flung Empire, New Zealanders and Maoris, Indian Sikhs and Gurkhas ; the Free French and, lone and fierce, the fighting Poles. It was a baffled, angry front. Something had gone wrong. They were stalled on the Rapido, which ran with American blood ; they were blocked before Cassino, which became a charnel-house. They found the vital gateway to Rome, in conjunction with their colleagues desperately hanging on at Anzio, shut and barried by that mountain wall on whose foothill perched, impregnable and all-seeing, the abbey of Monte Cassino.

Strange, thought Lieutenant Conway, as he stood on the bloody threshold of that terrain, how all his life, like a solemn bell, the word Cassino had tolled in his heart. There was an hotel in that little town intimately known to him, though he had never seen it. He knew the street, the name, the balconied room on the second floor, the very view from it of the great monastery on the mountain height dominating the town. Soon he would have the incredible experience of seeing with his own eyes the place of his dream through boyhood to manhood, and perhaps stand on that very balcony where one morning in May the finger of Death had touched his father.

The stubborn rage of battle was now defeating his hope. Cassino still eluded their grasp. In that growing ruin, desperately contested over every yard, the bodies of fallen soldiers, mixed with the rubble of collapsed houses, or sunk in the rain-logged shell-holes and slimy bomb pits, bore witness to the terrible price of that costly battleground.

At the end of February, 1944, following a saturation bombing of the Abbey, in which fifteen hundred sorties by their planes in support of the ground troops had failed to evict the Nazis, Charles Conway's battalion was withdrawn for a rest. Tired, dirty, with torn clothes and depressed by the heavy casualties, it was a sombre return to civilisation. The trucks carrying them to Naples were loaded with silent men, bearded some of them, who had long lost the high spirits that had brought them, triumphant, out of Africa and Sicily. There had been a terrible strategic error, it would seem. The whole Italian campaign had bogged down into a bloody ding-dong tussle. The world's richest museum saw its monuments and treasures buried under an avalanche of rubble. Scurrying out of it came the wild-eye peasants, the cursing men, the weeping women and children, homeless, hungry, unnerved by the bombings and blastings. Homes, farmsteads and vineyards lay in frightful ruin. The line of destruction ran from Gaeta, on the Mediterranean, through Pontecorvo. Never had he imagined that human eyes could look on a scene of such utter desolation. The beautiful little town in the valley had been utterly obliterated. Not a house, not a church, not a street remained. Fifteen thousand destitute people fled this desolation where not a single thing survived in the heaped rubble of a vanished town, beautiful through seven centuries.

But few could feel concern over this material destruction. The men coming out of the line, away from the shambles, thought only of sleep, quiet, cleanliness, and perhaps a little love-making and feasting. As their trucks rolled back along the highway of death they came to signs of returning life. There were less ruinous villages, pleasant vineyards and farms, and splintered trees. There were children and animals, and a gradual disappearance of the battleground's untidy reminders of the grim business in hand, the roughly-sketched skull-and-crossbones of a warning board, "Road Under Shellfire," the notices in English and Polish and French, the tangled telephone cables, the Red Cross signs of dressing-stations, the blown roads, shelled bends, general demolition, and abandoned sites.

Now the vanished loveliness of Italy began to return. There was a silence in the air, away from those incessant guns. A campanile or a church, amid sentinel cypresses, told of a civilisation that had escaped human fury. It was patchy, for here a bridge was demolished, a stretch of road was roughly restored, and an odd pile of rubble showed that the Nazis had passed that way. Then, finally, as their journey ended, they saw the sea, and ravaged Naples, crowded with hungry refugees, and smoke-plumed Vesuvius, and the shipping sunk along the demolished harbour. But it was civilisation, and peace, with clean beds, regular food, leisure, canteen bars, and smiling girls on the long, noisy streets.

Charles, with his friend Gervase May, was billeted in a large villa on St. Elmo. It had a pergola terrace, and a superb vista of the bay, with Vesuvius and the Sorrento peninsula to the south, Pozzuoli and Cape Miseno to the west. Below them, clothing the slopes, lay the multitudinous city, with its Villa Communale running along the bay to the old Spanish fortress of the Castello Nuovo, hard by the San Carlo Theatre. They were giving opera there, with an Italian irrespressibility, to soldier audiences of three or four thousand, that crammed the famous opera house from floor to ceiling and madly applauded the artistes. A scratch orchestra and company nobly maintained the ancient tradition within its gilded walls. They were performing *La Traviata*. Charles went down into the town with Gervase May to get tickets. They were cramming every hour of this ten days with delirious activities.

Successful in his quest, he was putting the tickets in his wallet when a voice suddenly exclaimed, " But aren't you Charles Conway ? "

The voice was feminine and pleasant. He started and stared at the speaker standing under the arch. She was a subaltern in the A.T.S., slim and neat in her khaki uniform. Her face was shaded by the peak of her cap, from which blonde hair escaped over the small ears. He stared at her, a little bewildered, a smile lighting his eyes at this pleasant accosting.

" Yes, I am," he said pleasantly.

" You don't know me—well, I suppose this uniform is a disguise, and it's a far cry from a misty morning with the Quorn ! "

He looked more closely, but she saw he was still puzzled.

" I'm Diana Burke," she said, laughing. " You haven't altered much in five years, except for height."

" Good God ! " exclaimed Charles joyously. " Diana, you of all people here ! "

" We girls get about these days ! "

" Lord, what fun—what are you doing here ? "

" Same as you, I expect—trying to prise the Nazis out."

He introduced his friend. This had to be a morning. Somewhere they must find something to drink. After a time they found it, at a little place with some tables and chairs in the sun. It was almost a spring day. At that moment life was supremely good. They began to go back over the years until they came to that distant wintry morning when they had been " blooded " together by the Leicestershire copse.

Gervase May left them still talking, for Diana had a girl friend she could bring. He went off to get two more tickets and came back jubilant. They had four stalls for *La Traviata* that evening.

A broken-down carriage came by with a derelict-looking driver on the seat. It had seen former splendour.

The famished-looking horse had a tasselled bonnet. They hailed the carriage and got in.

"*Un giro !*" cried Charles, using his scanty Italian.

"*Si, si, signorino !*" responded the old man. "*Un bel giorno !*"

"It's a hell of a *bel giorno !*" cried Gervase ecstatically. "Where are we going ?"

"Let him go where he likes," said Charles. "It's quite certain we shan't get up any hills with this outfit."

They piled in. First they must go to a hostel on the front to collect Mildred.

"Mildred who ?" asked Charles.

"Mildred Warner—she's my pal—a lovely kid," said Diana.

"Truly ?" asked Gervase. "You know, whenever you meet a really pretty girl like yourself and she fetches a friend, the friend is always awful ! Pardon this anxiety about my fate."

"You needn't be nervous—I'm the one to worry. Wait till you see her," said Diana.

They clop-clopped along the Via Roma, past the Royal Palace, and the church of San Francesco di Paola, Naples here showing its war wounds. The roads were full of bomb craters, amid which they picked their way. The hotels along the front had been severely blitzed. A survivor housed Diana's friend. She disappeared inside, and soon came out again.

"It's all right ! Delighted," reported Diana.

"But where is she—won't she join the *giro ?*" cried Gervase.

"We've got to give her half an hour. She's drying her hair."

"Blonde or brunette ?" asked Charles.

"Brunette."

"*Comme-ça* or *comme-ça?*" asked Gervase, his hands making a rod and a balloon.

"The former," responded Diana. She liked this exuberant young lieutenant with the dimple and baby-blue eyes.

"Oh, boy! Gee! *Formidable! Süss!*"

"You must excuse him. He's so parched that anything without bristles goes to his head," said Charles.

They ordered the man to drive on.

"Via Caracciolo. *Bella vista!*" cried the jehu, turning and waving his whip towards the bay.

"We take your word for it," said Charles. "Multo Mussolini pronto-phoscofornio!"

"*Si, si, signorino!*"

"I object! I'm not a sissy, Signor Fustytopper," cried Gervase.

"*Si, si, signor capitano.*"

"That'll cost you a thousand lire," cried Diana.

"No—one cigarette!"

The coachman turned on the box at the magic word, pulling up the horse.

"*Si, signor capitano—sigarette, signor capitano!*"

The old jehu might have been pleading for the life of his favourite daughter.

"Now you've done it. The old buzzard won't go a yard till you've given him a cigarette!" said Charles.

Gervase took out his case, extracted a cigarette and gave it to the driver.

"*Tante grazie, signor colonello! Buonissima cigaretta Inglese!*"

"He'll make you a Field-Marshal for ten," laughed Diana.

The staggering horse was provoked into a trot as they went towards the park.

III

That evening they touched the heights of happiness. The four of them dined together in a little *ristorante* recommended by an American officer met in the Red Cross Club. It produced a creditable meal and a bottle of Briolo chianti. They dined by a wide window at a candle-lit table. The moon came up and silvered the sea. They were noisily happy when they set off for the San Carlo Theatre. Gervase was staggered by his good fortune. Mildred was even more than Diana's promise. She was a ruddy-faced, sparkling-eyed girl, with tumbling black curls and a mouth so red that Gervase could scarcely credit that Nature had done all in these lipstick days. She had a merry wit.

" I say, aren't you Irish ? " asked Gervase.

" Half of me."

" Which half ? "

" The better half," retorted Mildred.

" It's the half that gets out of hand," said Diana over her wine glass.

Among Mildred's assets was an Alfa Romeo car.

" How did you get it ? " asked Charles, enviously, as they got into it, opera-bound.

" A wangle," replied Mildred, at the wheel.

" I'd say ' lifted,' my girl," cried Diana. " She saw its back end sticking out of a half-bombed garage, and just rescued it. A boy in the R.A.S.C. supplies the petrol, and a Yank in the U.S.A.M.C. the tyres. I warn you, Gervase, if you can't make some kind of a contribution, Mildred will drop you ! "

They arrived at the San Carlo Theatre, found a parking place in the military enclosure and entered the theatre. It was crammed with the Forces from floor to

Q

ceiling. They were even sitting in the aisles. Charles took a deep breath as he turned in the stalls and surveyed the famous opera house.

" It really is a sight ! " exclaimed Diana. " Look at the royal box stuffed with colonels and their ladies ! "

" I hope they're ladies—but I have my doubts," retorted Mildred. " The competition we have these days ! "

" This is where all the trouble started," said Charles.

" What trouble ? " asked Gervase.

" The job that brings us here. This is where they held the Fascist Congress in 1922 that led to the march on Rome," said Charles.

" Now how did you learn that ? " asked Diana.

" You'd be surprised what Charles does know—he's positively unhealthy," cried Gervase.

The lights went down. The opening bars of the overture pervaded the house. The atmosphere was electric. Eighty miles away, at Piedimonte, the guns were roaring. Three days ago they had been crouching in their mortar-shaken hovels on Monte Cassino, seventy miles away ; there, stark death and raw nature ; here, music and civilisation. Verdi's magic filled the darkened auditorium as it had done for eighty years in this theatre, but to what a different audience !

The curtain rose majestically, following the overture, the Italian voices soared out across that tense multitude of listening soldiers. Enchantment fell upon them.

When it was all over, when the curtain had fallen and risen to the thunderous applause, they streamed out with the noisy crowd. It was moonlight in the Strada San Carlo. They found their car. Gervase had an invitation for them to a villa on the Vomero, where his cousin, in the Royal West Kents, was billeted. They were having a small dance.

They found the villa, after some trouble. It was an old *palazzo* standing in beautiful grounds, taken over by the British. A series of ornamental terraces commanded a superb view of the Bay below them, sparkling in the moonlight. Inside the great villa, with its arcaded galleries and richly painted ceilings, a local Italian orchestra was playing, and on the floor of the great salon about fifty uniformed couples were dancing. Gervase found his cousin, who was delighted with the feminine company in his train. In one of the rooms there was a buffet supper. Wine flowed freely.

" How do you do it ? " asked Gervase.

" Don't ask me. The Adjutant's a wizard. This has been going on for a week," said Captain Stanlow. " But if you really want to see how wars should be fought, go over to the Villa Emma and your eyes will pop. The Navy boys have set themselves up in a style to make Nero blush."

" I'd call this good enough," said Charles, taking Diana into his arms. They moved into the crowd on the floor.

Little by little they divulged their personal histories to each other. Diana was stationed at the A.F.H.Q., in the Royal Palace at Caserta, in the Signals Branch. She liked her work in this vast building swarming with the Allied Staffs. She had been in Naples three months. Why had he not seen her for so many years, enquired Charles. He learned that on her father's death, five years ago, they had moved from Leicestershire to Shropshire.

" How much leave have you got ? " she asked.

" Ten days—and you ? "

" Five, but I can get into Naples quite easily."

" I'm glad of that," he said. " This marble floor's hard—shall we go on to the terrace ? "

She nodded. They left the *salon* and went out on to the wide balustraded terrace with its statuary and dark cypresses. The trees were black in the moonlight, a soft light lay over the hillside. The sea glittered.

"I suppose Capri's over there," said Diana, looking on the bay.

"I know heaven's here," he said with a laugh.

Like children, they held each other's hand. They went down to the lower terrace. It grew quieter. Other couples were sitting there in the moonlight. The night was warm. Spring was here. Charles thought how pleasant Diana's voice was, how comforting it seemed to find someone out of his own past, a link with his home, which had become a little unreal in these dreadful months. To be able to move, to talk to someone that was not male, to touch someone soft, and hear this musical laughter. He reminded himself it was all the enchantment of the Neapolitan night, the ecstasy into which they were lifted by the opera, the romantic setting of this villa.

"You are very silent," said his companion.

"Sorry—I'm not much good at small talk."

"Neither am I ."

"It's just heaven to be here—with you," he added quietly.

He felt her hand press his.

"Diana, what are you going to do after this?" he asked.

"Go to bed."

"No—I mean when this war's all over."

"Do you think it ever will be—it goes on and on!" she said.

"One day it must end—we've just got to smash 'em!"

She made no reply for a few moments.

"Funny, Charles, isn't it? Fifteen years ago you and

I at Hangman's Copse with two bloody smears on our cheeks."

" I was blubbering, you were disgustingly stoic, I remember."

" That was the first time I saw you. The second was at the Pearson wedding. You were about seventeen, at Eton then—rather frightening."

" Frightening ? " asked Charles. " I could never be frightening ! "

" I thought so—tall, stiff, with very solemn eyes. Of course, you never saw me."

" Oh, yes, I did—but your people scared me. I do remember—I got you a glass of champagne, and I thought your mother frowned when you drank it."

" Quite correct, you did. I'd forgotten that, and you had your mother and a nice old boy with you."

" Uncle Vin—Lord, how it all comes back ! I can hear the hounds baying in the kennels."

" You are still at Winton ? " she asked.

" Yes—my mother's there. Rather lonely, poor darling."

" It's such a beautiful place, Charles, you must love it very much."

" I do. How nice of you to like it."

" But why shouldn't I ?—it's something to hold on to these days, when everything's failing us," she said earnestly.

He looked at her alert face, fine featured, with beautiful colouring. The uniform fitted her perfectly.

" I'm glad you feel like that about it," he said. " It's not something I find easy to talk about—many people don't care about continuity,"

" Continuity ? "

" I suppose that's the word," he said, bending and stroking his ankle, a little embarrassed by his confession.

" It's something to feel the flow of Time, to live within walls that have echoed with the voices of people who've handed the place on. You know, I even feel my father there—and I never saw him. Does that sound very silly ? "

" Of course it doesn't. There is such a thing as tradition, although it's quite out of fashion. Your son——"

" I'm not even married ! " he said, with a short laugh.

" But you will be," she asserted.

" If I come out of this—perhaps," he said quietly.

" But you will come out of it. Everything's in front of you ! "

" You'd agree with my mother," he said, smiling at her. " One of the last things she said to me as we stood preening the old place——"

" Preening ? "

" Sorry, that's a family word—whenever we stand outside and look at the old place, and feel frightfully pleased with it, in other words, preen ourselves like the peacocks—we call it preening. Well, on our last day together just after we'd come back from church, we stood by the hall door, looking at the place, and indulging in a little continuity fixation—if you understand me ? "

" Perfectly. Go on ! "

" Well, when we were preening, she said to me, ' *La vita comincia domane* '—Life begins to-morrow."

" And it does—look at us ! Yesterday we neither of us imagined we should have met to-day ! "

" And will again to-morrow ! " he said quickly, pressing her hand.

" Of course."

" Diana, it's awfully nice talking to you—you're easy."

She laughed at him then. " I'd never say you were difficult."

" Well, there are some things——"

" Such as ? "

He hesitated. She noticed the habit he had of stroking his ankle with his fine hand. His face was very sensitive, and quite untouched by the horror he must have come out of so recently.

" Well—I suppose I've got what they call a fixation," he said.

" Another ? We've had the continuity one—what now ? "

She smiled at him encouragingly, and he was conscious then in the moonlight how warming her smile was.

" It's rather as if Fate had brought me here to Italy, to Cassino, of all places in the world."

" Why ? "

" You won't laugh at me ? " he asked earnestly.

Her hand reassured him, and he continued :

" I suppose it's because my mother has given me such a clear picture of my father that, in a sense, I've always been close to him. Never close enough, really ; there's always a frustration. If there were such things as ghosts and one had the power to conjure them up, then perhaps I would see my father. He died on his honeymoon. They were staying in an hotel at Cassino. They had been visiting the Monastery, where they met a mysterious young Englishman, a monk called Brother Sebastian. My father was an architect, and he was greatly interested in the abbey. The following morning when he got up he went out on to the balcony to have a look at the view, and the old monastery up on the mountain. My mother was in bed and after a time she called to him. He didn't answer. She went out and found him dead on the balcony. Heart failure—he had had rheumatic fever in the army, and they thought that accounted for it. You see, there was something very special about my father and mother. They were so desperately in love with each other—you can, if you understand what I mean, feel the vibration of it now when you talk to my mother, or when my father's name, or some incident concerning him comes up. I was born after he died—he couldn't have known he was going to have a son. My mother has a curious idea I was an answer to prayer—don't laugh at me, Diana."

" Charles, I wouldn't dream of laughing at you—this is frightfully interesting—go on," said Diana earnestly.

" Well, it seems that when my father lay in that bedroom—Number 14, on the second floor—the monk, Brother Sebastian, hearing what had happened, came in to see my mother, and asked if he could offer a prayer at the bedside. We're not Catholics, as you know, but my mother thought it very sympathetic of him. She knelt down with him and she remembers, after the Latin prayer, he paused, and then said in English, " Grant, Holy Mother of Jesus, that a sign of love be given to the sorrowing bride, for her comfort and in memory of him.' At the time she thought it was a symbolic wish, but when she learned I was to be born she had an absolute conviction she would have a son, and that Brother Sebastian's prayer had been answered. And here I am, fighting at Cassino, brought here by a great war, to this very place ! One day I shall get into that hotel, see the room, stand on the balcony, know——"

He paused, and she saw how his face shone in the moonlight as he sat beside her, his hand holding hers.

She waited, but he did not finish the sentence. After a long pause he said, very quietly, " It's so strange I should be talking to you like this. I've never talked like this to anyone—neither to my mother nor Uncle Vincent." He laughed, a little embarrassed as he looked at her, and added abruptly, " Shall we go in and get something to eat? I'm quite hungry. It must be midnight."

They rose. He slipped his arm through hers. They reached the upper terrace. The moon was high in the sky, the shadows of the cypresses and ilex were black and short. The marble balustrade was very white. The dance band played vigorously.

On the upper terrace before they reached the portico Diana brought Charles to a standstill, and looked up into his face.

" Thank you very much for telling me all that, Charles. I am glad you feel you can trust me," she said.

" Yes—funny, isn't it, I don't feel a bit strange talking to you—not a bit as I feel with others. Many people would think I'm cracked ! "

They went into the house.

IV

It was the fourth day, when she had only one more day of leave in Naples, that he knew the absolute truth concerning Diana and himself. The thought of losing her on the morrow, after these four enchanted days, with every hour spent together, became quite unbearable. They were inseparable now and Gervase had tactfully left them to their own plans. " Quite bitten, old boy, eh ? " he said one morning as he shaved. " Well, she's a jolly nice girl. P'r'aps there's something in the old blood sign of you hunting Johnnies—you know, tribal and all that. Fox blood's thicker than water ! "

He dodged the slipper that came at him from Charles's bed.

That afternoon Charles and Diana went out to Pompeii.

After an hour's strenuous tramping down dead streets and through half-ruined villas, listening to the guide's atrocious patter, they slipped from their party and found a quiet corner by the ancient amphitheatre. An old wall sheltered them from a recurrent wind, and it was warm sitting there in the sun.

" It's funny how the war puts this place out of the picture, isn't it ? " asked Charles. " All ruins look alike whether they're two thousand years or two weeks old. You'd think this place had been blitzed and the demolition squads had been in and tidied it up. Yet it's almost nineteen hundred years ago that Vesuvius blitzed it."

He lay on his back, with his head resting in Diana's lap. Her fingers played through his hair. He laughed happily, caught at her hand and kissed it. It was a day given by Heaven to youth. The tiny cloud was to-morrow.

He sat up suddenly, looked at Diana very earnestly, and said, " Darling, how short it all is—they were all here, twenty thousand of them, loving and laughing and working, and now look—a wilderness, with nothing but a few frescoes and statues to tell us something about them. Twenty, thirty or forty years alive, and now two thousand years dead ! "

" Why this solemn thought ? "

" Well, it shows we should live while we can, fully, intensely—that's what all this proves to us," he said gravely. " Darling, any moment something can happen to us—we can be wrenched apart. Don't you see, we must take everything we can while it's near to our hands ! "

" Meaning ? "

" Meaning, Diana, we must be married at once ! "

" But, Charles, darling—if this is a proposal——"

" It certainly is ! " he avowed.

" There are such things as regulations—we aren't free agents, we——"

" I won't admit it ! We are the two persons that matter most in the whole world, so far as we belong to it. I have five more days, after that, I'm back in the lines—would you risk what might happen then ? "

There was a silence while his eager young face watched hers. He found tears in her eyes as her hand clenched his.

"I would risk anything, Charles, dear," she said solemnly.

" Then this is what we do. To-morrow you go back to Caserta. You get five more days' leave—honeymoon leave. You get permission from your A.D.A.T.S., to be married—what's the old girl like ? "

" Oh, she's a honey. But I've never tried her with anything like this ! "

" Well, try it now ; she's only got to sign her name to it. I shall get hold of my C.O. and get permission. The day after to-morrow we'll be married. We'll have three days' honeymoon. We'll go to Camaldoli—Bill Frye's aunt has a villa there ; he went over the other day to talk to the couple who keep it for her until she can come back. He says it's a gem, with a little garden and terrace and beautifully kept—wonderful beds and linen and china."

" Oh, Charles, it isn't as simple as that ! "

" It's going to be. Darling, time's too short for us, we must defy it or we'll lose everything."

He jumped up, pulled her to her feet, grasped her by the shoulders and looked solemnly into her eyes.

" Diana, I'm not joking. Please—we must do this," he said intensely. " Will you try, Diana ? "

" I'll try, Charles, darling."

He drew her to him and kissed her. The silence seemed to sing around them. Then he stooped and picked up his cap. " Let's go," he said, glancing at his wrist-watch. " I want to see old Gervase, and to dig out the Colonel."

v

Charles's intrepid spirit had carried the day. Into the scene came Gervase May, best man in every sense of the word. He became the master of ceremonies and in twenty-four hours had provided a car, a small wedding breakfast, two dozen bottles of *asti spumante*, an American gift this, and a villa for the three days' honeymoon.

The wedding itself was the simplest affair. They were married in a few minutes in the office of an Army padre, surrounded by packing-cases filled with khaki New Testaments. Gervase and Mildred were present. A slip of paper certified that Charles and Diana were man and wife. The whole thing had taken only about ten minutes.

Gervase had secured a large room at the Terminus Hotel. About twenty officers and their girl friends came in. There was a small American contingent, some of them known to Charles from his time on the Allied staffs. Six girls had come in from Caserta.

How Gervase had provided the food for the buffet was never wholly explained, but America had again made a contribution from its illimitable stores. Both Navies were also represented. To crown it all, Charles's Colonel and the Adjutant came in, and Diana's C.O., too. The Colonel, tall and surprisingly eloquent, proposed the toast and kissed the bride to thunderous applause. An hour later, when the *asti spumante* had all been consumed and the buffet denuded, the bridal pair departed. Bill Frye drove them off to his aunt's villa at Camaldoli.

It was the first Saturday in March, sunny and warm. They arrived from their billet on the Vomero within three-quarters of an hour. The villa was situated near a famous monastery. Bill Frye had reported that it had the finest view from its windows of any place within fifty miles of Naples. As soon as their car turned in on the short gravel drive and stopped by the terrace of the old house they knew he must be correct. They wondered if there was a more wonderful panorama anywhere in the world. High up, they commanded a vista of the Bays of Naples and Gaeta, the promontories of Posilipo and Misenum, the islands of Nisida, Procida and the regions of Baiae and Cumae. To the south, faint over the calm blue sea, rose mountainous Capri, between sky and sea, and the long grey-blue line of the promontory, with Castellammare and Sorrento. Above the luxuriant plain beyond Naples towered Vesuvius, majestic, with its constant plume of smoke.

A white-haired old Italian and his wife, resident housekeepers, greeted them effusively. Behind a curtain of the kitchen window lurked six other Italians, all come to peer at the honeymoon couple, for the news had gone round. "È bellissima!" ejaculated a fat old woman, seeing the bride.

The villa was all that Bill Frye had reported. For twenty years his aunt and her friend, now in England, had lived here. Its furnishings were old-fashioned. It had a long pergola walk beyond the terrace, whose steps went down to a large *settecento* basin with a bronze fountain, a dolphin from whose mouth rose a shining jet of water. Its summit coincided with that of Vesuvius, fifteen miles away.

" I can't believe it ! " said Charles, when Bill Frye had gone and they were alone together. He looked at Diana standing at his side. " I suppose at this very moment we are the most fortunate pair in the whole world ! "

A noise made them turn. Giovanni and Marietta stood there beaming. A complicated conversation followed as they settled all the domestic details. It was all very good-humoured, with much gesticulation. Finally they came to understand they were expected to go upstairs and inspect *la camera di noce.*

They obediently followed Marietta upstairs. In a large front room, opening on to a wide balcony with a breath-taking view of the Bay, they saw the bridal bed. They could not miss it. It was a wide, brassy four-poster. Over it, like the drapings of a throne, rose the mosquito curtains, drawn back with large silk ribbons, for it was not yet the mosquito season. At the foot of the bed were two large brass knobs and a rail. Wide bow knots of blue silk ribbon decorated the knobs and festooned the rail. The bed itself was loaded down with fine Venetian lace ; it trimmed the pillows, it trimmed the sheets, it covered the counterpane.

" *Un bellissimo letto matrimoniale !* " cried the old woman in a hundred-wrinkled smile.

" *Si, bellissimo ! Tante grazie,*" responded Diana.

" *Prego !* " said Marietta, and with a little curtsey withdrew.

" She doesn't think we're going to bed now, does she ? " asked Charles, surveying the room, which was filled with flowers. He turned over the pillows. " My God, what can we do with these ; we'll have nothing but lace in our mouths."

" It's rather overwhelming—but she's gone to a lot of trouble."

"Very obviously. What puzzles me is what was Miss Frye, a heavy old spinster of seventy, doing sleeping in a bed like this, a *letto matrimoniale*?" asked Charles.

There was a peal of laughter from Diana, who had opened her kitbag and began placing its meagre contents on the dressing-table.

"Charles, don't you realise—Miss Frye never slept in that bed—it's been brought in! You can tell by the mark on the carpet where the other bed was!"

Charles's eyes opened wide. "You don't mean to say——"

Diana, convulsed now, pointed to the great love-knots on the brass knobs.

"Look at them! Blue, darling! Blue!"

"Yes, it does knock you," said Charles, staring at them.

"But blue! Don't you realise?" gasped Diana laughing hysterically. She saw Charles looking at her, a little bewildered by her mirth. Then she went up to him, put her arms round his neck, kissed him and looked into his eyes mirthfully. "You innocent lamb! Have I got to tell you?"

"Tell me what?"

"Darling, pink ribbon is for baby girls, blue is for boys!"

He was stunned for a moment and then recovered. Diana watched his face. Their eyes met. There was a moment of embarrassment and then laughter united them. He hugged her playfully, and then held her at arm's length.

"My God, Diana—so that's it! Well, I hope it's prophetic!"

"Charles, don't be silly!"

"Silly! I was never so serious in my life!"

They looked at each other in silence, in a long, word-less embrace.

"Oh, Charles, it hurts to love you as much as this," she said at last.

"I know, darling. There aren't enough words to express it."

They stood there, while the world in its beauty sang for them. Below, on the terrace, they heard the tinkle of the fountain.

"What time is it?" asked Diana.

"Two," said Charles, glancing at his wrist-watch.

"Wouldn't it be nice to have some coffee on the terrace?"

"A great idea! I'll go and order it."

He left her. When he returned a few minutes later, he was about to enter the room, then hesitated, tapped, and waited.

"Come in!" called Diana, combing her hair.

He was a little breathless. "Diana, the place down-stairs is alive with Italians," he cried. "I believe when we go to bed to-night they'll burst into a chorus from Verdi!"

"Poor dears!" laughed Diana. "Miss Frye never gave them a treat like this."

VI

How long is forty-eight hours to the condemned man in his cell, how long is it to young lovers in paradise? The night, the dawn and the day passed over that villa on the Neapolitan hillside. Night came again, with its stars and the still moonlight in that terraced garden where the dolphin spouted. An almond tree in early blossom stood like a ghost in the white night as they looked down on it from the balcony before retiring. In the absurd bed, beribboned and belaced, they lay in the ecstasy of their communion, youth in its strength and grace fused in the immortal flame. When sleep took them, thief of these wasting hours, they lay embraced, like Amor and Psyche in the fabulous palace. When the first light came through the unshuttered windows they stirred in the dawn, found each other again with familiar passion, then slept on until the impatient day strode, wide-eyed, into the room and they woke, prisoners of their inexorable jailor, Time.

They played together in the large marble bath, noisily and happily as children, and at a moment when Diana stood drying herself, he sprang from the bath, caught her up with a little cry of protest, her wet hair over his naked shoulder, and carried her out on to the terrace, so that Apollo from his chariot looked down with a warming smile on Daphnis and Chloe.

" Darling, I'm cold and wet ! " she protested.

He laughed, held her up, kissed her cool, wet body, and then let her slip down him to her feet.

" Stay there, Diana, like this ! You are the most beautiful thing in the world ! " he said breathlessly, his eyes shining in their worship as he looked at her. He went swiftly indoors, came back with a towel and slowly dried her in the sunshine. She chided his tardiness and laughed gently when he buried his face in her damp hair. For a moment they were figures on a Grecian urn.

" I didn't know I'd married a faun ! " she said, releasing herself.

" *Le matin d'un faune !* Oh, darling, if one could die now ! " he cried.

" Crazy boy—I don't want to die, I want my breakfast," she retorted, escaped him, and fled into the room.

He picked up the towel and began to dry himself. Looking out from the room, Diana saw his naked figure silhouetted against the light. He fitted the landscape perfectly, something Praxiteles might have shaped for this timeless scene.

An hour later they heard the car in the drive. Gervase and Bill had come for them. The idyll was ended. The old caretaker and his wife brought Diana a bouquet of spring flowers. They left to a refrain of *Arrivederci*. Back in Naples there was a sharp desperate farewell. By noon Diana would be back at Caserta, early the following day Charles and his company would be *en route* for Cassino. As the car bore Diana away it seemed as if the whole episode had been a delirious dream.

Charles wrote letters all that afternoon—to his mother, to Uncle Vincent, to Diana's mother, to his lawyers. At six o'clock in the evening, as he turned out of the Via Roma, he saw a little church. He entered. It was very old and dim, with two candles burning on the altar. Half a dozen poor old women were praying. A sacristan shuffled by, dousing the candles on a side altar. How old it was, its name, he did not know, but the centuries had spared it and the prayers of long dead generations had been whispered between its dark walls. He sought a chair, and slipped to his knees. It was not the Church of his faith, but his heart was very full. He prayed for Diana, for his mother, and, lastly, for himself, that out of all dangers he might be safely brought to live with those he loved in the land of his fathers.

VII

Cassino held. They took the castle up the hill, they threw a line across the railway station. The waves of battle flowed and receded in the streets of the shattered town. The New Zealand troops, after desperate onslaughts, having pushed their way along the railway line and into the town, were forced back by Kesselring's men, infantry, paratroopers, sharpshooters. On March 15 the Allied Command began an obliteration bombing of the place. The heavy air attack concentrated on a square mile of the town, and it was followed by a terrific artillery bombardment. One thousand five hundred tons of explosive fell upon Cassino. It did not seem possible that anything could be alive within that shattered town, but the Germans emerged from their shelters and fought back, men of the famed Parachute Division, Nazi thugs and rosy-cheeked boys—heroes alike in defiance of Death.

The torrential rain poured down, it flooded the valley, it filled the great bomb craters so that infantry advancing through the darkness slipped into them and were drowned. Every heap of rubble was contested. The tanks churned the mud and were bogged down. In every cranny of the shattered town, up by the Castle, down by the station and along the foothills of the mountain barrier on whose crest sat the ruined Abbey, death met men who fought tenaciously within a few yards of their foes. The New Zealanders crept into the rubble of the town, and the Allies, pressing constantly, seemed about to take possession of it two days after the terrible bombardment to which it had been projected. But Kesselring's obdurate Parachute Division began to flow back again and infiltrate the ruins, which gave them cover. The battle stalled. The break-through had not been achieved. The Allied Command decided to cut their losses. Monastery Hill still barred the way to the Liri Valley, Cassino was still a disputed heap of ruins. The Germans, the American and British dead lay unburied under the rains that lashed it and the guns that churned it up.

There was a morning towards the middle of May when the tanks went nosing through the rubble and the infantry crept along the walls of the broken streets, under a constant rattle of fire. Word went round that the Germans were drawing out of the town. There had been a new offensive along the Gustav Line. The despatch riders picked their way over the broken roads, the battalions were on the move, there was a quickening throughout the 78th Division. The jeeps, American and British, tore in and out of the moving columns. A spirit of tense expectancy swept all ranks. Were they going to crack that bastion at last?

"We're pushing in," cried a tank commander on the outskirts of Cassino. "The Northamptons are right ahead!" Charles's C.O. had just given orders to his company commanders. They were advancing into Cassino behind the tanks. So at last he was to see it, so much of it as remained.

They waited by a ruined church. The barrage lifted and moved forward three hundred yards. They were to follow in with Brens and bayonet work. The German shells were coming over. They plonked and fountains of dust went up. The unholy chorus swelled, Nebelwerfers, rockets, mortars, Spandaus and Schmeissers. Their own shells, salvo after salvo, were going over, and the tanks roared and blasted on their tracks.

Now! They advanced through mountainous piles in the blocked streets. Gervase was there with six of his men, ahead, wall-creeping. Suddenly he shouted, and waved frantically. For a moment Charles, with two of his company, halted, cautious. But Gervase seemed pleased and excited, shouting at him through a fog of dust. He pointed, and then Charles heard him clearly.

"There's your old dream-place. Look!"

Charles looked. Across the street stood a roofless

building. Still discernible on its façade ran its painted name—*Albergo Monte Cassino*. His heart stopped. He waved to Gervase, gave a brief order to his men and scrambled recklessly over the rubble until he reached the hotel. Its twin doors were still intact. He pushed and they opened. Out of the chaos of the hall, open to the sky, rose the stone staircase. He bounded up it. On the landing a large palm still stood in its tub, beside a bust of Garibaldi, white with fallen plaster. On the wall a painting of King Umberto, epauletted, with large mustachios, hung askew. Charles paused a moment, then turned left into the corridor, whose ceiling had fallen. Room 14 was the third on the right. Its door was unhinged. He pushed it and was in the room.

He stood there, and despite the noise of battle all around there seemed a great stillness within him. How often he had seen, in imagination, this place described to him by his mother. It was now full of wreckage. The walls had cracked, the plaster fallen, broken laths and rubbish lay over the stripped bed and the furniture. It was hardly possible to see the littered carpet still on the floor. Months of dirt and exposure obscured the long mirror.

Over the heavy bureau hung a picture. His heart gave a leap at the sight of this unbelievable relic from the past. It was a coloured portrait of Gladstone, with wide, tight mouth, intense eyes, and high collar and bow. Had Charles needed anything to confirm the miracle of his presence in the very room occupied by his father and mother, in the very same month, twenty-four years ago, this portrait would have assured him.

The glass doors of the French windows were shattered, the twin shutters hung askew, but the balcony was intact. He went forward, knowing so well what he would see, standing where his own father had stood and taken his last look upon the world.

He stepped out on to the balcony. The stream ran below him, the shattered town lay around, and across the valley he saw the steeply rising hill, and there, crowning it, the great monastery, heart-moving in its vast shattered majesty. He stared at it, transported in that moment of revelation, the light of it filling his eyes.

A staccato sound rapped the air. As the vision of the monastery lit his face Charles toppled forwards, over the balcony into the stream below.

CHAPTER XI

AMERICAN EPISODE

IT was strange how you went round in a circle, thought Private Arthur Blaine, of the Northamptons. Here he was, hoping that the next Nebelwerfer would not get him. This was undoubtedly It. The mountain was belching fire. Below, he could hear the scream of the Sherman tanks, the crack of their seventy-fives. The barrage lifted and moved on. Afar, in the valley, an ammunition truck was afire. For some reason its misty blaze recalled Guy Fawkes' night and their bonfire in the fog of the London backyard at Baron's Court. That was the night his kid brother Fred had been pushed into the fire by Mickie Farley and had burnt his hand. Fred had been taken prisoner at Singapore and was somewhere in a Japanese prison camp. Wild Mickie Farley had gone down in the North Sea, running lend-lease material into Russia. And he was here, one of the P.B.I., taking cover in this hovel, awaiting the order to advance.

Through a nick in their shelter they could see the old Monastery. Battered to pieces, it was still defiant, and they felt a sneaking respect for that old companion of their months of misery. Well, it might be theirs to-morrow. At least that was the report. The Poles had got a toe-hold, and some said the Jerries were drawing out. Someone was always saying something ridiculous.

No one believed him, of course, when he told them

he had been in that monastery. His officer had said, " As a monk, I suppose, Elaine? "—and the laugh had gone against him. They did not know life went round in circles. Last month, for instance, on leave in Naples, there was that Yank in the bar. His eyes popped out of his head when he told him he had lived for two years in Orange, New Jersey, for the Yank came from Orange, New Jersey. They knew the same drug-store. And Sergeant Louis Locattelli, black-haired, bright-eyed, who drove a truck in civilian life for Macy's Store in Herald Square, New York, and had played basketball for Orange High, had his own story no one could believe. He had driven a Sherman tank right into Cassino in the early days and stopped outside his grandmother's house. The family was at home and went mad. They had his own portrait standing on the dresser, sent by his father. Two months later his tank had gone right over the house, a heap of rubble just after the evacuation and the bombardment.

" Sure, a guy never knows, I might end up a tinned sardine on that heap of rubble the next time we go in," said Sergeant Locattelli.

Private Blaine felt the hovel shake from a near blast.

" Christ ! " said Mason, brushing debris off his gun.

The mist cleared again, revealing the Monastery. What a story there must be inside that place. They said over three hundred Italians, who had taken refuge in the cellars, and had not moved out because the German commander had assured them the Allies were bluffing and would never shell so famous a place, had been sealed in, alive, after the February bombardment. Blaine wondered if it was near the crypt. He remembered the crypt, with its mosaics, and the excitement of the Miss Wurzells, Anita and Jane.

The Miss Wurzells. They were still sending his

mother food parcels, bless their hearts, from Orange, New Jersey. And there had been a parcel of warm clothing from the Women's Club, of which Miss Anita had been Dame President. How often he had waited outside for Miss Anita and Miss Jane. The old ladies never missed a lunch or a lecture. They once went through three feet of snow to hear a long-bearded old Indian poet, and came back home all excited about life in India in an ashcan. " Ashram—a kind of retreat where one contemplates the soul," explained Miss Jane, correcting him. If this war had not come it was quite probable the ladies would have gone off to that Indian ashram to visit the old bearded fakir. The Miss Wurzells enjoyed life on an adequate income inherited from a father who had made a fortune out of hooks-and-eyes in Newark, New Jersey. They pursued culture with a tomahawk, but they had a shrewd eye for winnowing out the charlatans.

There was the famous occasion when they had entertained His Holiness Abou Achmed Sabu, all hair and flowing draperies and a voice of honey, collecting funds for a leper settlement in Sikkim. A few discreet enquiries of the Indian Minister at Washington had brought disconcerting revelations. A month's stay was abruptly curtailed, and he had been hastily summoned to drive His Holiness, and all his boxes, to the station. But the Miss Wurzells soon recovered their adventurous zest, and turning from contemplation of the navel, to reduction of the stomach, they imported a Californian doctor to lecture on the Hay Diet.

The bombardment increased in noise and fury. A great prong of masonry on the outside wall of the monastery crumbled into dust. When the whole thing had settled Arthur Blaine saw a bright blue patch of sky through the gap made by the collapse. Spring was here in Italy, with blue skies that reminded him of those sharp, sparkling mornings when he drove across the George Washington Bridge and saw down the Hudson the finely-etched skyline of New York's skyscrapers against the clear sky. What an odd succession of events had brought him to this murderous hillside from the old life at Baron's Court, via Orange, New Jersey, Phœnix, Arizona, North Africa, Sicily and Monte Cassino !

He remembered well the morning the telephone rang in the office of the hire-service garage where he worked in London. Mr. Jackson, the manager, had turned to him as he put down the receiver.

" Blaine, Miss Wurzell, at Claridge's Hotel, wants the Daimler at three o'clock. She seems to have taken a fancy to you—wants that ' nice pink-cheeked boy with the beautiful manners.' See that you keep it up ! "

" Yes, sir," he had replied, blushing. It was his twenty-first birthday, and when the Miss Wurzells were acquainted with the fact they gave him an extra large tip. A week later he was engaged for a three-weeks' tour of England and Scotland. Then they borrowed him for a Continental tour. He drove them through France, along the Riviera, into Italy. They went to Florence, Siena, Assisi and Rome. Naples, being so near, they made a fleeting visit and on the way, lunching at Cassino one September day, they visited the famous monastery. Becoming a little bored with mosaics and paintings of saints, he had slipped the Miss Wurzells and their guide, and found himself in one of the courts among a noisy flock of little priestlings playing football. He joined in the game, and learned with astonishment that the games master, a monk who was superintending these pupils of the seminary, was an Englishman. He was a man about forty and had fought in the British Army in the Great War !

One morning, after their return to London, he was called up to the Miss Wurzell's sitting-room at Claridge's and they made him a proposition. Would he like to go to America with them as their permanent chauffeur? It had to be seriously considered. There was his widowed mother and, above all, there was Mabel to think about. The family thought it a good chance, the wages sounded quite fabulous compared with the British standard. Mabel cried a little, said she would not stand in his way, and finally agreed to come out and marry him when he had settled down. So he sailed with the Miss Wurzells in October, 1937, in a state of great excitement.

He slept and boarded in the house along with five other servants. He was completely happy in his new life. He loved the bright, vigorous atmosphere of America. Being conscientious, he restricted himself in the matter of American girls, though his success with them was immediate and illimitable. He wrote faithfully to Mabel. The Miss Wurzells treated him as a son.

He had driven them out to Arizona in the autumn of 1938, when the bombshell fell. Mabel did not want to live in America; he must either give up his job or give up her. He left the letter unanswered for a whole fortnight, going to bed and getting up with the problem on his mind. At the end of two weeks of mental torture he wrote to her. He had no intention of giving up his job; either she came out and married him or the engagement was off. He received an angry reply, denouncing him as callous and mercenary, and breaking the engagement. Four months later his mother wrote to tell him Mabel had hurriedly married a young postman with whom she had been "carrying on." "So you've had a lucky escape," commented his mother, to whom he was sending a pound a week to help them out. Young Herbert had won a scholarship to St. Paul's School, but he would need clothes. He sent ten pounds for young Herbert's wardrobe. Then Fred had taken a job at Ealing and had to have a motor-cycle to take him across to his work early each morning. He sent Fred twenty pounds for a first instalment on the motor-bicycle. His sister Mary went into hospital for an operation. He sent twelve pounds for her medical expenses.

In the reaction from Mabel he got entangled with a young married woman of German-American extraction, in Orange. She was a ripe blonde, whose husband was a traveller. Twice a week he slipped out of the house to sleep with her. He knew it was perilous and idiotic, but he could not keep away. She was a leech and would not let go. The other servants began to gossip in the house and he knew that if it came to the ears of the Miss Wurzells he was finished. He had a tremendous veneration for his employers. They treated him with affectionate consideration.

When, in September, 1939, England declared war on Germany, he felt angry with life. His girl had jilted him, his family did nothing but extract money from him, he had been miserably underpaid in England, and lived grubbily in a cold, smoky, lodger-filled house in Baron's Court. Here he had a nice warm room, good food, excellent wages, considerate employers, an interesting life, and, down the road, that woman. He was very well off. Why should he throw it all up and go back and fight for a country that had done nothing for him except underpay him and whine for his money? Besides, he could help here. He doubled his remittance to his mother to ease his conscience.

But all was not well. There was a continuous war in the servants' dining-room. The butler was Irish and the cook was Dutch. They united to attack England, and he found himself in passionate argument. The local isolationists riled him also. They seemed to think they lived on another planet. You had only to drink the milk of pure democracy, as poured out by Jefferson and Lincoln, in order to grow peacefully sleek and prosperous. The lesser breeds in Europe were too sunk in ignorance and envy to behave sensibly. They deserved all they got. England specially deserved it. She had bossed the world too long.

In the week of Dunkirk he belonged, it seemed, to an heroic nation, and Mr. Churchill was so great a man that all would be well if America could have him for its President and not the dreadful Roosevelt, with his Communist friends and Jewish judges packed into the Supreme Court.

The sudden avalanche of haloes now pressed on his head, as England dug in under a tornado of bombs and conflagrations, and became a nation of heroes, was more disquieting than the former abuse. He could not feel entitled to the praise and when, one morning, he learned that his mother had been bombed out and five neighbours he knew had been killed he could stand it no longer. He saw the Miss Wurzells and told them he wanted to go home and join the Army.

"Arthur, we had been hoping you would feel like that about it. We're very sorry to lose you, but it is a right decision for you to make," said Miss Jane, who was always the spokesman for the two. So he had made his preparations. But the British Army did not seem at all anxious to have him. The authorities in New York kept him hanging around for three months. Angry, he went up into Canada, got on to a boat at Quebec, paid his own passage and after three weeks landed in Greenock. He travelled down through a blacked-out, bombed, cold and rationed England. His youngest brother was home on leave when he arrived and promptly called him a damn' fool for not staying where he was ; but his mother wept over him.

A month later, in his training camp, he had a shock. He received a newspaper cutting from Orange reporting an inquest on Mrs. Heidi Borsage, aged forty, who had gassed herself. It came in the evidence that she had been in despair since the departure for England of a lover and Mr. Borsage was suing for a divorce. It was a shock to learn that Heidi was dead and that she was forty. There had been a dreadful parting scene. For him it had been solely an affair of the flesh, but these German women were terribly sentimental. He was already tired of the affair and her voracious demands. She wept and talked of suicide. He was twenty-two when she had snared him into this unpleasant affair, and he did not take seriously her threat to end her life. Now the whole intrigue would be laid bare to the Miss Wurzells, and they would be finished with him. But the expected did not happen. Miss Jane's food parcels and letters came regularly, bringing news of life in Orange. There was no reference to the Borsage business.

A terrific burst overhead shook their hiding-place. Mason grimaced at him under his helmet, but no one spoke. They crouched there while the noise of battle mounted in a crescendo of fury. Sheets of orange flame burst around the walls of the monastery. It was being heavily mortared. He wondered grimly what had become of all those little monks he had played football with, and of the English monk in charge of them. Perhaps he was still in there, poor devil. They said some of the monks had refused to leave. The place must be an inferno.

" Hey, Blaine, you've been in America, haven't you ? "
asked a voice in a group on the floor of their hovel.

" Yes, why ? "

" This 'as been the 'appy 'ome of your gum-suckers.
Look ! " The soldier pointed to the wall over his head.
" Lucky sod, to be out of it ! "

On the wall someone had scribbled a name and address.
Arthur Blaine went over and read it. *James T. Bellows.
Raleigh, N.C.* He had motored through Raleigh, North
Carolina. Miss Jane had a nephew, a student at Chapel
Hill. He wondered where James T. Bellows was now,
and what was his fate. The inscription gave him a
pang and he felt suddenly homesick for a country that
was not his home. If Miss Jane and Miss Anita could
see him now, caked in dust, with a three-days' stubble on
his chin. It was the thirteenth of May. They were
always supersititious about the thirteenth, the old dears.

There was a general rattle and stirring. An order
had come. The lieutenant and the sergeant were at
the door. They were moving forward. The sky seemed
very blue and bright as they came out into the sunshine
and began scrambling up the rough hillside. The first
thing they saw was a Gurkha stretcher-party coming
down. There was a terrific shellburst overhead.

CHAPTER XII

MAY MORNING

I

THE light came early on this morning of May. Spring was in the valley and over the hillside. In the first faint light, Captain Carter, on the low bed, heard bird voices cheeping somewhere around the ruined farm. He lay on the ground floor of the shed where the peasants and his two companions had brought him. How many days he had lain there he did not know. He was so weak that he could not think consecutively. He knew he had been in Naples at Christmas, for he recalled how he had stood with the crowd inside the cathedral and heard High Mass. Before that, it must have been a month before that, not more, for winter lay heavy on the mountains, he had succeeded, after leaving the Monastery, in coming through the German lines, with incredible good fortune, and reaching the British Headquarters. What a lot of persuading they took to believe a man in his forties could be of use to them! They were suspicious, too—a monk wishing to be a soldier again in the British Army after twenty years of praying and fasting! He had convinced them at last.

How those boys in the paratroopers' school had stared at him, and then how kind they had been to him. The ordeal he had feared was so much less than the anticipation. There was that tense moment of his first jump, the youth out before him, the urgent young lieutenant behind him, but it was surprising how it all fell into the order of events. The night-jumping had seemed an experience in another world. There followed the briefing, the rehearsals with his stick of men, their careful equipment, the wads of Italian *lire*, hidden compass buttons, the small printed silk map. But he knew his terrain above the Liri Valley, on the heights commanding the Via Casilina, the German artery feeding Cassino. The Monastery owned farms there—he knew the people in the homesteads.

The door opened, a voice sounded. It was young Marsden, the most reckless lad of them all, but phenomenally lucky. He was liaison officer with a section of the Italian Action Party. The destruction of the German convoys filled his days and nights. He was wary as a fox and drew off his hunted men with supreme cunning. If ever he was betrayed it would be by the *donne*. He was as reckless in love as in battle. He had been out all night on a wild exploit and something of the excitement of it sounded in his voice, though he lowered it because of the man lying there before him.

" The Jerries are going ! They're drawing out ! The roads were jammed last night. We've been picking 'em off like flies ! " he said, crossing the room in the dim light. " The battle's coming up the valley. We're over the Rapido. We've breached the line and cut the highway north-east of Cassino ! "

The officer on the bed did not answer.

" How do you feel, this morning ? " asked Marsden quietly, and suddenly ashamed of his enthusiasm.

" Better—less pain," said the unshaved man on the bed. The growing light fell upon his ashen-grey face.

" With luck we might have the ambulances through by to-morrow," said the young lieutenant.

S

" Seldon and Marsh and Garrett ? "

" Fine—they had a great killing by Tre Croci. But the place is crawling with Jerries. They're savage and fearful. They hanged Martinelli and six others down in Aquino yesterday, and fired Roccasecca."

The door opened. It was old Eleonora, the farmer's wife. She had come across from the house with a jug of goat's milk and a piece of bread. She was fat, breathless, white-haired. The Germans had shot her husband over a matter of two cows whose commandeering the old man had cursed volubly. Three sons were out on the mountains with the Partisans and had been gone two months. She rarely spoke, but there was fire in her eyes. The Germans had searched the farm three times, and threatened to fire it, convinced she was conspiring against them. They failed to find anyone. She seemed to have a sixth sense of danger and moved her people in time.

She talked to the *Capitano*. He was one of the few who knew Italian ; with the rest of these *Inglesi* she gesticulated. She was very quiet in manner as she addressed the wounded man. Then she went out. She signalled to the young lieutenant. He followed her out.

" *Il Capitano è finito,*" she said quietly, and crossed herself.

" But no ! " exclaimed the startled youth. " He says —much better this morning—*molto bene stamattina !* "

She shook her head. " *No, signore, egli ha la luce della morte nella faccia, il poverino !* " she said. She raised her fingers. " *Due—tre ore !* "

She looked at him sadly, and walked away from the shed back to the farmhouse.

Marsden watched her go. The morning was bright, the sun struck the mountains, green on the slopes, deep violet in the folds. The olive groves were patches of silver-grey. Distantly, the Rapido river shone blue in the emerald plain. It was a smiling, pleasant world, but over these Italian hills there was a continuous booming, the dull rumble of guns below, the sharper vibration of planes above.

The old crone had said Carter was dying. She saw the death-light on his face. These peasants were chockfull of superstition. The hæmorrhage had stopped. His voice was clearer. With luck, in a day or two, if it was true there was a break-through, they might get an ambulance up, or a doctor.

He walked over to the outhouse where he slept, and found Garrett, back from an all-night sortie, getting into his blankets. He gave him the news.

" Too bad—we can't do a thing, the place is thick with Jerries, they're streaming up the valley. There's a hell of a strafe going on. God, you should see how we're plastering 'em ! If he can hold on till to-morrow our fellows may be through. I've got something to tell you about the old boy—what do you think ? "

Marsden stared at his excited colleague, shaking out a blanket, but said nothing.

" You know that Perelli kid who jabbers English ? " asked Garrett.

" In the Malvasia gang—yes ? "

" Well, what do you think he told me ? Old Carter was a monk in Monte Cassino ! Perelli was there as a kid. It seems they've a school there. Carter was a sort of games master. He even taught them to play football. They called him Brother Sebastian—the kids thought him no end of a fellow. It explains everything —that prayer book——"

" Breviary," corrected Marsden.

" Whatever you call it, and his knowledge of this country, and the way he talks the lingo. Just imagine it—a monk who hopped out of the Monastery to join in the fun ! There's a story for you ! We British are a very peculiar people ! "

" He's a damn' good soldier, anyway," said Marsden.

" You're telling me ! But what I'd like to know is why a fellow like that ever became a monk ? "

" If he gets better you can ask him."

" My boy, there's the remnant of a gentleman left in me despite this career of murder," retorted Garrett, ruffling his hair and wrapping the blanket around him. " Well, I'd make a good guess—I'd say it's for the same reason as makes a pretty wench hie her to a nunnery—if you remember your Hamlet—a disappointment in love ! "

" What rot you talk ! "

" Think so ? Well, well. Here's where Lieutenant Garrett has a shut-eye, after a night on the tiles. Call me at noon for tea and toast."

He banged himself down in the straw, and turned on his side. Marsden walked out of the shed. He saw a corporal hurrying towards him with some letters in his hand and he knew there had been a plane-drop. It was one of the miracles of this crazy life that letters from the civilised world fell on you from the skies.

He took the letters, two for himself, one for Marsh, one for Carter.

" Any field-dressings in the can ? " he asked.

" Yessir."

" Good. Let's have 'em at once."

The man went off. He sat down on a box and tore open his letters.

II

Gerald Carter put down his Breviary. He had finished
the Divine Office. He lay with closed eyes, a little
surprised that the pain had left him. He was no longer
troubled by the cold in his feet. Young Marsden and
old Eleonora had brought him relays of baked bricks
wrapped in a flannel to warm them, without effect,
but now he had no discomfort. The bleeding in his
loin seemed to have stopped. His hearing was very
acute for he heard an endless commotion in the sky.
The vibration beat through his head. He turned and
saw the milk the woman had brought, but he had no
hunger or thirst. Through the open door of the shed
he could see a Lombardy poplar, in bright fresh leaf,
against the clear blue sky.

He closed his eyes. It was 1944, May, May, the—— ?
They were coming up the valley, there had been a break-
through, Marsden said. A break-through—a familiar
word. Yes, he had it—on the Aisne, in 1916–17? He
wasn't sure. He was a Captain then. It was just after
the wiring party, after October 20th, 1917, after he
had brought in Dick's body huddled against the
post. Dick Falmouth, sent out on the wiring-party.
This was a farm, too, in the battle area. He had
walked out with Richard into the orchard and heard
his story.

" *When are you marrying Estelle ?* "

" *The next leave.*"

" *You won't expect me to be best man, I hope.*"

Estelle. Estelle Warren, watching him in the ring,
cheering for him, delicate, intense, wrapped up in her
camel-hair overcoat.

" *When! But, Estelle, don't you realise we're getting older ?
Time's rushing by ?* "

She laughed at him then, a silvery peal of laughter —a silvery peal, how clear it was! He opened his eyes.

"Estelle!" he called, seeing her standing against the light, with the poplar and the sky beyond. She had not changed in any way—dark, vivid, with her high colouring.

"Jerry!" she said, smiling at him. "You see, darling, you can't get away from me—I'm always with you really, Jerry, why did you run away?"

"Ah, if I dare only tell you, Estelle."

"You can tell me anything, Jerry. I should never fail you."

"But I am a coward, and worse, Estelle."

"Darling, that is silly of you. You would always be brave, at any time, everywhere!"

"No—I daren't tell you the truth. I sent Dick to his death, in my jealousy."

"Darling, what a ridiculous thing to say! Is that why you vanished from my life?"

"Yes."

"Oh, Jerry—had you told me it would have made no difference."

"No difference?"

"It was only a myth, Jerry, that you tortured yourself with. It was Dick's duty to go out; it was your duty to send him."

"You believe that?"

"Implicitly. Jerry, we mustn't waste our lives any more."

"I've wasted mine."

"Oh, no. We're only beginning. Look how green the poplar is—the leaves have just come, and spring is all over the valley. You remember the beech wood, and the stream, and the yellow daffodils you and Jack and Janet planted? I was there this morning with

Janet and the children. It hasn't changed, Jerry—nothing's changed, I love you just as ever."

Her eyes shone on him. No, she had not changed. She was just the same as on that day he had put his head in her lap and cried. He looked at her and smiled to see her, so beautiful against the sky and the poplar, so beautiful he could never lose her again.

III

When Marsden, carrying his lint and bandages came in, he found Carter drowsy.

"Will you let me dress you—or shall we leave it later?" he asked.

"No, now—she will help you."

"She?"

"Estelle—won't you, my dear?"

"That's all right, old boy—I'm glad of an assistant," said Marsden, realising the patient was "wandering."

He cut away the shirt and the temporary dressing, and was filled with a sudden dismay. The bleeding had not stopped ; it had soaked through and down into the mattress, which was sodden. Marsden said nothing. The lint and gauze were too coagulated, he had to be content with a top dressing, and a wad underneath to take up the suppuration.

"How are the feet?"

"Nicely—the cold's gone. What time is it?"

"Eight o'clock."

"I must have slept. Marsden, would you do something for me?"

"Certainly."

"I want to put on my uniform. It's not nice for Estelle to see me like this."

The request struck Marsden with dismay. Any movement was bad for him.

"Well, old chap, I don't think—but, of course!" he said suddenly, deciding it was better to humour him.

He found the uniform in a corner of the shed.

"We'll give it a brush—it's covered in dust," he said as he picked up the jacket.

Outside he batted and shook it. There was a row of ribbons above the breast pocket. They must have been gained in the last War. Marsden wondered how much truth there was in the story about his having been a monk in that monastery. Certainly he was mysterious, and it explained how he came to join the Army in Naples, which had always seemed a bit odd. He spoke Italian well and knew the district. He must be quite forty-five, pretty well on for a paratrooper, though he was cool and quick in a tight corner.

He went in with the coat. It was a difficult business getting it on. Spasms of pain crossed Carter's face, but when it was over he smiled and seemed very content.

"Will you brush my hair—to-morrow I'll shave. Estelle won't like this bristle," he said.

"Estelle?"

"Yes, when she comes in, tell her I'm much better."

"Of course."

Carter closed his eyes. Marsden waited for a time, and then quietly went out. He looked in again twice that morning. Later, he said to Garrett, who was shaving, "I don't think he's going to last long. I wonder if we could find a priest—you see, he's a Catholic."

"If he's a monk isn't he a priest?"

"I don't know, but I don't think it's as simple as that —he wants the last rites and absolution—something like that."

"We might try to get the priest at Roccasecca when

it gets dark—the road's alive now. It must be a break-through. Poor old boy—I wonder just what's the story!"

"If he pulls through you can ask him," commented Marsden. He started suddenly, one hand in his pocket. "My God, I've forgotten this letter for him. Come and have a look at him."

He waited for Garrett, then they went across the field.

"He's rambling a bit—someone called Estelle."

"Ah, not so monkish!" said Garrett with a glint of mischief.

They found Eleonora in the shed, persuading her patient to eat. The doors were wide open. The bright noonday flooded the place with light. Carter looked handsome in his ribboned coat. One could see he had been athletic in his youth. He smiled at them, and seemed better.

"I've got a letter for you," said Marsden, as the old woman went out. He bent down and gave it to Carter.

The sick man looked at it, and then said quietly, "I hardly know what it is to receive a letter."

He turned it in his hand for a few moments, and then put it on the cover. He asked the time.

"Would you like me to open the letter for you?" asked Garrett kindly.

"Yes—read it to me," said Carter quietly.

Garrett squatted by the bed. Marsden stood by him. It was written on light blue paper. The handwriting was bold.

"Sunridge, near Godalming," he read, "April 10th, 1944."

"When was that?" asked Carter, his eyes on the youth kneeling by him.

"About five weeks ago," said Garrett, and began to read.

" *Dearest Jerry,*

You cannot imagine what a wonderful surprise your letter is. It is like a message from another world. So you are back in the old Army again! I have wondered all these years, twenty-four actually, how you have fared in your far-away monastery. I learned where you were soon after you went to Monte Cassino, and wondered if you would ever send a word to the outside world. Jerry, my dear, you are still very vivid in my eyes and nothing of you has faded. You will be fighting in the hills, a paratrooper, you tell me. My prayers will be with you every hour. And when it is over, what will you do? Won't you come home? I see Janet and her husband. They were very brave when Frank was killed . . .

"Frank? My nephew Frank?" breathed Carter, quietly.

. . . when Frank was killed, and I tried to be equally brave when Eric was lost at Singapore. He was just twenty-one, my eldest. John will be going overseas soon, Mary is at school. Did you know that I married Ernest Folding—your old sparring partner in the gym? I went out to India with him. He died there five years ago and I brought the children home. So I am alone now. I work very hard at the . . .

A motion of the sick man's hand stopped Garrett. It reached for the letter, and gripped it nervously. They saw his mouth work convulsively, his eyes looking at them in great anguish.

Garrett did not move, Marsden stood silently behind him. They saw a man's soul in torment, and they could offer no word to ease him.

Carter's hand, holding the letter, lay still on the blanket. His control returned. "Thank you," he said very quietly, and they knew he was dismissing them.

IV

Early the next morning they brought in a little fat priest, who had made a night journey across the mountains from Roccasecca. Carter was sinking and only just conscious, but he made the responses in the last Office. . . . " *Ego te absolvo in nomine Patris*," said a voice in the dim light, and the two young officers saw the priest make the sign of the Cross. Before he left they talked in Italian a little while.

The light was breaking over the mountains when they went outside into the cool air. And with the morning came great news. They had made contact with their forces coming up the valley and a Canadian ambulance had come through from Pontecorvo. General Juin's men, the re-equipped veterans from North Africa, were infiltrating along with the Canadians and the Irish. A dressing-station had been established five miles back.

They decided to move Carter down in a litter. He seemed to have rallied. He smiled at the tearful Eleonora as they carried him out.

At the dressing-station they attended to him, but when the ambulance drove up and they moved him into it, already overcrowded, he was unconscious. He did not feel the pressure of young Marsden's hand in that farewell moment. Half an hour later, down Highway Six, the *via dolorosa* of all those months, the attendant reported the officer in the second tier was dead. They put the body out at the next station and took in a living patient. Every space was precious. All that morning Captain Carter lay with his face to the brilliant blue sky. Later someone pulled the sheet over his unseeing eyes.

CHAPTER XIII

MAN OF THE MOUNTAINS

I

LITTLE Chandra Jung was glad when his father stopped for a rest. They had been coming down the great Chandragiri Pass for four hours, and the thin mountain air left them breathless. The path was rough and although Chandra's feet were hardened to the earth, they ached. He was now eleven and too big a boy for his father to carry. The scenery had quickly changed from the grim pines into the soft tropical vegetation of Nepal, a rank growth of vivid bamboos, sisu trees, palms, great banyans and spreading tree-ferns, all looped together with flame-vines and creepers, amid which sudden blazes of colour revealed wild orchids, yellow mimosa and sweet-smelling acacias.

Across the deep valley below them the banks of cloud obscured the far mountain range, the Roof of the World, beyond which lay the Forbidden Land whence came the yellow-robed monks on pilgrimage from the lamaseries of Tibet.

When they had rested a while, Girja, his father, rose to his feet, pointing across the valley.

" Little Son, behold ! " he cried, looking northward. " The Master of the World ! "

Chandra scrambled to his feet, his eyes following the direction of his father's hand. He made no sound, no motion, his dark eyes, sunk deep in his Mongolian features, looking in awe upon the stupendous panorama spread before them.

The wind-driven clouds had parted fitfully to make a supreme revelation. Range upon range, snow-clad and brilliant in the crystal air, from east to west, the last rampart of the world, lay the sun-smitten Himalayas, peak after peak scintillating like diamonds in the bright noonday. There was mighty Dhaulagiri, and to the east Gosai Than and great Kinchinjunga on the borders of Sikkim. But it was not these mountains that held their gaze. Afar, clear on the vast horizon, one hundred and fifty miles distant, rose the peerless one, monarch of all, untrodden, unconquered in its terrible beauty, mighty Everest soaring in the blue of heaven.

Father and son stood dumb before the majesty of this brief revelation, then the curtains of cloud were drawn again and the vision of the Eternal had faded. Slowly they resumed their descent into the long valley below them, mountain-ringed Nepal, aloof, mysterious, their native land bastioned by the mighty mountains, and shut off from the traffic of the world. Their goal was in sight now, and among these cities of the plain, their golden roofs shining in the sun, they saw great Khatmandu, its temples, palaces and dwellings spread over the green valley.

They had been gone two weeks, visiting a relation in the wild Terai, the hunting-ground of elephants and tigers. Now Girja and his little son were home-coming to beloved Khatmandu. They were two days early, for Girja wished to miss nothing of the great Treaty-signing, where he would stand in the King's Bodyguard, proudly arrayed in his bright blue uniform, wearing his round black cap, and upon his breast the ribbons of his long service with the Gurkhas, in Gallipoli, in Persia, and in

France in the Great War. Girja was a far-travelled soldier.

In this year of 1923, when the Treaty between the British Government and Nepal was to be signed, Girja had prayed that his retirement might be deferred so that he could march with the Gurkha Regiment to the Singha Durbar. His prayer had been granted. For the last time he would wear his uniform guarding His Highness the Maharajah, and His Highness, Sir Chandra Shum Shere Jung, hereditary Prime Minister. For this great day Girja was hurrying home, son Chandra trotting at his side.

They came to the city and wound their way through the busy streets. They passed the Hindu temples, the houses with fantastically carved balconies, the great white dagobas, the idols, the shining pinnacles, the gold-tiled roofs with curving eaves, the bazaars, the walled palaces with their latticed windows and peacock-feather screens, the street of the fashioners of brass, the street of the temperers of *kukris*, the stalls of the roasters of chestnuts, the bazaars of the vendors of carpets, the workshops of the armourers. They jostled the People of the Far World, lamas out of Tibet, in robes of brown wool with hoods of orange, the verminous Tibetans in quilted garments of saffron and vermilion, with round fur hats and high red-leather boots, the holy men from India, the pilgrimage-making Hindus going for virtue to the fabled shrine of holy Pashpati.

Chandra would fain have lingered before the conjuror, the acrobatic Dombers, or the Hindu juggler who charmed his poisonous cobras, or the beater of many drums, or the holy man with his begging-bowl, naked, smeared with white ash and cow-dung, or the wild vermilion-haired Bhotra, or the crop-headed praying Brahmin. But his father hurried on, blind to the alluring pageant of these alleyways were the Gurkha soldiers strayed, squat and taciturn, amid a babel of voices speaking Chinese, Tibetan, Sanskrit, Hindustani, Urdu and Newar.

For a thousand years through Khatmandu the many-coloured pattern had been woven by these pilgrims from over the mountains. Girja moved through them with a high disdain. A Gurkha of many wars ignored this haggling filth. Was he not of the mighty brotherhood of the clean Splendour of the Blade, the Light of Valour, the Sun of Unsetting Victory? Aloof as the snow-peaks above great Khatmandu, Girja hurried through the town towards the foothills, where his home rested in the jungle clearing.

He came to it quietly, in full view of the slender tower of Bhim Sen, down by the Maidan where the Fourth Regiment drilled. To-morrow, in thanksgiving, he would sacrifice a buffalo before the statue of Kala-Bhairat, God of fear in the Durbar Square, but to-night he would enjoy his young wife Shri in the moonlit silence while the nightingales sang in the sisu-trees. Shri was young, and he drowned in her sweetness like a bee in the honey of the red lotus. When Kali had died, the twenty-year-old mother of Chandra, he had taken sixteen-year-old Shri, the poor woodcutter's seventh daughter. For five years now youth had leapt within him again, his forty-five summers lit with the flame of her spring.

Holding Chandra's hand, he mounted the balcony that ran round the house. He pulled aside the rattan curtain. The cool dim room seemed empty, but against the light of the open window he saw a slim male body, naked, ungirdled, briefly pass. It leapt the far balcony and there was a rustle of sisal leaves in the plot below.

Girja did not move, nor the boy by him. The wolf

had gone to cover. It was useless to follow in that viscid jungle behind the bungalow. He waited, knowing who was within, where the darkness cloaked her shame.

He called her after a space, in a low voice.

There was a stirring, and into the light a young woman moved, clad in a saffron skirt. Girja put off his shoes and upon them the curved *kukri* knife, for a symbol of pursuit and vengeance. She stood before him, making no answer. Her beads glinted, moved by the undulation of her naked breasts. In her glossy black hair there was a champak flower.

" Abide thee, betrayer of my house," he said quietly. Then, turning, he stepped out through the portal. Shri did not move. Chandra withdrew to a corner. There was no sound in the room until Girja returned.

Girja knelt on the floor before his young wife. He had brought in from the garden a lump of earth, some bamboo shoots and a pot of water. He poured the water upon the earth and began to knead it. Shri paled as he laboured, her black eyes fixed upon the thing her husband fashioned. She knew the ceremony of divorce.

Girja made the mud balls, and taking two pieces of the bamboo, he tied them together and placed them across the balls. Then he rose and from his purse counted forty rupees. The price of a wife's divorce was one hundred, of a husband's forty. He placed the money beside the mud balls. Only then did Shri take her eyes away from the floor. She noiselessly went to the far end of the room. She put on a short red zouave jacket that just met the band of her ballooning saffron skirt. Into a large cloth square she placed her selected belongings, making them up into a bundle. She returned to where Girja waited. Kneeling, she picked up the forty rupees. Then out of her hair she removed the three gifts of jade, pearl and bronze, then her earrings and her ankle bangles, placing them on the floor. She rose and stood motionless.

Girja took up the *kukri* and with a swift stroke sliced off her nose. The red blood spurted and ran down the channel between her breasts, darkening the red jacket and splashing upon the cedar boards. The mark of shame forever upon her, Shri picked up her bundle, and with no word, no look, walked from the room, across the balcony and down the steps, the trail of blood marking her way. Girja and Chandra watched her slim, bare-footed figure until it passed from sight under the banyan tree. The unfaithful outcast woman had gone forever from the house.

Girja moved at last. He wiped the *kukri* and pressed the curved blade to his brow. One task remained, to find the betrayer. It would be fulfilled, whether it took a week, a month or a year. He called Chandra to him and gave him the knife. The boy pressed the blade to his brow. Should the father in the span of his life fail in revenge his honour would pass to his son's charge.

II

Before the day of the great Durbar Girja called Chandra to him. He stripped the boy and bathed him in a bronze bowl in which the juice of bruised verbena and jasmine had been strained. He fastened around his son's naked waist a waxed cord of black goat's hair. It carried a threaded pearl which he fitted into the boy's navel—a symbol of courage. He washed and combed Chandra's black hair and anointed it with perfumed oil. Between the boy's thighs he crushed a bel-fruit until the aromatic golden juice ran down to his strong

T

young knees, symbol of faithful service. Then he dressed him in a yellow robe, with a crimson cummerbund.

It was the day of Chandra's twelfth year and Girja knew that manhood had come to the only son of his loins. It was time for the boy to go forth in service. He had spoken to the Great Sahib, the Lieutenant-Colonel O'Connor, Envoy to the Court of the King of Nepal, and had been bidden to bring his son Chandra.

In the early forenoon they went down into Khatmandu. They came to the Durbar Square, with its shrines, pagoda and temples. The little bells hanging from the eaves tinkled in the breeze, the gold and cobalt tiles glittered in the sun. Tibetan pilgrims, fifty days from Lhassa, bare-armed in their saffron robes, lay prostrate before the temple. Murmuring, *Om mani padme hum, O jewel in the heart of the lotus!* they made the circuit of the shrine, acquiring merit. Girja came to the stone steps of another temple, worn with the feet of untold generations. Chandra would have liked to linger. Before the shrine sat the fire-eaters, the jugglers, the snake-charmers, the nude fakirs, the cheek-skewered and sitters-on-spikes, but they went into the temple past the orchid-garlanded idols, bulbous-eyed and fanged, studded with gems and splashed with *ghee*, that leered at the stream of worshippers.

When they emerged, crossing the pavement that often swam with the blood of buffaloes sacrificed in the great festival of Kala-Bhairat, they made their way out of the city, coming at last to the walled compound, where, amid its trees and gardens, lay the British Legation, surrounded by offices, barracks and guest-houses. They passed the guard of Indian sowars and came to an inner court. Here, by a giant helianthus tree, they waited some two hours until at last they were ushered into the presence of the Great Sahib. He knew Girja and,

Master of Countless Tongues, he spoke kindly and smiled on the trembling Chandra until the boy lost his fear. The Great Envoy was a tall, thin man, with twinkling eyes and at once the heart of the boy was conquered. The Envoy took Chandra by the chin, raising his timid face until their eyes met. He asked him his name and pulled his ear. " Send him, Girja, he can serve here until he goes to the regiment," said the Great Sahib. It was as simple as that. Half an hour later they left. In a week Chandra would return to the servants' compound, in the service of the Great Sahib, representative of the King-Emperor at the Court of Nepal.

On the morrow they were up early. By his rank of subahdar in the Gurkha bodyguard, crimson-coated and decorated, Girja took his son into the inner gardens that led to the great hall of the Singha Durbar. They passed through the great white gate and saw, beyond the eucalyptus trees and the pools of green carp that rose between the lotus leaves, the immense façade of the palace, glistening white with double Corinthian columns. Here his father left him, to join the bodyguard in the lustre-hung and mirrored Singha Durbar where the Treaty would be signed.

A seething multitude had filled Khatmandu, shaken by the salute of nineteen guns, and flocked to the gates. Chandra watched the arrival of the Nobles, the Bharadars and Lamas. Then came the Procession of Elephants, bearing the carved howdahs. After them followed the Newar guards in skin-tight breeches and embroidered jackets, the vermilion tom-tom beaters, the naked giant, bearer of the great sword of *Kot-bar* with which the great Manju Sri had cut the wall of the mountains so that the lake they cupped had run out and the dry bed became Nepal. After the elephants, the chained and spotted hunting cheetahs, the cymbal-clashers and drum-beaters, the palanquins of the Chinese mandarins in yellow silk, the wealthy Tibetans on pilgrimage from Lhassa, the shaven-headed Brahmin priests and the *gurus*, came more soldiers, squat Gurkhas in cobalt jackets. They were the bodyguard of the Hereditary Prime Minister, the Shadow of the Throne, the Voice Omnipotent, Field-Marshal His Highness Maharajah Sir Chandra Shum Shere Jung, Bahadur Rana, T'ung-ling-ping-ma-kno-kan wang, G.C.B., G.C.S.I., Commander-in-Chief, Prime Minister of Nepal. His breast was as the setting sun, his glance was as lightning. The jewels of his Orders flamed in the noon. His helmet was made of closely sewn pearls, fringed with drops of rubies. From a clasp of diamonds rose the plume of the bird of paradise, a fountain of brown, orange and white feathers. The hilt of his sword was a kingdom's ransom. Chained tigers of Terai brought up his cavalcade.

For Chandra the supreme moment was the arrival of the Great Sahib, his master the Envoy of Great Britain, Lieutenant-Colonel O'Connor, riding to the hall of the Singha Durbar to look upon the face of the King, to speak to him, and sign the Treaty. His servant Chandra looked on the Great Sahib with a swelling heart. Two days of feasting and illuminations, of free food and clothes, of music and entertainment and the working of magic and temple ceremonies would mark this miraculous year of 1923. He, Chandra, was twelve, the proudest boy in the world. His father Girja was in the Palace, his master, Lieutenant-Colonel O'Connor, talked with the King.

III

Six years passed. Chandra rose, office by office, in the service of the Envoy, and then a day came of mingled sadness and pride when he went to the Regiment, as his father and his forefathers had done. Chandra, son of Girja, put on the uniform of the King. In the tenth year of service, when he was the father of three sons and two daughters, came the World War. On the high pass of Chandragiri he turned and took his last look at golden Khatmandu in the valley, at the Roof of the World, snow-capped, remote, before descending to the Indian plain. In the fourth year of the war he stood upon other mountains, out of Calabria northwards, out of Campania beyond the Matese and the Valley of the Volturno, toward the Rapido River, and Cassino, where the Liri valley was barred. So, a man of the mountains, with his fellow soldiers he came to mountains, harsh, and snow-capped as those of far Nepal.

Oddly sad, the little Gurkha burial plots dotted the grim mountain-side below Monte Cassino. They had their curious distinction : at each grave's head a helmet, at each grave's foot a tiny pair of boots. No religious symbol marked their temporary lying-place, no memorials carried their curious names. They fought and died in a quarrel that was not theirs, for a cause they could not comprehend, men of forbidden Nepal who came in the service of a foreign Emperor-King to kill Germans in Italy. But fighting was their trade, and loyalty to their vows the sum of honour ; for the rest their courage was their fame.

In the third week of April, 1944, while accompanying a stretcher party down the mountain, Chandra drew aside to let some English soldiers pass. A shell burst on the ridge and an English boy lay dying beside him.

For a while he moaned, crying out something Chandra could not understand. Then he lay still, his agony ended. The noise of battle filled the air, but they were alone.

Chandra could not move, some part of him was numb, but he heard birds singing, singing so full-throated that he knew them ; the clear contralto notes of the tree-pies, the noisy scimitar babblers, the bush-chats, the black-naped orioles, the laughing-thrush, and the red-vented bulbul. He saw a girl with a necklace of pearls, golden bangles on her slender arms, golden anklets above her brown quick feet, in a robe of yellow silk, and in her blue-black hair a champak blossom—Maija, his wife, laughing as she fed with locusts the emerald carp among the lotus stems. . . . His father explained, giving him the small phial. On a proud day with the Prince of Wales, two years before the signing of the Treaty in the mirror-hall of the Singha Durbar, on the great *shikar*, when they had shot elephant, tiger, and rhinoceros, he had caught the magic blood gushing from the nostrils of the fallen rhinoceros, for was it not written that this was a viaticum, and smeared upon the brow of the dying it ensured a happy reincarnation ? So it was greying Girja's farewell gift to his warrior son.

Chandra, through a sudden searing pain, searched deep in a pocket. Dizzily he found the precious phial, and with his small strong teeth bit off the metal top. The dark red liquid flooded his palm. He could see no longer. He pressed his wet hand to his brow, smearing it with the precious blood. " *O Bhairava ! O the jewel in the heart of the lotus !* " he muttered, and then lay still on the mountain-side.

CHAPTER XIV

THE LIGHT

I

SERGEANT MORRIS scrambled down the rocky footpath until he came to the ruins of a wall. The bright sunshine of the day had gone. Over Monte Cairo great black clouds, with ragged edges, were piling up and a stillness in the air foretold a thunderstorm. It had been hot all that day working among the foothills. The old Abbey of Monte Cassino, sharp against the blue Italian sky, had looked beautiful in its utter ruin. The tide of war had passed and now it rested, a monument to the fury of men.

The landscape began to smile again. Trees that had escaped blasting had put out their leaves. The olive groves shimmered silverly in the wind. The orange and the lemon trees had blossomed. Here and there venturesome peasants were returning to their farms on the uplands, often to find them burnt out, but, like the people in the valley, they scraped among the ruins for a few domestic utensils, erected an awning and camped out on the spot that had once been home. No one was yet allowed in Cassino. An immense heap of brown rubble, it was full of booby-traps and mines. The stench of death lay over it. But the homeward trek had begun, to the despair of the authorities. Northwards the Allied armies were still fighting for Rome on these last days of May.

An American sergeant came down the path. He belonged to the Graves Registration Unit. They were working together over the same terrain. Sergeant Morris could see their trucks down in the valley near to his own. The American paused. He was tall, with a long bony nose and dark eyes in his sallow face, about forty years of age.

"Howdy?" he said, leaning against the wall.

"Storm coming up," commented Sergeant Morris.

They both looked at the threatening sky. The ruined monastery had lost its colour and was now black on the horizon. Below them the town of Cassino lay in a cold grey light. Somewhere in the clouds they could hear planes, returning probably from a sortie northwards. They were a reminder of the battle line beyond these mountains.

The American pulled out some cigarettes, offered one to the Englishman, and then passed his lighter. He noticed how the Englishman's hand shook.

"Hell of a job!" he said, quietly. "Who'd have believed it? I had a nice little business in Brooklyn before they pulled me in for this—same line, been handling corpses all my life, but this—Jesus!"

He removed his cigarette and spat. Sergeant Morris listened while the American talked. A mortician by trade, made caskets, had a funeral parlour in Brooklyn, so naturally was posted to the Graves Registration Unit. Undertaker, coffins, private mortuary, translated Sergeant Morris mentally. "What did you do in civvy street, brother?" asked the American.

"Worked in a hosiery factory," said Morris, and added, "I can't go on with this—it's getting me down!"

There was a note of desperation in his voice. His hand trembled as he held the cigarette that he puffed at spasmodically. It grew darker on the mountain-side.

Some men came down with stretchers, others carried bags. Heavy spots of rain began to fall. The evening hurried on.

"Aw, don't take it to heart. A guy gets used to anything," said the American. He took off his cap and rubbed his head. Three of his men went down the path with their burdens. "Helluva mix-up in this gully— our boys, yours, New Zealanders, Gurkhas, Poles—it takes a bit of sorting. I don't mind digging 'em out whole, but it's the bits and pieces, when their dogtags have gone and you have to start opening their mouths to look at the poor bastards' teeth for identification— an' fingerprinting ! That sure gets me. When I'm pressing their cold fingers on the pad I always feel one of 'em will claw hold and say, 'Hey, buddy, you come along with me ! ' An' ivery one a mother's son ! Sure, it's a bitch of a business to be in, but some guy's got to do it ! And we don't get no Congressional Medals, brother ! "

He threw away his cigarette, pulled out a hip flask and took a drink. He passed the flask but Sergeant Morris refused it. The American looked at him and saw he was shaking violently.

" C'mon—do you good, it's the real widow's hootch," he cried, genially, pressing the flask into his companion's hand. Sergeant Morris put it to his lips and drank. The gaunt American watched him, smiled, and in turn drank again. " Sure, it's a corpse reviver ! " he said, corking the flask.

The rain spattered heavily. It was quickly growing dark. Men with shovels were hurrying down the path. A sudden crack of thunder split the silence.

" Hell ! We're going to be drowned. I'm beating it. So long ! " cried the American, and started off down the path. Sergeant Morris did not move. He stood while the rain angrily beat down on him. He could see his men gathering down by their trucks. They were pulling tarpaulins over their loads. The lieutenant had joined them.

They would be waiting for him. He began to descend the path. It was the end of a particularly ghastly day, and there would be months of this, miles on miles, as they cleaned up the battlegrounds northwards. He felt he could carry on no longer. He would have to tell them, and get out of it. He was heading for an asylum. He began to hear the dead men talking to him, staring at him reproachfully for moving them from the places where they had rested so long. The living men in his company were looking at him curiously. Only yesterday Captain Hadden had reprimanded him over some muddle in the registration sheets. "Morris, you don't seem to have your mind on your work!" His mind on the work! What an idea!

II

When in the last light of evening, in the torrential rain, Sergeant Morris's convoy reached the collecting station between Cassino and Cervaro it was sent to a new centre, much to his annoyance. Up the hill there was an old villa, in spacious grounds, that by some miracle had escaped destruction. His unit had taken it over to deal with the overflow. The villa, in the Palladian style, had been looted of its contents, probably more by the local peasants than by the Germans, but a few unwieldy articles of furniture, and some grandiose portraits, studies of a local *nobilita*, emphasised the disorder and desolation of the place. A grand salon, with a painted ceiling, a massive marble fireplace of heraldic design, with one great

Venetian glass chandelier still intact, and walls from which
the crimson damask had been roughly torn, opened off
the pillared hall.   This room and the long dining-room
had been converted into a mortuary for the bodies of
soldiers with incomplete identification.   They had still
to be sorted and re-checked.   They lay in orderly rows,
in brown bags, mattress slips, and under covers, tagged
and numbered, impersonal as the baggage in a railway
receiving shed.   The floor of the grand salon was occupied
from end to end when Sergeant Morris's trucks arrived.
The dead crowded the room as perhaps the living had
never crowded it.   The shutters were closed, but the last
evening light filtered through them and half lit the awe-
some scene.

The sergeant and his men began to unload their freight.
They found space for it in the dark dining-room with the
Pompeian frescoes, but this was soon full.   On the left
of the hall with its curving marble staircase and statue
of Cavour in the well, they found a room that had once
been a library.   A few books still occupied the shelves,
and the panels of the coffered ceiling were painted with
scenes from the tales of Boccaccio.   The curtains of the
long windows at either end were missing, the velour
palmettes had been torn down.   There was a long red
leather settee by the wall and some Empire gilt chairs
had miraculously escaped the looters.   The long windows
at the north end overlooked a wide terrace with classical
statuary.   There was a view of the valley below, and of
the ruins of shattered Cassino.   The great hill, the
demolished abbey crowning it, and the mountains
guarding the Liri valley, were shut off by a screen of
torrential rain.

Sergeant Morris superintended the emptying of the
trucks.   The overflow, when the dining-room was filled,
was carried to the library.   Three bodies were taken

from the stretchers and lay covered with sheets. It was astonishing how small dead men always looked. Along with these they left four bodies in canvas bags, labelled according to their identification tags and the papers collected from them. Like the bodies in the salon and the dining-room they would have a final classification and identification check. On a battleground so covered by the Allied armies, correct distribution was an exacting process. Americans, New Zealanders, Poles, Indians, Frenchmen and Englishmen had to be sorted out in this great brotherhood of the dead in battle.

According to the check list in Sergeant Morris's hands the seven soldiers in the library were a mixed lot—a major, a captain, a lieutenant and two privates, all from British regiments, and a Polish captain and a Gurkha private. Four of them, in the canvas bags, were too fragmentary for personal identification, but their tags and papers were decipherable. The ‘unknowns’ were always carefully set apart. To-day there had been none.

When they had finished their task it was quite dark. Sergeant Morris came out of the library and one of his men, a corporal, closed the door, turning the key that was still in the lock. His companions laughed at him. The sound of their mirth echoed eerily from the walls of the empty villa.

“You don't imagine they're going to walk out, do you?” asked Sergeant Morris irritably.

The corporal looked at him and made no reply. The sergeant seemed more scared than angry. They hurried out of the hall, now quite dark for there was no electric light in the villa. At the foot of the steps leading from the colonnaded terrace they entered their trucks and drove down through the grounds to the highway. Their quarters, on the other side of the valley, were in an old house above the olive groves. From their elevation they could see the villa on the opposite hill. The rain still fell in torrents.

As soon as he arrived Sergeant Morris went upstairs and reported to Captain Hadden, who shared the upper floor with two lieutenants. He did not like Hadden, who was unsympathetic and a martinet. Nor could he understand a man who exhibited such a positive zest in such a job as this.

III

Sergeant Morris could not sleep that night. His mind raced through the events of the past two years. He had been slightly wounded in the head in North Africa, but to his chagrin he was not sent home after his discharge from hospital. He was sent to Divisional Headquarters for administrative duties. He had been a good soldier and he brooded over this relegation to duties behind the line. He was moved from Palermo to Naples, from Naples to Caserta, and now he found himself sergeant of a corpse-collecting company around Cassino. He suspected malice in high quarters, and so far his appeals had been unheeded. Nor were his domestic affairs in any better shape. His home in Coventry had been blitzed, and his wife had gone to live with her parents. She worked in an arms factory. She was ten years his junior, pretty and flighty. She seldom wrote to him and he had a feeling that she was enjoying the war and his absence unduly.

At two o'clock he turned on the light, sat up, and lit a cigarette. The night was warm. He tried to read, became drowsy and turned out the light. His room was on the ground floor and he thought he heard rats running across the floor. The rain had ceased. Through his open window he could see the moon, in its second phase, shining intermittently between the white clouds. He slept but woke again, and lay in the dark thinking he must get away from this dreadful job. He envied the cheerful American who had talked to him. He was a professional, hardened. " I give 'em quite a nice little job for three hundred bucks a time—dignified," he had said, alluding to his funeral parlour in Brooklyn.

Sergeant Morris closed his eyes. It must soon be dawn, another day of it. The horrors swept down on him. He got up from his bed and in the darkness went to the window for the cool air. The farm buildings and the olive groves were silver-grey in the moonlight. He could see in the valley the ruined church with its shell-struck campanile in which the bell still hung. One tolled last evening for vespers and the old priest had held a service in the half-demolished sanctuary. A dozen women, two old men and some children had been all the congregation. They had come through the rain. It was the eve of Pentecost, said the padrone's wife who had been present. The church was very old. There was a legend that Saint Scholastica had performed a miracle in it.

Two tall cypresses stood like sentinels on the little piazza in front of the church. Its wall shone white in the moonlight. The valley was very still. The air was cool and slightly aromatic after the rain. Suddenly Sergeant Morris saw something that rooted him to the ground. Across the valley, on the rising hill, sat the villa where they had left the bodies last evening. It lay dark and sprawling in the faint moonlight but at one end, the north end, there was a light in the lower windows. He could not be mistaken. It glowed, breaking that long dark façade with a curiously intense bluish light.

The three illuminated windows were on the ground floor. They were the windows of the library.

Sergeant Morris stared, incredulous. Who had gone into that room of the villa and for what purpose ? For a few moments he could not move. He felt the light would vanish, a trick of the imagination, of the moonlight perhaps. But the light in the villa was constant in its intensity. Some one, for some purpose, was in the villa, among those seven dead men, and had somehow lit up the library. For what purpose could anyone be searching there at this hour of the night ?

He drew back from the window, then looked again and knew it was no illusion. He turned on the light. It was half-past four. With shaking hurried hands he put on his shirt and battledress and hastily laced his mud-coated boots. He picked up his revolver, buckling on its holster, and in a few minutes was out in the still night, moving down through the olive-grove to the highway. It was a ten-minute walk across the valley to the villa gates. For most of the way the villa was in view. The light in the room was still visible. As he walked up through the grounds, past the avenue of ilexes, black against the sky, and the neglected parterres, he noticed how strange was the light streaming through the library windows. It glowed with a singular incandescence, like moonlight turned to flame, faintly bluish and ghostly.

He approached the terrace and mounted towards the open colonnade, trying to soften the sound of his footsteps in the silent night. At any moment the light might go out, the trespassers warned by his approach. He gained the loggia and walked towards the light streaming out over its tiles. Cautiously he drew near, his heart thumping, alert and tense. Taking advantage of the cover of a column, he came in view of the first window and looked in.

Two men were standing by the fireplace, talking with a third who sat looking up into their faces. By a marble caryatid supporting the mantel a small figure, almost as monumental as the form behind him, squatted on the floor, calm and withdrawn. Further in the room three men were standing before an old man occupying the settee. He was venerable as a prophet as he looked up into the young faces regarding him. He wore a dark loose garment and his face shone with a striking benevolence as he talked.

Sergeant Morris, paralysed with wonder, stood motionless by the column. It was then that he observed something that chilled the blood in his veins. With the exception of the old man they were all in uniform, denoting their rank and nationality. There were a major and a captain, one young, one older, and a tall lieutenant, almost a boy, all in the British uniform, as also two young privates. The flat nose and the high cheekbones of the figure squatting on the floor, dark in complexion, proclaimed him to be, as much as his uniform, one of the Gurkha contingent that had fought so fiercely in these hills. One other, young and handsome, wore the uniform of a captain in the Polish brigade.

In an overwhelming wave of consciousness Sergeant Morris knew who these seven were. They were the corpses left last evening in the darknesss of this room. They were now talking, animated and full of life. Seven out of eternity stood there, restored to their mortal frames. Seven, but in this room there were eight. Seven only had been left. He had checked the list. How came he here, this strange old man of such a commanding yet kindly presence?

The light glowed, and the voice of the Gurkha was uplifted. He rose and went towards his companions, who listened and smiled, comprehending his native speech. He was answered by the Polish lieutenant, and the English captain, and the old man whose glance rested upon them like a benediction. Different tongues they spoke, but it was as if a flame were upon each head, mingling in one light of perfect understanding the thought each would convey to the other.

As in a vision, unfearing, Sergeant Morris watched and listened. Then, as quickly as he had comprehended, a terror of the unknown swept through him. Suppressing a cry, he turned and fled from the loggia down through the garden towards the valley.

CHAPTER XV

WHITSUNDAY

I

THROUGH the long windows they could see the valley and the village in the moonlight. The tower of the church on the hillside shone faintly. The cypresses on the foothills above the olive groves rose dramatically in a night-piece almost theatrical in its beauty. The mountains to the north, where the Liri valley opened, were shrouded in mist. The heavy rain had ceased and into the room of the villa on the hill there came the sound of a rushing wind, so that the seven soldiers and the old man sitting by the wall looked at each other until the sound had passed. The room which had seemed dim and indefinable was filled with light and the landscape through the windows was no longer visible to them.

The old man, the only one of them not in uniform, sat quietly on the settee by the wall and talked to three young men who responded from time to time. Their voices as they conversed were calm and pleasant. But like a dark cloud drifting in upon a serene sky, within their minds there was the shadow of something crossing their consciousness. Was it yesterday, or a year ago, or even a decade, that the thing troubling them had been part of their experience ? Among them the old patriarch alone seemed to have nothing invading the peace of his mind, no anxiety marring the serenity of this quiet room on the Italian hillside. They became aware that he was fortified by a faith that gave him an aura of inviolate peace, although they felt that somehow he comprehended all the anxieties touching them.

He was dressed in a long loose robe, of a dark cloth that contrasted with the silver of his hair. A very young officer, Lieutenant Charles Conway, talking with him, was aware that he had instinctively comprehended the anxiety within his own mind. He had scarcely uttered, with the utmost diffidence, the thought obsessing him when the patriarch spoke, with an assurance that dispelled all his doubt.

"Do not be troubled," he said quietly, "for very soon you will see all those you love."

For the first time Charles Conway felt assured that the quest of his boyhood and youth was certain to be fulfilled in some manner beyond his comprehension. He would at last see his father, and in that same moment those others he loved, his mother, and Diana, his girl-wife. It was almost as if they awaited him in the next room.

A young man, a private of the Royal West Kents, raised his voice in a protest that seemed addressed to them all as much as to the patriarch. There was anguish in his boyish face and clear eyes.

"But why do they keep me here? I've not been home for three years! I've a wife and a child—a son I've never seen. It's so long now!" cried Private Parker, in a voice charged with rebellion. "My kid won't know his own father! Why can't I go home?"

The air was troubled by his distress. He was about to speak again when the patriarch addressed him gently, and regarded him with compassion.

"My son, be not anxious. It will be well with you. Love restores all things we think we have lost. In God there is no time, no forgetfulness, no loss. Can you believe that ? " he asked.

The boy looked at him, his mouth trembling.

" I don't understand what has happened to me," he replied.

Major Westell, standing near him, put a hand upon his shoulder in a gesture of sympathy. Then he turned, addressing the patriarch, his face earnest and sensitive.

" If as you say," he asked, " Love restores all things we think we have lost, I could then have hope for myself, as Parker too could have hope. But it seems to me that life cheats us, or perhaps we cheat ourselves, blinded by self. We are all so terribly alone and often we hurt each other, thoughtlessly cruel in our pride and selfishness. But what shall we do ? The past's so irrevocable. You are an old man, with much knowledge of life. Why do you believe love restores the things we've lost ? I broke the heart of one who loved me unselfishly, unfailingly. Being dead, how can he know of my contrition ? It seems to me the worthy have no just reward, the unworthy suffer no retribution."

The patriarch observed the troubled face before him, conscious of the suffering in the young major's eyes.

" It is not so," he answered slowly. " God's justice is not of the hour or the day, it flows through all time and always prevails. You cry out in the anguish of your spirit. Is not that your punishment, and the proof that God has not deserted you, for otherwise why should you be troubled ? "

The young man made no answer. The patriarch looked from the private to the major, compassion in his mien.

" My sons, you are not lost to grace, nor will your virtues be forgotten. Why should I lack faith in the ultimate perfection of His great design ? Did self entirely triumph in you ? ' Greater love hath no man than this, that a man lay down his life for his friends,' " he said, and seeing they did not comprehend, added, " All that we take from the one and all that we give to the other are truly weighed in the balance of His righteousness. I have seen so much I thought destroyed prove imperishable in the grace of Him whose mercy keeps us in remembrance. Behind the shadow of the world, the momentary projection we call life, is His eternal purpose, the light that gives us being. If we have failed it is but in the mortal moment of our experience. We are encompassed by Eternity, God's own reality, in which resides the justice and the mercy of His plan. One of you feels robbed of those whom he loves, one of you sorrows for the love he has misused. A discord does not destroy the symphony ; it may help to build it. In the harmony of His plan, in God's time only can we learn the nature of our contribution. To strive, to know error and repent it, to hope and to believe, are all that our brief mortality vouchsafes to us. For the rest, my sons, let us await the revelation of the Everlasting."

They had not noticed the Gurkha who had risen from his place by the hearth and come over to their group. He listened and when the patriarch had finished he moved forwards and slowly spoke to them, with a singular dignity.

" The *guru* has wisdom and holiness. Time is but the shadow of the Universe. Out of the Dream we come and into the Dream we go, as it would seem. But who shall say, Sahibs, this is reality ? Are we not told by the holy ones that the rim of the Eternal Wheel briefly touches the path of our mortal progress ? How vain is he who exclaims : ' This is the Whole ! ' Man revolves around the hub of the great Wheel, coming whence he knows not, going whither he knows not, briefly aware of this earth he treads as the servant of the All-seeing. It is in the journey that we acquire merit."

Having spoken, the little man in the rough uniform made obeisance to the patriarch, who regarded him with a benign grace. As he turned away their eyes followed him, for his voice had a quality that deeply moved them.

By one of the windows the Polish captain, Stanislas Morowski, was talking with the middle-aged English captain wearing the white and red shoulder tab of the Special Services. They had listened intently to the group by the settee. When the Gurkha left them, the Polish officer glanced at his wrist watch and addressed his companion. " My watch stopped at six, it doesn't seem to be going. Have you the time? "

" I'm sorry, I haven't," said Captain Carter.

" That old man's quite a character. Why did our Gurkha friend call him a *guru*—what does that mean ? "

" It is Hindi for a spiritual teacher."

" Oh ! Do you know who he is ? It's very odd, but there's something about him, something—I don't quite know how to express it—that makes me feel I could confess everything to him. And what a story that would be ! " He gave a nervous laugh. " I'm afraid I've been a pretty bad lot, but never with malice aforethought —just circumstances which were too much for me."

" That is true of most of us in our human frailty."

" Yes—and we do have odd moments of what the old fellow called the revelation of the Everlasting. Myself, for instance. I've given up everything I struggled to get because I have an odd idea that fighting for my lost country, and perhaps dying for it, would soothe my conscience. Can you understand that ? "

"I can indeed. I am here for a similar reason," said Captain Carter.

"Ah, then you'll know my problem. I ask myself is patriotism next to godliness, or is it just a delusion, a racial prejudice we blindly support? I wonder what our old prophet would make of that! It seems to me, in the matter of acquiring merit, on the lines of our Gurkha friend, that I've only done one thing creditably so far—played the violin, if I may say so without vanity. I brought it with me and somehow mislaid it. I always feel that the angels of the Lord should play violins, not harps!"

He smiled at Captain Carter a little sadly. He was handsome, with dark expressive eyes. Then he looked out of the window into the moonlit night. They were both aware of the mountains of their travail and the great hill crowned with the ruined monastery, though blanketed in a white mist.

"I suppose we shall soon all be out there again," said Captain Morowski. "You know, with all its horrors, it is so much better than the tawdry life I've lived. I feel I might achieve some kind of redemption there if it chanced that——"

He checked himself and said, apologetically, "Forgive me for talking like this. Somehow this place invites confidences. There's something about that benevolent old fellow that gives me a feeling—how shall I put it—that——"

He paused, seeking for words in which to express the nebulous thoughts in his mind. But they did not formulate. Instead, he began to talk about his boyhood in Poland.

The soldier, Private Blaine, who told Parker he had lived in the United States, rose from his chair when he saw the patriarch was no longer surrounded. He went and sat beside him. They began to talk. Their conversation was long and earnest. Captain Morowski, glancing towards them in the course of his story, became aware that Private Blaine was weeping quietly as the old man talked with him.

When at last the soldier got up to go he was calm and grave as though no longer troubled in his mind. He joined the Gurkha and Parker and was soon absorbed in a story that Chandra was telling of his life in Nepal. The little man spoke quietly, with a narrative gift that held them enthralled. The patriarch sat alone, his eyes closed, his hands resting in his lap. Later they all began to gather about him again, drawn by his presence.

A discussion grew up about the abbey of Monte Cassino. Should it have been bombed ? Something had perished from the earth that could never be replaced. How far could military necessity justify vandalism ? Vandalism ? Yes, said one, the whole campaign in Italy had been an act of vandalism, a useless military excursion, costly in lives and negligible in its result. There was strong disagreement. The Germans had used the abbey for an observation post. They were the vandals. The Germans had not used the abbey for an observation post, not until it was, like Cassino, a heap of ruins made advantageous to them. The discussion grew passionate. Presently the patriarch, who had maintained silence, put forth his hand with a commanding gesture and spoke.

"Are you not all in error ? For many centuries the Abbey of Monte Cassino has been a lighthouse of the Faith. It has diffused wisdom and grace. Its fabric rose with the labour and prayer of generations of godly men. It was founded to nourish the truth of His Word and through the darkness of the ages its light has endured, a beacon never quite put out, though kingdoms fell and the rage of the wicked assailed it. Think you it has been destroyed? My sons, how mistaken you are! Its walls will rise again, its altars and courts sound with God's praise. Who can destroy that which was righteously loved? I tell you the abbey exists. It was not wholly built by man. How then can man destroy it?"

No one made answer. He rose and going towards the window looked out into the night. A great quiet fell upon them all. Presently he turned and addressed them, speaking as if to each one apart, his voice low, his face beautiful in its benevolent old age.

"This is the day of Pentecost. Under the working of this gift of God a renewed spirit of love takes possession of all who believe. Through the course of the Church's history it has been the mission of the Comforter to convince the world of sin, of righteousness and of judgment, to glorify Christ to his believing people, to lead the Church into all truth, to show her things to come, to sanctify them that believe, and to bestow grace upon all who serve in any ministry according to the requirement of the office which they fill. It is His Mission still, and the great hope of the Church and the world lies in the renewal of Pentecost, with its breath of refreshing and its tongue of fire, in each successive age. My sons, we are in God's keeping, let us journey unafraid."

There was a stillness in the room when he had spoken. His words had a kindly authority, and they looked upon one another with a question in their minds concerning this venerable man whose face seemed lit with the radiance of the Holy Spirit. It was Captain Carter who broke the silence. He approached and asked in a voice that trembled—"Are you not he, founder of our Order and

Abbey, whom Dante met in *Paradise* and to his query
made reply——

> *I will answer even to the thought*
> *Which thou hast such respect of. In old days*
> *That mountain, at whose side Cassino rests,*
> *Was, on its height, frequented by a race*
> *Deceived and ill-disposed ; and I it was*
> *Who thither carried first the name of Him*
> *Who brought the soul-subliming truth to man.*
> *And such a spelling grace shone over me*
> *That from their impious worship I reclaimed*
> *The dwellers round about, who with the world*
> *Were in delusion lost."*

He quoted the soft Tuscan words of the twenty-second
Canto, with burning eyes upon the face before him.

" My son, I am that Benedict," said the patriarch.

The soldier fell to his knees, casting his eyes to the
ground. The saint put forth a hand that rested on the
head of the bowed figure at his feet.

" Brother Sebastian, be not troubled in your mind
concerning a broken vow. Higher than the spoken
pledge He ranks the spirit of self-sacrifice, knowing all
the tumult of your heart. Nor be you troubled for a
fancied crime, the fantasy of conscience. Your friend
will greet you soon, as in the days of your youth together."

The captain lifted his head, gazing upon the face of
the saint who, with a gesture, raised him to his feet.

II

The urgent knocking of Sergeant Morris woke Captain
Hadden, always a light sleeper. He got up and went
to the door. The agitated sergeant confronted him.

"What on earth is the matter?" he asked, irritably. The story that Morris poured forth, with characteristic incoherence, confirmed his opinion of the man's unreliability.

"But the light is there, sir! You can see it now, from your window," cried Sergeant Morris.

"Then one of you must have left the light on in the room."

"There's no electricity in the villa, sir. We had to use our torches when we came away last evening."

Captain Hadden went to his window and looked out. There was a light in the villa across the valley.

"You say you saw them walking about in the room?"

"Yes, sir."

"Eight of them?"

"Yes, sir."

"How could that be possible anyhow? You say you left only seven bodies in the room."

"Yes—but there are eight live people in there. I counted them, sir."

"Morris, I think you are quite mad!" said Captain Hadden.

"Yes, sir. I expected you to say that. I couldn't believe my own eyes. But there are eight men alive and talking in that room. You'll admit it's lit up, sir?"

"Yes."

The captain stood still for a few moments, looking out of the window. Then he turned to Morris.

"I believe I'm as big as fool as you are. We'll go over and take a look," said Captain Hadden. He began to dress hurriedly.

In a few minutes they were crossing the valley. The moon had gone down. It was still dark but the dawn was near. The light burned steadily in the windows of the villa. It had a spectral quality, bluish and cold.

They came to the gate and mounted through the grounds, a little breathless. Something of Morris's excitement and apprehension communicated itself to Captain Hadden. He felt angry with himself for coming on such a fool's errand.

They reached the terrace and went up its steps, proceeding to the north end where the light streamed out over the marble pavement and flushed the round columns. Quietly treading, Captain Hadden came up to the window and looked in. Without any doubt eight men were in the room, talking together. Seven were in uniform, the eighth, a white-headed old man, was dressed in the habit of a monk.

Captain Hadden turned to Sergeant Morris behind him, whose blanched face shone in the light.

" We'll go in," he said, brusquely, and led the way down the terrace towards the main door. The hall was quite dark when they entered, but some light came through from the library. Captain Hadden tried the door. It was locked. He turned the key. Then resolutely he opened the door and stepped into the room.

Their presence seemed to be unnoticed by the saint and the soldiers. He was talking to them in a quiet voice, his tranquil gaze upon them.

" Of this festival of Pentecost it has been written in the Acts, ' And it shall come to pass in the last days, saith God, I will pour out my Spirit upon all flesh ; and your sons and your daughters shall prophesy, and your young men shall see visions, and your old men shall dream dreams ; and on my servants and on my hand-maidens I will pour out, in those days, of my Spirit ; and they shall prophesy. And I will show wonders in heaven above, and signs in the earth beneath ; blood and fire and vapours of smoke ; the sun shall be turned into darkness, and the moon into blood before that great and notable day of the Lord come ! ' "

There was a silence when the saint ended, and such a peace as seemed inviolable. Then, down in the garden, a bird's voice sounded. St. Benedict turned towards the window, lifting his hands, and they all saw what he saw. The dawn was breaking, and in a shaft of light, high over the dark valley, they saw the monastery on the hill illumined. It stood, solitary and immense, but it was not the abbey they had known in the days of their trial. It was no longer a ruin, impressive and sad in its shattered majesty. This was the abbey before the fury had blasted it and the mountain was soaked with their blood. The morning light sparkled on its eastern windows and touched with gold the Cross upon its dome.

" It is there—as my father saw it ! " cried young Conway in a voice ringing with wonder.

The saint smiled upon him, saying, " It was always there, my son. Whatever we build in love, whatever we create in the grace of His Spirit, is there eternally."

The dawn, spreading, pervaded the room. With a great effort Captain Hadden moved forward to speak.

" Who are you ? " he cried, in a strange voice that echoed from the walls.

The saint gazed upon him.

" We are the spirit of the Eternal which your mortality has seen," he answered gently.

The voice died and there was nothing there. The captain and the sergeant stood transfixed. Dawn had flooded the empty room. Captain Hadden's eyes travelled from the window, with its prospect of mist-clouded Monte Cassino, to the floor of the library. There he saw three shrouded figures and four canvas bags, with their identification labels hanging from them.

Sergeant Morris looked at his officer, white-faced and trembling.

" Sir, what was it ? " he asked in a whisper.

Captain Hadden made no reply for a moment, and then in a tone that had a gentleness the sergeant had never heard before, he said, " Morris, it was something no man will believe when we speak of it. It was a moment's vision of the living God."